JAVELIN THROWER

Copyediting by Robin Martin, Two Songbirds Press

Book Design by Lisa Ham

Published by AMV Novels

http://amvnovels.com

Available for purchase at Amazon, etc.

For my wife, Jeanette

PROLOGUE

The rock was not a large one.

Compared to the one that bumped it out of orbit, it was puny.

Out of a black silence the porous rock tumbled toward a half-sunlit planet like an unsupervised child on the loose. The mostly blue planet swathed in browns, greens, and whites directly in the rock's path waited for it.

If not for its impeccable timing, the wandering interloper would have been nothing more than another insignificant rock plummeting from the vacuum of space into the planet's thick atmosphere.

Behind the rock, some two hundred and ninety trillion miles behind, a massive shock wave flared across the universe at incredible speed, generated by an exploding giant red sun—another inconsequential celestial event timed perfectly. The supernova's brilliant flash would not reach the planet for another forty-nine of the planet's years. Herdsmen tending their flocks would marvel at the wondrous, bright light hovering in the evening skies. Nobility and peasantry alike would draw near from afar and be awed for days before the majestic star would fade away.

And if the rock and the supernova were not enough, a comet was soon destined to make a return visit from eons past, not to return again for eons more. The heavens—and therefore the gods—were busy.

The gravitational laws of the giant, multi-colored orb engaged and beckoned the little heavenly body to come closer. The innocent rock obliged and flung itself toward the giant as commanded, into waiting skies.

Unseen forces buffeted the speeding chunk of rock and batted it around. Sparks flickered from it like small fireflies abandoning their home, increasing in number by the second, aware that the end was near. The incandescent rock flared brilliant red and blue as the first layer of thin air devoured its elements with a voracious appetite. The fiery mass screamed toward the planet in rapid disintegration. It slammed into the planet's thicker atmosphere leaving a death throe of a thunderous boom thousands of feet behind. The rock was dying.

Down on the surface of the planet at the transition line where night turned to day, a column of Roman soldiers confronted a narrow, cascading stream. The water in front of them ran clear, quick, and unspoiled, prancing over smooth riverbed rocks as nature intended. At the head of the column, a general, his red cloak draped heavily around him for warmth, straddled his cold horse and appeared to be contemplating options and consequences. Behind him, the general's legions stood waiting, like the trees along the riverbank, mere dark silhouettes against a developing chilly lavender morning sky.

Vapor clouds snorted from the general's restless horse, for this was the winter month of *Janus*—the god of doors.

One of the general's most trusted aides sidled forward on his own cold horse. "What are your orders, General?"

The general sat hunched, a heap of red cloak deep in thought, looking beyond the river crossing, a boundary, a doorway, a point of no return.

It wasn't the aide that drew the general from his trance but the flaming star breaking up in flaring splinters, each piece racing one another and blazing across the heavens toward the general's focus of attention.

The general's burden was no more. This was a sign, an omen—

an answer. A multitude of bronze helmets cocked back in unison with uplifted eyes and witnessed the fiery pieces of rock shoot across the horizon. There was no question: the god *Janus* had opened the door for the general. The decision had been made for him.

Julius Caesar turned to his aide. "Are you a gambling man, Lucius Cornelius?"

"I've tossed the dice a time or two, Gaius. Unfortunately, I do not have your luck."

Caesar scanned the heavens once more.

The aide waited.

The general's horse kicked at the riverbed.

Standards and eagles shifted and rose a little higher and straighter.

"Advance and cross the river."

The once-pristine water of the shallow river stream churned murky as horse hooves and hobnailed boots splashed their way across.

CHAPTER
I

Lucius raced death down the shadowed alley, peering over his shoulder with nervous eyes just in time to see them, at the far end: two silhouettes, Roman legionaries with weapons drawn. The glint off one of the swords was like a searching eye. The fleeing youth slid to a halt and plastered his body against a wall. He was sure his galloping heart gave him away.

The two soldiers split. One disappeared from view; the other marched in measured steps towards Lucius, his weapon held out in front like a torch guiding him in the darkness. The legionary's echoing footsteps let everyone know of his cautious advance.

Lucius could only guess at one of the reasons for the encroaching legionary's slow approach: human waste and filth littered the darkness. Luckily, the legionary's slow march gave Lucius extra time to think.

Lucius hugged the wall. Probing fingers explored the dark and found an unlocked door. What incredible luck, the gods were with him, he thought. Like a cat, silent and confident, he broke in and sauntered into a small room. Firm hands pressed the door closed. Seconds taken to see objects in the blackness were agonizingly long, but necessary. His heart pounded. His head throbbed. And his chest heaved while he leaned against the door. Heavy breaths and deep sighs forced their way through flared nostrils and an unconscious rub of the nose with a finger helped him get in control. Wafting aromas of spices, flour, cured meats, musty cheeses, and something—gamy—replaced the stench of the alley.

Not far from the other side of the door, hobnailed boots splashed their way through a puddle of water—or something worse. The echoed splashes gave Lucius goose flesh. He looked down at his own sandals but it was too dark to see if a wet trail had given him away.

A faint suggestion of light under a door caught Lucius' attention and drew him toward it. He tiptoed to the light.

Something brushed against his face, soft, like feathers, lightly stroking his right cheek. He grabbed for the creature and found himself about to strangle an already dead bird suspended from a hook. He recovered from the bird and eased his way past the door of the storeroom into a hallway lit in a gilded haze. His instincts guided him to the right, toward another open door. Soft steps carried the intruder a short distance to a reception area, the *tablinum*.

He entered the soft-lit room and caught the highlighted features of someone's ancestors, pious-appearing figureheads, generations of them, resting on pedestals all in a line. Vacant eyes stared at him and watched his every move. On the walls, in command of the darkness, hung weapons and trophies of all shapes and sizes. The objects reflected the barest amount of light that seeped into the room.

Heavy footsteps broke the silence like the sudden crash of shattered pottery. Lucius' head spun in all directions, looking for another exit.

There was none.

Half of a fleeting thought suggested he hide in line with the figureheads, but the other half said that was stupid. Trapped, he felt his best chance was to leave the way he entered, but he would have to be quick. He made it to the doorway in three swift steps when every muscle in his body locked and refused to move further.

Up close, the dark figure rooted at the threshold looked more like an arena gladiator than an ordinary legionary. His cropped horsehair-crested helmet had no face, only an ominous blackness. The pectoral mold of his breastplate gave the appearance of someone very strong and menacing. Shoulders and arms were pure muscle. The glint off his sword flashed again, causing Lucius to gulp air. Before Lucius could formulate his next move, the shadowy figure marched forward and plunged the sword deep into Lucius' chest.

The blade felt strangely ice cold, yet scalding hot at the same time when it sliced through him. The two bodies stood fixed in place, the only movement coming from the *gladius* as it pulsed with Lucius' heartbeat, which was getting slower and louder with each beat. Lucius' eyes drifted from the faceless void in the helmet to the impaling sword. Gawking in disbelief and awe, he wondered why he just stood there and let the monster shove that thing into him.

At the hilt of the sword gripped a strong, scarred, muscular hand, holding it in place. The beginning of a scream fell backwards into Lucius' gaping mouth when the hand pulled the unwelcome *gladius* from Lucius' torso, allowing only an ugly, guttural gasp. The flat, smooth blade slid out with a sucking wet sound.

Lucius' head swayed. His knees buckled. Then he crumpled to the floor and gawked at the boots and the tip of a bloody sword that dripped crimson blood—his blood. A glossy pool of dark liquid spread from him. It flowed thick and flooded the floor like seeping oil from a ruptured vase. Lucius thought he could see the reflection of the monster's face in the dark pool, staring back with eyes filled with evil. Lucius' draining heart felt tired and barely cared to beat. Slower. Slower. Softer. Each beat spilled blood to the floor.

Lucius' eyes exploded open and he bolted upright on his cot. His chest heaved in giant spasms, sweat poured in torrents down his face, and probing hands crawled to his lower chest to explore the wound that wasn't there. His breaths eased—each one of them cherished.

The other seven legionaries around him slept; only one stirred. "Knock it off and go to sleep, pervert, or take it outside!" the stirring form from the other cot hissed.

Lucius, one of the new recruits, closed his eyes and let himself fall back, breathing deeply through his nose—which he had to rub, it's what he did at times like this. He couldn't help it.

It was only a dream—another one.

The sun would rise soon, and there would be little chance of a few minutes more of some much needed sleep, real sleep—peaceful sleep. Tired as he was, slumber evaded him at every toss and turn. It hovered near, teased, and provoked, but would not grace him. Fragments of the dream flashed in his head and chased sleep away. He scanned the color of the changing sky through the partly open flaps of his tent. His heavy eyes confirmed the fast approach of the early hours of the Roman day. There definitely would be no more sleep for him this morning.

No sooner had the eastern sky hailed the arrival of the first of the twelve daylight hours, *hora prima*, than it ushered in the centurion of Lucius' cohort—the tenth and least experienced cohort; the ones who had a lot to learn yet; and the ones most likely to die first. Like an angry ogre, the centurion barked orders and kicked at anything and anybody in his way. He marched along row after row of tents filled with tired legionaries.

The tired recruit didn't see the tyrant: that bulk of hardened sinew and muscle moving like a bull dressed in uniform. Scars decorated his arms and face like old badges of valor. Neither did he see the centurion swinging around in the air that royal, twisted baton of good vine wood, but he sensed it. The centurion's marching boots crunched to a stop just outside Lucius' tent and the morning went quiet.

"Get your lazy, worthless asses out of there. NOW! You think you're still in your mother's womb? Well, I've got news for you. OUT!"

———

Helios climbed the morning sky with authority and took charge in his rightful place. This was his part of the world. He and the centurion would deny Lucius and the others any further sleep. In obedience to the sun, and to the centurion, tents regurgitated and spewed their contents of sleepy and slow moving legionaries.

The huge, growing giant climbed even higher and brighter. It first appeared as a glistening, orange gem, but then transitioned to a sparkling diamond, warming the air and all that it commanded with its divine powers.

Mornings in Illyricum, across the Adriatic, just east of the heel of Italy, were normally like that: beautiful; Helios worked his magic well. The ball of gas would continue to climb and progress to nothing more than a vague smudge of light, lost in the haze of dirt and smoke created by all the mortals and animals. Thus, the Romans took the day from the deity. They were always in the habit of taking, making things and places their own; it was the Roman way.

The month was *Quintilis*, one of the many Roman lunar months they had brought with them across the sea from the Republic; the seventh month; the middle; the *Ides*. It was time for some serious campaigning.

Lucius and his companions were up and busy within minutes. Somebody got the fire restarted and a meager morning meal was underway. The eight legionaries assigned to the tent, their *contubernium*, squatted at the fire and began their day the way they did everything else—together.

"How long have we been here in Dyrrhachium?" someone asked, poking at the fire with a long finger of a crooked stick. It was Macro, the big guy. No one was sure if his name was by design or by accident.

"Since *Martius*, four months," Lucius answered, staring at flying cinders kicked up by Macro's stick.

"By the gods, it seems longer than that," Secundus, the hairy one said as he squatted and rubbed sleep or smoke or both from his eyes.

"How long have Cicero's troops been here?" Decimus, the skinny one, asked, having a turn at the fire with his stick.

"They came three months after us, in Junius." Again, Lucius had the answer. He squinted and turned away from flying ash and smoke coming his way.

"I say that would give us . . . 45,000 men just on our side alone, not counting the cavalry and mercenaries," Decimus said while he blew away smoke and ash now flying in his direction.

"I'm glad we're under General Pompey's command. Feel much safer," Didius said, yet another one of the eight. He grabbed Decimus' stick and claimed it for his own. "Hope Magnus has as much luck as that Julius Caesar. I hear that man has more luck than Fortuna herself."

"Nobody can have that much luck," Lucius murmured.

"I hear he leads from the front all covered in blood by the time the battle is done. Not his blood, though," Didius continued, wiping his burning eyes of the irritating smoke with the neck of his tunic.

"Doesn't seem right," said Marcus, one more of the eight.

"What doesn't seem right?" asked Didius, eyes fixed again on glowing coals that he probed with the stick.

"That he should be covered in our blood; I mean, we're Romans, too."

The voices fell silent, carried off with the smoke and shifting morning breeze. Shouts from bellowing centurions, the clamor of equipment, and braying of animals from nearby surroundings filled in the contemplating silence.

"You sure impressed Centurion Caelius with your javelin throwing yesterday, Lucius. You made the rest of us look like a bunch of fumbling farmers," a quiet Remus said, joining in and changing the subject.

"Yeah, what's your secret, Lucius?" Didius asked, trying to blow out the flame at the end of his stick.

"No secret. My father taught me when I was a kid," he answered. His face flashed a proud smile. "He was a legionary in one of Sulla's legions, an *optio*, could have been a centurion. He was more skilled than anyone I know at the javelin."

"He still in the army?" Secundus asked, spitting at the coals just to hear the sizzle.

"Nah, he was discharged after more than twenty years of service and given land in Venusia, where I was levied."

"I bet he had a lot of stories to tell, huh?" Macro remarked.

"Nah, he never talked about his battles much. Had his share of scars about him, though; but didn't like to talk about them," Lucius said with a fixed stare, but not at the fire.

"Sulla. Now there was a real general," Macro said.

"How would you know?" Didius quipped. "He was way before your time and you're not any older than the rest of us. How old are you, Lucius?"

"Twenty."

"See. You couldn't be older than the rest of us by a couple of years," Didius chided Macro.

With twenty years to his name, Lucius was as tall as most of his tent companions and carried as much weight about him, except for Decimus; but then, everyone out-weighed Decimus.

Lucius had well-defined, dark tanned arms covered with fine golden hair and was framed in a lean, youthful body that fit well into a uniform. He favored his mother in the eyes: dark brown to match his wavy hair that had just the slightest curl at the nape of his neck—when not butchered short, like now—and long lashes to keep out the sun and debris. His facial features were well-cut and proportioned, nothing too big or too small. His nose was straight with just the slightest hump in the center for a good Roman nose, like his father's—his mother had always told him that anyway. And his smile could always put one at ease. Back home, women had always considered him pleasant to the eye, even as a young boy. The gods felt compelled to give him a habit of rubbing the under part of his nose with his finger when extremely nervous; nobody could be as perfect as the gods.

Lucius trained well and was especially keen with the Roman *pilum*—the javelin—as his tent mates had noticed. He could out-throw any of his peers and hit the training post at one hundred marching paces—thanks to his father. He received no particular punishment or admonishment from his optio, other than the normal, harsh conditioning needed for a disciplined Roman legionary. Lucius kept up with the other new recruits, wishing only to be a good legionary. It was what his father would have wanted, and he was going to make his father proud, or die trying. Twenty years to his name and not a single battle scar—yet.

The group of eight finished their meal of bread, honey, and a very salty *suppa*—broth, when Centurion Caelius returned to haunt them.

"You ladies done with your morning chat?" he bellowed. "Wouldn't want to interrupt anything important, but there's a little matter of training we need to see to, so if you don't mind, get your lazy asses up and moving! To the *palus*!"

"By the gods, not that damn training post again," complained Didius.

"Yeah, and maybe today you might even kill the damn thing before it kills you, Didius," Marcus said in a mocking laugh. He got up and led the way. The others joined in with their own little smirks; they all knew, however, there could never be enough practice at thrusting and jabbing if they were going to stay alive.

The young, yet-to-be warriors grabbed their weapons and *scutas*, their curved shields, and started for the training area. Lucius kicked dirt at the fire and limped away.

"What's with the limp?" Didius asked.

"Ah, nothing; think I have a rock in my boot," Lucius lied.

He didn't feel inclined to tell anyone about the tightness and soreness plaguing the back of his right, lower leg. If the recurrent bad dreams were not enough to sour his disposition, he now had to contend with a new dilemma: a sore ankle. Before his ankle, it was his feet. He had been tortured with ill-fitted boots, losing his share of toenails and suffering ugly blisters. His feet had become hideous from miles and miles of marching and training, sometimes through tracks of thorns and thistles, trudging along with disciplined indifference. He felt lucky, though; he had seen soldiers marching—no, limping—ahead of him with leather digging into their flesh, raw tissue glistening where skin used to be, and then becoming infected. His mother would hurt for him if she saw his feet. His father would have shrugged it off as part of the rite of passage, something all good legionaries had to bear.

The recruits reached the training field and prepared to do battle with the training posts. The posts were splintered and scarred from many battles and were ready to take on the recruits one by one. The wooden foes would receive many more strikes and take on additional wounds, but they would never succumb to a bunch like Lucius' group.

The optio yelled at Didius again and again for "chopping at cabbage" instead of thrusting his gladius. "Jab, you idiot! Thrust over your shield. Now thrust under it. Go for the legs! No—no—no! Don't chop, THRUST, and JAB! IDIOTA!"

Poor Didius, every unit had one; Didius was theirs. The vanquished youth walked away, tired and sore. The old wooden veteran stood its ground and waited for more.

While waiting his turn at the palus, Lucius examined his hands. Fresh blisters from hours of trenching two days ago covered his palms. Painful feet, aching ankle, and now sore hands, too. His chest inflated and his head shook in disgust.

"You got 'em, too, huh?" Marcellus, who had been silent all morning, asked. He was a listener.

"Yeah," Lucius answered, aware that Marcellus was looking at his own glistening, raw tissue where blisters had been.

"How can anyone be expected to use his gladius and scuta properly if his hands are nothing more than ugly meat? We need a strong grip for a good thrust and stab," Marcellus lamented.

"Caelius said they would become tough and callused, remember?"

"I hope so," the listener said, grimacing as he wrapped a thin piece of hide around his hand.

You need to be able to dig a trench quick and deep after each march at the end of day, every day, if you don't want to be dead by morning. Lucius could hear Caelius' voice echo in his head. The centurion's words mirrored the very words of Lucius' father. The young recruit received his fair share of digging defensive trenches, building ramparts, and earning new blisters. It would not be so bad, but the land here was more rock than dirt and digging was not easy, especially up here on the slope of the hill looking down upon the Bay of Petras.

Lucius tried not to let negative thoughts enter his head; his father may be listening. Complaints were to be kept in the head, not gushing forth from the mouth—another lesson from his father. Give thanks to the gods that one was born to be a legionary, doing soldier's work; one could have been born a slave, or worse, if there were worse.

CHAPTER
II

From the moment Rome levied him in Venusia, his home, Lucius found himself thinking too much. "Not good for a legionary" his father would have said. He thought of the coming battle where Roman would battle Roman, soldiers like himself. It was like Marcus said: "It didn't seem right"—Lucius was not the only one thinking about it. He dared allow himself to think: was he on the right side? Of course he was—or hoped anyway. The Republic was important; otherwise, Rome would not be the great power it was. It had been in existence for at least 450 years, 450 years since the kings.

Normally, a foot soldier would not bother with such thoughts or concerns. Lucius was different. His mother had encouraged him to question and think for himself. His father didn't think that wise. Better to do what all disciplined Roman legionaries did best— follow orders.

Again, like always in the Roman world, there was a difference of opinion as to whose idea of the Republic was best; or more importantly, who should guide and protect the good people of Rome. Should it be the *optimates*, "the best of men," the conservative senatorial oligarchy, those blessed with birth and wealth? Or the *populares*, "the men of the people," who wanted more power shared with the assemblies.

This, of course, was over simplified. The truth was that it was about egos and personalities, of strong-willed men having it *their* way. Moreover, it was about power, always about the power. Lucius' fate was in the hands of some great men who were about to determine who was right, and who was wrong, and who would be the last man standing. And, in turn, their fates would be in the hands of the very gods to whom they all offered prayers and sacrifices. Lucius wondered about the sacrifice part.

He wondered to whom the gods would listen and grant their grace: Pompey, or Julius Caesar. It would all be resolved on the battlefield; one would win, the other would not. Lucius felt stuck in the middle. His father was probably right—too much thinking was not a good idea.

Lucius cared little about the dilemma neither wanted nor needed by Gnaeus Pompeius Magnus—Pompey the Great: His one-time colleague, co-triumvirate, former father-in-law, and now nemesis—Gaius Julius Caesar—had decided to champion the cause of the populares. Whether Caesar's motives were honorable and truly for the sake of the people could be debated in the Senate for days, if not weeks, but that time had passed.

Caesar could not return to Rome from his present domain without facing a few issues concerning criminal law for alleged conduct on his part. Rome had outgrown its feeble and archaic legal system, but the Senate could always find a law to suit its purposes. He definitely could not return with his army. That was war.

Civil war once again reared its ugly head in the Republic when Caesar marched his troops across the Rubicon, that silly little creek of a river that served as a sacred boundary up north in the Po valley. The war would be civil in that the violence and mayhem would be among the civil people of the Roman Republic, unlike the unrefined carnage and brutality of the *un*civilized barbarians farther north.

Caesar had defied the law, defied the Senate, and defied Pompey.

That was all above Lucius' pay grade, what little he got, when he got it.

—◆◆◆—

Unusually kind this particular day, Caelius let the new recruits break early—only two hours at the posts. Nobody would complain. They marched with brisk paces back to the staging area where other legionaries rested, mostly older vets from the first cohort, the most experienced. The vets busied themselves with inspecting personal equipment, sharpening weapons, or just checking for defects in their eyelids.

The boys plopped next to the vets. The old men ignored them and all the noise they brought with them. In staccato-like glances the recruits eyed the vets, emulating the elder legionaries' actions: inspecting shields, fixing loose pieces of body protection, and sharpening weapons.

Lucius took this time to alter one of the leather straps of his *caliga*, hoping to solve the problem of the hobnailed boot and sore ankle. The pleasant warmth of the sun, the lack of sleep, and the two hours at the palus played havoc on his tired eyelids as he worked the straps. He felt drunk with fatigue. His eyelids were as heavy as his twenty-pound curved shield. It was impossible to complete any task without his lead-heavy lids drooping and his head bobbing to his chest. He willed himself awake but his body ignored him. It took several violent recoils and snaps of his head to keep awake, but necessarily alert.

The boot alteration was complete. An inspection of his personal body protection came next. He cast his sleepy eyes to his chest and he ran his fingers alongside his torso and abdomen, checking for an open wound. The dream seemed so real; the wound was not. He could not help but rub his nose again.

A conversation from four vets next to him drifted his way like smoke and he averted his attention from the imaginary wound.

"I hear Caesar's trenches to the south, near the sea, aren't done yet," one old vet, Phoebus, said. "If I were Magnus, I'd hike my ass down there and take Caesar at his weakest spot. That's what I'd do."

"If you were Magnus, your ass wouldn't be sitting here with us, eating this dung they call food," his friend Mario said, earning him some laughter from the others.

"Yeah, I can't wait to get some real food," said a third.

"How in Hades did Caesar manage to surround us and cut us off from our supply ships in the first place?" asked the forth.

"Skill," Mario answered.

"Nah, it wasn't skill. It was luck! That man has more luck than gold," Phoebus said. "In fact, I think he has Fortuna herself for his second-in-command."

"No, the man knows tactics," Mario insisted. "He used the same tactics up in Gaul."

"You mean against . . . ah . . . that king . . . Genver . . . Gen—"

"Vercingetorix," Lucius answered for him, which earned a respectful nod from Mario.

"Yeah, that's the one, the Gaul king, up in . . . ehhh—"

"Alesia," again Lucius answered.

"You want to finish my story, boy?" the irritated vet shot back.

"Ah, let the boy be, Phoebus, he just knows more than you," Mario said, flashing a wink at the boy.

Lucius returned to inspecting his equipment, deflecting leers from the peeved vet.

It was now common knowledge that Caesar, with his ubiquitous luck, had surrounded Pompey and cut him off from the sea. Caesar's experienced legions constructed double entrenchments some ten plus six miles west of Pompey's own lines, including twenty forts, just as he did three years earlier against the Gauls.

Something in the distance disrupted the controlled chaos of the camp. The elderly vets next to Lucius eased themselves up and struck familiar poses—familiar only to other vets. Their heads turned in unison towards the ensuing commotion like wolves sniffing information in the wind. Lucius looked first to the experienced vets and tried to read their faces, like a subordinate member of the pack cuing in on the alpha member would, and then turned towards the ruckus coming his way.

Not far away, other cohorts were trotting at a quick march with purpose in their steps. Word somehow managed to precede the disciplined mass of troops like a shock wave before a falling tree in the form of shouts from others scrambling to their tents—"Pompey is taking the battle to Caesar at the southern portion of the unfinished trenches!"

Phoebus turned to Mario and let a gratified smile stretch across his face, and then followed with a wad of spit flying for the earth.

The veterans gathered their weapons and other gear and barked orders to all the new recruits. Centurions barked even louder orders to organize the growing chaos and add to the flow of a mighty war machine on the move. Lucius picked up his scuta and gladius and ran to his tent with the others to gather the rest of his gear, ignoring his painful right ankle.

Centurion Caelius was right behind the recruits, like a raging bull. He marched faster than the recruits could run. "Don't forget your javelins and spears or by Jove you'll have me in your tent tonight! Then you'll wish you had more than your scuta to protect you!" the centurion yelled, stirring the air above him with his baton.

Lucius gathered all his important equipment and secured it onto his *firka*, the pole used to carry his gear, like a little boy getting ready to run away from home in a hurry. He ran to the assembly area, glanced over his shoulder just in time to see his tent disappear within a cloud of dust, and prayed that they would remember to bring everything else he owned, including his extra bedding. He trailed behind the others, trying to work out the cramp at his ankle and still manage to keep up. More importantly, he kept out of the reach of Caelius' cane.

By chance, or chaos, he fell in line but was not in his usual place. He found himself next to other recruits he had not seen before. Didn't matter, he was in formation and ready. The order *"Move!"* flew through the air and he began marching, more a nervous shuffle at the onset. He prayed to the gods for a good show of valor should this be his first real fighting experience. Up until now, his only combat consisted of short skirmishes with probing elements of Caesar's legions, no major casualties, just the exchange of a few javelins and insults. He had yet to be tested, toe-to-toe, with somebody trying to kill him and he trying not to be killed.

The adrenal hormones responsible for the pounding of the heart pumped into his bloodstream and he marched with measured purpose, slipping in step with the others as centurions barked last-minute commands and went about with their batons smacking a few poor souls just for good measure. Up front in the dust, the eagle and standard of his unit bobbed and swayed in unison with the animal-skin-covered *aquilifer's* cadence. Lucius' dust merged with the dust of his fellow legionaries. A rhythmic slapping of leather and metal developed as troops marched in the direction of their eagle, that gold bird that pulled them along like children, leading them to victory, or to slaughter; didn't matter, they followed in blind obedience.

Wave after wave of undulating bronze helmets flowed like a powerful metallic river, coursing and winding along the rocky and semi-dry landscape. The thunder of hobnailed boots pounded the earth and became trance inducing to the soldiers' ears, a metric beat that took control of their lives, yoked them to an invisible chain, and pulled them along. The combined effect was of an ominous machine on the move—a killing machine, and Lucius was in the midst of it.

The river of legionaries marched for a long hour, swaying and pounding, moving the earth beneath their feet back toward the end of the line; and then—*"Legio—Sta!"* In three thunderous stomps, the machine came to a halt as commanded. The large dust cloud that had encompassed and accompanied the troops continued on its way, completely oblivious to the legionaries that had stopped. The new recruits panted, coughed, and gasped. They wiped dust from their eyes and nostrils at the risk of being clobbered by Centurion Caelius' baton for movement in the line. The veterans were not bothered at all.

Lucius welcomed the stop; his firka, which normally carried about sixty pounds of stuff, dug into his shoulder like a dull axe. He was thankful for the chance to rest it to the ground. He was grateful, too, for his right ankle was killing him. He was sure he could not have gone another hour more. The order to "rest" flew into the air and shoulders and arms relaxed.

"Of all times—why now?" he murmured. "What ills have I given you gods for this?" he said, looking up to the heavens.

"What? What did you say?" the legionary standing next to him whispered.

"What?" Lucius echoed. The noise level was picking up from all the troops transitioning from a disciplined machine in motion to one of a purposeless, loitering formation.

"You say something to me?" a new legionary said, spitting dirt and dry grass bits from his mouth and picking at his ears.

"No, just talking to the gods."

"You do that often?" the legionary asked with a half-smile and a wink.

Lucius offered a bracketed, thin smile of his own and looked away.

"Sthenelus. Sthenelus Regulius, but you can call me Sthen, it's easier."

"Lucius. Lucius Pontius."

Sthenelus examined the skies with a grimaced face. "I hope they're friends of yours—the gods. We're going to need all the help we can get. Caesar has some experienced troops and you know what they say about that man's luck."

Regulius was slightly taller and stockier than Lucius. Out of uniform, he had the appearance of an unbeatable wrestler. His skin had seen more sun than Lucius', his face a little fuller, eyes rounder and darker, hair short, thick, and wavy. He had more Greek about him than Italian. His family came from the coastal area near Tarentum. His grandmother loved reciting parts of the *Iliad* to him, the part where an ancestor, his namesake, was one of the Greek warriors hidden within the Trojan horse pulled into Troy.

Centurion Marcus Caelius patrolled the formation as an alpha wolf would his pack, exerting dominance and authority, putting all subordinates in their places. *"Silentium! Silentium! Mandata captate!*—standby for orders!" he shouted as he went about swinging at the recruits with his baton. He looked skyward to the vague light, shielding his eyes with a salute. "Must be *hora septima,*" he said more to himself than to the formation, the sun positioned just past directly overhead. "Covered some good ground on that one, a good little march indeed," he whispered.

"Centurion Caelius, why have we stopped?" a voice in line had the audacity to ask. It was Didius; poor, poor Didius.

The centurion's chin caved to his chest in disbelief and his eyes rested shut. The air around the formation stilled, like the sound of crickets giving alarm. He cast a cutting glare in the direction of the inquiry. Aligning himself with a fixed stare the centurion marched in slow measured paces to the location of annoyance, coming to a stop abreast of a legionary several bodies deep in front of poor Didius. Narrow glinting eyes stared full-bore on the youth. Caelius took a deep breath. White knuckles clutched his baton as he sliced through the formation like a sword entering a torso, effortlessly parting bodies about him until he reached Didius.

A pause of several heartbeats filled the air before he spoke. "The good General Gnaeus Pompeius Magnus saw how tired you were getting and decided to stop the army so that you could get some much needed rest." The centurion's stone face and voice hit hard.

Didius stood fixed in place, muscles paralyzed, not even able to generate a simple swallow; he did, however, a good job controlling his bladder.

Looking left to right, Caelius shouted, "You ladies have any other questions?"

Even the flies and other insects had the sense to silence themselves.

In a cloud of the ever-present dust, a young tribune galloped to the centurion and ordered him to meet with the other centurions once he put his troops at rest. Caelius responded with a thudding fist to the chest and an extended arm. He gave orders allowing the men to be in loose formation, but not before fixing Didius with one last glare for good measure.

The flies and fellow insects picked up from where they left off.

Baggage and supply wagons caught up with the cohorts, bringing some hard tack, stale wheat bread, and water. The old veteran, Phoebus, was at the side of the trail emptying his bladder, announcing his presence as always: "Ahh, Phoebus *hic*!—Phoebus was here!"

Didius slid in next to Phoebus and offered his own scent to the ground. "Old man, why do you think we stopped?"

Phoebus, his wrinkled, leathery face carved in a perpetual smile, displayed a party of discolored, broken, and missing teeth. His eyes, lost in slits, glowered at Didius. "You heard the man. We stopped for your rest! Wouldn't want you to be too tired when the rough stuff starts. You might get yourself hurt." The old man turned and ambled over to where Lucius and one of the other vets were sitting.

"Watch out for that one, Mario. Make sure he's not covering your right, if you know what I mean, eh?"

It was late in the evening when Centurion Caelius returned to his men. The plan was for an early start of action; at dawn. With any luck, the developing cloudscape would continue to provide cover for the first group of attackers and archers from the moon's light. Once the attack got underway, the others would follow, including the cavalry. For the present, the clouds served only to paint the evening with pinks, crimsons, and grays; ironically, the dominant colors for the coming events.

For Lucius and his cohort, Caelius had some good news and some not-so-good news. The good news was that it would be someone else's turn to dig trenches and build ramparts this evening. The other part of the news was that they would have the honor of leading the attack tomorrow, in front of the archers.

A wave of nausea swept over Lucius briefly, like the shadow of one of the swiftly moving clouds.

The end-of-march camp completed, an exhausted Lucius staggered and fell into his cot. Sleep smothered him within seconds. Unconsciously, he probed for the phantom wound in his chest, rubbed the under part of his nose, and then let his hand fall limp to the side like a cadaver as he slipped into a dreamless coma.

CHAPTER
III

Pompey studied his unfurled maps. Aides, young tribunes, old senators, and a former, once-trusted legate for Julius Caesar, Titus Labienus, mulled over the maps along with him. Oil lamps cast exaggerated silhouettes of the attendees on the hides behind them, giving the appearance of a very crowded tent. A few more pieces of information trickled in from informers and scouts regarding Caesar's troop placements and movements. Ever the wise and astute military man, the general was well aware that Caesar, too, was accumulating information about Pompey's status.

"We'll send in the first elements, including the archers, before daylight, under the cover of darkness. Their goal—the trenches, to fill them in the best they can, with what they can. Should the gods be with us, these first troops should be able to approach under the shadows of the clouds," the general said, pointing to strategic points on his map with his thick, stubby finger. "That moon can be brightest when you wish it otherwise. My *1st* and *15th* will be here—and here, my right wing. The cavalry and mercenaries will be to the rear and on the left, here—and here."

Tribune Marius broke a brief silence. "General, we have some fine experienced legionaries ready to serve you and the Republic. Your *Legio I* will serve you well, as they have always. We'll be ready."

The general tilted his head and eyed the young tribune. "We also have many young, inexperienced recruits. They'll get their first taste of real battle, or serve as fodder for the gods. In any case, all will serve."

A few more minor logistical matters were addressed and orders given to take care of them. Everyone stood, gave the formal salute, and exited to make final preparations, and get some rest. There was no real rest, however, before a major battle, at least not for the mind. Old veterans of previous battles thought of all the things that would go bad when least expected; veterans-to-be thought only of how valiant they were going to be.

Titus Labienus loitered behind as the rest of the war council trickled from the tent. Pompey remained fixated on the map. There was always something overlooked. "The plan looks good, Magnus," Labienus said, his eyes focused on his own areas of responsibility.

"Yes, but it will go awry with the first arrow, or javelin. It always does."

Titus shrugged, offering a confirming smile.

"The gods will be looking down, making their own moves, toying with us. They will have it their way. I only pray that they would be so kind as to throw a little of Julius' luck my way for a change," Pompey uttered.

"Luck. That man has more luck than women, and he has plenty of those, too," Titus said.

"Surely, he has no more favor with the gods than the rest of us," Pompey said, rolling up his maps. "I know that man well. He is no less mortal than you or I, Titus. I've had my share of glory, wins, and triumphs, too."

Titus Labienus wanted to remind him of that one triumph refused him by Sulla, but thought better of it.

Pompey gleamed with pride as he reflected on how he had been showered with accolades and laurels upon the capture of Spartacus' army. Of course, Crassus did all the work, Pompey just happened to stumble on the rebels at the right place and the right time.

And then there had been Africa, Sicily, Pontus, Armenia, Syria, and Jerusalem. Yes, Jerusalem, what a piece of work that was. The treasury and the coffers were filled to capacity. Nobody, but nobody brought back to Rome so much in territory and riches. He was better than Caesar. He could have brought his army into Rome, just like Sulla. But no, he was the good citizen, the honorable citizen. He disbanded his army. And did the Senate give him recognition and land for his veterans? No. That pious bunch of old—

And Crassus, he got his riches only through the bad luck of those who lost property through fires, fires he probably started himself; more, always wanting more. Fool of a general, getting himself, his son, and all those good men killed. If he had just waited for reinforcements and not have pushed those tired men—what a fool.

Unaware of how long he'd been adrift in thought, the old general realized that Labienus was still present, looking intently at him. "Sorry, I was just thinking. Better get some rest. Big day tomorrow."

Labienus gave a nod, saluted, and exited the tent, leaving Pompey to the rest of his thoughts.

Delicate hints of morning crept in from the east. As hoped, irregular shadows from slow moving clouds slithered across the landscape and provided cover for the initial raiders and archers. The trek in from the camp in the dark to the assault area was unnerving; truly, the gods were on their side, considering all the noise from colliding metal, broken twigs, kicked rocks, and heavy breathing. The guides that ushered in the first elements did a good job; it could have been worse.

Lucius was down on one knee. The rest of his contingent was in its assigned position not far in front of the archers. The trenches would be close at hand; they knew; they built the very same trenches for their own forts. The situation felt awkward and strange and went against all that had been drilled into Lucius: close order formation, moving in blocks of men acting as one entity, with complete discipline to signals, orders, and commands that directed the order of battle.

He was ready and waiting, holding onto his scuta and weapons with death grips, recalling the threats from Centurion Caelius. Painfully aware that he would be in the forefront of the ensuing battle, his heart raced, reaching a point where it would just explode from his chest, he was sure of it. Hammering pulsations in his ears echoed within his helmet. Sweat trickled down his forehead, down his back, and down his arms. His brows could not stop the rivulets that seeped through and dripped past into his eyes. Fast blinking lids cleared some of the sting, but like an invading army more drops just kept coming. His throat was dry and his stomach churned. Waves of nausea washed upon him but he held them at bay the best he could.

If the anxiety was not enough, small crawling insects and buzzing mosquitoes persisted in getting their fair share of blood first, plaguing him to the point of near insanity. He knew better than to slap at them or make any sudden gross movements; worse yet, he was in desperate need of a nose rub. And this was no dream.

Sthenelus took a knee directly behind him, breathing heavy in anticipation. Lucius cocked his head just enough to throw his voice. "You make too much noise," he whispered. "Are you doing something obscene back there?"

"Yeah, I was just thinking of a young slave girl back home I once got to know one night like this, behind our house," Sthenelus shot back in a harsh whisper. "Sure would like to have her with me right now. I'll just have to be happy you're here instead."

Lucius twisted about and glared at Sthen. He could just make out parts of a smile and bright teeth through Sthenelus' face guards. He didn't need to see it. He knew what it looked like.

Out of the darkness behind the crouched attackers and without warning, a line of fire flared in the darkness. Lucius was flashing a hard stare at Sthenelus when it lit. Sthenelus saw the developing light reflect off Lucius' face and turned to see the source.

Brilliant flames destroyed Lucius and Sthen's acclimated night vision and etched burnt images on their retinas. Blinded for the moment, they thought they heard the flight of a hundred winged birds taking to the night sky directly overhead. Nearby legionaries heard the same soaring birds and looked up. They sensed them more than they could see them. Those who caught a glimpse saw black slivers streaking skyward in the beginning of an arch. Continuous waves took to the air. Their feathered wings did not beat, flap, or flutter like game birds being flushed in a hunt; they hummed in a chorus of vibrations and sounded more like large insects on the attack, pouncing on the fort in the near dark.

———

The black slivers of death came in clouds, bringing with them a horrible calamity. Some slammed into wood with vibrating thuds; others found metal, leather, flesh, and bone. Metal on metal rang out as arrow points hit, glanced off, or penetrated bronze helmets of those who could not hide fast enough. For a few unlucky souls, a blur was the last thing they saw before arrows found their eyes. Arrows punched into leather-covered torsos forcing air to rush from lungs, leaving victims breathless. Neither arms nor legs were spared. It all happened so fast, like a great tidal wave striking with little warning and leaving much devastation in its wake. Following the destructive clouds was a brief air of silence as the last of the arrows arrived, found their mark, or continued on in the darkness.

Somewhere in all the awesomeness, alarms shouted from those who survived the initial wave; the dead and dying could care less. A daring few peeked in the direction of the onslaught and witnessed the approaching flight of a hundred missiles more. This time they were aflame and appeared as hundreds of phoenixes, coming to take anything in their wake to die with them. Death was coming again.

Again, there was the thunderous crash of speeding missiles

slamming into anything in their trajectory. Sparks flew everywhere as flaming arrows hit with sudden impact. Wooden structures and raised shields started burning, as well as clothing on the dead and wounded.

Eternity had lasted seven minutes—seven minutes of pure terror.

Word rushed north to Caesar that the fort was under attack. Troops materialized from nowhere to man the walls, put out fires, and move the dead out of the way. Archers from the burning fort rushed to take positions and return their own version of Hades.

Lucius and Sthenelus recovered their night vision in time to catch the feathered-end of the chaos that befell the defenders of the fort.

"Thank the gods we weren't on the receiving end of that," gasped Sthenelus.

"Hold your tongue lad, we're next," said a voice of experience from somewhere in the dark.

Sthenelus brought his large curved scuta close to him. He huddled tight. And then he began to whisper prayer-like pleas. He looked to the top of his shield and listened. He waited for the sound of approaching birds. The only sound he could hear was heavy breathing—his.

A harsh whispered command came from up front. "Advance. *Equaliter ambula!*—stay in line!"

The shadow of a fort against a less dark sky was now a burning inferno—a beacon. Lucius, Sthenelus, and the others advanced in line as commanded.

Thick brush bit and clawed at exposed legs not covered with shin guards. High grass swished in resistance as troops plowed through in slow measured steps. Burning sweat continued to stream into eyes of many, making it difficult to see the ground they traversed, but they advanced anyway. One dared not let go his shield or weapon to wipe the burning liquid. Disciplined as they tried to be, legionaries stumbled as they tripped over unseen rocks and tree stumps in shadows and uneven terrain.

Somebody crumpled to the ground. Lucius turned to see if it was Sthenelus. It wasn't. Sthenelus looked to the poor fool who was dancing to get back in line. Lucius and Sthenelus exchanged relieved glances followed by nervous smirks, each thankful it was neither of them.

Lucius somehow managed to rub his nose with a free finger.

Didius scrambled to get back in line within seconds, praying no one could see him quaking in fear, his shoulders convulsing in frenzied spasms.

Sthenelus heard it before Lucius. It sounded different when coming for them.

Somebody shouted, "Shields! Cover your—"

The alarm wasn't finished before a thunderous roar of metal slamming into metal, metal into leather, and metal into flesh and bone echoed all around. The cacophony was like a sudden downpour from a cloudburst of hail. The lucky souls who recognized it crouched beneath their shields quickly, making like small insects. Those in small groups tried to form the *testudo*, or tortoiseshell, as fast as they could, locking their shields together overhead and to the sides.

The missiles came in torrents, pounding on and piercing through shields. Failing to find shields, the arrows spiked exposed feet, legs, torsos, arms, heads, or anything they could find. Lucius closed his eyes tight and prayed to the gods and his father to let him survive this horror. He held his breath, panted in huge gulps of air as if breaking through water, and then held his breath again.

Still the downpour continued. Two, then three arrows pierced his scuta, smashing down on him like the pounding of a forger's hammer. Arrow points appeared like magic. He opened one eye with a squint and saw them staring right at him, like snakes from Medusa's head. Close by, he could just make out the sound of a body slumping to the ground, not a cry uttered.

The rain of arrows diminished and the thunderous roar subsided, only to pick up again with a new vengeance. More shields fell to the ground. The crescendo of incoming missiles faded as the last of the arrows looked for and failed to find prey. Painful moans drifted through the air like fog after the downpour.

"Lucius, Lucius, are you there?" It was Sthenelus.

At first, Lucius didn't answer. He had found himself thinking of his mother and recalled some vague sensation he once felt as a child: the want of his mother's embrace. He quickly snapped out of it as soon as he realized someone was calling his name. Was it one of the gods? Was it father? Was he dead? Was he in the Elysian Fields? Strange, there was no pain and he still felt all the fatigue and fear of a mortal.

"Lucius!"

He allowed himself to move the slightest bit to hear better but remain under the protection of his shield. "Yeah. Is that you Sthen?"

"I hope so," Sthenelus said, unsure of it himself. "You okay?"

"I still seem to be among the living, if that's what you mean!"

Again, the deadly, feathered missiles hissed, only this time flying past and not upon them, the impacts heard just ahead. The recruits were acclimating themselves to the new learned music of killing and death.

Somehow, they made it to the trenches just in front of the walls of the burning fort. Their job was to fill in the trenches the best they could with what they could find: tree limbs, branches, rocks, bodies, anything. Fortunately, the trenches were not as deep as they could have been—a gift from the gods.

Arrows, spears, and javelins continued to fly in both directions. Though his limbs felt like heavy wood, Lucius continued on. He grabbed the body of a legionary that lay in front of him and rolled it over to toss into the trench; it was Didius. The sight of his dead tent mate's face caused him to let go his grip, which earned a bellowing admonishment from behind. "Throw him in! Throw him in! That's an order!"

Lucius grabbed Didius by the arm and rolled him into the trench, where other bodies were accumulating. Live legionaries flew past the hesitant recruit. They trampled over the pile of bodies and debris, and climbed to the opposite side.

Lucius was bumped from behind and he toppled into the ditch, coming to rest on top of and staring directly into Didius' lifeless, pale eyes. His trance was broken when the full weight of another soldier trampled across his back and pressed him further down upon the corpse. The unmistakable sound of arrows zipping past, piercing bodies next to him, urged him to move fast. He pulled himself together and sprang to his feet, clambering for the rim. Lucius managed to bring his shield and gladius, but nothing more.

Out of the ditch, the assault on the rampart was next.

The raised earthwork itself was once the contents of the trench. Lucius pedaled in the loose dirt and rock as fast as he could to reach the top. The pounding on his scuta from the other side was relentless. It didn't matter what it was, rocks or arrows. What mattered was that it remained on the other side. The tired recruit used the curved scuta to dig into the loose earth and claw his way upward. Arrows and javelins flew past and overhead like angry wasps.

From atop came a body, sliding headfirst back into the trench, a javelin impaling its chest.

It was Marcellus.

Lucius' feet dug in faster and faster, churning deeper and deeper. The soft dirt grabbed at his ankles and pulled, sucking at what little strength he had left. Every muscle in his body burned, each fiber on fire, especially in his legs.

He turned and watched the quiet listener slide limply, descending into the pit of hell. Exertion and nausea filled Lucius' body by the second as he scrambled for the top of the berm. Groping and gasping for air, he faced his next obstacle: the wooden palisade.

Legionaries appeared from the other side of the burning structure, which was falling apart. They came yelling their war cries. Lucius paused for just a heart's beat: the charging legionaries mirrored Lucius and the others of his cohort. Six other legionaries from Lucius' element materialized from the confusion, forming a line with Lucius in the middle. In the chaos, Lucius recognized the encouraging cries from Sthenelus coming from somewhere in line off to his right.

The legionaries of both sides clashed, more pushing than fighting, like boxers and wrestlers sparing at some game, but scoring no points. Lucius and Sthenelus were now backed by more of their brethren. More shoving and pushing ensued with shields clashing and grinding. Groaning and gasping filled the air. Tips of *gladii* showed themselves on each side of opposing shields, prodding and probing, thrusting and jabbing, like vicious snakes looking to strike.

Lucius had fleeting glimpses of his opponent's eyes, eyes tucked away under a bent and scarred bronze helmet, much like the one he was wearing. Eyes filled with determination, hate, desperation, survival, and bewilderment; all of it revealed in rippling seconds. So it had come to pass: he was finally fighting toe-to-toe with someone truly trying to kill him, and he desperately trying not to be killed.

It was nothing like going against a languid, scarred, and splintered old wooden post. This was real. And it was terrifying.

The battleground filled with blaring horns, shouted commands, angry curses, clashing metal, more shields grinding, and exasperated grunts and moans. The battle tasted of sweat, bile, and salty blood. Slices and crescent wedges of pink, open wounds glistened. Crimson jets spewed in all directions. Gray and purple lifeless lips rimmed gaped and silenced mouths. And Lucius and Sthenelus were in the thick of it all, sandwiched between the enemy and comrades alike, the living and the dead.

Lucius pushed his shield with all his body weight. Pain gnawed at him as if a mad dog had attached itself to his calf. He ceded ground, partially to pain, but mostly fatigue. His opponent surged forward to take advantage of the situation. The gap created was just enough for the legionary to Lucius' right to find an opening. It was Sthenelus.

Sthenelus thrust his sword deep into the oncoming enemy legionary. The look of triumph on the surging legionary's face changed to one of surprise, and then to one of grief. Sthenelus shoved his shield forward and pulled the buried sword from the young man's torso. The dying foe slumped to the ground, only to be replaced by another. The defenders of Caesar's burning fort faltered and inched away from the bloody and littered frontline. Fighting for their lives, they ceded ground.

More of Pompey's troops charged from behind, including Marcus and Decimus, leaving Lucius in their wake in the pursuit of enemy combatants. Lucius recognized Decimus easily enough; he looked like a scurrying training post in uniform next to Marcus.

The tired recruit found himself limping, searching for strength to catch up with the others, so he leaned against the palisade wall to catch his breath. From the other side he could feel heat as fire licked at the dying fort. Vibrations from soldiers fighting above and on the other side thrummed through his body; it wasn't over yet.

Nausea and projectile vomiting assaulted the exhausted legionary without warning.

With his stomach empty again, he moved on, ignoring the aftertaste of war. He picked up his shield and staggered forward to catch up with the fighting that was leaving him behind. Thundering hooves and flying clods of dirt startled him from behind. The ground shook and rocks pelted him; it was the cavalry, swarming and charging, heading for the beaches.

Lucius had become part of the breach sorely needed by Pompey to reach the sea and his supply line.

The defeated troops were under the command of Caesar's deputy, Marcus Antonius, his *8th Legio*. They were due for discharge and their hearts were not with Caesar, or Marcus Antonius. Many of them had already defected to Pompey, just as Antonius' legate, General Titus Labienus, had.

Word reached Caesar of the breach and he gathered the bulk of his army, already preoccupied with a planned feint simultaneously at two other points of attack along the lines and other locations further north, to meet and engage Pompey at the break.

Caesar and his legions charged in from the north, fighting for ground and their lives, moving like a swift colony of ants, rushing to attack an invading colony of rival ants. Pompey's troops were increasing in number as well. The battlefield swelled. Soon, both Caesar and Pompey were close at hand, commanding, shouting, and leading by example.

Pompey had the greater number in legionaries; Caesar had the most experienced. Pompey relied on his increasing momentum; Caesar relied on his luck. Pompey knew from the beginning there was no choice but to engage Caesar, he would have been impotent if he hadn't tried, and doomed if he failed. Caesar hadn't given it a second thought; his course was set after he had crossed the Rubicon.

Dust, smoke, and curses filled the air. Shields clashed, swords jabbed, flesh was sliced and punctured, and blood splattered everywhere. Like combatant ants, the armies tried to sort themselves out, fighting en masse, arms and weapons flashing in the air. Chaos and confusion reigned as Roman fought Roman, and so there was the occasional "friendly kill" due to the closeness of battle, flowing adrenaline, disregard for discipline, and the poor luck of those involved.

Lucius was back in the thick of action again, limping and stumbling, trying to make a difference for his general, his centurion, his comrades, himself—but more importantly—his father.

A perceptible change permeated the air as Lucius limped on to follow the battle. He could hear it, smell it, feel it: Caesar's fighters began a retreat, developing from a slow withdrawal to a full rout.

Pompey yelled orders to stand ground, but the commands were lost in the cacophony of battle, or just plain ignored. Blasts from horns fell on deaf ears.

Pompey's troops were startled at first to see the veterans running from the fray. The general gave further commands to his nearest deputies to have the troops cease action. The troops would have stood down had they heard the orders. But that did not happen; not this time.

New recruits, filled with bravado and that ever-flowing adrenaline and who had somehow evaded death, started after the retreating veterans. Others followed and soon the whole of Pompey's army joined the pursuit. Magnus could not believe his eyes. How could they disobey his orders? Lucius, too, was caught up in the rush and was pulled into the chaotic madness that ruled the moment.

He pushed off with his right foot to join the others when his leg gave way. There was too much noise from the battle to hear the loud "pop" when the tendon ruptured. The snap and separation brought him down, down to the ground in incredulous disbelief, anguish, and with a horrid sense of failure.

He sat on the ground, hot, sweaty, and quivering in exhaustion. Something, or somebody, drew his attention, as if calling him by name. Through vision blurred with tears from pain, dust, and frustration, he saw old Phoebus. The old vet still had that perpetual smile on his face. The body of Phoebus lay on its side, with an intense stare, fixed straight at Lucius, looking into his eyes, right into his very soul.

"Why are you looking at me like that old man?" he asked in gasping, rapid breaths. That smile—or was it now a grimace—was unchanged from all the time Lucius knew the man. This time, it was as if Phoebus knew something Lucius didn't know, and he was trying to tell him. Had he found peace and rest for himself? Did he know who the victorious would be at Dyrrhachium? Or, was there something else? He followed Phoebus' outstretched, dirty, and bloody arm to its partially opened hand. The fingers pointed to an object. Lucius blinked the tears and dust away and the object revealed itself. It was a javelin.

Horror struck like a point of a dagger. He couldn't remember what had happened to his own javelin. Somehow, somewhere, he had lost it during all the fighting. Was Phoebus now reprimanding him?

Rage and anguish returned. He had let his centurion—and his father down.

He labored to his knees, cringing in pain from the uncooperative ankle. He reached over and seized the javelin. Back on his aching knees, he removed his helmet and cast it aside. His eyes painfully let him know that the army was leaving him behind. He grasped the javelin in his shaking right hand and with all the will he could muster, struggled to his feet like a newborn colt, using his excruciating pain as an energy source. He closed his eyes and put forth his left arm, his right hand and arm holding the weapon steady and cocked. He lowered his head in concentration, digging deep again for any residue strength he may have left in his life blood, he let the javelin fly with a powerful, superhuman throw, screaming, "O—mighty—Jupiter, please——"

The javelin disappeared into the haze in an upward arch and Lucius collapsed face down to the dirt, the light of day telescoping into darkness.

The javelin was airborne, a predator looking for prey.

It flew over men fighting below. It glinted and whirred through the air, wobbling ever so gracefully. It danced. It spun. It continued on in perfect flight. All the mortal creatures below, barely visible in the dust and confusion, ceased to move; time had stood still. Tops of helmets and extended arms, frozen in midair, flashed by as the javelin soared toward a target that only the gods would designate. The deities reached out and touched the speeding implement of death, giving it their blessings as it sped by. Janus, the two-headed god who sees both the past and future, the god of doors who seeks new beginnings, the god of transition, was the last to touch the javelin before its earthly descent.

On the ground, Caesar fought to control his horse and command his men at the same time. He yelled orders and insults at his troops as they ran past, in the wrong direction. His bodyguards, large, blond Germans on horseback, simultaneously leaned forward with their long swords to ward off soldiers who were getting too close to Caesar.

That's when it happened.

In battle, the unconceivable is always possible; the unforeseen always foreseeable; the impossible, most probable; and the lucky, well—

The spiraling javelin began its descent, earthward, gaining

speed and energy. It sailed straight for Caesar. He did not see its earthly approach, nor did he hear its sound as it cut through the air, hell bent for whatever, or whomever, lay in its path. It had taken on a life of its own, endowed by the gods and the fates with power to spare or take life as it pleased.

Caesar took this moment, this place, to look right. And, as he did, he offered his neck to the on-coming missile.

The javelin struck him in the space framed by the two neck muscles that form a triangle, just above his clavicle, above his breastplate. It came down with all the force it could gather in its descent, impaling him with a sudden, sharp, spiking force. The point sliced through his vital neck structures, glancing off one of the upper vertebral bones that supported his mighty figurehead. It severed major nerves and blood vessels that lay in its path.

Caesar's right arm came up toward his neck, half-ways with a limp hand, as if to stifle a cough; his left arm could not move at all. The javelin ceased it journey when it finally pierced the back of the breastplate.

Known for his superb horsemanship, Julius Caesar could ride with straight back, arms behind him, and strong legs grasped around the animal; but this was not the case now. His horse sensed something terribly wrong and started a circular prance, counter clockwise; there was no command coming from the rider to do otherwise. The rider finally listed to the right and dropped to the ground in a fine plume of dust.

Everybody in the near vicinity ceased fighting to take in the event that had just stopped the world. Half the bodyguards froze in motion, looking at the man in awe as if they'd never seen him before. The other half ordered their horses away and galloped off, struck with silence, peering back in disbelief and confusion.

The great Caesar was on his back, left arm and hand twitching ever so slightly, gray lips quivering as if trying to speak, and eyes staring but not seeing through half-opened lids. Crimson blood oozed from his neck, blotting his cloak with spreading dark patches.

Men gathered around him, but left him space. They all gazed upon him, taking in the last moments of a god-like mortal; a mortal who had left his boot prints in much of the known Roman world; a mortal who commanded great armies, and had contributed much to the Roman Republic—but wanted more.

Pompey materialized out of a haze like a phantom summoned by temple priests. He dismounted in measured motions, as if coming upon something sacred itself. Those who heard his approach cleared a path so that he, too, could come and pay homage. He kneeled near the fallen Caesar to catch the last gasp expired from Julius' blue lips. Except for the distant muffled sound of galloping horses and fleeing soldiers, the air was eerily still. The leather of Pompey's uniform and the pebbles under his boots broke the revered silence as he stood, eyes fixed on the corpse.

"Put him on my horse," he said, speaking to no one in particular. "And take him back to my tent."

CHAPTER IV

Subdued, solemn, and tired, Pompey led his bodyguards, tribunes, and a small contingent of legionaries back to his command post. In tow, a lone horse followed with a cloaked body across it. A strip of torn red cloak covered the animal's eyes. The smell of blood and the saddled dead weight of the cadaver had made it jittery.

Senator Cicero, who fled Rome as an ally of the optimates but not necessarily as a collaborator with Pompey Magnus, emerged from a large tent to take in the procession. The former consul planted himself, hands clasped together at the back and chin aloft; his fidgeting fingers and toes did not appear so regal. He attired himself in an officer's uniform, looking like an emaciated turtle in a shell too big for him; it fit his ego perfectly.

The general and his entourage stopped just short of Cicero who greeted them with a much-practiced, professional smile.

"Greetings, General. I pray you have returned with good news for the Republic." Leaning to the right to peek around the much larger man in front of him, Cicero eyed the horse with the body draped across.

"I come with more than just news, Consular. I come with Caesar."

Cicero scratched at his head as if to unfetter some words, important words, words he could quote himself saying later in some future speech or writing. "Ah, I see, well . . . the Republic will remember this glorious day and the services you have performed. My congratulations to you, Sir; of course, you will share the details with us so that we might have it all together for prosperity."

Pompey leered at him, not offering a single syllable whatsoever. He turned to the nearest tribune and ordered him to gather a detail to place Caesar's body on Pompey's cot. The tribune saluted, pivoted sharply, and pointed to three legionaries. The general observed with guarded eyes, making sure it was performed respectfully. The legionaries grasped Caesar's body and pulled it from the horse. The horse side-stepped in nervous prances and then relaxed when relieved of the corpse. The legionaries carried the corpse by its legs and torso into the tent and gently placed it on the cot as ordered, part of the javelin still in its neck. Its face remained covered with a blood-soaked cloak, which started to attract annoying flies. An air of reverence prevailed during the whole little ceremony, in spite of the attacking flies.

Cicero followed the informal honor guard, turned, craned his neck, and searched for another horse with a body on it. "And what of Marcus Antonius? Did you not bring anything of him as well?" he asked, interrupting the solemn act.

"No. I bring nothing of him. He and his legions, or what's left of his legions, escaped to the East," Pompey said flatly as his exhausted body and mind slumped into a chair.

"Caesar is really dead," Cicero said, making a declaration, his eyes roving over the corpse on the cot as if he'd never seen the man before in his life. "It's hard to believe. I didn't think that man could ever die. He'd always been . . . been so—"

"Lucky? Yes, he was a very lucky man. Fortuna watched over him as if he were her own son," Pompey said, admiring the body. "But why should it be a surprise? That man tempted death so many times on the battlefield, and elsewhere."

"Still, I didn't imagine he'd die this way," Cicero continued. "I could see him dying at the hands of some jealous husband, a woman spurned, or the likes of those pirates so many years past. Yes, they could have dispatched him easily enough then. Or, even in the Forum at the hand of an assassin or two, or a mob, or—"

"Like the Gracchi brothers."

"Precisely!"

"Maybe he gave Pluto the evil eye; who knows? And what does it matter how death took him. The man is dead," Pompey pronounced, as if to make it official. "Get over it. Besides, I think this is how he would have preferred death—in the thick of battle.

"Oh, but it does matter. A man may be remembered more for the way he died than the way he lived. Pity. It could matter much, indeed. Look at Spartacus. Crucifixion. All those followers. To this day there are those who whisper his name in reverence and worship him in secret. In death, he still has a following."

"That may be an exaggeration, Cicero. Who would worship a rebel instigator after crucifixion? That should be example enough to make people think. They'll soon forget. You'll see," said Pompey. "But Caesar, I doubt anyone will forget him, no matter what form of death befell him. I dare say he will be remembered . . . as Alexander himself. Some men are just born to live forever, no matter what form of death takes them. Only his mortal corpse is dead, my friend. I doubt either you or I shall be remembered for as long, Consul."

"One never knows. One just never knows," Cicero exclaimed as he turned and was gone.

Out on the battlefield, a young legionary—one of many—lay sprawled in the dirt. The earth quenched a thirst as it drank in blood, much blood, blood seeping in through cracks and crevices from the dead of both sides. Bodies littered the field, remnants of mothers' babies; vestiges of teetering toddlers with tiny teeth flashing loving smiles; relics of mischievous boys agilely running and jumping through the countryside, carefree and unencumbered; residues of teenage youths plagued by raging hormones and the want of . . . something . . . that unknown—something.

ANTHONY MICHAEL VILLANUEVA

For some, that something was the excitement of being a legionary and going to battle, all fun and glory—until someone got killed. For others, it was to make someone proud, like a father. For those who did not want to go, there was that beleaguered, constant fear that death loomed near. Like a green wheat crop, the battle laid waste much unripe stalk cut down too soon.

In a dream state, the sprawled legionary was working the fields, cutting wheat, fresh golden stalks ripe with grain. There was a stone house in the distance reflecting a warm sun and he could just make out the image of a woman waving at him. It must be time for the noon break. He continued to sweep the sharp, shiny, curved blade from side to side with bits of gilded straw floating effortlessly into the air. Oddly, the blade morphed to a Roman sword, the twenty-one inch gladius. The sun beat down on him and all was good.

He stepped forward for the next row of uncut wheat when a stabbing pain bit at his right ankle. Muffled humming in his ears grew to a roar of men yelling, horses whinnying, wagon wheels rolling on dirt and rock, and flies buzzing about his head. Boots, more than one pair, marched in his direction. The crunching of the ground grew louder and louder until the boots stopped just short of where he lay.

"I think he's one of ours," said an accented voice, the inflection different than Lucius'. "Turn him over, but be careful. Have your swords ready."

Lucius felt his body levitate with the help of several pairs of rough hands. They tossed him unto his back. Pain at his ankle shot up his leg as if some unseen monster had just bitten his foot off; he grimaced and then cried out.

The shout of pain took to the air and disappeared over the battlefield, leaving behind a train of panted breaths gasping for air.

The sun was warm on his face, yet an errant breeze swept across his body and made his body shiver. Another set of boots approached at a quickened pace, stopping near his head. A silhouette blotted out the sun and cast a familiar voice.

"That's Lucius. Pontius I think is his *nomen*, Lucius Pontius. He was with my group, with Centurion Marcus Caelius." The familiar voice belonged to Sthenelus Regulius.

"He doesn't look wounded, get him to his feet," ordered the person in charge. Two soldiers reached for him and yanked him to his feet. From a distance, it looked like they were trying to hitch a scarecrow to a pole.

"My foot, my foot!" Lucius cried out in pain again, unable to stand without support. Sthenelus noted the extreme swelling and purple skin at the ankle before anyone else and pointed it out. The foot was in an abnormal position and definitely discolored.

"Good then." Not really meaning a good situation, just an acknowledgement of the predicament. "Fix a litter or get a walking stick," the legionary wielding authority ordered.

Two men tossed Lucius onto a stretcher and carried him off to the triage area. The two bearers served as veterinary orderlies as well as medical aides. The trip to the designated area was long and bumpy. Lucius held on for dear life during the white-knuckled ride, mostly to keep his lower leg from being jostled about.

"W-w-what happened y-y-you?" asked the bearer at the foot of the stretcher in a strange, broken accent. His chopped words came out nasal and covered with spittle.

"Don't know. One minute I'm fighting, the next—" Lucius grumbled, but stopped himself. He had no idea why he was even talking to this person.

"Y-y-you lucky. See no b-b-big cuts, no b-b-burns. Y-y-you very lucky. Not like C-c-caesar. He not lucky n-n-no more. Foot look b-b-bad. If you horse, we k-k-kill you! Eat you l-l-later."

Lucius studied this bearer hard. Was he on our side? He

appeared as strange as he talked with facial features bordering on extreme ugliness: half-lidded, bulging eyes that fought to stay even, crossed with a single, thick eyebrow that looked like two, fat, hairy caterpillars going head-to-head in battle; ears set low, sticking out from an oily, filthy, leather cap, like small shields often carried by those barbarians way up north; pegs for teeth that were encrusted in brown food stuff from at least the past month; and a vast swarm of flies that kept him company.

Where did creatures like this come from? What was going on? What did he mean not like Caesar? Is it over? Too many thoughts to sort out for now as another wave of fatigue, nausea, and somnolence rushed at him. He slipped into unconsciousness once more.

Pompey stared at the draped corpse before him. Until today, that man had been incredibly lucky. He had survived Sulla. Marrying that tyrant's granddaughter was certainly the smart thing to do; Sulla had his death eye on him. By the gods how he could eat—enough for many at the table. And he loved his women—and other men's women, too. Pompey wondered if it was true what was said about the other gender as well. How was it said? Oh yes, "every woman's man and every man's woman." Rubbish, jealous talk, that's all.

In silence, in sincerity, and in reverence, Pompey thanked Caesar for one gift to this world—Julia. The tired general focused all his cerebral awareness on that wonderful child, scent, sight, and sound. He leaned forward so that only Caesar could hear and whispered, "You know, we truly loved each other, Julia and I. I would have given it up, all of it, the politics, the army, everything, just to be with our lovely Julia . . . just the two of us in the countryside."

There would have been three had Julia survived the birthing. She was too small and delicate, didn't have the proper pelvic structure to allow a good birth, no matter what the midwives did or to whom they prayed. It had been horrible: the hours, the screaming, the wailing, the pleading, the exhaustion, the bloody mess. The young girl—a child really—was brave like a soldier, like her father, going to war with nature knowing that she would either be victorious, or would be death's next prey. In the end, both mother and child lay lifeless in a heap of bloody linen on the grotesque battlefield of her laboring bed. Gnaeus Pompeius Magnus lost a loving wife and child; Gaius Julius Caesar lost a loving daughter and grandchild.

"My life ended when the gods took them, dear friend. My spirit roams this world, looking for them, while my body suffers life. Sure, I have Cornelia, but she's no Julia. I mourn the gods have taken the wrong man this day, Gaius."

The corpse did not answer back.

Elongated, stabbing shadows inched along the inside of the tent, etching a scene of impending evening. The old general, fifty-seven years old being exceptionally old this evening and with another year to add in two months' time, laboriously stood up with the help of some small groans. He stepped outside to stretch his weary body and survey all that was his to command this evening.

Once out of the tent, he encountered Cicero again. The man had been busy writing his account of today's events, even though he was not present. He had been dictating the events to his secretary, former slave, but now freedman and close companion Tiro. Like most men his age, Cicero's eyesight was faltering—as was the bladder, the hearing, the strength, the balance, the back, the body in general. It was much easier for someone else to write— he would simply provide the words.

Pompey himself suffered poor vision, as well as other maladies. He had been dreadfully ill not too long ago and the people of Rome were most concerned. They prayed to the gods for a quick recovery. Even now, he felt unwell: that nagging discomfort under his rib cage plagued him again. It was tough getting old. It took much stamina. Every new morning was a gift; or a curse.

"Ah, General, I see you have been resting. It's been a busy

day for you and the gods. Jupiter Invictus appears to have been in league with the goddess Fortuna today, even though she gave up her favorite son. Yes, victory and luck, it's always best to have them both on your side. The omens couldn't have been better," Cicero said with authority. "You know, five years past I was appointed to the *college of augers*. Yes, being responsible for studying the auspices can be a serious undertaking. The gods can be very fastidious."

Pompey shot Cicero another leer. The man was forever boasting.

In a slouch to inspect the gravel before his feet, Cicero continued, "I must confess, however, I really don't give all the credit to superstitions and omens. It just seems so . . . illogical at times. I mean . . . well, we mortals must take control and be responsible for our deeds, our lives—our destinies. Events can happen by chance, luck if you will—or lack of it. What do birds, animal intestines, clouds, and countless other portends have to do with the outcome of actions and events we set in motion, huh?"

Pompey raised a brow and flashed a cutting look in disbelief. Was he really hearing this from Cicero?

Cicero collected himself and came to attention, he apologized. "We must, however, maintain the traditions . . . for the public's sake . . . for the good of the Republic . . . for the people . . . or all of Rome," he countered loudly, casting a quick peek with raised eyebrows and a flick of his head skyward, following with a sheepish grin, as if someone up there might be listening in. Pompey followed Cicero's eyes, glancing upwards. He saw only sky and the changing cloudscape.

An uncomfortable silence followed as Cicero moved some small rocks around with the tip of his boot, rearranging the earth to his liking. "What of Caesar? What is planned?" he continued, satisfied with the new arrangement of the pebbles.

"Tomorrow we'll commit his earthly body to the fire. I'll take his ashes to Calpurnia when we return to Rome. He would have done the same for me, I'm certain. She may wish to have him rest with Julia, in the *Campus Martius*—the Field of Mars." The mention of Julia's name summoned a twinge of pain to the scar on Pompey's heart, not for Caesar, but for himself; he missed his beloved wife. The scar hurt less, but nonetheless, it still hurt.

"And his army, what will become of it?" Cicero inquired.

"Many have come over to our side. His veterans were due for discharge. They'll swear an oath of allegiance and our army will be increased by that many."

"Can they be trusted?"

"Ask General Titus Labienus," Pompey shot back. "He was one of Caesar's best and most capable generals. Now he's one of ours."

"That's rather lenient, Magnus."

"Caesar would have done likewise. He was most magnanimous to a fault," Pompey said.

"And Marcus Antonius?" the elderly statesman and orator asked.

"Thank the gods he was not the victor today, Marcus, or both our heads would be on the first boat to Ostia in the morning, for display in the Forum, for all of Rome to admire."

Cicero cleared his throat and dismissed himself. "Yes, well . . . well maybe there is something to be said for the gods after all . . . huh? Well, then . . . suppose we will continue this tomorrow. *Kalinihta*—good night," he said in Greek, turning away but stopping in mid-turn. "You may want to do something with our friend in there," tilting his head to the tent and wrinkling his nose. He turned away again and disappeared into the evening.

Cicero marched to his tent in quick steps, thoughts drifting to

Julia. She was such a pretty young thing, and appeared to really love that old man, Pompey. All of Rome said they were quite fond of each other. It's possible. If the situation presented itself and the gods felt it necessary, even he, Cicero, the elderly but respectable statesmen he was, could take to a young pretty wife.

Now thoughts of his own precious daughter, Tullia, flooded his head, his little "Tulliola." If ever there was pleasure in this world, it was in the form of a divine daughter like Tullia. Julia was pretty, but Tullia was the fairest of all daughters in the Republic, if not the world.

Cicero was not only blessed with the gifts of speech, intellect, and philosophy, but also with a little goddess in the form of a child—now a woman. A floodgate of images opened up and filled his head: a little girl with long, dark, curly hair and little wisps of fine threads floating at the upper corners of her broad forehead; a fine cherubic face gleaming with innocence; a beautiful smile accented with little giggles as she ran with tiny flowers in her delicate and petite fingers; and eyes large, brown, and round, like small olives with dreamy upper lids to flash when she blinked. She was love in motion.

The *nones* of next month, Sextilis, the eighth lunar month, would be her birthday. That month was always special to the household with celebrations and feasting. Now she was heavy with child and having a difficult time of it. If only there was word of a grandchild, a little boy; what a blessing that would be.

His chest inflated deeply and expelled a suffering, single sigh. A flicker of a peek in the direction of Pompey's tent cleared the way for him to wipe the beginnings of a few tears with his fingers. No one saw and he continued on his way.

CHAPTER
V

A pair of fast ducks hurried in disciplined formation over Roman campfires flickering below which appeared as glowing coals strewn across a darkened landscape. Their wings beat the air severely, carrying the birds east, climbing to a sky not yet blessed by Helios. In their wake among the fires below, men lay scattered, exhausted, wounded, or dead.

Lucius woke from a lifeless sleep, tired, cold, and shivering violently. In desperation he tried to sponge warmth from a woolen cape placed on him during the night. The pain at the ankle was cold and throbbing, feeling much worse when he moved his leg.

Coughs and moans in nearby shadows grew in number around Lucius as others stirred. The silent ones cared less about blankets or anything else; they would be moved later for mass cremation.

Hours passed, yet there was no sun. All the colors of cold, especially dark gray, dominated the morning as trumpets called and the camp pulsed with organized purpose. Cohorts and legions were preparing for a busy day.

Lucius' trembling arms propped him up on one elbow and he scanned the direction of the trumpet calls. Must be a mustering of the troops, he thought.

An attendant wearing just enough skin and very little fat to cover his bones appeared out of the dark. A blood-encrusted leather apron that was much too large for him draped his skinny frame and skimmed the ground as he waddled. Used and dirty dressings dangled from his arms like dead animals. He reminded Lucius of some of the mangy, wild dogs seen roaming the area looking for something to eat, but without the apron.

Lucius reached and grabbed at the attendant's leg. "What's happening?"

The attendant stopped. He turned to the direction of the blaring. "The commander is going to give a speech to the troops, and then I guess they'll put Caesar to the fire."

"Caesar? Fire? Is he really dead?" Lucius asked, oblivious to the world the last twelve hours or more.

"No, we're going to roast him alive, like the Parthians!" snickered the attendant as if gasping for breath.

"You know what I mean," Lucius snapped back in a stern mask.

The attendant blinked wide, nervous eyes, wishing he hadn't answered as he did. "Forgive me, I only meant that, well . . . Caesar died, Pompey was victorious, and today they commit Caesar to the funeral pyre. Pompey is going to address the troops sometime this morning.

"That fire should be nice and warm, the day being cold and all." He hesitated, blinked rapidly, and then tried to look serious. "I mean . . . it should be a very nice, uh . . . honorable fire . . . ceremony."

"I need to talk to somebody about getting out of here, back to my unit," Lucius said, grimacing in pain as he sat upright.

The attendant shrugged his bony shoulders, wrinkled his runny nose, shook his head, and went on his way, leaving behind the stench of his work and his body.

"I've got to get to my unit. Got to find a way," he whispered to his surroundings as he searched for parts of his uniform or anything else that looked like it may belong to him. His ankle pained him to move, but he was learning to slink about in measured doses.

"And where do you think you go?" said a Greek-accented voice, which startled Lucius.

Turning to the deep voice, Lucius faced an elderly man with wisdom and experience etched in his face, especially around the eyes. He, too, wore an apron splashed with medical, veterinary, or meat cutting skills. "I need to get back to my unit," the cripple answered. "I just need some help, a walking stick, or crutch of some fashion."

"I'm afraid you go nowhere, young man, least of all to your unit. Your fighting days are . . . how you say . . . *finis*—over," the old man said.

Lucius glared at the old man, attempting to process those words into something his brain would accept. "My fighting days—over?"

The old physician lumbered to a knee, laid hands on and gently manipulated the ugly ankle. Lucius stiffened and panted through clenched teeth. With squinted eyes and wrinkled nose, Lucius controlled the shooting waves of pain that attacked him.

"You know, in my country, many, many years ago, in the times of . . . well, you wouldn't know my people, anyway . . . the victors would take a sword to this part of the lower leg and slice this sinew, this flesh we call Achilles flesh," pointing to the backside of the swollen ankle with his hairy, fat, yet delicate finger, "thus . . . making them slaves." The old man and the young recruit locked eyes, one stating the obvious, and the other refusing to believe it. Lucius shook his head in denial, flinging sweat from his wet hair.

"What will become of me?"

"Ah, well, I believe your army has . . . how is it you call them?— *immunes*, workers who do other things than fight. Cooks, medical helpers, people like that."

"You mean . . . like slaves?"

The old man shrugged and offered a half-smile.

Lucius' mind flashed images of the litter-bearer and the dressing attendant. He felt another wave of nausea welling, like an angry pool of bubbling bile seeping upward. The old physician regarded the young man for a moment or two, and then continued on his way to evaluate other wounded warriors.

Lucius' eyes followed the old Greek. Was he serious, or just trying to scare him? I'll die first before I become one of those creatures, he vowed. He contemplated alternatives, skills, options—there didn't seem to be very many. "I'll go to Centurion Caelius, he'll tell me what I can do," he whispered. Lucius assumed Caelius had survived the battle.

An uncertain future preoccupied the young cripple. He didn't notice the display the gods were offering in the developing morning sky. The rims of the eastern, gray clouds ignited and burned scarlet as if heated by a great oven. The fiery hue spread beyond the edges and soon the whole blanket of ruffled clouds glowed crimson. The cloudscape was of a great conflagration afar, as if a great city was aflame and dying underneath, the vaporous blanket above reflecting the heat. The inflamed sky finally caught Lucius' eye and he found it absolutely beautiful, yet terrifying. "What is this? What is it that you are showing me? Is this my future? What have you planned for me now?" he asked the gods.

Finally, Helios broke through in all his glory with the points of his crown, blazing shafts of penetrating rays, shooting outward from a bright yellow ball. Clouds once bright scarlet cooled to dull yellow and then back to gloomy gray. The giant orb climbed into the cloud layer and disappeared from view, not to be seen again for the rest of the morning.

By midday Lucius had ceased his shivering and felt much warmer; thanks to the old cape used as a blanket. Horn blasts from the curled *buccina*—the war horns, sounded again. Legionaries obeyed the blaring calls and assembled.

Lucius worked himself up to a sitting position where he could just see the back end of troop formations with the tops of their respective standards and eagles at the front. He could imagine Pompey addressing the victorious legions and cohorts. "I should be there," he said, letting a sigh, heavy with hopelessness, topple from his chest.

He listened intently, making out the drone of a voice echoing off nearby structures. Now and then he could hear a word or two from the general, something of "victory . . . the Republic . . . Rome . . . people . . . He wished he could hear more clearly, but he wasn't in the best place. There were hundreds of troops in his way, and that's where he wanted to be, in line with them. If only he could have contributed his part.

Only the gods knew of his contribution.

A sudden, thunderous roar erupted from the formation: *"Hail Imperator!"* The pulsating reverberation slammed and pounded into his chest like a gigantic fist, causing his lungs and heart to shudder. The deafening salute rumbled on like a huge tidal wave, rolling and echoing into the distance. The shock wave woke the dead—Lucius was sure of it.

Draped in his royal, red cloak and absent the javelin, Caesar's body rested atop a giant funeral bed. The fort and palisades near the breakout provided the wood—Marcus Antonius' contribution. Though it couldn't be seen, a gold coin rested on Caesar's pale, cold tongue to pay his fare across the Styx—Pompey's contribution. The victorious general stepped forward, gave the formal Roman salute, and then tossed his torch up onto the stacked wood. Likewise, at Pompey's signal, a nod, five tribunes tossed their torches as well.

There was smoke only at first as everyone watched. Hissing vapors gradually became small flames, combusting to a larger fire, then developing to a roaring inferno. Those closest had to step back as the heat on their faces and bodies became more intense.

In Rome, at Caesar's house, dressers busied themselves attending to Calpurnia Pisonis, Caesar's third wife. A new *palla* had been designed for her for a special occasion, the occasion being a private birthday party in honor of her husband, who turned fifty-two, near the *Ides* of Quintilus. He would not be present for he was away conducting his campaign against Pompey and the rebel optimates; but, as she would advise her guests, he would be there in spirit.

The attendants finished securing the final clasps that held the garment in place when they were all assaulted by a wild and chaotic squall from a nearby window. Curtains lashed out in violence like long arms reaching out for prey; the pleats of the beautiful palla flew undone; and her hair, neatly put in place with pins and netting, attacked her face.

The tumultuous whirlwind stormed into the next room like a loose, crazed beast. Metal and ceramic objects clattered and smashed to the floor. And then—as suddenly as it had arrived—it was gone; only a still, cool air remained.

Calpurnia trembled in fear but did not move as everyone awaited a further assault. The curtains, however, fluttered softly in an effortless and innocent breeze, as if offering a gentle caress.

Screams of panic and the scrambling of sandaled feet emanated from the room from which the beastly wind charged. Calpurnia gathered her torn palla and ran to the room from where the screams flew.

A large oil lantern rolled rhythmically back and forth on the marble floor next to decorative drapes framing a bust of her husband. One end of a drape disintegrated as a metastasizing flame climbed for Caesar's figurehead. Oily, black smoke smudged the wall. All the while, soot snowed upon the bust.

Servants rushed to the scene with containers of water and

extinguished the flames, leaving the floor a pool of black liquid and burnt fabric. They looked to Calpurnia for further commands, but she stood motionless, frozen in place, unable to speak, let alone breathe without shaking. Nausea assaulted her and she had to run to an open window to either get some fresh air or expel the contents of her unsettled stomach.

Lucius pulled his way to his feet, avoiding undue weight on his ankle. He leaned on a tent pole and looked over toward the burning heap: A giant pyramid of fire leaped for the heavens and burned a hole in the sky. Amidst the blaze, spears of pirouetting, orange flames danced atop the pyre, like reveling nymphs.

The formations had moved on. Only a select few stood guard, or waited further orders.

Ash and soot rained down on the cripple, collecting in his hair and arms, like snow on a winter day. He remembered the crimson, morning sky and how it appeared to be ablaze. The ash had finally arrived.

The cripple collapsed back to earth. An insatiable thirst and hunger invaded his body as he fell to his back. He stared up at the raining ash and soot, and couldn't remember his last meal.

CHAPTER VI

Gray gave way to blue as the evening crept in.

Food found its way to Lucius: a hard piece of wheat bread with a bit of olive oil, wheat meal mixed in the usual suppa, a few small, dried fish, and some wine cut with water. It wasn't like home, but it partially satisfied his hunger. Along with the food came a surprise: a visit from a friend.

"Sthenelus! The gods let you live, huh?" Lucius couldn't remember the last time the muscles in his face had allowed a smile. It felt good, as good as the sun's warmth on his skin. Sthenelus was intact with clean face and arms; his uniform, however, was crusted in dry blood—but not his.

"Looks like they weren't too sure about you, though," Sthenelus said. "Are you hurt badly? Is it grave? You look to be in one piece."

"I'll survive," Lucius said, managing to keep the smile as he examined his ankle again. "My ankle gave way. Something under the skin tore or broke. I can't move my foot." He was trying to remember what the old Greek physician had told him.

"Don't worry, you'll be back marching with us in no time, you'll see. In fact, we're getting ready to move again, not sure where to this time."

"I don't think so, Sthen. The old physician said my days as a legionary are over." Lucius scoped up a handful of dirt and let it fall back to earth through a narrow channel made in a clenched fist, watching the granules and small pebbles funnel to a small mound. He repeated this several times. Sthenelus scanned the horizon as if expecting something of significance to happen. A breeze and the commotion of winged insects filled the silence.

A simultaneous start of trivial chatter stammered and clashed into unfinished and broken words, followed by awkward smirks.

Again, silence.

Sthenelus started again, first. "What are you going to do? I mean, if you can't soldier, what then?"

"Don't know for sure, yet. I still have the use of everything above my feet, which should count for something. Maybe I could scribe, you know, copy writings and letters. Or maybe I could draw portraits for people on walls in their homes. My mother said I was good at etching pictures and copying images. I've seen some beautiful frescoes painted on walls. I can do it. I know I can." He examined his hands intently, his eyes roving over extended fingers as he rotated and inspected them at different aspects. "Surely the gods could find something important for these, other than killing. Besides, I never made a kill in battle anyway." He cringed the second the words slipped past his lips and looked around to see if anyone else had heard him.

Sthenelus flashed Lucius a smile as he tried to make a crude circle in the dirt with his own finger, quickly brushing through it in disgust—he would leave the sketching to Lucius. "It just wasn't your day for fighting, that's all. Mighty Jupiter has other plans for you. I bet you could have taken ten foes if the battle wasn't over so soon. And if Jupiter doesn't have plans for you, then I bet one of the other gods has."

"What happened anyway? Caesar is dead, is he not?" Lucius asked.

"Dead as dead. His troops gave way, turned and ran. I hear Pompey had ordered us to hold, but . . . well, there was so much yelling and noise and a rush from our side chasing those fleeing cowards that . . . well . . . we just didn't stop," boasted Sthenelus.

"You should have seen it! It was magnificent." Sthenelus gestured in wild animation and excitement as his arms and hands told his story. "Caesar was trying to hold back his retreating army when he took a javelin to his throat, I've been told anyway. I didn't see it happen."

In disbelief, Lucius fixated on a point a hundred miles behind Sthen, his smile failing him, his eyes wide and blinking, and his brain trying to digest and absorb all that Sthenelus was saying. "A javelin," he whispered. "Are you sure a javelin?" he asked.

Sthenelus fixed quizzical eyes on Lucius. "That's what I heard. Why?" he asked, a little confused as to what difference it made what weapon killed Caesar—Caesar was dead.

Lucius returned to the moment, the trance broken by Sthenelus' question. "No good reason, just wondering if I heard you right." Lucius willed another smile to his face, his brain clamoring for more information. Could it be? No, impossible. It was a battle. There could have been any number of weapons flying through the air. And the field was thick with fighting.

His ears cleared themselves of a humming before Lucius realized the humming was Sthenelus' voice.

"You look pale. Are you well?"

Lucius met his eyes and nodded. "Yes, I think so."

"Well, I have to get back before they start looking for me. Get well. I'll see you later my friend." With that, Sthenelus was up and gone.

Lucius sat in stunned silence and found that place he had drifted off to again. "Javelin. It couldn't have been mine. It was . . . it was the god's."

The funeral fire died and the earth was sprinkled with wine.

A special detail combed the pile of debris for Caesar's ashes, or what they would claim to be, including some bone fragments. The sacred material was placed into an urn obtained from the nearby city of Dyrrhachium and delivered to Pompey. Cicero was present when it arrived.

"Ah, Caesar is once again with us," Cicero said, eyeing the urn. "You will take him back to Calpurnia soon?"

"That's right. First, I need to get enough sailing vessels prepared to take my legions with me. An 'Honor Guard' if you will."

"Take your army back into Rome? But, Magnus . . . isn't that what all this carnage was about? You can't take your legions into Rome!" Cicero started to stutter, which was so un-Cicero, in the Forum anyway.

Pompey turned and advanced on Cicero, like the dominant wolf pack leader forcing submission with his assertiveness. "I'm taking half my army. I can and I will. The Senate will not deny me this time."

"But, Magnus—"

Pompey felt empowered and confident and was thankful it was only Cicero he was confronting. Had it been the likes of Cato, it would not have been as pleasant. Cato would have challenged him, with a sword even, and be his unwavering defiant self, demanding that Pompey rethink his plans. Fortunately, Cato was back at the garrison where Pompey could keep an eye on him. The general had a suspicion that with both Crassus and Caesar dead it would be highly advantageous for certain members of the Senate if he, too, were dead, in order for the optimates to take back their Republic. It would be wise to keep someone like Cato close—closer than his friends. He could be trouble.

Cicero used his best weapon against the general—his words: "For the sake of the Republic and the constitutionality of the government, it is unwise, let alone unlawful, to bring your troops into Rome! Think of the implications, the consequences, the . . . hypocrisy of it all," Cicero stammered.

"Then, I'll have you to defend me," Pompey retorted in a calm, assured voice. "You were part of my operations here."

Cicero was speechless, which was awkward for such a great orator.

Tiro, Cicero's efficient secretary, waddled in a hurry toward his master's tent in his usual characteristic gait: feet jutting outward like a duck; hips swaying from side to side to keep up with his flat feet; knees slightly bent; spine and head straight and chin extended; hands effeminately clasped in front as if in prayer; eyes fixed straight with lids at half-mast; and mouth completely empty of muscle tone. His lofty mannerism prevailed when addressing anybody but his master, at which point he would revert to his former, subservient, slave self: humbly bowed; a wide smile plastered across his face forcing his cheeks up into his eyes; and his head inclined to the right. He was in his aristocratic mode when he came upon a young cripple.

The cripple was on the ground, stick in hand, sketching unique images in the dirt. The images were akin to a large mural, created flat on the ground.

Tiro came to a stop and cast a long, ominous shadow on the images. The dirt pictorial was remarkable, he thought, and would look marvelous if painted on one of the master's walls.

The ghostly silhouette looming over the cripple's creation caused the cripple to cease his etching. The being that blotted out the sun stood rooted before the artisan and his dirt mural. The silhouette's tilted head looked like it would topple off the shoulders at any second. The stranger uttered not a word until the cripple began a slow destruction of his work with the same stick he used to create it.

"No, please, not yet," Tiro beseeched. "You seem to have a gift."

The young cripple said nothing, not even acknowledging Tiro's presence.

"Can you write?" Tiro asked.

The cripple caught the stranger's lordly, yet cold eyes. "I can write."

"What are you doing here?"

The cripple squinted at the stranger before him in puzzlement. Couldn't the man see? He was wounded. Any fool could see that, he thought to himself.

Tiro stared at the cripple, waiting for a reply. "You have a name?"

"Lucius, Lucius Pontius."

With an occasional blink and an expressionless gaze, the stranger remained engrossed with the cripple.

The cripple could feel the stranger's eyes roaming up and down his body, lingering on his legs, shoulders, and arms. It made him nervous. And then, saying nothing further, the stranger turned away and continued on, taking his shadow with him.

With the intruder gone, Lucius went back to his creation: soldiers in the thick of battle, men on horses, one of them resembling the dead Caesar. In the middle of it all, a single javelin coursed through the heavens. The figures were unlike stick people; they had substance and form and were more than one-dimensional. He imagined the figures yelling, fighting, and dying.

Cicero continued his argument, adamant against returning soldiers to Rome. "The Senate will not take it lightly. There will be a concern regarding . . . regarding the past repeating itself . . . the proscriptions," he said in as calm a manner as he could possibly feign.

"So, you think I plan to do the same? Make a list and decrease the Senate of good people? Confiscate property? Tip the scale in my favor?" Pompey said with a crooked smile on his rotund face, his brows lifting three thick pleats of skin of his forehead.

"Gaius Marius and Lucius Cornelius Cinna did it. Lucius Cornelius Sulla did it with a vengeance," Cicero exclaimed.

"That's true. They did, didn't they?" Pompey let his words hang in the air, like a threatening storm cloud for Cicero to ponder. "My good Cicero, fellow Roman, compatriot . . . we are all from the same animal, but not necessarily the same litter," he said, pausing for effect, gathering his thoughts, choosing his words carefully, and moving cautiously as if stalking prey. "Sulla took many lives, tipped the scales back to his liking, towards the optimates. I even contributed my own private legions to his cause. I'm well aware of my 'butcher boy' reputation."

Cicero stood silent, listening as Pompey circled.

"I was young, strong, and a fit wolf cub. The great Lupus, our dear she-wolf, reared me well, as well as her Romulus. It is part of the natural law of things, don't you think? I have gained much experience and knowledge with all that I've become. The populus have no need to fear me, nor do the patricians. I was more loved by the people than Caesar ever was. It is with no great vanity that I say this, only the knowledge that it is so. I won more battles, conquered more for Rome, and brought more riches for our treasury than he ever did. I did more in less time. The people will receive me well. The Senate, the people, and Rome have nothing to fear from me."

Cicero inhaled deeply. "Reared well, as well as Romulus," he echoed Pompey. "Romulus slew his brother Remus. The she-wolf's offspring are always killing one another. She-wolf indeed, Lupus, the wolf, our most excellent protector of sheep."

Pompey stood resolute before Cicero, smiling as if he possessed a much-guarded secret. "I repeat, my dear Consular, citizen, fellow descendant of Romulus . . . and Remus, you have nothing to fear from me. Save your fears for the kin of Caesar and his loyal followers, like Marcus Antonius. It is not from this friendly lupus that you should lose any sleep. Now, if you'll excuse me, I have much to do." Pompey waited for Cicero to depart.

Cicero exited Pompey's tent and left behind many quick and irate footsteps. Missed commentary and razor-sharp rejoinders that had come too late filled his head. So full was his head that he thought it would split open, like a ripe melon. He had to calm down, he told himself. Be civil. The tongue can be as sharp as any blade. Control the situation or the blade will do much damage. He tried very hard to convince himself this was so.

From a short distance Cicero saw his man Tiro approaching. It didn't take much to recognize that waddling gait and stubby short hair. He closed his eyes and offered a quick, brusque nod.

Tiro acknowledged with a stuttered bow. "Good day to you, good grandchild of Aeneas. Did you have a good meeting with the general?" he asked with a façade of a smile.

Narrow, hard eyes flared at the freedman, but the master's mouth could not find anything to say, it was clamped shut and tight.

Tiro fell in line and followed his master, waddling as fast as he could, like a duckling in its mother's wake. "Shall we be returning to Rome soon, Dominus?"

Cicero answered with a robust shake of his head and a frown clearly creased in his face.

Tiro's smile shrunk and his eyebrows constricted. The thought of spending more time on this remote tour settled in like a severe case of dysentery. He missed all the comforts and conveniences of civilized Rome; but mostly he missed the master's villas. To be away much longer didn't bode well with him, not at all. "Can my master give a hint as to how much longer I . . . well, that is . . . we . . . are to be here?" he asked, trying to keep in step.

"Not sure," the master grumbled as they marched to their tent. Nothing more was said. And now, both heads ached.

Upon reaching his tent, Cicero took the time to examine the heavens and cleanse himself with deep breaths and wide, circulating arms that drew the tension away from his body to elsewhere.

Tiro sensed it might be safe to ask questions again. "What are your plans when we do finally return, wisest of all Romans?" he asked.

The master cast a long, searching stare to the sky, as if seeing through a time portal. "Write. Yes, I plan to write quite a bit. I've been formulating many ideas as of late. I have a lot to say before I cross that river Styx." Then a change, a sense of warmth and love washed over his face, as if a ray of sun had broken through some dark storm clouds and found him. "My daughter, yes, my daughter Tullia; I shall spend time with my daughter, and with all hope, a grandchild."

Tiro thought of the writing, more writing. Of course, there would be copies needed, many copies. More help, more scribes so that the master's work could be available for everyone to read. More copies to be sold in the bookstores. His mind processed thoughts in rapid succession, jumping from one idea to the next when he had a flash of an image—the cripple sitting in the dirt, etching.

"With your permission, kind sir, I have a thought or two about your impending works. We may need some extra help with these works and I think I know where I can get some quality help," Tiro interjected. "I may, however, have to use the services of your good name."

"Oh?" Cicero said, wondering where this conversation was going.

"I happened upon a young man, a wounded soldier I believe, who has a good eye and talented hands. And he can write. If his writing ability is as good as his artistic talent, then we may be able to reap the benefits of two services, a skilled scribe *and* an artisan."

"An artisan?"

"Yes, Noble Lord. I saw a wondrous creation of art etched in dirt, of all places. One can only imagine what wonders he could do with a palette of paint and a wall in your *domus*, or any of your villas, Tiro exclaimed in excitement.

"Hmm—he's not one of our own?"

"I don't believe so, Dominus. He is one of Pompey's men, wounded in the recent battle."

"A Roman soldier . . . an artisan? Who ever heard of such a thing? And he would do such a thing willingly?"

"I cannot imagine a better option for the poor cripple," Tiro replied.

"Cripple?"

"Yes, my lord, this is so. I do not know the full nature of his infirmities, but . . . as we are not leaving immediately, I can pursue this further—with your good graces that is, Sire."

"One of Pompey's men, huh?" Cicero pictured in his mind scenes he would like depicted on his walls.

CHAPTER VII

Eight days passed since the battle, a full Roman week.

In Rome, news of Pompey's victory filtered in. It started as a small ripple, but like a tidal wave it gathered momentum and cascaded through the city with a powerful surge. Creative gossip and embellishment filled in incomplete or missing information; the number killed increased by the thousands each time the news passed on from one mouth to the next; soon, no armies were left at all. Two things remained true: Pompey was victorious and Caesar was dead.

At the house of Caesar, hurried footsteps and guarded whispers were received with screams of disbelief, sobbing, and wailing cries.

Calpurnia napped in a small room just off the colonnaded courtyard of the domus when the news arrived. The room was quiet and dark. The only sounds in the room, other than her soft, stertorous snoring, were the buzzing of a honeybee trapped when it inadvertently entered a ventilation slit, and the flute-like warble of a small bird singing in the courtyard, her notes filtering in through the doorway.

Calpurnia stirred, irritated by the distant and foreboding din not associated with the peaceful sounds of nature. In her stupor she couldn't wholly comprehend the droning aggravation that disturbed her nap, but she wished it to stop. She rolled onto her back and focused on the noise. The agitating hums pulled her from her comfortable couch. At the doorway, she glided through a curtain of colorful, stringed beads and ran into Sabina, her chief servant.

With watery eyes, cheeks streaked with tears, and quivering lips, Sabina stood speechless in front of her lady. Calpurnia knew in her next breath what had befallen them: her husband, Gaius Julius Caesar, former consul, Pontiff Maximus, and general of legions, was not coming home.

In an instant she recalled that strange event a week past, that ominous portend, that gust of wind followed by the fire. Her skin crawled and she felt chilled.

The two women embraced each other, Sabina sobbing and the widow consoling her.

"Oh, *Domina*. What are we to do? What will happen to us now? Our good master is gone," cried the servant.

Though she was the one with the greatest loss, Calpurnia was the pillar of support for Sabina. "Let us wait for news of substance . . . from someone of authority . . . someone with *imperium*. This is the House of Caesar! A noble's house! A patrician's house, not some *insulae* of common people. We will receive whatever fate befalls us with honor and grace. We will wait and be strong, Sabina. How many times have we received false news from afar before? Mercury himself will have to deliver such grievous tidings of our good Caesar before I rip the cloth from my breast," Calpurnia said, her voice cracking and the pallor on her face betraying her self-assuredness. They remained embraced, rocking and consoling.

The honeybee orientated itself to the sunlight and shadows and made its way to the ventilation slit, freeing itself to the outside world, free from temporary confinement; the bird ended its song and flitted away. The notes of peace and serenity—gone.

—⁂—

Gnaeus Pompeius Magnus—Pompey the Great—gathered half his legions, 22,000 men, and prepared to head for the city of the seven hills—Rome. It had been a week since the battle at Dyrrhachium and illness spread amidst his troops. Contagion was common after battles; Pompey knew he had to keep his healthy legions moving, especially to unoccupied areas with fresh water to minimize disease. Once a contagion started it could decimate an army just as efficiently as any well-trained and better-equipped enemy. Generals Pompey and Labienus agreed Marcus Antonius was likely heading further east, toward a large plain in Greece, near a place called Pharsalus. Labienus was tasked to take the healthy legions and shadow the renegade and his legions.

Sailing conditions appeared perfect. Pompey needed to ferry as many men as he could with the fleet at his disposal: 110 battle-ships and some fifty smaller ships. The larger battleships could man a crew of up to 800, including oarsmen, regular sailors, and sea warriors. Logistics for ferrying the men back to Brundisium required making room for some 200 to 250 legionaries per ship. Supplies, horses, food, water, and the legionaries' baggage needed to be brought across as well. This was no small undertaking. It would be a far greater task, however, if he were taking his entire army. The task force needed to make several return trips, two days each way with good weather, favorable winds, agreeable currents, and the blessings of the gods. Pompey had sacrificed well, only the cleanest and purest beasts. He prayed that Fortuna would look his way and offer a kind hand and a warm smile, now that she had forsaken Caesar. All the ships' captains reported that their sacred chickens ate well and were satisfied—good omens.

Lucius sat at an ideal viewing point looking down on the ship activity out in the bay. From his vantage point he could see small boats ferrying men from shore to waiting battleships. The water was calm. Small craft, packed with men and their baggage, bobbed rhythmically as they rowed to their respective ships. Lucius recalled the journey from Brundisium to this place. It was pleasant. All had gone well. Good weather and even sailing. And no seasick-ness like the stories he had heard from some of the old veterans. He remembered the dark blue waters with thin streaks of white, the wind fresh and cool, and the dolphins playing with the ships, jumping and zigzagging in front of the prows.

A few of the larger vessels pulled away for the open sea, their forty-foot long oars grabbing at the water in synchronized cadenc-es, sails not yet unfurled. Faint echoes from drums onboard pulsed like heartbeats as the ships came to life and yearned for the sea. It wouldn't be long, the cripple thought, before the bay and the sea would have a forest of wooden masts and oars moving away from this forsaken place.

"I should be on one of those boats," he muttered. "I pray the gods have not condemned me to this place. There has to be a way back. They can't just leave me here. They can't." He wondered if there was really anything to his gods; or just maybe, they were all too real and demanded much—much more than he could offer.

He labored to his feet using a crutch fashioned to fit under his arm, padded with wool and leather. One of the medical aides had instructed him in how to make it so that it would support his weight and enable him to move about with ease. The ankle was much less sore than before, almost completely pain free, except when applying full body weight. His foot flopped about when he walked, slapping the ground and announcing his presence. The old Greek assured him it would heal, but not be as before.

He'd been given temporary duties at the camp food lines, helping with the kneading and baking of bread, distributing cured meats and vegetable rations to the troops, and whatever clean-up duties the old cooks threw at him. He did his job without complaint, but also without interest. He wanted to be on one of those ships headed west, or with the troops headed east, anywhere but where he was now.

By evening more than half of the large ships that once nestled in the bay were gone or could be seen at the far horizon as a faint debris field of giant shields resting atop of wooden blocks with the suggestion of long, shimmering legs grabbing and pulling at the sea. Lucius felt alone and abandoned. Melancholy hid in his shadow, gnawing on what little spirit he had left.

He hobbled to his tent, fell into his cot, clasped his hands behind his head, and stared up to nothingness, filling his tent with deep sighs and wandering fantasies. Finally, he allowed sleep to conquer him, not caring if he dreamed or not.

Sleep brought images—still images. There was a large battle scene: men, horses, arrows, and of course, javelins. Then there was the blush of two figures—a couple, motionless, posing, holding objects in their hands, objects of interest or significance. When he awoke his aching head recalled nothing more than the smoldering remnants of distant dreams, no images or actions, only the sensation that he had dreamt.

Helios ushered in another morning and it was time to start whatever chores awaited the cripple. Filthy and already feeling tired, he promised himself a bath and a washing of his clothes at some point in the day.

A familiar figure approached the cripple who was now sorting a heap of dirty pots. It was the man impressed by the dirt etchings some days past.

"Lucius Pontius?" asked the stranger with no smile.

"Yes"

"My name is Tiro. I am the secretary to Consular Marcus Tullius Cicero."

Expressionless eyes from the cripple leaning on a crutch with an encrusted pot in his hand were the only response.

"I have come to offer you . . . an opportunity, an opportunity to leave behind this . . . this work unbecoming of a young man with your talent." Tiro surveyed the immediate surroundings with an oblique glance. Obviously uncomfortable with the griminess and filth about him, he retrieved a scented scarf from his belt and wiped it across his nose, letting it linger there for several deep breaths. Flies darted about his head and face, making each minute, if not each second, more and more intolerable.

"I offer you a decent job as a scribe . . . and maybe some other opportunities using your unique skills with your hands and eyes," he said as he fidgeted, swatted, and dodged, not wanting to be in this area and in the company of the flies any longer than necessary.

Lucius didn't trust his ears. It must be the lack of sleep. Or maybe he was asleep and stuck in some bizarre dream. It could be the gruel he tasted this morning but couldn't stomach; even the flies wouldn't touch it.

Were the gods toying with him? Were they tempting him with such fruits and luring him into some wicked trap? This dream was too good to be true. What door was good Janus opening? What was Fortuna weaving for him? Or was this the work of the Larvae, those mischievous spirits of the dead? It certainly was alluring, and it would get him out of this place, out of this filth, and just maybe closer to home. Odd, he hadn't really thought of home seriously until just this very second. A spark ignited some kindling of hope within.

"What do I have to do for this—opportunity?" the cripple asked as he rubbed his nose.

"Well, first, I would like to see how well you can write, or copy. We can discuss any future endeavors afterwards. I've made arrangements for you to come and scribe for me . . . for us that is." Tiro ran his eyes up and down the cripple's condition and closed his eyes. He brought his scarf to his mouth and subdued a petite retch. "Someone will come for you later, after you have . . . bathed, barbered, and rid yourself of the . . . airs of your present duties; perhaps a nice clean tunic?"

Lucius was well aware of his abysmal self, his grungy clothing, his body odor. Tiro's remarks only intensified the stink, making it more malodorous. It was one thing to be basking in one's sweat and honest body odor after a hard workout or battle; it was another to wear the fetid stench from work usually delegated to slaves, work demeaning to the soul.

Finished with his camp duties, the cripple limped from the work area and found clean water and a poor substitute for soap. The water was fresh and cold. It helped awaken his spirit again. The bath was finished off with a nice clean shave from a sharp blade and some clean clothes materialized by way of the old Greek physician. Lucius didn't ask from where the clothes came, but he was most grateful.

Early evening arrived and as promised, someone came for Lucius. He was probably a slave, a freedman at the most, he thought. Whatever he was, he looked well fed, clean, and had a pleasant air about him. Maybe being a scribe wouldn't be so bad, he mused.

The cripple hobbled along agilely, keeping up with the man, and followed him to Tiro's tent. There he saw other young men, sitting comfortably on pillows, pens in hand, bowed forward in intense concentration at short desks, copying letters and manuscripts. One of the busy scribes stopped penning long enough to sneak a peek at Lucius, offering a flash of a smile—a welcoming smile.

"Ah, Lucius Pontius." Tiro appeared from the shadowed end of the tent like a manifestation. His eyes flashed and then feasted on the clean cripple, allowing a twitch of a smile to flicker at the corner of his mouth. "Welcome. You look much . . . different; more relaxed; and more alert." The secretary moved in and let his nose inhale Lucius's freshly washed hair.

Tiro then led the cripple to a desk and gave him several documents to copy, one in Greek, and the other in Latin.

Lucius studied the documents, drinking in all the characters, concentrating on the lines and curves of each symbol. He eased into a cushion and picked up his pen, caressing it, twisting and feeling the texture with his callused hands. He measured its weight and balance in little bounces, as if it were a miniature javelin. Lucius wanted to know it and all its nuances. He dipped the pen into the inkwell and in a delicate pull, drew it across the rim. A steady hand let the pen glide on the paper and copied symbols and letters from the template. He penned with authority, yet with tenderness, as one writing a love letter.

For several minutes he said not a word or looked elsewhere other than from the template to the page before him. Each and every muscle in his hand contracted and relaxed in such perfect harmony as to make the letters appear just as they were on the template, if not better. Other scribes busy with their own documents peeked at him now and then, measuring him. He continued his work without stopping, making no mistakes. The glances from the others became more and more frequent. One of the scribes stopped abruptly, having made a mistake in his work.

The cripple paused just long enough to stretch the stiffness from his back and take a deep breath while he pondered his work. He was pleased, very pleased.

Tiro came up from behind, looked over the cripple's shoulder, but said not a word.

He dove back into scribing until he noticed the others putting their tools away; the day of letters and penning had ceased. He glanced around, unsure of what to do next. Tiro approached, this time offering a semblance of a smile of satisfaction. He took the cripple's copies and examined each with hard, critical eyes.

"That will be all for now. You are done for the day. Return in the morning and we'll continue with some other . . . challenges," Tiro said, speaking to the documents in front of his face, not directly to Lucius.

Lucius put aside his writing equipment, being careful not to mess the desk. It felt so rewarding, he thought; so different from soldiering, digging trenches, or using weapons. He hadn't thought about it at the time, but a man could be just as efficient and deadly with a pen as he could be with the gladius, that other important Roman instrument of power.

With crutch under arm and enthusiasm in his step, Lucius returned the next morning as ordered. This day's lesson differed: he practiced using the stylus and wax tablets. The battle order of the day was to transfer the spoken word to the written word, which he did. Both his father and mother had taught him to write. He even had an uncle who introduced him to the Greek alphabet.

"Is your father a schooled person?" Tiro asked, impressed with Lucius' skills.

"No. Not really. He was a man of many talents, but not an artisan of just one, except for killing."

"For killing?"

"He was a Roman soldier, under Sulla," Lucius replied for clarity.

"Was? Did he die in battle?"

"No. It was illness, something under his ribs. He lingered for some time, spilling much bile and turning the color of yellow squash. Some of the old villagers said the little bag under his liver had failed him. By the time we found a good Greek doctor to treat him it was too late.

"I see. He was a soldier, not an *equite*—a knight?" Tiro asked, knowing it to be highly unlikely, but he asked anyway.

"No, he didn't have that kind of money. He was a good foot soldier, very keen with the javelin. Taught me. He was given land to farm in Venusia after he was discharged, but I think he enjoyed the army more."

"You, too, were very skilled with the . . . javelin?"

"You could say that."

"Hmmm."

A long silence intervened. Both sensed they were probably at the boundary of too much information asked and given; for now, they would remain at the limits of their comfort zones. They both went back to the tasks at hand: scribing and observing.

Lucius progressed daily, rarely bored with his work and making few mistakes. Cicero, and therefore, Tiro, was pleased with the young man's work and potential. Lucius struck up friendships with the others, comrades in common duties. His artistic talents cinched the bonds: in his spare time the cripple drew or etched portraits of the scribes on used portions of papyrus. The sketches were high quality, the likenesses true and flattering.

One of the new acquaintances, Caius, asked if he wouldn't paint a portrait of his parents at their home in Pompeii when they all returned to the mainland. They would be most grateful and sure to pay him well.

"You praise me too well, Caius. I'm just a soldier. I do pictures for fun and because it reminds me of my mother. She's the one who taught me how to put to my hands what my eyes can see. But for you, I'll do it because we're friends. I can't boast of its quality, though. I'm not a polished artisan. I'm . . . or was . . . just a soldier."

"May Minerva, good goddess of crafts and industry, lay her hands on yours, Lucius, and give you that polish," Caius said.

Lucius' face managed a half-smile followed by a smirk.

———

Word came: Cicero would be sending three ships back to Italy. Lucius and Caius were to be onboard one of the three. Their final destination would be Tusculum, south of Rome, on the northern side of the Alban hills, an area rich in villas and vineyards.

"Have you heard? We're bound for Italy! We're going home, or at least to the mainland." Caius could not sit still; he was like a young lamb. Lucius was much more reserved, on the outside; on the inside, he was just as excited as Caius. "The master won't be joining us on this voyage. Word is that his daughter Tullia has lost a child, a boy."

Death was no stranger to Lucius. Until recently, it was part of his craft; produce it skillfully, or sustain it honorably. He felt something for the old man. Surely, it must be terrible to lose a child, even a grandchild. He just couldn't identify with the loss. He wondered if it was like when he lost his father. No, it had to be more like when his mother lost the baby girl, his sister. The baby did not live very long, a couple of years perhaps. It had been a long while ago. The child came in the cold months and was always sick, dying of a high fever and a terrible cough. His mother had cried for days and days. She was an empty shell, a body without a soul for months after. Lucius was very young then, but remembered the isolation and the emotional wall his mother had placed around herself. Then one day, she came to him, caressed him, kissed him, and then gently rocked him in her arms; he felt his mother's love and warmth again. Yes, it must be that kind of hurt.

He stood next to Caius, offering no words, just being very—Roman.

Chapter VIII

Day of departure came; time to set sail for the mainland.

Lucius and Caius gathered at the embarkation area as instructed by Tiro. Their possessions were inverse in proportion to their excitement: very little of the former, much more of the latter. Lucius was still in need of his walking crutch, more out of habit than necessity. The foot-slapping continued, but without much of the pain.

A dreary sky displayed all the coldest colors conceivable, requiring extra layers of tunics and cloaks. The seascape offered various shades of pewter and ash under a thick blanket of gray. Wind gusts played with everyone's hair. The air had a severe chill to it producing watery noses, watery eyes, and cold feet. The ocean dampness penetrated poor clothing as ghostly spirits might seep through thin walls. One could almost hear their moans as the wind shuttled the spirits about.

Seabirds hovered fixed in the air, into the wind, hardly needing to flap at all, bobbing in a separate sea of air currents. With the slightest adjustments of special feathers in their stretched wings, they changed their angle of attack as needed, shooting upwards or diving. In jerky little head movements, they scanned the ground and sea for any sign of food scraps, diving quickly and complaining scandalously whenever a crewmember from one of the moored boats tossed garbage in the surrounding water or land.

The captain of the expedition walked out onto an outcropping of rocks to read the situation, looking to the sea for signs, omens, and answers. "Good Neptune, what do you have planned for me?" he asked the sea.

The answer from the sea was nebulous.

Distant gray skies met and merged with equally gray waters of the sea. To the north a huge, angry gray—almost black—cloud with a pale curtain of mist falling from its underbelly crawled along the sea. To the south, the captain could see bright patches of emerald sea where the sun was stabbing at it with warm rays. The seascape was tempting the captain with all sorts of displays, deferring to his expertise, experience, and his luck. The morning sacrifices and auspices were in favor of the captain; even the sacred chickens feasted on cakes without fear—the omens were good, despite the portentous cloudscape.

Small skiffs, loaded with travelers and baggage, delivered ten passengers each to the waiting ships. Each ship had twenty-five oars to a side and a single mast with the ever-present square sail, currently furled and secured. Lucius and Caius were assigned to the same ship.

Lucius' small craft collided and bounced off the side of the larger ship as choppy waters toyed with and slapped it around. The cripple and the others clambered aloft from the skiff, scaling a fortress that rose from the churning waters and then plunged back into the cold depths. White-knuckled grips fought with wet rope and strained shoulders pulled heavy bodies up slick nets. The sea's freezing spray soaked and chilled the bones of all those attempting to board.

Normally, Lucius would have climbed with ease and been done with such a trifling exercise. But his foot flopped about and was use-less; the act of boarding had become a labored fiasco. Once onboard, he collapsed and was reunited with the pain of his healing ankle.

Lucius, Caius, and the rest of the passengers were shown their quarters below deck: spaces with just enough room for each person and what little baggage they carried with them. Lucius flung his bag to his space and it let out a resounding "clang" as it hit the wooden floor.

Their quarters were gloomy and dank, smelling of mildew and old rope that never dried. The new passengers were welcomed with a serenade of creaking old lumber and the stretching of large ropes as the boat gently rocked.

After another hour of consternation and further readings of omens, the captain finally conceded and decided it was time to sail. Before doing so, however, he had the crew add additional stones to the bilge area for peace of mind; the boat had plenty amphorae of wine and other heavy cargo to stabilize it if encountering rough seas, but a little more weight wouldn't hurt.

At a given command, the lead boat headed off in a southerly direction, a course set for Brundisium. With luck, they would be back on dry land again in two days' time. The other boats followed in line. Lucius and Caius were in the second boat.

———

From a rocky crag near the shoreline, Cicero watched the flotilla pull away as the vessels' oars lifted, crashed into the sea, and pulled in a synchronous motion, again and again. The cadence of their muffled drumbeats floated across the choppy waters toward the shore and beat a farewell to those watching, including Marcus Cicero.

The elderly statesman stood there encased deep up to his eyeballs within thick, woolen cloaks. Sparse, graying hair thrashed wildly atop his statuesque, implanted frame. Except for small, teetering corrections made to compensate for gusty wind bursts that played and got pushy, he remained motionless for minutes on end, thinking of everything and nothing. The blustery sea breezes whipped past his ears and whistled an old tune that made sense to only those with a melancholic heart.

His head filled with Tullia and the grandchild who was not to be. A rent opened along the side of his heart, ached, and then began to spew a leak, a leak that was part of the old man's future. It was best he had not seen the infant—not dead anyway.

Nothing could be crueler in this world than to see the lifeless body of a child, especially a child with one's blood. Juno had ways of making women stronger than men; giving birth to a child after nine months of nurturing and love only to lose it in the end certainly had to be one of them.

Once the boats had charged out to sea, he could see the unfurling of sails. The wind, the currents, and the gods were now in command.

The ships disappeared into the blending of the sea and sky and Cicero left the viewing point for his tent. His mind needed work. "Oh, my little Tulliola, I grieve for you and me," he whispered. "I do miss you so."

In Tusculum, Tullia languished in bed, ready for her grave. Attending her were her mother, a Greek midwife, and a small army of family slaves.

"More water! Bring more water and clean sponges!" ordered the midwife, Althaia. "And make sure it is of the boiling pot! Not the other!" The youngest slave of the group scrambled as Althaia continued to sponge blood seeping from between Tullia's thighs.

"Domina, her color is not good. She is as white as milk. She needs liver of a young calf, liver not completely cooked. I've made a suppa with special herbs and spices to make her strong," the slave said to Tullia's mother, "but she needs more than just the broth."

Althaia used all the skills she could recall from her Greek upbringing. The slave's mother was the village person everyone called upon when it was time for birthing. Terentia, Tullia's mother, felt fortunate to have Greek slaves as they usually came with much knowledge, and most could read and write their own language.

"Do what you can, Althaia. Whatever you need is yours," Terentia said, pacing around the bed.

"I will do what I can, Domina. It's been a week. And the afterbirth did not look complete—a bad omen. And there is still much bleeding. Sadly, Lady Tullia needed the infant to suckle her breast to help slow the bleeding," Althaia said. After an extended silence she added, "There is one treatment . . . oh, but it is so dangerous."

"What is it Althaia? Please tell me," Terentia begged.

Althaia pursed her lips, looking extremely anxious. "There is a seed—no, not really a seed—more a blight, from the wheat fields that might help . . . oh, but it can be so dangerous!" again she said. "I've heard of people who are of child and wish to lose the child will eat of the cursed bread. It is an awful thing to see, I've been told. The most careful amount in Tullia's case just might work. My mother used it once or twice."

"If we do nothing, we may lose Tullia. If we try the seed, or whatever it is, it may stop the bleeding," Terentia murmured. She looked at Tullia, helpless, dying. "Do what you must, Althaia. We will sacrifice a young calf to Aesculapius, god of health and medicine for divine intervention, and then the liver you suggest. Lucina, our dear deity of childbirth, was not pleased with our initial offerings. We must try again."

Althaia disappeared from the villa for several hours. She returned with a small pouch, which she handled gingerly. In the cooking area of the domus she sprinkled most of the contents onto a wooden slab. The medicinal herb—or poison, depending on the disposition of the gods—resembled a dry, crumbled bulb of a dead flower, with little black seeds. Using the backside of a wooden spoon, she crushed the dry material to a fine dark powder, separating it in two small mounds. With trembling hands, she cut one of the mounds in two parts again, using the sharpest knife she had.

"O Aesculapius, I pray you, guide my hands for the right amount of your magic for the poor young Tullia. Mother, please be with me, help me, I beg of you," she implored of the immortal and mortal. She selected the smallest portion on the right of the two for no other reason than it seemed to be the one calling to her. Using the knife to scoop up the finely crushed material, she reverently placed it into a cup of boiled water. She stirred and repeated her incantations to the gods, and her mother, over and over with each swirl. Looking in the broth, she let herself believe that it was her mother's reflection she saw staring back—a good sign.

The slave ceremoniously brought the cup to the room where Tullia lay, semi-conscious. With the help of Terentia and a young slave, the midwife lifted Tullia's wobbly head, eyes appearing lifeless, and skillfully dribbled the brew past the young girl's desiccated lips and into her mouth. Tullia's reflexes took over and allowed a swallow. The deed was done; now, it was a matter of waiting.

Before the end of an hour, Tullia grew restless. With pale and thin outstretched arms, she reached out in front of her, her fingers clawing for some invisible object. Terentia and the slaves could only guess as to what she was grasping for.

"Papa—papa, please help, help me!" Tullia cried out in a whisper belonging to someone else. If she could have, she would have told her mother and Althaia that she was reliving the labor from the week before. Pain hammered her lower back and her insides felt twisted and pulled. Noxious cramps rolled in on waves, each more menacing than the previous, like the pounding surf from an angry and punishing sea. "Aye! Make it stop! Please make it stop! I don't want to! Make it go away! Mama—don't let them do this to me, please! Aye! I can't do this!"

Althaia clutched her loose apron to her mouth and her eyes welled in tears. "Oh, my child, my child," was all she could mutter.

Terentia went to the bedside and tenderly took her daughter's hand. In a blur, Tullia deftly reversed the hold like a body possessed and put a death grip on her mother's hand. Terentia screamed. She struggled and fought to pull free, managing to do so only after Althaia and the other slaves came to her rescue. She cradled her discolored and contorted hand to her breasts, sobbing in pain.

Tears trickled down Terentia's red cheeks as she hovered near her daughter's side, but out of reach of trap-like hands and clawing nails.

Tullia rocked from side to side, screaming and pleading, her blood saturating the bedding again.

"More linen, get more linen, hurry!" Althaia cried out to the other slaves.

Tullia let out a grunting scream, followed by deep panting as Althaia changed the vaginal dressing. A large, dark—almost black—malodorous clot oozed and then dropped from between her legs after the scream. Althaia scooped up the glob and ran outside with it. Blood dripped from between her fingers as she hurried away from the house, leaving a trail that led to a small clearing under a gathering of tall trees. The midwife buried it in a small plot, praying in Greek that this would be the end.

When she returned to the house she found Tullia quietly sleeping, surrounded by her mother and the other slaves. Althaia and the gods knew it was not sleep she was looking at, but something closer to death. The young girl's heart raced, her skin was cool and clammy, her respirations fast and shallow, and her complexion ashen gray. The blood was very thin now, but not as perfusive as before. Every now and then, her face would grimace, giving evidence of pain somewhere.

The family stayed at her side, cleansing her and whispering personal prayers to whomever would listen.

CHAPTER
IX

Out at sea, the three ships made good time. The winds and currents had been kind. The sun even made a brief appearance. All was good and fair sailing.

On deck, Lucius tried to acquire his sea legs. He walked up and down the length of the vessel, using his crutch for support. The rocking motion of the ship challenged him with every step but he prevailed—most of the time. Twice he lost his balance and skipped sideways, his crutch skipping across the wet and slippery wooden planks as the ship leaned toward the sea.

Caius hugged the railing of the ship. His color waned and his stomach rolled with the sea. One of the ship hands offered him a cup of wine, assuring him that it would help him feel better. That's all it took. Caius leaned farther over the railing and heaved the contents of his tormented stomach as an offering to Neptune. The sailor laughed and drank the wine himself.

Lucius skipped and slid over to poor Caius, who was still retching. "This happen to you often?" his friend asked. Caius could only nod and continue to offer profane oaths to the gods.

Helios, who made the start of the journey promising, withdrew his offerings of sunlight and warmth and gave way to ominous clouds and threatening dark skies again. Even the sea birds had abandoned them. The rocking of the ship became more intense and the crew scurried about stowing and securing everything down with extra rope. The other passengers grew more alarmed and sick.

Whitecaps on gray and pewter crests flicked sprays of stinging salt water at anyone brave enough to be topside. Legions of angry, rolling waves took turns mugging the boat. Escarpments of ugly gray grew tall and ominous, and then sank, disappearing past the rim of the railings only to reappear again. They lapped and pounded. And then they became angrier.

The crew brought down the large, square sail as it was showing signs of tearing from the increasing, angry winds. Lashings used to bind and hold the sail in place cracked and snapped like vicious whips seeking someone to punish. Swells climbed tall and sank deep. Cold rain pelted all those who dared come on deck. Hours blew by and the tempest tossed the three ships about like play things for the gods. The vessels managed to stay within sight of one another for most of those hours, but not for long.

Caius slithered below deck for a brief spell, unable to tolerate the violent rolling and the cold, thrashing waves; but the stench of vomit and other bodily wastes below deck overwhelmed him and drove him back up.

Lucius hobbled and skipped up after him to make sure the seasick friend was safe as the ship heaved about at the whim of the gods. Only a few of the crew dared to stay above deck to manage the ropes; inevitably, they, too, gave up and went below.

Topside, the wind howled like a crazed sea monster. Rain came in freezing sheets, sideways most of the time. And giant waves washed the decks with cold, foamy sea. Lucius had to scream to be heard, yelling at Caius to hold on tight to the mast. The crashing and punching waves became more violent, knocking the cripple off his one good leg. He hugged the wet and lathered deck, tying Caius to the mast with plenty of thick rope. Lucius looked over his right shoulder and saw one of the other vessels climbing high on a giant wave above and next to their own; it fascinated his mind to look up and see the bottom of the neighboring ship as the huge swell lifted it towards the clouds. The ship lingered in the air for an eternity as lightening stitched across the waves like a crooked hand reaching out for a gift offered by Poseidon. The ship eased back down and disappeared into the next trough with just the top portion of the mast showing. The mast rotated slowly and the ship drifted into a blackness that swallowed all light.

There was no sign of the third ship.

Lucius' ship lurched forward and downward, tossing anyone not anchored with white-knuckled hand grips to something solid like rag dolls strewn across a cluttered floor. Lucius felt weightless and airborne as the ship plunged, diving sharply into the sea. The vessel ceased its dive with a sudden, hammering impact and the cripple was hurled to the bow where he was engulfed by a monster of tangled ropes. The entangled cripple grew heavy under the compressed weight of the massive wad of wet rope as the ship began its ascent again.

The vessel climbed and crawled along the next giant wave. The rope monster held Lucius tight and dragged him past Caius and on toward the aft section. The smothered cripple couldn't breathe. His air had been hammered from his lungs while going from a state of weightlessness to weighing a ton when he was slammed to the deck. There was a great brawl between man, vessel, and the sea, and the sea had the upper hand.

The ship roared upward, creaking and moaning, and when it reached its apex it teetered on the precipice of another giant wave. It then yawed, shuddered and vibrated violently as its giant rudders buffeted against the wind's wild turbulence. The violence of it all, along with yet another giant massive, gray wave, tossed Lucius overboard into the frigid water.

He found himself at the bottom of two gigantic waves and his ship nowhere in sight. His heavy woolen clothes soaked up the sea like a sponge and the octopus-like rope cluster put a death grip around him. It was intent on dragging him under. As much as he thrashed wildly about, the sea, with the aid of the rope creature, persisted in its attempt to swallow him. He fought to gulp air. His nose and sinuses filled with large mouthfuls of briny water and he coughed and choked. He took in more water than air and sensed the end was near.

Despite the howling, the frigidness, the darkness, and the loneliness, a strange calmness seduced Lucius. His fatigued body relaxed and became one with the sea. The rope creature lost interest in him and relinquished its firm hold. It disappeared languorously into the deep murkiness, its undulating tentacles waving farewell as they released him. Flashes of lightning illuminated his surroundings and he could see where it was he was going to die: amid giant, gray, striated walls with saltwater spray blown wildly by unseen, screaming giants. There was no panic, only peacefulness. There would be no pain, only the numbness of the cold. A thought crossed his mind, as if he was remembering a funny story: *I always thought I would die by the—*

Serenely, if by magic, he felt himself floating upwards, upwards towards the heavens, carried by the gods themselves. He swore he could hear them singing as they gently lifted him aloft, up to where his father would be waiting. It would be over soon and there would be nothing more to fear.

Propelled by a giant surge, Lucius lofted upwards like a large cork only to come crashing down again on something hard and slimy—it was his ship. A hand grabbed him by the nape of the neck and pulled at him. It was Caius. He grabbed hold of a friendly rope and slung it around Lucius' chest.

Caius couldn't be heard in the raging and howling storm, but he was laughing hysterically—crying, at Lucius. "The gods Neptune and Poseidon didn't want you in their domain! They spat you right out, like a piece of rotten meat!" He roared with laughter again. Lucius, coughing and choking, laughed, too, when he realized what it was that Caius was laughing about. They latched on to each other and continued to howl, choke, cough, and ride out the storm.

The storm died and the seas calmed. Lucius' ship had lost eight oars; the sail was torn, but repairable; the entire store of amphora remained intact; and everyone was present and accounted for—even Lucius.

There still was no sign of the third ship.

———

Pompey marched into Rome, his eleven *lictors* at the lead, all but two carrying the bundled *fasces*, but without the axes. Behind him, a contingent of handpicked legionaries and centurions paraded with authority—Pompey's. And behind them all, Pompey's *clientela* strutted along, almost dancing, blessed to be in his shadow.

Laurel wreaths and red ribbons wrapped the bundled fasces—a sign of victory. The general decided not to include the axes—the signature of authority that one could wield capital punishment; not just yet, anyway.

They made their way through the winding streets, the lictors calling: "Make way, make way!" Life in the normally busy, crowded, and noisy streets died as the victorious general and his entourage triumphed past, but revived in his wake.

Vendors and buyers of all classes milled about, trying to get from one end of a crowd to the other. Songs of enticement to buy their goods serenaded the cavalcade from merchants, offering deals of a lifetime. Outstretched arms bore merchandise and valuable wares from the farthest corners of the world.

The procession maneuvered through thick, fragrant hazes and savory clouds of smoke from sizzling lamb and other cooked meats that clung to clothing like scented perfume. Street jugglers and musicians performed and called for donations. Extended palms with skeletal fingers sprung forth from lumps of rags along the walls calling for alms. Languages and songs in foreign tongues floated and reverberated all along the hectic corridor, seeking attention from the parading convoy that was Pompey and his people. Some offered blessings on behalf of the gods to the victorious general. A few offered whispered curses behind broad smiles.

The procession met up with a contingent of city military personnel who pushed with their shields and shoved bystanders back out of the way. Hobnailed boots stepped on feet that did not move fast enough. "Make way you clumsy oxen, move out of the way!" the soldiers yelled and cursed.

At the corner of two intersecting streets, a large vat of collected urine owned by a local textile fuller toppled when another crowd got caught in a melee attributed to Pompey's procession. Bystanders scrambled, but not before being drenched by the contents of the vat. There would be no more bleaching of fabric for the rest of the day by the textile owner. The best he could do would be to petition someone for restitution.

The entourage made its way for the Palatine Hill. Its destination: the residence of Gaius Julius Caesar.

On entering the Via Sacra, Pompey and company reached Caesar's residence. Two of the lictors pounded on the large, wooden door and announced the presence of "Gnaeus Pompeius Magnus!"

One of two large, wooden and bronze doors creaked opened cautiously. Two, three, then four knobby fingers appeared, crawling around the rim of the door, like little snakes slithering out of a hole. And then two large eyes peered from the shadows. On seeing the important group before him and assessing the situation—the presence of the lictors and all the people behind the nobleman— the slave scampered off to summon another slave who announces the presence of guests. The *nomenclator* materialized instantly, bowing with respect, and then swept his extended arm in the direction of the *ostium*, the small chamber just before the atrium. All but two lictors remained outside. The two who entered with Pompey carried gifts, one an urn of high quality, and the other, a small box.

The nomenclator, having made the announcement, returned and ushered the guests to the tablinum, where other household servants appeared with stools and small chairs.

Souvenirs and battle memorabilia—swords, shields, spears, and the like, decorated the colorful walls of Julius Caesar's reception office. Pompey's reception room bore a similar decor. In fact, he had just added one new trophy to his exhibit. All old men of war have need of these things to display and admire—a connection with the mortal.

Off to the side stood an armless, wooden mannequin sporting a very handsome ceremonial cuirass. Atop the mannequin's head rested a gilded helmet with brilliant red plumage. The sculptured ebony and gold breastplate was surely for a god-like figure, its pectoral and abdominal sections cut perfectly to represent the anatomy of the wearer. The plumed helmet and impressive breastplate was in command of the room—a connection with the immortal.

The general and lictors stood when Calpurnia Pisonis entered the room.

"Greetings, Lady Calpurnia."

"Greetings to you, General," she answered, plying a warm smile and a regal posture, like many a statuette in Rome.

Pompey looked upon her as if for the first time. She was shorter than what he remembered, lean, but not skinny. Her attendants had pulled her coiffure from the front, coiled it at the back, and held in place with braids. At her temples thin silver threads of gray peppered her natural auburn hair, which did not detract from her handsome features. Her dark, round eyes showed no mourning; they were bright and dignified. A beautiful, dark-umber *palla*, made of rare linen, adorned her petite frame. He saw in her features that which reminded him of all his five wives. His friend Julius had chosen well.

"As you know, I've just returned from Epirus," was all the general was able to eke out. *How foolish, of course she knows, and she knows why I've come*, he reprimanded himself. He had a well-rehearsed little speech all planned for this moment, but it crumbled and fell apart. The great general had met this woman's husband on the battlefield and was victorious, yet completely disarmed and exposed in her presence. Her regal bearing and resoluteness repelled his planned assault on her presumed weakness and vulnerability. He was dead in the water.

"A pleasant and safe journey, I pray."

His advance checked, he regrouped and changed tactics.

"Lady Calpurnia—" He turned to moisten his parched lips with a sweep of a dry tongue, and then looked to his lictors. An unspoken command given with a sideward nod of his head and squinted eyes ordered the civil servants/body guards to leave. They placed the urn and small box on a table and marched out.

Calpurnia did likewise with her servants and staff.

"Calpurnia, if I may, your husband . . . Julius . . . and I . . . we knew each other for a long time. We both performed our duties for Rome, each in our own capacities. We each left scars on this good earth, in far off and different places that are now graced with the governance and power of the Senate and Rome. We were part of that Senate, working together for the common good of our people, for the good of Rome. As our world got bigger, the complexities and our ideologies changed. We found ourselves politically misaligned and on the battlefield again, only this time at opposite ends. The legacy of Romulus and Remus once again has been passed on to us, their ancestors. In a way, it was the natural law of things. I do wish you to take comfort in the knowledge that he perished a hero, and not by my own hand. The gods have reasons and ways."

It's not how Pompey wanted it to go; but, he thought it a good little speech, if not at least a good excuse, and it would have to do. The reality of it all was: egos got too big and the world got too small to accommodate them both. Pompey chose to believe he was acting on behalf of the Senate. But they were using him to counter Caesar, who chose to believe he was acting on behalf of the people. But Caesar was really leveraging his way for bigger and more regal opportunities. The gods knew that the Republic was in its last throes no matter what the statesmen chose to believe.

He picked up the urn and presented it to Calpurnia. A male servant appeared out of nowhere, took the urn from his outstretched hands, and stood next to Calpurnia. Pompey next handed her the small box.

"But for the gods, I am sure Julius would be presenting these items to my wife, Cornelia."

Calpurnia's eyes flared and her chest inflated. Petite fingers peeled back the lid of the small box. Inside sat the signet ring that once belonged to Gaius Julius Caesar, deceased husband, former consul of Rome, *Pontifex Maximus*, distinguished general, conqueror of barbarians, and former ally and friend of Gnaeus Pompeius Magnus. The ring looked barren without the finger and hand she was so familiar with; the hand that had been used in so many loving caresses; the hand that used to touch her face; her husband's hand.

The Lady's glistening eyes met Pompey's strong, yet averting eyes. She smiled graciously. With a slight nod and heavy lids, she accepted the items.

The widow turned to the servant and exchanged the small box for the urn, affectionately taking it from his hands. It was difficult to believe that the contents of the hard, cold metal urn contained the man who was once tall, in excellent physical shape, had well-kept hair and dark, penetrating eyes; the man she slept with, held intimate conversations with, and shared private and personal secrets with; entertained friends and acquaintances with; and was sure to always come back to her when he departed.

Odd, those fifty-four years of a man's life should weigh so little in one's hands—and she shared only the last dozen years of it. Surely, the ashes of Julius Caesar should far outweigh those of a simple, mortal man who made no mark whatsoever on this earth. She wondered how much her years would weigh in the end.

Before leaving, Pompey turned to Calpurnia. "As Julius died within days of his birth date, I plan to proposal to the Senate we rename the month of Quintilus to Julius, in honor of his greatness.

"He would have been honored," Calpurnia whispered, her eyes struggling with tears.

Pompey exited the great house and receded in the direction from which he came, lictors and military guards at the front, and his gaggle of followers, wishing him good health and devotion in his wake—the more numerous the clientela, the more prestigious the patron. He was bound for one of the rich villas in Tusculum to spend time with his wife. He would return to meet the Senate later.

―――

Out at sea, two of the three ships that belonged to Cicero followed the sun, their sails engulfed with cool but dry winds. The crews occupied themselves with repairs. The passengers worked on regaining their strength after being weak from the wild sea. The skies cleared by the hour and the waters calmed. This day, the second day out, should be a promising one with land in the not-so-far distance.

The captain of the lead ship reckoned they had been swept too far south by the storm and that it would take additional time to reach Brundisium as planned. They would have to tack north along the coast. The alternative would be to continue south along the coastline, round the heel, and then head for the old Greek port of Tarentum. He opted for the former.

The sun slid from the western skies behind the two ships as they made their way up the coastline. Approximately two hours of daylight remained—*undecima*—when one of the lookouts on Lucius' ship spotted sails in the distance, on the left side, the side where land would most likely appear soon. Had it been thirteen years earlier, the chances that the sails belonged to marauding pirates would have been certain. But Pompey had cleared the seas of pirates by special imperium given him by the Senate those thirteen years prior, the seas were much safer now.

Passengers and crew alike gathered on the "sinister" side—the left side—of their respective ships to see the distant vessels. They were just able to make out the dim and hazy suggestion of land and hills beyond the sails. Excitement and levity mixed with the cool, evening breezes that pushed the little ships northward. Sea birds flew out to greet them, calling out their welcomes.

The fiery, giant, orange-yellow globe grew in size as it eased behind the ever-developing landscape, leaving in its wake layers of scattered clouds distinctly painted in salmon-pink, dark gray, and a lighter gray with silver rims. The captains read that as good omens.

Lanterns appeared along the coastline, their reflections cast as long, wavy streaks reaching out to the ships. It was a beautiful evening and Lucius and Caius were there to take it in.

"We should be on dry land by late morning I would think," Caius said.

"Can't wait," Lucius replied. His eyes fixed on the gilded sunset. "I couldn't be a sailor. I'd rather face the fates on good *terra firma*. Which reminds me, I want to thank you for . . . you know . . . extending me a hand the other night."

Abrupt laughter broke up an awkward silence as they both recalled the storm and Lucius being thrown back on deck by the angry sea, each with his own mental recollection of what happened.

"Well then, you owe me," Caius said.

Night claimed the ships and though they were close to their destination, the captains decided not to head inland just yet. Unseen rocks in the night could bring disaster, which would be a travesty after making it this far in one piece. Losing one ship and its crew was enough. The two vessels bobbed in silence under a magnificent black sky dappled with thousands upon thousands of sparks of light. The Milky Way appeared as a spreading mist in the heavens. Lucius and Caius were ready to go below and get some sleep, but not before taking in the spectacular night one last time.

"You know," Caius started, "the Greeks call that the 'Milky Circle.' Master Cicero once wrote about it in his . . . let's see . . . it was in his *De re Publica*—On the State. Yes, in his book he says that is the place we all go to after we die and leave our flesh. We copied that about three summers ago, I believe."

Lucius was awestruck with the quantity of stars that could be seen out at sea. Oddly, he couldn't remember all these stars on the trip over. "It must be beautiful up there. There's a good reason not to fear death, huh, Caius? Do you think they can see us from there?" he asked, eyes fixed to the heavens. "Father, can you see me?" he whispered.

CHAPTER
X

The night had been fitful for Calpurnia and now more guests sought an audience; so early in the mid-morning, too. Yesterday's visit with Pompey had left her tired and not in the highest of spirits. She put on her best face and entered the tablinum as the nomenclator announced, "Gaius Octavius, son of Gaius Octavius and Atia, great-nephew of Gaius Julius Caesar." Three young men milled around the reception room instead of just the one, more adolescents than young men. Unsightly facial eruptions plagued two of the three. Young Gaius Octavius had the best complexion of the three.

"Greetings, Lady Calpurnia. On behalf of my mother Atia, my sister Octavia, and myself, I offer condolences for the loss of your husband, my uncle," said Octavius.

Calpurnia nodded politely and offered a receptive smile. She glanced over to the other two youths accompanying Octavius like double shadows. He caught the glance and continued, "Excuse me, My Lady; these are my close friends and acquaintances—Gaius Maecenas and Marcus Agrippa." Each of the youths gave his best attempt at respectful bows.

It was no surprise that all three would be there, at least not to the gods. The three boys—Octavius was fifteen and his friends equally young—were inseparable and did everything together: learned, traveled, plotted, everything.

Octavius had fine features: a handsome face with clear eyes, golden hair, and a confident, disarming smile. Maecenas stood behind and to his right, more attentive to the floor than anything else. He looked up now and then with dark-olive eyes that matched the hue of his long, unkempt mop on his head. He avoided direct eye contact; fearing one might see what was going on behind his. Agrippa appeared carefree and confident. His eyes explored the contents of the room and measured everything and everybody around him. He looked the strongest and fittest of the bunch, with large shoulders, muscular arms, a thick neck, a square jaw with a bit of cleft in the middle, and a prominent ridge of thick brows that covered and protected his recessed, hazel eyes.

"Your uncle spoke highly of you, and often. He had great affection for you, Gaius," Calpurnia confided. "I believe you two would have been very close, very close indeed. I remember him discussing an idea, a plan . . . a plan of taking you campaigning with him."

"That would have been an honor and privilege, I am sure."

"Are you aware that General Gnaeus Pompeius Magnus was here yesterday to bring your uncle's remains back to Rome?" the lady asked.

"No. No, I was not," answered Octavius.

"Would you like to see the urn?"

Held in the grip of indecision for several breaths, thin lips pursed slightly, he nodded. Calpurnia led the three to an adjoining room where once there was a bust of Caesar, but now the urn in its place. The small audience of four gathered round and gazed in silence at the cold receptacle.

Octavius reflected on the urn, pondering all that could have been with a great mentor like his uncle. It may take longer to climb the rungs of that required political ladder, that *cursus honorum*— the honors race, to become consul, now that his uncle was no longer mortal. How much easier it would be if his dead relative were a god or something, not just some ash in a metal jar. Octavius' own father died too soon. Octavius was only four at the time. The death left the family without pedigree of its own, other than his stepfather, Lucius Marcius Philippus, who was consul eight years prior, and his sister's husband, Gaius Claudius Marcellus, who was consul two years ago. Uncle Julius would have been his—"in." Now—

Calpurnia glided over to a tall, beautifully carved wooden desk and retrieved a small box from a single drawer. She brought it over to the young men, one of them watching her every move in quick glances. She opened the box and pulled out the signet ring, holding it for all to admire. The three youths leaned close to inspect it. Maecenas measured it even closer, as a fox eyeing a stray chick, unprotected and vulnerable.

"This was . . . is . . . Julius' signet ring," Calpurnia said with sad eyes. After displaying the ring for a few minutes, she placed it gently and reverently back into its sacred little box and returned it to the desk where it was entombed; all the while, Maecenas followed it with penetrating eyes, straining to see around Octavius, observing Calpurnia's every move.

Octavius made the first move. The other two followed his lead as subservient wolves of the pack. "I thank you for allowing this visit and I wish you well," the young Octavius said. "I fear I will miss him greatly, though we did not spend much time together as of late. Mother did say he might have thought of me . . . in his will. He did leave a will, did he not?"

Calpurnia smiled politely and ignored the question. Octavius returned the smile and turned to the door. A senior servant rushed forward and escorted the three young men out. They left without looking back. Maecenas had Octavius' ear, whispering something of importance. Agrippa just looked around, taking in the neighborhood.

Across the Adriatic, on the plains of Greece at a place near Pharsalus, three giant birds of prey rode rising thermals, their extended wings allowing them to soar with little effort. They orbited over two large armies just under way in a great battle. The large birds were a good omen for one army, bad for the other—only the gods knew for whom the laurels would go.

It was still summer, very hot and dry. A towering, thin dust cloud developed and ascended to meet the birds, a sign cavalry from one of the armies was on the move and engaging its objective. A thicker, more compact cloud was in the making from foot soldiers.

General Titus Labienus commanded one end of the battlefield; Marcus Antonius held the other. Labienus thought that he had shadowed Caesar's legions to these plains, but he was led into this engagement by design: Marcus Antonius'.

Labienus' horsemen charged at Marcus Antonius' cavalry, making good penetration. The situation appeared decisive. In the middle of the fray, Pompeian troops led by Pompey's father-in-law, Quintus Caecilius Metellus Pius Scipio, clashed with Antonius' main line. Javelins and spears flew from the Antonian troops. The Republican army stood ground and rode out the onslaught of arriving missiles, waiting to launch its own version of hell in turn. Most of the front line survived the initial wave of *pilum*.

One of the survivors was Sthenelus Regulius. At the trumpet calls, he let loose his own javelin, grabbed his sword, took a stance behind his shield, and waited the arrival of the other army.

"Steady—Steady!"

He didn't have long to wait. Caesar's veterans surged towards Sthen's line like a huge wave rumbling for shore after an earthquake. The ground under Sthen thundered and shook. The air in front of him gelled and roared.

"Steady!"

Sthen's heart pounded with the ground and his hands trembled. He braced himself.

"Steady—Steady. *Ordinem servate*—Hold the line!"

The hoard of charging soldiers arrived like a tidal wave: a wall of leather and metal, crazed legionaries in a cloud of war cries, swords and shields held out like plows.

The first legionary to reach Sthenelus was older than Sthen, definitely a veteran. Like a vicious, raging bull, the on-coming warrior collided with Sthenelus, the impact driving the younger legionary back. Sthenelus dug in with his boots. All he could see was the top of the other helmet. They pushed at each other, like wrestlers locked in a hold, muscles bulging, their defined anatomy glistening in sweat. Saliva drooled from Sthenelus' clenched teeth, sweat poured down his face, dirt and rocks seeped into his boots. And all the while, he watched for the thrusting point of the attacking sword that would try to find him. He sensed that his comrades next to him, at his flanks, were giving ground. He did the same so as not to be exposed and unprotected, especially at his right; besides, he was exhausted already. The bravado and abundance of confidence he had brought to the battlefield from Dyrrhachium rapidly evaporated.

At the far end of the line where horsemen engaged in battle, Marcus Antonius' cavalry fell apart. They turned and ceded ground to the advancing Republican horsemen. Cavalry officers were of a different class than the foot soldiers and had more to lose. Besides noble looks and status, they had property and enterprise; they did not stick around for very long when the situation was not to their liking.

Titus Labienus' Pamponian cavalry gave chase and broke through only to find a wall of fresh troops held in reserve for such this very purpose. The troops were put together from different legions of experienced and disciplined veterans. The wall was solid and displayed no fear.

Instead of throwing their javelins, the solid line of veterans used them to thrust into the faces of the on-coming horses and riders. A few of the horses managed to knock some of the veterans to the ground just from the laws of mass and velocity generated in the charge.

One of the downed veterans rolled to his back and thrust his javelin upwards into the belly of the horse upon him. The horse reared in panic and dropped his rider to the ground; the rider was immediately swarmed upon and impaled by swords, javelins, and spears from line troops. The impaled horse, screaming and raging in pain, collided with other horsemen, prompting a cascading chaos. More horses collided and fell, bringing riders down in a cloud of dust. A few of the fallen riders managed to get to their feet before they were cut down; others were butchered where they lay.

The initial wounded horse reeled in a chaotic circle and fell on the legionary who had impaled it, crushing the man's ribs and dislocating his shoulder. Miraculously, the legionary survived the horse, but did not get to his feet. A fellow legionary ran to his aid and covered him with his scuta and let fly his javelin toward a crowd of disoriented horsemen, impaling both a rider and his horse. The javelin pierced the rider's thigh and entered the horse's flank. Horse and rider galloped off, the horse kicking and jumping, trying to free itself of the rider. The rider flew off the horse's back but was fastened tight to the animal's side. The rider's leg broke and his body flung about like a rag doll nailed to a rolling barrel. In the ensuing chaos, the horse sustained successive arrow hits as it bucked in wild gyrations. With three arrows to its neck and rider still attached, the crazed horse stumbled and crashed to the earth, bringing the rider down with it.

Behind Labienus' cavalry, archers and slingers waited. Stampeding horsemen stunned the footmen as they flashed past in a panicked gallop, retreating from the battle. The archers had no time to organize and let fly any kind of volley before they, too, were cut down and massacred by the fresh troops. Many of the troops in Caesar's legions were from the Cisalpine and Transalpine country, Caesar's province north of the Italian boundary—they had no reservations in cutting down true Romans.

All along the lines, the battle did not go well for Labienus. The enemy penetrated the center. The failing flanks separated and his army fell apart as a fighting unit. The well-experienced, attacking veterans wheeled around to the Labienus' rear, and the river Eniperus cut off the only escape route. Some of the Republican horsemen and foot soldiers managed to make it to the foothills of nearby Mount Dogandzis to gain some high ground—that's as far as they got.

By mid-day, it was over. Victory went to Marcus Antonius and Caesar's troops. A number of legionaries who at one time had been with Caesar, but found themselves battling on the side of Pompey, dropped their weapons and stood ground, awaiting whatever fate to befall them.

Tired and confused Sthenelus stood among the vanquished, his sword lying at his feet.

Antonius' officers gathered survivors and herded them into ranks. They offered the beaten legionaries the opportunity to submit an oath of loyalty and join the victorious. Or they could take to their knees and submit to the point of the gladius.

Sthen's head was heavy and low. His eyes slid left and right as he watched crestfallen legionaries step forward to take the oath. Others stood fixed in their shadows.

He took a deep breath and planted a boot forward. He followed with the other and continued on to flock with the others.

A quick glance to his rear revealed a handful of soldiers slumped to their knees, their heads bowed in prayer, or shame.

The oath of allegiance was taken and the defeated were now part of Caesar's army under the command of Marcus Antonius, Sthenelus included.

The survivors stood at attention in silence, their backs to the handful that refused the oath.

Streamers on standards fluttered in playful breezes.

Dust clouds scudded across the landscape.

Horses snorted in boredom.

Crows cawed overhead.

Flies darted.

And then the unmistakable sound of killing and bodies toppling stirred the horses.

CHAPTER XI

Lucius and Caius were finally on land with belongings slung across their backs. Lucius used his firka, to carry his gear, as was the custom of all legionaries.

Unsteady sea legs carried the two for a stretch of time and road, until they found their land legs. They navigated the streets of Brundisium, searching for the way to the Via Appia and then on to Rome. Before leaving the port city, they resupplied with fresh foodstuff: bread, cheese, dried meat, and fresh water. It would be a long journey.

The two made their way for the open road after getting directions from shopkeepers and venders. They were like two ships headed for open water again. This time, there would be no drumbeat to mark their cadence as they set out, only the slapping of Lucius' sandaled, right foot.

"I wonder how long before we reach Tarentum?" Caius asked.

"I would say in two days of good marching and good weather," Lucius replied, not looking at Caius but to the ground that needed to be put behind them. "And no bandits or thieves."

Caius flashed a casual glance, not knowing if Lucius was serious, or just trying to frighten him. "I'm afraid they would get nothing much in the way of coins from me."

"Well, in that case, I guess they'd either kill you or take you as a slave."

"Lucius, you can be so full of it sometimes," Caius said.

"Ah, don't worry. Remember, I owe you," Lucius said with much confidence and assurance in his voice. "I'll watch your right."

They marched at a comfortable pace, taking in and enjoying the countryside. It was peaceful and picturesque. They kept one eye open for beauty, the other for bandits. Except for birds and farm animals, it was quiet; eerily quiet.

Caius felt safe with Lucius marching next to him. "What month is this, Lucius?" he asked. "I lost count of the days."

"Not sure."

"I haven't been paying much attention to the moon. Have you?"

"I think it is Sextilis now, or maybe the end of Quintilus, Caius. It's hot enough still to be Quintilis."

"Wasn't the battle near the Ides of Quintilus? Don't you remember? And it seems like a full lunar month since then."

Lucius shrugged.

"You're probably right, though. Yes . . . Sextilis," the young scribe said. "It must be Sextilis."

"Or, it could be the beginning of Septembris—"

"Lucius!"

"Or maybe even Octobris—"

"Don't confuse me more than I already am."

"Hey, you're the scribe. You should know what month it is!"

"A scribe, yes, but not an auger or a priest," Caius said as he scanned the sky, searching for any sliver of a moon. He couldn't see any.

Lucius interrupted the sound of the slapping sandal. "That storm sure didn't feel like summer weather."

"That's for sure. But I guess the gods can make the seasons feel anyway they wish."

The two travelers trudged on farther in longer stretches of silence, trading words for strides. The marching changed to a leisurely stroll, the slapping of the cripple's foot still keeping time.

"What day do you think it is?"

"Come on man, let it go, Caius! Okay? We'll find out in due time!"

Caius cloaked himself in silence again. In the upheaval of the civil war, the calendar had been neglected and most mortals were about two months ahead of themselves. In any case, Caius knew it was hot, dry, and felt like a summer month.

Giant verdant trees along the road provided plenty of opportunity for shade, which was a relief; the day got warmer with each mile. Lucius slipped into an uncomfortable hobble as his walking stick repetitively pierced and moved the country road under and past him. His ankle swelled, and it ached. He tried hard to hide his discomfort from Caius, and did well—for a time.

"I think we should stop, rest for a while, maybe have something to eat, don't you?" said a tired Caius. He was shorter than Lucius by two ears, equally tanned and lean. Short, wavy, almost matted, dark-brown hair capped his head. And large brown eyes separated by a small, sharp nose. He could eat forever and never gain a pound or inch. His body liked the softer, gentler life, not long marches.

"We haven't marched a full day and you're tired already? If you were in the army, you would have to walk at least twenty miles, build an end-of-day camp, dig trenches around it, and then rest," retorted Lucius.

"Well, I'm not in the army; and neither are you!" Caius countered.

Lucius limped to a halt, locked eyes with his marching companion, ready to justify his reasons for continuing on, but decided against it. "Okay, but not for long. We've got a ways to go yet." Frustrated, Lucius knew that without the injury he would have covered much more road by now. His ankle convinced him to rest.

A large, leafy tree bid the tired travelers to seek refuge under its cool shade. They eased themselves onto a soft blanket of shadow, latticed with patches of gilded sunlight that filtered through the tree's thick canopy. They lolled against the giant's trunk and were instantly beset and serenaded by flying insects. The soft songs of bees made it easy for weary bodies to melt like warm wax to fatigue. It would be hard to get back on the road again.

Caius pulled an inviting piece of cheese and a bit of bread from his cloth wrappings. Insects didn't wait but a second before attacking the fragrant morsels. Caius lashed and batted at the invaders, but they swarmed in repeated attacks.

Lucius was content just to lean against the tree and rest his eye lids. His lungs were in charge now for a change. His mind faded to black. Unconsciously, he crossed his right leg over onto his extended left leg. Pain from his torn ligament raged and roared to his brain, bringing him back to daylight. He winced and opened an eye to Caius to see if the scribe had noticed. He hadn't. Caius's mouth was too busy munching on cheese and bread and his eyes were too dead to the world, insects or no insects.

"How did you become a scribe?" Lucius asked.

The question stopped Caius' mouth in mid-chew. His eyes fluttered open and skipped about, examining the tree branches and foliage overhead for the answer. "My mother's sister and her husband," he answered. "They have position and status in Pompeii. They took me in for a while and taught me what I needed to know. And then they introduced me to the house of Cicero, through Tiro. Cicero has a villa not far from my aunt and uncle's house. I love Pompeii. Have you ever been there?" Caius asked.

"No."

"You'll love it. We'll visit my relatives when we get there."

"Are we going there?"

"Of course, we must," Caius said, more animated now.

"If you say so," Lucius said.

"If I say so? Of course I say so. How could we not go to Pompeii?" Caius said more to himself as he gathered his food scraps and refolded his grub cloth like precious cargo. "Lucius, do you remember me asking for a favor, the favor being that you paint or sketch portraits of my parents in Pompeii?"

"I recall something of that. I also said that you praised me too well. Remember?"

"Well . . . it's like this, Lucius, my real parents are dead. They died from an illness that took many lives in our village, a fever and cough. Many people, whole families, end up buried in large pits. I was away with my aunt and uncle at the time. They took me in as if I were their own child. I thought maybe if you painted a portrait, like some of the paintings I've seen at some of the other great homes in Pompeii, it would be some small way for me to repay their kindness."

"Caius, you place some heavy weight on my shoulders. I can't promise something like that. They deserve a real artisan, don't you think?"

"I've seen your work. I know you can do just as well as a real artisan. It's in your blood. The gods have touched you and given you a special gift." Caius was almost begging.

"Let's leave it in the hands of the gods for now. They'll do what they do. Enough said." Lucius gathered his belongings and labored to his feet. Grimaces highlighted every move he made as he climbed his walking stick to get to his feet.

It was a slow start but they were on their way down the road again.

They had just settled into a comfortable pace when galloping horse hooves from behind startled them. They turned in time to see a rider and horse closing in on them, fast. Lucius and Caius jumped to the side of the road as the rider sped past, completely oblivious to their presence, leaving them in a wake of dust and a scent of wet horse. They hid their faces in their tunics to deflect the flying clods of road and fine dust that pelted them.

"He's in a hurry; must be a courier with urgent news. That means we're bound to come upon a way station up ahead sometime soon," Lucius said.

"That's what we need, fast horses," Caius answered back.

The rider rode as fast as he could with the news of a battle across the Adriatic: Marcus Antonius was victorious, his army bigger and moving north. General Labienus fled to places unknown with a small contingent of officers and a few senators.

The cripple and the scribe resumed their march in the direction of the cloud that was once horse and rider, which gradually became more faint and distant, until it was completely gone.

Sol, Helios' brethren on this side of the Adriatic, took his time sliding behind the tree line, sparkling through leafy trees as Lucius and Caius trudged along the road. The air turned cool. The trekkers' tired feet screamed; it was time to call an end to the marching.

"Caius." Lucius spoke in a hushed tone, eyes fixed straight ahead, and a finger rubbing at the tip of his nose.

"What?" was Caius fatigued reply.

"Did you notice the two men behind us, behind the trees to our right? Don't look, keep your head straight."

Caius' fidgety and spastic head tried not to turn. Neck muscles fought one another and strained to keep his head straight. But his eyes cheated and took a quick peek.

"I said don't look!" Lucius exclaimed in a harsh whispered shout.

"Who are they? What do you think they want?" Caius asked. His mouth was dry as the countryside and his heart raced in his chest.

"Could be just a couple of farm boys, nervous about us."

"Or?"

"Just keep your senses high and don't look directly in their direction. Use your side vision. Did you come armed with anything other than your stylus?"

"No."

"Okay, just stay calm, but alert."

They reached a small clearing protected well on the windward side by tall Cyprus trees. Lucius decided to make camp. The pair tossed their gear to the ground, Lucius' gear hitting the earth with a heavy clang. They each gathered stones and wood for a fire and prepped the ground to bed down for the night, all the while using side glances and their ears to keep alert for any sign of unwanted visitors.

A thick blackness rolled in, chased away the evening minutes, and swallowed up dusk. A fire tried to comfort the two travelers by dancing for them. The flames cast drunken shadows on the trees and ground about them which only fueled Caius' nervous state. His eyes slid in all directions, trying to decipher what was real and was not.

The fire died to a few small surviving yellow flickering spears and glowing embers. Dying coals popped and sizzled as trapped gas escaped and fled the pit, denying the weary travelers any rest. Their eye lids fluttered wide at each sharp pop and changing shadow. It would be a long night.

———

The same night fell softly on Tusculum. In a bedroom of one rich villa, Gnaeus Pompey lay with his wife Cornelia. It was warm night, warm enough not to need the heavy, woolen bedding. They lay facing each other, resting on long comfortable pillows, talking as husbands and wives do.

"Husband, you were gone for such a long time. I was afraid you were not going to return. I feel sorry for Calpurnia, but I'm relieved that she is the widow, and not I. Is that so bad?"

"No."

She placed her slender fingers on his cheeks. Her hands were soft, but her fingertips were hard and callused from years of playing the lyre. She was still a beautiful woman. Her reddish-brown hair had less silver in it than Calpurnia's and her teeth were neat and intact, giving her a beautiful smile. Pompey felt lucky to have such a woman with him at this late stage in life. She was his fifth wife. She and young Julia, however, held the highest places in his heart. He loved her sincerely for the fine woman she was. Cultured, well read, and intelligent, she could hold her own with the best of men when it came to discussing philosophy and some principles of math.

"I did miss you, dear," the old man said.

"And what was it you missed of me most?" Cornelia was toying with him.

"Well, let's see, where shall I start?" He kissed her gently on the lips, then on each cheek, nudging her ears. He inhaled the bouquet of her hair, her unique delicate scent that held her stimulating pheromones. His coarse soldier's hand touched her soft, small shoulder, followed her arm to her hand and embraced it. It was small and delicate. He marched his hand back up to her shoulder and let it slide down her side and then to her waist. His resting hand could feel her smooth, abdominal muscles contract at his touch.

Her clothing felt too rough for such a fine, soft body. They removed their loin clothes and returned to each other in familiar embraces. He let his lips touch and glide over her soft stomach and breasts and kissed her flesh with tender, exploring touches. Turning her to her stomach, he gently lifted her hair at the nape of her neck, kissing her just at the hairline. The kiss generated a brief shiver followed by a giggle. He then followed her spine, kissing each space between her vertebrae as he coursed down her back, and then gave each dimple at the back of her hips their own little loving peck. They wrestled passionately, but not all night; he was definitely feeling his fifty-seven—soon-to-be fifty-eight years. The lovemaking was not of the young, hard, lusting type, but of the much more mature, respectful, and experienced technique of man and woman in their golden years.

At the roadside camp, two flickering shadows crept along the tree line, approaching the sleeping mounds from the left. The snap of a twisted branch stirred one of the sleeping mounds. The covered bundle changed shape for several seconds and then was still again. The silhouettes froze, remaining motionless until the mound appeared to be sleeping once more. The other mound never moved, except for restful respirations of someone truly slumbering.

The shadowy figures continued their advance, closing in on the nearest mound without further noise. The lead figure reached for the traveler's possessions with an outstretched, trembling hand.

Before another breath could escape the intruder's mouth, a deft left hand shot up from the dark mound, grabbed the man's wrist and held him in place. A well-hidden gladius in a right hand lunged upwards, thrusting soundly into the man's torso. The dark form under the blanket then pulled the man's arm down and to the left and pushed with his sword, causing the dying man to cart-wheel to the ground. The energy and rolling motion of the two bodies allowed the dark mound to come upright and standing—it was Lucius. With eyes fixed on the second intruder, he pulled the sword from the dead man. The blade was wet, sticky, and ready for another kill.

The second intruder had no idea what to do next. In the dark, highlights of the man's dirty face revealed itself to Lucius; the terror in it was unmistakable. The surprised and terrified intruder turned and ran, dropping his knife to the ground. Lucius moved in fluid motion and picked up the weapon, exchanging sword for knife. He hurled it in the direction of the fleeing man. The only sound heard was a thud as the knife glanced off a tree in the dark.

The man was gone.

Switching the gladius back to his right hand and peering into the darkness where the escaping intruder had fled for his life, Lucius heard footsteps from behind. Wheeling about sharply, sword in hand and ready to strike again, he met Caius face to face. "By the gods, don't ever come up on me like that!" he shouted, the tip of the gladius inches from Caius' throat.

They scanned the darkness and listened. The only sound they could hear in the darkness was heavy breathing—theirs.

Lucius collapsed to the ground, quivering, gradually becoming aware of the pain at his ankle. He cast a glowered stare at the dead man, who had the appearance of nothing more than a deformed log in the dark.

Caius also eyed the corpse. "Is he dead?" the young scribe asked.

"I believe so, as dead as Caesar," Lucius said. Caius made no connection other than the two were not of this world any more.

"What do we do now?"

"I don't think it's safe to wait around to see if the other has friends or kin who may come looking for us," Lucius answered.

"What do we do with him?" Caius asked, pointing to the lifeless figure on the ground.

"Bury him fast, or burn him," Lucius said. "Bury him. A fire would only give us away."

The task was done quickly. With Lucius' experience at digging, the man was in the ground in no time. The grave was not very deep, but enough to make him disappear.

"We need to gather our stuff and leave, *now*, Caius." Lucius did not have to repeat himself.

The miniature army gathered its gear and was on the move again, no small talk, just quick, silent steps. The intrepid travelers marched with heightened senses, gushing streams of endorphins, and the stamina needed to leave quick footsteps behind. Lucius ignored the pain as he moved at a sharp pace. Caius focused only on the road that should be there in the dark; he didn't notice Lucius rubbing his nose raw in the dark.

The night was active everywhere. In the house of Caesar, another shadowy figure was busy. He managed to gain entry, find his way to the tall wooden desk, locate Caesar's ring, and sequester it from its box. He did not take the ring from the room, though; instead, he took a wax tablet from under his cloak and imprinted the face of the ring into the wax. He examined the impression with a keen eye and was satisfied. He closed the tablet and put the ring back into its sacred box, returning it to its rightful place. This intruder had a successful night and exited the premises as stealthily as he had entered.

CHAPTER
XII

The first blush of morning spilled on the countryside and life continued—for most anyway. Lucius and Caius were still planting tracks on the road and were much farther away from the man in the ground.

"Lucius, I'm—very—tired."

"So am I, Caius."

"You have blood on you."

Lucius looked down at his tunic and wiped at it with his hand. The blood was mostly dry and flaky to the touch; much of it was soaked in the fabric.

The exhausted cripple and his equally exhausted friend heard the distinct sound of cascading water from a nearby brook. They abandoned the road and followed the sound of the brook until they came upon the winding stream. On tired knees they drank by cupped handfuls. It was so cold, Caius thought, as he felt it trickle down and plunge into his empty stomach.

Lucius removed his stained tunic, immersed it in the water, rubbed briskly with his hands, and then used small rocks to pound at the stains. The caked blood returned to liquid again, flowing out and downstream, leaving a rusty cloud of what was once life-sustaining blood. The stain was almost gone after several rinses, and the water clear again. Strong hands and muscular arms worked to ring the tunic to at least a damp state. Snapping the damp tunic in the air with authority managed to flick off more moisture.

"There, that should take care of that," he muttered.

Caius hardly flinched at the sharp snaps. His arms were dead weight across his chest, his legs loosely attached to his body, and his face resembled a cadaver: mouth agape and lids almost closed. Lucius stared at the body and then relaxed when he saw the chest rise and fall in peaceful waves.

The cripple contemplated taking a little nap himself, but the chilled tunic brought his senses back to full life when he put it back on.

He scanned the surroundings and took mental notes: A morning sun penetrated the thick tree awning with angular, stabbing beams of warmth that carpeted the forest floor with a dense mist. The playful haze floated and teased at the trees like a cat rubbing against a leg. Winged insects caught and reflected the light as they fluttered around the pillars of bark that reached for the canopy above. Aurora and Eros dazzled Lucius with their work.

Normally, an employee on task for his master, or a fugitive on the run, or whatever he was, wouldn't stop to notice such things, but Lucius was different. He felt his mother's presence in all that he observed.

A sudden rustling of dead leaves nearby disturbed the serenity, and Lucius frantically looked for his sword; it was not close at hand. More rustling grabbed at him. He stilled and became one with the trees and shrubs around him.

In a clearing stood a young deer, ears tall and fixed on Lucius. They eyed each other, man and animal, for a long, soft minute. The deer turned, high-stepped away, and disappeared into the thicket. The man felt the tension slide from his shoulders; his arms succumbed to his sides and a sigh of relief followed. "Please tell me, reverent Diana, goddess of wild things, let this be a good omen for today."

"What?" Caius stirred.

"Nothing, Caius," Lucius said, opening his meal bag to get some food into his famished stomach.

"I thought you were talking to me," Caius slurred as he recovered from a gaping yawn and extracted foodstuff from his own bag.

"No, I was saying my morning prayers to the gods for a good day."

"I hope they favor you, Lucius," Caius mumbled with a full mouth of bread, looking like a squirrel.

"Me, too, Caius; me too." A vague recollection of someone saying something similar to him wafted through his head. Sthen?

They ate in silence, eyes set in separate trances, both thinking of the night before.

He came from the south, another horseman riding fast, leaning hard and urging the horse on. Without breaking stride, the rider turned askance and made eye contact with the two at the roadside. He returned his full attention back to the road and rode on at breakneck speed, on to his destination—wherever that was.

Lucius and Caius' eyes followed the rider. They watched until rider and horse were no more.

"Shouldn't be long before we reach a rest station," Caius said.

"Um," was Lucius' reply.

———

The old man attempted to roll out of bed, not wanting to disturb his wife.

"You did not sleep well, my husband." A soft voice floated from a mound of bedding.

"No, I suppose not; too much drink before bed. I needed to get up several times last night. Getting old is neither as graceful nor pleasant as I expected. The gods give us these maladies for pure entertainment, I'm sure. Can you imagine old Jupiter having to awaken often during the night to empty his bladder? But then, they don't have mortal bodies as we, do they?"

"Three or four hours of good barbering will restore your energies, good husband," again from the lone body in bed, comfortable and content.

"Yes, a good bath, hot and cold, a good oiling and rub down . . . yes, that would be just the morning I need." He labored out of bed, groaning all the while.

"You sound like an old man."

Pompey, working out the kinks, turned to his wife. "That's because I am an old man, old woman."

Cornelia rolled to a propped elbow. "I wasn't that old last night!" she said in a playful huff.

Pompey walked away from the bed and rubbing his lower back. "No, no you were not. We were both much younger last night than we are this morning, my dearest wife, especially you." He disappeared from the room to have himself pampered; but first, he had to empty his bladder again.

Across the Tiber, in one of the many suburbs populated with the poorer inhabitants of Rome, a young adolescent made his way down a winding, shadowed alley, dark from tall wooden structures that housed these poor citizens and non-citizens alike. He passed a partially collapsed and burnt *insulae*—apartment block, to a blacksmith shop where many things could be fabricated. Anything could be acquired in this part of Rome—for a price. The youth gave his wax tablet to one of the artisans working in the shop. The man examined the tablet at different angles, nodded, and held out a hand. A small purse was placed in the outstretched and waiting hand. The dirty, blackened hand bounced and weighed the contents as accurately and precisely as any scale in a merchant shop.

"I'll be back tomorrow at this time," the youth said.

"Aye, tomorrow, it'll be ready," the blacksmith said.

"And not a word to anyone," the young man said with implied authority.

"Of course not, not a word."

The young man retraced his steps and exited the strange underworld, back across the Tiber, to the world he was more accustomed and more at ease; back to his books and poetry.

Things were going as planned.

⸺

Octavius' eyes appeared to be glued to his Greek manuscript. "Mother . . . ." The word drifted to Atia, who was enjoying some fruit and bread at a small table nearby. "Do you believe Uncle Julius thought of us in his will?"

"I don't know," she answered. "Has there been a reading of a will? I have not heard from anyone that there has been a will, or a reading. When did you hear of a will?" Atia asked.

Octavius stirred. "Oh, I don't know if there has been a reading. I just assumed that there was one. I mean, Uncle was more than just some other patrician . . . surely he had a will."

Atia's mouth stopped chewing and paused, her eyes rolled left to right and then back again, looking at nothing in particular. "He really had no family other than us, with poor Julia dead and there just being Calpurnia, and, of course, the people of Rome, who dearly loved him. His legions loved him more you know."

"I had always thought that he would be around to help me, you know, make my way up the *cursus honorum*, the *quaestorship*, *aedileship*, someday even a *praetorship*—to be consul someday."

"Octavius, you're young. You'll have plenty of time for that. Besides, your father will mentor you—"

"He's NOT my father!" young Gaius shot back. "MY father is dead!"

Atia glared, mouth agape, struck hard.

Gaius Octavius, son of Gaius Octavius, great-nephew of Gaius Julius Caesar, left the house of Lucius Marcius Philippus, taking his bad mood with him.

It wasn't more than ten paces when he came upon his companion, close confidant and associate, Gaius Maecenas. Octavius quickly donned his stoic, marble-esque face. Maecenas just as quickly had Octavius' ear. He had news of some importance again. Octavius' face remained impassive, except for the flaring of the eyes and a fine twitch at the corner of the right side of his mouth as his friend whispered. When Maecenas finished his message, they continued on, deep into the city, young wolf pack members leaving the den for their own territory in the wilderness.

They had plans.

CHAPTER
XIII

Late, sultry, summer weather greeted Cicero upon his return to Brundisium from Greece, not the refreshing, cooler days of Octobris the mortals would have expected, if in fact it were Octobris—but, of course, it was not. Chaos had the Roman lunar calendar two months ahead of the natural law of things. Luna and Sol knew exactly the time of the year; someone needed to do something about bringing the calendar back in line with extra calendar days—normally the job of the *college of pontiffs*. Cicero would see to it when he returned to Rome.

The old statesman looked up and down the dock as the boat glided in. He did not see his daughter Tullia there to greet him as in the past. He scurried to the back of the boat to get a few extra seconds of search time; still no sign of her. She'll probably show up any minute now, he thought.

The boat's wooden hull collided with the dock. Cicero and everyone else onboard lost their footing and grabbed for something solid. The crew scrambled to moor the creaking and rolling boat as the old man peered left and right.

He listened. But no one cried for "Papa."

Yearning eyes continued to search the dock; still no reason to rush to the dock.

Greek slaves, soaked in sweat and looking like glistening eels, began unloading Cicero's baggage. Sol cast various shades of sunburn on exposed skin each minute crew and passengers mingled on the waterfront.

Cicero bore a wide-brimmed, straw hat that helped battle the sun's rays, but not the heat. His heavy, dark clothes sapped his energy.

"Tiro, we need to get our things unloaded soon and delivered to the villa before we all perish from this un-godly heat," the master shouted.

"Right as always, Good Savior of Rome. I will get them moving the best I can," the secretary shouted back, fanning his face with a makeshift straw fan. He picked at his formerly fine, white tunic, now soaked in sweat. The darkened material clung and irritated his skin at every point of contact as he waddled over to the part of the dock where a small mountain of luggage grew. He called out in Greek—the common language of all the coastal cities in Italy—to the larger of two slaves. "You! You there. What is your name? Yes, well, Kostas, get this entire luggage organized and loaded onto the carts as soon as possible. We need them delivered to the villa just outside the city gates, the villa with the apple orchard, patrician Flaccus' villa. You will get further instructions from one of my men," Tiro commanded. "And I will deduct two *denarii* for each hour of the sundial that you delay."

With eyes of a jackal, the dockhand, his dirty long hair plastered to his scalp, sweat plunging from his forehead and nose, skin reeking a pungent odor of ammonia, leered at Tiro. He said not word. He turned his head askance, but not his eyes, and spit a wad of ugly sputum to the dock.

Tiro's head reeled in revulsion. He reached for his handkerchief, brought it to his nose and blotted out the image with closed eyes and a quick shudder.

By evening, Cicero and his entourage were at the villa, a fine comfortable place with plenty of room to relax, private baths with hot, tepid, and cold water, and excellent slaves skilled at full body massages. The day's heat finally dissipated and Cicero lingered in the colder *frigidarium*, awaiting the night air to cool off even more. From the cool pool, the statesman dictated some ideas to Tiro for future reference. The scribe squinted in an anemic light from a few oil lamps and shorthanded the dictation onto his wax tablets, which proved quite difficult due to the day's heat. This day grew unusually hot, according to the locals, but the following day should be much cooler—prized chickens were sacrificed and the omens promising. The remains of the sacrificial foul were most tasty as a gifted cook prepared, and despite the hot weather, baked them with the finest olive oil and just the right spices and herbs, easily found in this port city. More importantly, they were flavored with the epicurean seasoning—hunger.

One of Cicero's clientela dropped by and presented an exceptionally good wine and begged him not to cut it with too much water as it held its own with flavor and body. The man was right; such an excellent wine, Cicero enjoyed it immensely.

Pleasant and cool breezes replaced the evening's stillness. The night would be bearable after all—thanks to the gods for those divine and delicious chickens. And thanks to Bacchus for that marvelous wine. Cicero was truly a pleased and happy man this evening.

A week before Cicero's arrival, Lucius and Caius found the way station they were so hoping for. They also found a friendly station keeper who offered them a place to rest as well as food and drink. They even found a home-built bath where they soaked, relaxed, and shaved—Lucius, anyway. They felt like new men. In the evening, they caught up with the world and the news.

"Caesar's army defeated General Titus Labienus under Marcus Antonius in Greece," the station keeper had said.

"What of the army? Was it totally destroyed?" Lucius asked.

"I don't believe so. Who knows? We just get bits and pieces from the riders. They're always in such a hurry."

"Where is it now?" Caius asked. "General Antonius' army, where is it?"

"Word is that they are moving back toward the sea, maybe to move north and over to come down into Italia," the keeper responded, gesturing with a shrug and extended fingers that held an invisible orb of the world.

"Do you believe he will bring the legions to Rome?" Caius asked Lucius.

Lucius ignored the question, gazing down at the table, as if analyzing the movements of armies on a great map. The only armies on the table, however, consisted of a few ants on the move; no particular strategic or tactical design, only in search of food scraps to take back to the others.

"You walked all the way from Brundisium? Without problems?" the station keeper asked.

"What do you mean?" Lucius said, eyes locking hard on the keeper.

"Just asking," the keeper said. "With this civil unrest, there are all sorts of people out on the roads these days. Some are traveling for safe places. Some are preying on those traveling to those safe places—wolves and sheep. One has to be careful—very, very careful."

"Yes, I think I know what you mean," Lucius said.

"You appear to be afflicted with some sort of ailment," continued the station keeper, flashing a quick look at the cripple's ankle. "You use a walking stick for your limp."

"I injured my ankle. Tore some gristle under my skin, the one that connects my foot and leg muscle, but it is mending well enough."

"Ah, yes, I see," the keeper muttered. "Young man, you must be careful. Wolves, and some men, will seek out the injured and lame. They'll pounce on them. It's the nature of things. Is it not?"

"You don't need to worry about Lucius, he can take care of himself," Caius said. A kick under the table quickly silenced him. Caius' furrowed eyes glared at Lucius, but the return stare in his friend's face said *let it be.*

"We thank you for the warning. We'll keep our eyes and ears open and pray to the gods for a safe journey," Lucius said. With that, the two travelers were shown to their lodgings: fresh straw and a good space in the stables. They planned for another day and night at the way station, preparing for the next leg of their journey: north to Venusia.

A slave cleaned up after the guests and like a hovering, gigantic god, swept away the ant soldiers on the table with a mighty swipe of a dirty rag; there were no victors, only losers.

Lucius tossed and fussed. He couldn't find a comfortable position in the soft, clean straw. His mother claimed his mind and his dreams. *Was she safe? Was she healthy? Was she alive?*

The station keeper bounded into the stable just as Lucius' eyes were ready to close for the night.

"I have news of a caravan of sorts and armed escorts, taking some horses to the next station at Silvium. I can't promise anything, but maybe there's a chance to get passage if they have room," said the old man.

"Let's hope, huh?" Lucius said.

Silvium, that's only about fifteen miles or so from Venusia, he pondered. He found himself fully awake again and in a fitful rest. To ease the fidgeting, he command his eyes shut and concentrated on drawing a sketch of his mother's face on a slate of darkness. She wouldn't come. A faint silhouette lingered behind a veil of half-sleep, but would not push through from the other side.

I'm trying too hard, he thought. He inhaled deep, recalled some cherished memory, and then—there she stood. He pulled her through and played scene after scene of the past.

A smile crossed his face.

And then sleep.

———

Lucius and Caius were up with the hens and the rooster. Washed, refreshed, and revived, they were ready for whatever the morning, and the gods, were going to bring their way. And, as advertised, a small caravan of four armed riders arrived, escorting two small carts pulled by one horse each and a team of three horses in tow.

The riders appeared to be old legionaries, vets from another time. They wore an assortment of body armor: old leather cuirasses, some old chain mail around their necks, and swords at their right sides. One vet had what appeared to be an old javelin tucked alongside his horse. They were unshaven. Their faces and hair were powdered with road.

The station keeper met the riders, exchanged morning greetings, and then invited them in. The riders dusted themselves off, leaving a cloud of debris that once belonged to the Appian Way outside the station.

Once inside, they milled about the tables, not ready to sit just yet, their bottoms fresh off the saddles. Lucius and Caius appeared soon after to hear of any important news and find what the chances were of hitching a ride up to Venusia.

"So, my friend, what does the world look like today?" the station keeper, providing water, asked the most dominant-looking of the four, the one with a large scar across his right eyebrow and cheek, sparing his eye.

"Depends," replied the old vet, empting the wooden cup of its contents in four huge gulps, water cascading from the corners of his mouth and onto his chest. "If you're for Pompey, things don't look so bad. If you were for Caesar . . . well . . . who knows, huh?"

"And Marcus Antonius? What of Marcus Antonius and his army?" the keeper asked as he refilled the man's cup.

"Only the gods know for sure, but word on the road is that he is coming this way, to Rome."

"How far off is he?" another question from the keeper in rapid succession.

"Umm, weeks away," the scarred vet replied, finally sitting at the table. The other three followed his lead and sat as well. "It takes time to move an army like his," the old vet continued.

"I say he'll leave his legions up at the border," one of the other vets volunteered. Thracian tattoos covered his neck and arms.

The scarred-eye leader cast a sidelong look at the tattooed man for half of a moment, and then added, "Excuse my 'general' friend over here; he seems to know exactly what Marcus Antonius' plans are." General may have blushed, one could not tell from all the dust and crud on his face. His eyes just glared back through the dirt at the lead vet. He threw his head back and downed the water as quickly as the others.

Lucius and Caius had been quiet, standing in the background, just listening. They moved closer to the table. The station keeper approached the lead vet.

"My friends here are traveling to Venusia," said the keeper.

Four heads turned to measure the pair.

"Do you think you could provide passage for them, at least to Silvium?" he asked.

The scarred vet regarded Lucius and Caius and scratched at the stubble on his neck, contemplating an answer, weighing the pros and cons, factoring in any advantage for him.

"I don't know. They might slow us down," he said, not committing either way, just yet. "What is your trade?" the old vet asked, to neither one in particular.

"We're scribes for Consular Marcus Tullius Cicero," Caius answered.

"Scribes!" exclaimed General with a half of a laugh of stale breath, wiping his wet mouth with his tattooed arm. The wet smear on the arm revealed more of a tattoo. Lucius noted that almost every bit of the man's skin under the dust might be dyed as well.

Lucius limped towards General. "I was a legionary in Pompey's army; at Dyrrhachium."

Again, four heads drew Lucius in their sights, simultaneously, scrutinizing him much closer.

The scarred vet grabbed Lucius' right wrist and turned the palm up, inspecting it as if reading the future. "So, you've dug a trench or two, huh?" the old man said, letting the wrist fall away, looking down at the cripple's feet. "Are you a deserter?"

"No. I injured my leg and they let me go, or left me behind, rather."

Caius stepped forward adding, "Consular Cicero levied him as a scribe on his staff."

None of the vets bothered to look at Caius.

"Can you still handle a sword?" asked General.

"He can," said Caius, which brought a harsh glare from Lucius. Three of the four heads turned to Caius, awaiting more information. He silenced himself, stepping back without offering another word.

Scar-Face angled his head as if re-evaluating Lucius, looking closer, regarding the cripple again. There was something there, he could feel it, but not put his finger on it.

"What's your name?" Scar-Face asked.

"Lucius—Lucius Pontius. My father was Lucius Pontius Gavius, a soldier in Sulla's legions, retired to Venusia after his service. He was from a long line of fighters, Samnites. His father gave him the cognomen Gavius for one of the Pontii who fought at the battle of *Fureulae Caudinae*—the Caudine Forks."

Scar-Face eyed Lucius closer still, squinting, again tilting his head from side to side, looking for a face from another time, another army from the past.

"Who was your Centurion?" asked General.

"Caelius. Centurion Marcus Caelius."

The vet scratched at his tattoo at the back of his dirty neck, shaking his head. "Can't say I know anyone by that nomen."

"Any old legionaries in your group?" asked Scar-Face.

Lucius' mind went searching, eyes moving about as his brain scanned his memory for names and faces; then he saw him— Phoebus, staring at him, pointing to the javelin with his outstretched hand; those eyes, those old eyes. The words spilled slowly and with reverence, "A veteran, by the name of Phoebus. I don't know his other name."

Three of the four stirred, sitting more erect and giving Lucius their full attention.

"Could you see his eyes?" asked one of the vets who up to now had not said a word.

"Just barely," Lucius answered.

"Did he smile much?" again asked the vet.

"Always. Even in his sleep."

"Phoebus, that old bastard, what's he still doing in the army?"

the vet who asked about his eyes said with a snort that could have passed for a laugh. The others shook their heads with half-smiles on old faces.

"Doesn't he know he could get himself killed?" Scar-Face said, following with a laugh. The others joined in a chorus of laughter, too.

Lucius recognized the same leathery old faces shared by these men and old Phoebus. In turn, after a round of jocularity, the old vets noticed Lucius' solemn look, they'd seen it many times before; old Phoebus now belonged to that Greek Milky Circle.

The merriment ebbed and died like a flame consuming the last of its fuel. Silence replaced the vaporous memories that hovered, dissipated, and then wandered away. Scar-Face stirred and every-one came back to the present.

"I suppose you could come as far as Silvium, can't guarantee anything after that. Who knows, maybe you'll be lucky enough to find someone going to Venusia. We leave first thing in the morn-ing."

Caius looked over to Lucius with a broad smile. Lucius acknowledged the smile with a hint of a nod.

The remainder of the day came and went uneventfully. The vets snacked on bread and cheese, drank wine, and talked of old times, old scars, and old wars; old vets always talked of the old times, scars, and past wars.

Night befell Rome as it did the way station. Marcia, a Vestal Virgin in training, was on duty in the Temple of Vesta. She inspected the sacred flames to ensure the safety of Rome. The flames were healthy and alive. She moved on to see about the baking of the sacred cakes.

Scampering-like noises upstairs where important documents

and wills were stored for safekeeping grabbed her attention and she froze. Her eyes honed in on the ceiling and she listened for more sounds of tiny feet. And when she heard none, she started a slow ascent, taking each step as if it were her last. "I pray it isn't one of those ugly, huge rodents," she whispered. "I hate rats." When she reached the top, she crept to the room where she thought she heard the noises. She peered into a room dimly lit and dark at the corners.

"Shoo—shoo," she commanded with authority. An eerie silence answered back. No telltale sound of tiny claws running across the mosaic floor, nor any evidence of small black droppings.

Something out of place caught her eye, on the floor: scrolls and documents strewn about. She eased her way over to the little pile of scrolls with cautious, deliberate, and measured steps, unaware of the shadowy figure creeping up from behind.

CHAPTER
XIV

Marcia looked to the disheveled scrolls on the floor and then to the empty pigeonhole boxes on the wall. She glanced over the neighboring boxes and saw they all had their documents with identifying tags suspended from the ends resting in place. She scanned left to right. The other shelves appeared undisturbed and intact. Her probing eyes drifted back to the empty spaces when a sharp blow to the back of her head sent a blinding, white flash to her eyeballs followed by a black curtain of nothingness. She crumpled to the floor.

A dark-hooded figure stood over the Vestal as she lay sprawled on the floor with the scrolls. He had a walking crutch in his right hand. The hem of her gown rested at her waist, revealing her alabaster white thighs, left hip, and fleshy, curved bottom. The intruder's strong, adolescent heart pumped wildly; his blood surged and pulsated with each pounding beat. The sight of the young girl's exposed flesh and his raging hormones caused him to become excited in more ways than anticipated. He stooped low, left hand outstretched to the unconscious girl. Steady fingers reached for her smooth skin. His chest pounded. His breaths came easy but deep. His pupils dilated like black little moons.

And then a sane thought managed to break through his mesmerized brain: there was nothing more sinister than the raping of a Vestal Virgin; nothing more revolting to the Roman people than an assault on one of the protectors of Rome; no crime more heinous or reprehensible than the one he was contemplating.

He stopped.

Reluctantly, he pulled away from the girl, want and reason raging within him. A slight movement of the body on the floor and the beginning of a petite groan tipped the balance toward reason and he continued his withdrawal from the Vestal. Hurried footsteps moved him to the door. He looked back, his adolescent urges still strong with him, and then he was gone.

Lucina, one of the other six Vestals, happened to pass by the doorway and cast an eye in the direction of the room. On the floor was a quavering Marcia. She swayed awkwardly as she tried to sit. Her tousled hair covered her face, giving her the appearance of some eerie creature growing from the floor.

Fear seized Lucina. She couldn't move. When she recognized the creature on the floor, she ran to her in a panic. "Sister, dear sister, what is the matter? What has happened?" she cried.

Stunned, confused, mute, and with eyes glazed over, Marcia stared blankly into Lucina's face. The wounded girl's senses kicked in and she registered severe pain at the back of her head. She reached behind and felt a warm stickiness. Blood painted her hand. She began to sob and shake uncontrollably, but still uttered not a word.

Lucina surveyed the surroundings and saw only the spilled documents on the floor. Again she questioned Marcia. "What's wrong? What happened to you?"

After a stretch of more sobbing, Marcia finally answered. "I . . . I don't know. I heard . . . a rat. I found the scrolls . . . on the ground . . . and then—my head, it hurts so—and then . . . you were here."

The Chief Vestal happened by next, taking in the scene in the room. She said nothing to the girls, but gathered the documents, examining the titles on the tags as she collected them. She examined the empty cubbyholes in the wall, regarded the weeping girl, looked over the rest of the room, and then returned her interrogating gaze to the storage bin.

"Lucia, take Marcia to her room and see to her," the Chief Vestal ordered.

"Yes, Mater," Lucia answered as she assisted Marcia to her feet, the young girl still weeping.

The matriarch studied the documents in her arms, returning each to its rightful place when one of the documents caught her attention. The tag at the end indicated that it was a will—*The Will of Gaius Julius Caesar*. The imprint of Caesar's signet was clearly visible on the wax seal, and intact. The document appeared genuine enough.

"Strange, I don't remember registering this will," she muttered, her face contorted in a severe frown. She looked to the floor, replayed the scene of finding the girls, thought of the documents strewn about, and then prayed somebody would soon appear and explain it all to her.

But no one came.

"Dear Vesta, what has passed here?" she whispered. "What am I to do? Our dear protector, the good *pontiff*, our dear Caesar, is dead and there is mischief." She invoked the name of the previous Chief Vestal and asked—or prayed—"Fabia, dear Fabia, what do I do?" All the documents were now back in place, except for Caesar's will, that she took with her, clutching it tightly against her chest.

———

Horse's hooves echoed in the morning air as a lone rider bound for Pompey's villa in the Alban Hills moved at a fast gallop, headed in the direction of the rising sun. Bright gold and yellow sunlight from the future god-to-be, Sol Invictus—the unconquered sun washed the landscape along the road to Tusculum. The rider took no note of the beauty, only of the road under his horse taking him to his destination. He could see a large lake in the distant Alban valley as he rounded the hills. He knew the road was much shorter now, the villa much closer.

Long shadows shortened by half when the rider on his tired horse arrived. One of the villa slaves acknowledged the rider's arrival and summoned the nomenclator.

"Sire, there is a courier from Rome with an urgent message. He says it's from the Chief Vestal," announced the nomenclator. "Shall I have him wait, Sire?"

Pompey had just met the morning in peace, not quite ready to engage in any real crisis; he knew, however, that eventually he would have to return to Rome and take charge. Marcus Antonius and his army continued to pose a real threat. Plans had to be made. The Senate considered Pompey its man and depended on his protection, for the good of the Republic, and, of course, the property and wealth of all those old men.

"Have him wait in the tablinum, I will be there shortly," Pompey commanded.

The slave bowed reverently. "By your command, Dominus."

The nomenclator ushered the dusty rider into the reception area and instructed him to wait.

The rider took in all the war trophies on the walls as he waited. Pompey had a similar den to this one in his domus in Rome, near the Esquiline Hill, the *Domus Rostrata*, but with greater and more recent trophies.

Heavy, sure-footed, echoing boots brought General Pompey into the room. He took his place at his desk and glared at the rider.

"Well, what urgent message do you have for me?" demanded the general.

The rider pulled a rolled parchment from his pouch and handed it to the general. It had an official wax seal affixed to it. Pompey snapped the seal free and unfurled the document with authority. He squinted as he read; he had to do more of that as of late. He brought the document directly under an oil lamp, extended it a little further from his face, and then read in silence. Questioning eyes under raised brows and three deep fissures in his fleshy forehead locked onto the courier. He had prepared his mind for some information of importance concerning Marcus Antonius, or some other matter requiring his military opinion.

The messenger shifted, uneasy with the quizzical look, unsure of what to do next.

"Do you know the nature of this letter?" Pompey asked.

"No, General, only that it comes from the Temple of Vesta, from the Chief Vestal herself," was his nervous reply.

Pompey rolled the document back up, stood sharply, and paced slowly around his desk, his face set deep in thought.

"Venius!" he called out.

His nomenclator appeared in a span of a breath, obviously being very near all this time.

"Give this man refreshment and see to his horse. Then arrange for a scribe. I will have a message to return with him within the hour."

"Immediately, Dominus," the slave said as he ushered the rider out of the reception room.

Pompey returned to his desk, contemplating the situation, casting mental nets for ideas, and composing thoughts in his head. A young scribe arrived, wax tablet and stylus in hand. The general motioned for him to sit on a stool nearby. Pompey looked to the ceiling, waiting for the words to fall into view—

Greetings to you, good Chief Vesta. Have received your message of the will. I plan to be on the road this time tomorrow to meet with you. I am most grateful that you contacted me in this matter. You are wise to do so. As you are the guardian of our good Rome, I am sure the gods are pleased with your thoughtfulness and attentiveness and making the right decision in reaching me with this important matter. May the gods protect and keep you well, as you protect and keep Rome well.

The scribe etched as fast as he could, keeping up with the general, making sure to get it right the first time around and not miss a word.

Silence filled the room.

The scribe flashed probing eyes between the general and the wax pad, awaiting further words. There were none.

"Get that on parchment and prepared for my seal," Pompey ordered.

"As you command, Dominus," the young scribe replied, leaving the general alone with his thoughts.

Again, Pompey called for Venius. "Make preparations, we leave for the Domus Rostrata." Venius acknowledged the command and hurried out of the room.

Rider and horse rested, their stomachs filled, were back on the road, message in pouch.

———

In Brundisium, in a garden area sheltered by tall Cyprus trees, Cicero called for his man, Tiro. The secretary waddled briskly to the master and bowed in his usual subservient self, hands clasped and grin in mouth. "Yes, Your Graciousness."

"Tiro, I've decided it's time to leave for home, for the villa, for Tusculum. Plan appropriately," he commanded.

"Oh, yes Dominus, I will make arrangements immediately," Tiro exclaimed as he began to leave the room, barely able to control his enthusiasm, hands clapping like a child.

"Wait. We need to be frugal in our planning. I am not especially pleased with the messages I've received from Terentia and the management of . . . of my finances." The mention of finances took a softer tone of voice. In addition to the two legions he had contributed to the cause, he had lent Pompey a large sum of money; funds were tight.

"We won't be taking all the staff with us this trip. I need to do something about the lictors. They've become a small burden, I'm afraid. So, too, we shall have to dismiss some of the scribes. By the way, where is Caius? I have not seen him."

"Sire, we sent him ahead of us, on to Tusculum, do you not recall?" Tiro smiled, praying that Cicero had not given much thought about the young man's absence. It was Tiro who had taken the liberty to act on his own accord and sent Lucius and Caius ahead with limited funds.

"And the young cripple, the soldier . . . what of him?" asked the elderly statesman.

"He accompanied Caius as well, Sire," Tiro said, wilting his head to the side in his usual manner, his face veiled with that façade of a smile. Had he been a dog, his tail would have been wagging incessantly.

Cicero pulled his trusted aide by a sleeve to the side and whispered. "I fear I am slowly losing my mind, Tiro; my memory anyway. I have known many a good man to lose his fine edge in his late years, a mind as keen as the sharpest blade, dulled as if used to pound stone. I've much to write and pass on to the good people of Rome before my mind, too, becomes muddled. Like I always have said, the best or finest asset a man can possess is his mind, a 'first-class' brain, with impeccable morals; mental and moral excellence go hand-in-hand."

Cicero stood rooted, eyes fixed a thousand feet past Tiro. The secretary, smile still in place without strain, waited. The master blinked himself back to the moment and then parted. Tiro's eyes followed the patron as the elderly man left. The strain was too much and the smile collapsed. But the squint in the eyes hardened.

—∞—

Lucius and Caius traveled with the vets north to Silvium. There was comfort and safety in being more than just two. Along the way the small army of six passed several caravans of migrating people and animals moving in the opposite direction, away from Rome. They passed in silence. The refugees obviously had what little possessions they owned in rickety old carts drawn by hand, or a lone ox, and their livestock close by. Faces flickered hints of fear as they scurried past. Whipping sticks urged the animals to move a little faster. Caius, nervous as a barn mouse, spied about and searched for signs of predators ready to pounce on him. Lucius seemed not to worry at all.

They reached Silvium intact. Without a lot of ceremony the vets delivered the horses and departed, continuing on to a Roman garrison at Beneventum.

Lucius and Caius rested, replenished food rations, and then headed towards Venusia on foot again.

CHAPTER XV

The scribes marched all morning, all afternoon, and most of the early evening, stopping only to eat a brief meal and cool tired, sore feet. Idle chatter occupied many boring minutes and silence filled many weary miles. The end of day loomed down the road a ways; just a few miles more.

"Do you not miss being a soldier, Lucius?" Caius asked.

"Sometimes, yes. Sometimes, no. Long marches like today remind me of the not-so-pleasant times. Of course, I would be walking faster, farther, and with a lot more weight to carry. And at the end of the march, I would be trenching, you know, digging ditches for the night encampment. I tell you, by the end of the day, I would be one tired mule, one of 'Marius' mules,'" Lucius said, letting his crutch take on more weight.

"Whose mule?" Caius asked in a puzzled glance.

"Marius. Gaius Marius, consul some . . . some many, many years back, way before our time, Caius. My father called him the 'father' of the Roman legions. The soldiers were as good as mules, marching all day with packs, carrying everything they needed."

"Were you ever afraid of being killed?" Caius asked.

Lucius studied the dirt road before him for several paces. "I don't remember ever being really frightened to die in battle," he said, avoiding the real fear—the fear of failure. "I remember my heart pounding in my chest, but nothing like that short time I spent in the water during the crossing. Funny, now that I think about it, I remember the fear in the water being replaced by a peaceful calm when I thought the sea was going to swallow me up, and the end was at hand. What a rude awakening to be thrown back into the boat to see your face laughing at me."

Caius thought about the incident and smiled. He did his best to stifle a full-blown, hysterical laugh.

"If I could sketch images like you, Lucius, I would draw a large painting of Neptune tossing you out of the sea with his trident pitchfork. I would have him saying, 'and stay out!'" He broke down and unleashed uncontrolled laughter.

Lucius, brows furrowed, glared at him in mock anger. "I saw a little fear in your eyes some nights back, if I remember clearly."

Caius' laugh ebbed to a chuckle and then faded back to a smile. "Lucius, what's like to kill someone?" The words fell out of his mouth before he could stop them.

"You mean, knowingly kill someone?"

"Well, yes, I guess that's what I mean."

Lucius continued to measure the road for five more paces.

"When you're a soldier, you're taught to kill, that's your trade, that's your art. If it's done well, then I guess there's pride. After all, somebody's trying to kill you, too, so you've got to be better.

"The other night, on the road . . . that . . . that all happened so fast, it was like . . . as if the gods were doing all the work . . . I just held the sword. I didn't feel good about it. I didn't feel bad about it. I just felt . . . it had to be done. I was more angry than afraid. It had to be done.

"If one kills just for the fun of it, well, that's different. It has to be against the nature of things to kill for malice. That's evil. People that kill with malice must be possessed by evil spirits."

"Lucius, you said to kill—knowingly."

"Well, yeah . . . if you fire an arrow into the air, or launch your javelin, you don't know what's going to happen, do you? You may hit a target, or you just might miss. Only the gods know what will happen."

"Do you really think the gods control everything? What if there are no gods. I've heard of a people, the Hebrews, they say there is only one god."

"Caius! You think too much. Let it be, man," yelled Lucius. "Next thing you know, you'll be discussing whether the gods made us, or if we made the gods! We're not Greek. We're not philosophers. What do we know of these things? What difference do we make in the . . . in the nature of things? Do you think anything we do can change what the gods have planned? Or had planned? Rulers of countries and gods make history, Caius, not us. We're just scribes, and me especially, less than that. I can't—I can't even—"

"Can't what, Lucius?"

"I can't even—nothing, Caius, forget it."

"Now that you're not a soldier—and less than a scribe—what do you want to do the rest of your life?"

Lucius didn't answer. He only examined the road where his next footsteps would take him. He marched. He just kept marching. Private thoughts and the sound of a slapping foot on the road, kicking up small clouds of dust, filled his head.

"Live."

"What?"

"I said—live. Who knows, maybe a wife, children, and grandchildren for my mother. Soldiering certainly didn't work out. And I don't know about this scribing business. Maybe an artisan, I don't know. The gods have it all planned, Caius. Leave it at that, okay? For now, I just want to live."

Caius accepted the words in silence. Lucius knew his friend wanted to say more. He would just save it for another time. That was okay, another time would be fine.

They finished their philosophical discussion and found themselves approaching the next destination—Venusia. Off in the distance, from the inclined and curved road, they could see the rim of a mesa where Lucius' home would be waiting.

Elongating shadows from trees crept like snails across the road and slithered upwards along the hills that surrounded Lucius and Caius. The tips of the trees captured the last of the sun's rays, giving the tree tops a reddish-orange glint, as if a guiding light beam had been cast from a powerful light tower.

Lucius stopped, Caius followed his lead.

"At the base of the hill, we turn right. There's a small dirt road that will take us to a house," Lucius said. His face flashed subdued excitement and pleasant expectancy in blinked twitches.

———

The Vestals were notified of Pompey's arrival and that he would visit the following day—this day.

Again he traversed the city streets, lictors and bodyguards at the front, well-wishers and clients to the rear, following like a gaggle of geese. They traveled east on the Sacra Via until they reached the Temple of Vesta and the House of the Vestals.

The lictors pounded on the doors, made their announcement, and then cleared the way for Pompey.

"Greetings, General, may the gods protect you and give you great wisdom," said the Chief Vestal, Aemilia the Younger.

"Thanks be to you, Protector of Rome and all its citizens," replied the general. "You have some information about a will, I believe." Pompey wasted no time getting to the point.

"Yes, please do come in," said the Chief Vestal. Two of the lictors accompanied the general to a reception area. Aemilia disappeared and then returned promptly, clutching a scroll in her arms. She extended and offered the document to Pompey.

He squinted and held the document at arm's length, attempting to read the title on its small tag. In frustration he handed it to the lictor standing next to him. The man took the scroll and read the tag for Pompey.

"Sire, it is the will of Gaius Julius Caesar." He inspected the imprint within the wax seal. "The seal appears to be that of Caesar's," said the lictor, returning the scroll to Pompey.

Pompey regarded the scroll, hesitant, yet ready to plunge into it, pondering what spirits or mayhem may be unleashed when unfurled. He was more decisive when it came to ordering his legions into battle. Beads of sweat seeped from his forehead. His eyes bore into the rolled parchment. An idea; he looked to the Chief Vestal and handed the document back to her.

"Good Vestalis Maxima, Guardian of Rome and its people, the contents of this will would ring more true and venerated if read from your lips on this hallowed and sacred ground," Pompey stated diplomatically.

Aemilia guardedly took the document in hand. She rotated it until the seal with Caesar's mark faced her. With a firm twist, she broke the seal. The tiny crack shattered the confines of the room, along with the earth. All eyes fixed on the Chief Vestal and all ears awaited each syllable and consonant to follow.

She read the beginning of the text in silence and looked up to see hard eyes boring in on her. And then she began—

"I, Gaius Julius Caesar, son of Gaius Julius Caesar and Aurelia, of the house of the *gens Julia*, descendant of Aeneas and Venus, empowered with imperium by Rome, the Senate, and the People, do by declare that: my property with the gardens across the Tiber shall be enjoyed by the good people of Rome; that the same good people of Rome shall each receive a gift in the amount of 300 sesterces; that my good wife, Calpurnia, shall retain all villas and estates owned by me with the present staff; that my grand-nephew, Gaius Octavius, son of Atia, shall be lawfully recognized as my son in name and being and thus be inducted as a patrician with all rights and privileges as such—" The vestal stopped briefly, eyes raised. "My lord, some of these words are of a slightly different dialect from that which I am accustomed." But she continued on—

"Therefore, to my adopted son, Gaius Julius Caesar Octavius, I leave the remainder of my wealth, the respect and loyalty of my legions and veterans, as well as my *clientele*. Upon the occasion where as my son sheds his youthful toga for the *toga virilis* of manhood, I, Gaius Julius Caesar, *Pontifex Maximus*, decree that he shall fill the first vacancy of *pontifices*, with all rights and duties that accompany that honor, at the earliest opportunity. Furthermore—"

Pompey stepped forward and gently retrieved the document from Aemilia's hands. A scrutinizing eye under a raised brow inspected it closely. The words were blurry, but they were there. He squinted harder and willed the words to be clearer. Extended arms helped in the search for the right depth of field and then finally, in frustration, he handed it to the nearest lictor. Obediently, the lictor took the document in hand and read the words. After reading the document, the lictor met Pompey squarely in the eyes and nodded. Pompey stood silent; eyes fixed somewhere else other than the Vestal chamber.

"Well, good then; there it is," Pompey declared. "We will have a formal reading in the Senate House as soon as feasible." He started for the door, pausing briefly only to return the will to Aemilia. "Good Vestal, I place this will in your hands as the gods have placed the protection of Rome in your hands." With that, Pompey marched off again.

Just outside the gates of Brundisium, Cicero, Tiro, and entourage took on the Appian Way, headed for Tusculum. The statesman and his secretary enjoyed the comforts of a carriage—more a decorated box on wheels than a formal carriage. The rest rode on horseback, accompanied by pack mules. Four Roman soldiers, garrisoned in Brundisium, escorted the convoy—a contribution as recompense for favors rendered previously by the former consul to one of the magistrates of the port city.

In a small comfortable house of stone and cement at the base of Venusia, Lucius and Caius feasted on a delicious home cooked meal. Lucius, who could devour a meal in a few mouthfuls, ate leisurely, savoring each bite of his mother's food with every taste bud he possessed. Nothing spectacular in culinary invention, the meal consisted of some cooked vegetables in a thick zesty gravy; sliced cucumbers and chickpeas soaked in olive oil and topped with thick slabs of feta cheese; the juicy leftovers of a small chicken, speckled with fresh spices and herbs; and fresh baked bread, warm and pliable. Simple and filling, but most importantly, it emanated from his mother's hands.

The young, ex-soldier kept replaying the scene from the night before in his thoughts: the gentle knock on the door as the last rays of the sun washed the upper hills of the countryside; the cautious opening of the door; and the excitement in his mother's face when she recognized her boy.

She looked older, frailer, and leaner than he remembered. Her hair, which he recalled as ebony, now dappled in gray. She couldn't wrap her arms up around his neck, but did manage to hug him tightly about the waist with her head burrowed in his chest, sobbing softly with happiness. Her eyes, when not swimming in tears, still had a beautiful, dark luster.

Caius, for his part, took in the homecoming in silence, looking to and fro, mother and son, listening to all the stories Lucius related: the army, the training, the sea crossing, friends like Sthenelus, and more. Not discussed was the battle, nor the killings. He just barely mentioned his injury and assured her that he would be fine—the Greek physician had said so and Greek physicians know what they are talking about. To her relief, he informed her that he no longer wore a legionary's uniform, but rather a scribe's tunic.

"Lucius, I'm so proud of you. And more important, you've come home to me. Better that you are a scribe than a soldier. Your father would still be proud of you, no matter what. You learned well from him, your father. He was a very smart man," said his mother, Junia.

"All that time he spent with you learning the letters and writing, it bore fruit didn't it?"

Lucius cast a smile and nodded, chewing another savory morsel.

"You haven't forgotten your *Oscan*, have you?" she asked.

Caius looked to Lucius.

"You probably noticed we slip into our native Oscan from time to time. *Mater* is more comfortable in Oscan, it's her comfort language. People do it all the time, mixing Oscan with Latin—sort of an '*Oscantin*.' We're a proud people. Venusia was one of the last holdouts to the Romans, even to its *linqua*, which they stole from the *Latiums* I'm sure."

"Yeah, I know what you mean. As a child, I remember speaking Greek and Etruscan before relying on Latin. That's the way of things, huh? When a fire scorches the land, it changes everything, except a few pockets of the original earth," Caius said, attempting to be philosophical.

Lucius' face pinched in a pained expression, but said nothing.

Again, Lucius' mother slipped into her Oscan. "Your father knew what he was doing, Lucius. It's important to be learned. Your father knew a man here in Venusia, I don't recall his nomen . . . oh, yes . . . now I remember, Horatius . . . Horatius—something . . . oh, I can't remember his full name . . . anyway, the father devoted all his time and energy in teaching his boy, Quintus. Took the boy to Rome. Someone in the village said that he even took the boy to Athens. That boy will be somebody—you'll see. When parents devote their total lives to the children, how can they not be something, huh? Now eat. Look how skinny you are, nothing but skin and bones. The chickens have more meat on them than you do. Eat."

Caius looked to Lucius for translation. Lucius closed his eyes and shook his head briefly, translation: forget about it for now.

Caius let it go.

Caius eyed the walls around him as he ate his meal. They were decorated with paintings—roughly done, but striking nonetheless. Lucius caught him admiring the artwork. The small house certainly was not a home of an aristocrat, but the walls would have been suitable in any noble's domus.

"My mother painted those. Had she the proper material and powdered color, they would be even more beautiful," he boasted.

"I can truly see where you get your talent, Lucius. Your mother is gifted as well." Then Caius glimpsed some very faint painted subjects at the lower levels of the walls, obviously not of the same quality as those above. And next to the figures were two sets of small, faded handprints in blue paint, one set smaller than the other— very, very small.

"The larger ones are mine," Lucius managed to say with a mouthful of his mother's food. "My early days."

"And the others?"

"My sister's. Mother planted them there on the wall just before . . . just before the little one took to the fever. I don't remember much of her. I do remember how sick my mother grew after my sister's death. I don't mean sick with the fever; sick with melancholy.

She cried for days," Lucius said in almost a whisper.

Caius finished his meal in silence.

For the next week, Lucius and Caius allowed themselves the luxury of leisure time in the little house at the base of the hill. They went for short walks into town to see the local sights. Lucius looked for old acquaintances but found but a few. They helped with the garden and tended to partially collapsed stone walls around the property. Life was good again.

Five suns rose, four of them set, and everything in between had been pleasant. Good food, good conversation, and good laughter filled the time, along with intimate silence shared by mother and son. And now the road beckoned.

Junia sat on her little stool in the shade next to her stone house, cleaning vegetables, humming a soft, comforting tune. A small wren alit on a tree stump directly across from her. They eyed each other and began a song in concert. The little wren warbled in its finest notes and chords. Junia followed along in the same key. The song chirped and hummed of beauty and of happiness, but sadness, as well.

Footsteps approached and the song ended. It was the son.

The wren skipped and hopped to an about-face and fluttered to a higher perch in an adjoining tree. Lucius' mother peered into her son's face and read sadness. She knew it was time for him to leave.

"Mater, it's time. The time has come for us to go."

Junia smiled a mother's smile, a loving smile. "I know, a little bird told me."

"Oh, and what else did he say?" Lucius asked, flashing a son's smile.

"*She* said you would be back."

Lucius laughed lightly at that. "And you know what? She's right. I will come back. It's not like I'm going off to battle again or anything like that. I just have to see to my responsibilities. For all I know, things may not work well being a scribe, in which case I'll be back sooner than you think."

"When do you leave, my son? Where do you go?" Junia asked with hurt in her voice.

"We'll be on the road in the morning, to Tusculum first, to meet with our employer, Consular Cicero, and then probably on to Rome," Lucius said.

"To Rome?" Junia exclaimed. "You better be careful, my son. I feel Rome is no different than a battleground itself," she said with a mother's worry.

"Now, how would you know, Mater. Have you ever been there?"

"No—but I've heard. Some of the town's people have been there. They say it's wicked and evil. I'm afraid for you, Lucius. Can't you stay here in Venusia? Find a good woman and give me a grandchild—no!—many grandchildren!"

"Don't you worry about me, Mater. I will take care of myself." Lucius tried to reassure her with a tender embrace.

A large, burnished raven swooped out of a thick canopy of a nearby tree and invaded the one where the wren had flown. It chased the smaller bird away, crowing its ugly, raspy tune the whole time. Mother and son picked up the basket of vegetables and went indoors, ignoring the intruder and its ominous forebodings.

CHAPTER XVI

Weather-wise, it was a fine day for traveling.

Cicero's wagon ambled along the old road at an unhurried pace, its occupants at the mercy of the wheels that encountered the stones and ruts of the Appian Way. The four Roman escorts led the way and the staff followed.

"It will be good to be back in Rome again, my good Tiro. Don't you agree?"

"Indeed it will be, Good Protectorate of the Republic," the secretary replied in his velvety-smooth, even-sounding, beguiling voice.

"Ah, the Republic. I can't help but feel I'm visiting an old, sick friend; a friend who has seen better days; younger and healthier days. It's been some 460 years or so since that good Lucius Junius Brutus brought forth the Republic and threw off those Etruscan kings. We owe a debt of gratitude to our fathers, to their fathers, and the fathers before them, for honoring that sacred oath and not allowing the return of kings to rule over us. It was necessary for the good of the people, the Senate, and for all Romans," declared Cicero as if addressing the Senate.

"Truly spoken as no other countrymen could claim with such truth and righteousness, Sire," Tiro assented.

"We've been through some real fights, huh, Tiro? Verres. Clodius. Catilina. And now this damnable civil war, what possibly could be next?" Cicero asked, not really expecting an answer from Tiro. "When we get to Rome, we must properly assess and evaluate the situation, Tiro. Determine how healthy the body of the

Senate is. Be prepared for fallacies in reasoning by unreasonable men. And most of all, we must be prepared to argue the good argument. We will be Greek in mind, but Roman in heart. Our weapons and shields will be logic and the sound use of rhetoric."

"You are certainly the master of rhetoric and reasoning, Dominus,"

"Thank you, Tiro; that is very kind of you."

"Oh, no, Sire; it is only the truth."

Cicero's wagon and entourage had just passed the vicinity of Aquilonia when in the distance they spied two travelers walking along the road, their backs to Cicero.

<hr />

Lucius had Caius' complete attention, giving his version of the epic battle that took place in this area many years ago between the *Samnites*—his ancestors—and the Romans, the Romans being victorious, when they heard horse hooves and the creaking approach of wagon wheels from behind. They shuffled to the side of the road to let the parade pass.

First, the four escorts passed, offering sidelong glances filled with indifference. Their horses offered blustery snorts, spastic nods, and wide eyes. Then the horse-drawn coach squeaked and bounced past. The driver tossed a condescending look, and then looked back to his horses.

From deep within the combined clamor of clopping hooves, forceful snorts, and creaking wheels an excited shout emanated. "Caius! Caius, is that you? Driver! Driver, stop the coach! Stop, I command!"

The wheels locked and skid for several yards before horses and coach lurched to a stop. The escort soldiers continued on before realizing that the wagon had come to a stop. Cicero's frantic shouts got their attention. The horsemen yanked their reins hard and kicked and kicked and kicked at the sides of their animals— more of a clumsy exercise in turning large beasts in a confined area than an orderly military maneuver. They charged at the wagon to head off the two strangers advancing toward it.

"Halt! Stay away from the coach!" the lead military horseman shouted.

Lucius and Caius were already at the coach.

"Caius, my dear fellow, what are you doing here?" Cicero bellowed as he pushed at a stuck door to get it open.

"We're on our way to Tusculum as ordered, Sire," Caius said, pulling on his side of the stuck door.

Before either could utter another sentence, the military escort was upon them at a fast gallop, forcing Caius and Lucius to falter backward and stumble.

"All is fine! All is fine! These are my people!" Cicero shouted, finally managing to free the door.

The lead horseman acknowledged Cicero in glares of annoyance. "Very well then, as you command," he managed to eke out before sauntering back up the road to wait further orders. He measured the two road refugees and decided there was no real threat.

Cicero clambered from the coach and leaped for the ground. "Oh, it feels so good to get out of that box and stretch my legs," he said, as he rubbed his butt. He then gave Caius a fatherly bear hug. "Caius, my lad, it is so good to see you," Cicero sang. "How is it that you are not at Tusculum?"

"I'm afraid that's of my doing, Consular Cicero," Lucius said as he limped forward and intervened.

"Oh?"

"Yes, Sir. I'm afraid I've slowed us down with my leg, which is mending well, but not fast enough. And we stopped along the way for a personal reason, a short visit with my mother in Venusia."

"Your mother? Well, indeed, that certainly is a good deed. Good morals, young man, never forget your parents. I pray she was happy to see you?"

"Yes, very," answered the cripple.

"Well, then, you see, it all worked as planned. Not planned by us, you see, but nonetheless, as planned," Cicero said. "Now we are all together and we can travel as one to Tusculum.

"Tiro! Tiro, see here; Caius and Lucius are with us again. We shall make room for them. They must join us for the rest of the journey," Cicero exclaimed and did a little dance to the coach.

It pained Tiro to smile and actually appear happy to see the two here on the road. "Clearly, clearly, of course," Tiro rejoined, his hands flitting about in the air as if rearranging invisible objects. "We can make room somewhere, let's see—"

"Young Lucius, you can ride up top with the driver, and Caius, we'll make room for you in the coach," said an animated Cicero. Tiro wilted his head and managed to keep a pasted smile from sliding to the ground.

"I couldn't possibly burden you, Dominus, I could ride in the back with the others," Caius said. At that, Tiro's smile became genuine.

"No—no—no, Caius; I insist. You must tell me all about your journey. Come, my young intrepid traveler, you Argonaut of the Appian Way. Tell me everything. It couldn't have been half as boring as my journey."

Cicero, Caius, and Tiro labored into the coach. The driver's strong arm pulled Lucius up to his seat. With everyone onboard and most everyone happy, Cicero's troupe started for the next stop, Benevetum, where business awaited, and then on to Tusculum.

In Rome, in the comfortable house of Lucius Marcius Philippus, young Octavius confronted his mother, Atia. "Mater, I've been thinking. I'd like to have my toga virilis ceremony moved up," he announced. "I see no need in waiting for the waning moon of Octobris."

"But, Octavius, it's been planned, people have been contacted," she bemoaned.

"It's no big thing, Mater," Octavius stated with the all-knowing, superior wisdom of an adolescent.

"Why are you suddenly of want of your toga? For weeks you opposed the whole idea of the ceremony. And now, you can't wait? You know, it's supposed to be the point in your life where you advance to adulthood. Adulthood? When one becomes an adult and accepts all the responsibilities and actions of an adult? When one reasons and thinks like an adult?" Atia said, frustration straining her voice to near hoarseness.

"I just feel I'm ready now," Octavius said, in his usual stoical manner. "I'm ready to accept manhood and move on and find my proper station in life."

Atia filled her lungs. The question as to what his "proper station in life" looked like poised itself on her tongue, ready to leap. Instead, she let loose an exasperated sigh. Narrowed eyes tore into Octavius. Her head shuddered as to clear a fog from her brain. And then she flew away with the question roiling in her mouth, unable to escape.

Octavius pivoted and retreated to regroup and meet up with his friends and confidants. As far as he was concerned, the decision had been made. Plans were needed.

In the North, at the upper reaches of Italy, Marcus Antonius created a chokehold by stringing out his legions from Patavium in the east to the port city of Telo Martius in the west. At his command, his troops would to jump into the peninsula either by sea or land or both. The citizens of Telo Martius found themselves placed in the capable hands of Marcus Aemilius Lepidus, a one-time loyal and trusted friend of Caesar's. His task: blockade the nearby Roman colony of Massilia, whose residents remained loyal to Pompey.

In addition, Marcus Antonius planned to meet with the ruling family in Alexandria, Egypt, who were feuding, brothers against sisters. He had a simple objective: divide and conquer. Divide the strongest from the weakest and establish a strong Roman influence with the goal of controlling the grain export to Rome. He, himself, would negotiate with the Ptolemies and do what was necessary. A contingent of Roman legions garrisoned there, and over time had grown accustomed to the pleasant, soft life and easy duty. Surely, they would be susceptible to whatever plans worked to their favor; they were not eager to return home to strife and battle just yet.

CHAPTER
XVII

The gods were angry.

A horrendous end-of-summer thunderstorm raged over the city of the seven hills all night long. Sunlight flashes and thunderous, rolling echoes reigned for hours at a time, accompanied by hammering rain and hail. Torrents of fallen drops surged from the high ground and charged through the streets like gangs on the loose, taking what they liked with them to the swollen Tiber.

By morning, the deities had appeased themselves. Debris-filled streams calmly cascaded downhill and poured into the city's drains in an orderly fashion. The upside to the god's angst proved to be in the cleansing of the air and alleys of human stench and other wastes that littered the streets. Many of Rome's citizens welcomed the refreshed air that followed the weather cells by opening their windows wide and inviting in the cool air.

Senators, honorable old men of Rome, made their way for Pompey's Theater this fine, early, and refreshed morning. Most arrived by litter, sneaking in a few extra minutes of sleep as the slaves carried them to the meeting place. The litter-bearers carried their precious cargo with extreme care as they maneuvered through miniature lakes, mud, and slippery debris.

The senators had agreed to meet in the *curia* at the opposite end of the theater, near the gardens. The meeting place seemed appropriate, for Pompey had the temple of his favored deity, Venus Victrix, built there some seven years prior; it was by no coincidence that the temple dedicated to "Victory" would be near, towering over everyone, making a statement following Pompey's defeat over Caesar's legions.

Not all senators would be present. Many hadn't made it back to Rome since the battle at Pharsalus. An uncertain political environment and the absence of major players were cause enough for many to be cautiously late in their return to Rome; yet, a few returned early after the battle at Dyrrhachium to leverage themselves for elective offices, extremely confident in Pompey's military and political might.

One by one, occasionally in pairs, the old men ascended the steps and entered the meeting place, acknowledging one another with semi-warm embraces, or just a friendly nod. Pompey arrived on foot as usual with his normal complement of lictors and clientela.

The last litter to arrive remained parked at the bottom of the steps, curtains drawn shut; the bearers stood their places—more sentinels than bearers. The dignitary remained sequestered within.

Pompey marched into the curia and immediately locked eyes on Lucius Marcius Philippus, who immediately turned aside and averted his, as if spying an old, lost friend.

"*Salve te*—Greetings, Lucius, and congratulations," Pompey offered as he walked over to the senator and made himself obvious.

"Greetings and congratulations to you, also, Gnaeus Pompeius. We have reason to offer you congratulations, your victory at Dyrrhachium, of course; but . . . my accomplishment?" Philippus asked with furrowed brows.

"I speak to your household, young Gaius Octavius, heir apparent to our deceased Gaius Julius Caesar."

Several breaths of silence followed, breaths needed for some quick thinking on Lucius Philippus' part. "Surely, I'm not really certain of what we speak, General." Excessive swallowing betrayed Philippus; news traveled with the speed of its importance. It wasn't official yet, but many knew.

"Oh, well then, I shall save my congratulations for the appropriate time," Pompey said smoothly, head cocked and jaw forward. He pivoted sharply and left the red-faced Philippus standing alone. Philippus wondered if he should have confirmed what most people might have suspected or already knew.

When it was obvious that all who were going to attend were present, Pompey took to the center of the floor and started the proceedings.

"Senators—Senators, if you please," Gnaeus Pompeius Magnus announced. The loud drone of voices ebbed to low indistinct murmurs, and then finally to quiet whispers.

"Thank you. Thank you for coming. I realize this meeting is highly unusual and we do not really have a quorum, but these highly unusual times call for the unusual. The state of the Republic must be addressed, and addressed quickly, if we are to remain a Republic.

"For those who need the formality of points of order and require a *Princeps Senatus*—House Leader—I would like to nominate our dear friend, most trusted, and most honorable of honest men, with impeccable credentials and amicable to all fellow senators—Senator Lucius Marcius Philippus."

A low rumbling of voices erupted and then faded to a soft hum.

Philippus came forward with raised hands and a sheepish smile. "Fellow Senators . . . please. I am most humbled and honored, I'm sure, but there must be someone more qualified," he begged.

Pompey hesitated but for the briefest second, adding, "Well then . . . if there are no objections . . . I will continue the meeting with a brief agenda I feel warrants our most immediate attention."

Lucius Cornelius Lentulus Crus rose and spoke first. "I think I can speak for all of us, General. We have no objections." He faced all directions, looking hard into the eyes of those peering his way.

They all avoided his glare.

"I concur, General. Please continue," said another statesman, Senator Gaius Cassius Longinus, commander of one Pompey's fleets in Greece during the recent conflict, and very anti-Caesar. He, too, searched the sea of faces, looking for opposition. Finding none, he and Pompey exchanged a fleeting glance and confident smiles.

"Thank you. For those of you who were with me at Dyrrhachium, I give you my most sincere thanks and gratitude. The gods of fortune and victory were with us that day, and with reason—the Republic and the constitution. If I may speak for some of our colleagues and defenders who were at the battle, Senators Quintus Caecilius Metellus Pius Scipio, Marcus Porcius Cato, both of who are presently in Africa; Marcus Tullius Cicero; and countless others. I assure you, they would agree with what we do this day."

"And what of Pharsalus . . . and Antoni?" The lone voice belonged to Servius Sulpicius Rufus, a member of Caesar's party. All eyes fell hard on him. No one wished him any ill will, he just happened to be in the wrong camp.

"As of Pharsalus, our good General Titus Labienus is not here to give us the details. We can only speculate," Pompey said. "I understand he is presently at the Greek island of *Kerkyra*, but will be making his way for Africa."

"And of Antonius?" a familiar voice drifted over the heads of the assembled. All eyes turned to see Cato entering the chamber. A hundred questions filled the air at once.

"Marcus Porcius, this certainly is a surprise. A most welcomed and pleasant surprise, I assure you," Pompey said, not with the greatest degree of enthusiasm. "We thought you were in Africa."

"And I assure you I was on my way but stopped to conduct some personal business." The noise level settled and everyone wanted to get back to the question at hand—Antoni to some,

Marcus Antonius to most.

Pompey gave Cato a brief cutting look, and then continued. "We do know for sure that he has his legions, eighteen to be the count, maybe more, spread across the north from Patavium to Telo Martius."

"Ah . . . Telo Martius. He wants to secure the purple for himself it seems!" Longinus had the floor again, referring to the purple dye made from snails harvested at that particular port. A senator standing nearby looked to Longinus in a baffled glare. Longinus returned the glare and flicked a nod to the purple border on their senatorial toga. The puzzled senator thought a second and then mouthed "ahhhh" as he nodded in little yeses.

"Our supporters under siege in Massilia are holding strong," Pompey said.

"If he secures Egypt and the grain shipments and controls all of the northern territories as well as the ports, then—"

"—Then it seems we have Antoni right where he wants us," Cato interjected, cutting off Longinus.

This initiated another round of loud murmurs in the curia.

"Senators, please," Pompey urged. The curia settled down to a vibrating hum and gave Pompey their attention again. "I, too, might venture to Alexandria. Ptolemy owes me . . . rather, the good people of Rome, much in the way of his sovereignty, and his heirs are in my guardianship. The Roman garrison there will do as I say."

"Ah . . . you will stomp your boot then," Cato uttered, just perceptible to those around him, triggering another round of subtle laughter.

"The fleet is still intact and will protect our shores. As for my legions, I have sent them north to the garrison at Mutina."

Cassius Longinus stood to be heard. "Good friends and noblemen, as the good general stated, these are unusual times, and I agree, the unusual is called for. A handful of years past, during the time of Publius Clodius and the burning of the Senate House, we asked—no—we implored, the good general to restore order, in which he did, most posthaste. In our gratitude, we, the Senate, the whole Senate," Cassius cast a conspicuous, sidelong glare to Cato, "rewarded him with the honor of Sole Consul, when in fact we considered the office of—dictator. I hereby entreat you, good honorable and wise men, to pass a *Senatus Consultum*—the Ultimate Decree of the Senate—to offer the Office of Executive Magistrate—Dictator—to Gnaeus Pompeius Magnus!"

The curia came alive with old men jumping to their feet, some shouting in favor, others expressing concern. Cato had been here before, and as before, said nothing; but his mind burned in thought: where were men like Cicero when we needed them?

Pompey stood silent, as silent and daunting as his statute to "Victory." His proud face fought to suppress a creeping grin. He had not seriously considered this possibility. In the earlier event— the election to Sole Consul—he was content with the office of consul bestowed upon him. The gods continued to heap fortune his way and this time he would not be so complacent. He would take what came his way and maybe a little more. Fortune would rule this day; not wisdom.

Pompey raised an arm and a booming voice, the way he usually brought a military formation to order. "Senators—senators— please! Most honorable of men of the Senate!"

The cacophonous and volatile old men, some grasping and tugging at togas of fellow countrymen in their zeal to make themselves heard, finally succumbed to order and became civil again.

"I am most honored. And if you pass this final decree and appoint me your protector, your dictator, I assure you—though I do not own a farm to retire to as our most honorable ancestor, Lucius

Quinctius Cincinnatus—I, Gnaeus Pompeius, will retire the office once the clear and present threat to the Republic is resolved."

Pompey evoked the good name of the Roman hero, Cincinnatus, as opposed to the tyrant, Sulla. Better to associate with a hero than to be guilty by association. From a distance, Pompey caught Cato's eyes set in a stern, stoic face and fancied that Cato had thought the same. He was right; Cato's mind had been there and back already.

Every school boy knew the story of good Cincinnatus, the Roman Senator, gone into retirement some four hundred years ago to a life of farming. A Roman army had found itself in trouble and under siege by a nearby tribe. The Senate pleaded for Cincinnatus' help and so appointed him dictator. The noble hero saved the army, retired the dictatorship, and then returned to his farm—simple as that.

Silence staved off further debate. Longinus asked for a show of bodies in favor of the final decree. It was unanimous—Pompey would be dictator.

"Before we take our leave, there is one more matter, one last item on the agenda," he announced to the crowd of honorable men. All bodies and eyes turned to Pompey. "Gaius Julius Caesar has an heir."

The announcement met subtle murmuring; no real surprise; some already had heard or suspected as much. The news only confirmed the rumors being spread in small social circles and dinner parties.

"As a matter of formality, I invite our Chief Vestal, Aemilia the Younger, to join us." Pompey turned to one of his lictors and gave an order with just a look. The lictor ran to the litter parked at the bottom of the steps, retrieved its waiting passenger, and then escorted her into the curia.

"A woman in the curia, now that is highly unusual," said one of the gawking senators.

"It's not without precedence," Cato chided. "Did we not often have the 'Queen of Bithnyia' in our chambers?" The remark was a slur in reference to Caesar's rumored affair with the King of Bithnyia.

The Vestal cradled a document in her arms. She approached the center of the curia and the newly elected dictator.

"Good Senators, I beg you give your most serious attention to our cherished Vestal, Aemilia, and the words she has to pass on to your ears," Pompey said. He gave Aemilia a nod.

With delicate fingers working in no hurry, Aemilia unfurled the *volumen*—rolled parchment. She peered over the top of the document and caught a sea of eyes locked on her. She forced a petite swallow and gave several attempts to clear her parched throat. And then she began—"I, Gaius Julius Caesar——"

Her soft, angelic voice echoed in the chamber of the curia, a voice so serene and kind, so out of place in a room filled with old testosterone, avarice, covetousness, and phobias born of the optimates; a bird trapped in a lion's den.

When finished, her small hands rolled the scroll tight and she hugged it close to her chest.

"Well . . . there it is," Pompey said.

"Is the young Gaius Octavius aware of his inheritance?" Servius asked.

Pompey let his eyes casually drift in the direction of Philippus. "I don't know for sure. Do you, Lucius Marcius?"

The question struck Philippus like an unseen arrow. "Of course not . . . I mean . . . I don't think so. He had some question as to whether he would be mentioned in a will, but—"

"Well then, I shall make it my mission to inform him and his mother . . . unless . . . you would rather do it yourself, Lucius Marcius," Pompey suggested. "Or, we could do it together."

"Yes . . . together. That would be very good . . . yes, that would be an excellent idea," replied Octavius' stepfather, Philippus.

"Forgive me, good men of Rome, one more item before we disperse. As our calendar is in such disarray following the disturbances to our good Republic and we are again in disorder with the seasons, I propose that we mend the present calendar with the appropriate number of intercalated days to bring us back in order. In addition, as our young Octavius' great-uncle, Julius, died on or near his birthday, I propose we rename the month of *Quintilus* to—*Julius*," Pompey declared.

Until that moment, the attentive assembly had been as impassive as marble columns dressed in white togas. They quickly transitioned to a mob of fractious old men. Not one, however, objected directly to the newly elected dictator.

"The next proposal will be to declare him a god!" remarked one of the senators as an aside. Laughter leaped from the old men. Cato's stoic face didn't think it so funny.

"Good then, the collegium of augurs will be contacted and the process for sanctioning the change will begin," Pompey affirmed.

The old men drifted from the curia in small groups, discussing the day's agenda. There would be plotting. There would be planning. There would be a need to leverage themselves in a most favorable and opportunistic position, for themselves and their fortunes; for now, what worry of a boy inheriting his uncle's property when a greater threat still existed—Antoni.

CHAPTER
XVIII

Mauve-tinted shadows of evening marched eastward right behind Cicero and his people. The shadows subdued everything in their paths—trees, villas, small homes, hillsides, travelers, everything—washing away any glint of gold left from the setting sun. The shadows called for farm animals to start for home, and for the nocturnal predators to prepare for a night's work.

A rider raced the shadows to alert the villa of the master's arrival. After receiving the message, a welcome party rushed about and prepared the villa, and themselves. They waited outside in excited little twitches and bounces as a suggestion of coach and riders neared the villa.

Dark silhouettes of horses, coach, and lead escorts appeared in a haze, crossing to the right. A row of tall Cyprus trees and a thick hedge grove swallowed them up. They appeared again, as if by magic, this time racing left. They made another turn and headed for the entrance into the villa, accompanied by a fresh cloud of new dust, a gaggle of excited children, and a pack of barking dogs.

The coach staggered to a stop in front of the waiting staff, and the children and dogs were chased off by one of the grounds men. One of the more senior slaves, Felix, rushed to the coach and opened the door to receive the master.

"Master Cicero, good Patron, Honored Father of Our Country, welcome home, Dominus. Please, let me assist you," the slaved begged.

"Ah, my good and fortunate Felix! How good it is to see you again," Cicero said as he nearly tumbled from the coach. Felix caught him in a warm embrace and then brushed off some of the heavy layer of road that covered the master. Pulvilla, Felix's plump little wife, waddled over with a large goblet of cool water for the master's thirst and a handful of fresh flowers.

"Pulvilla, dear sweet Pulvilla, thank you, my little cushion," Cicero said as he took the goblet in hand and emptied it, spilling not a drop. Pulvilla grinned from ear to ear, her plump round cheeks hiding her sparkly, little eyes. The remainder of the staff rushed forward and wished him well and showered him with praises and adulation. Cicero loved it; next to life and his daughter Tullia, he loved nothing more than attention and praise.

During the informal veneration for Cicero, Caius and Tiro eased their way out of the coach and Lucius quietly descended from atop, unnoticed.

On tired horses, the mounted soldiers approached Cicero. "By your leave, Consular, our mission is complete and we must depart," the lead horseman said.

"Yes, if you must. You are welcome to rest and water your horses," Cicero replied.

"Thank you, we will water the horses, but we must leave before the night hours grow much older," the soldier said.

Cicero returned to his adulating clientela. "Come, come, my children, let us retreat to the comfort of the domus."

Lucius and Caius gathered their gear and fell in behind the rest as they headed for the house.

Before he reached the house, Cicero faltered to a stop. In his wake, the adoring crowd collided and stumbled to a clumsy heap.

Tullia, frail and wan of color, stood at the doorway. She wore a heart-melting smile that collapsed her father on the spot. An unrestrained sob burst from his chest and his eyes flooded with tears, making it even more difficult—if not impossible—

to see his precious daughter.

"Oh—my child, my Tulliola, my Tulliola," Cicero cried as he flung himself to her, partially crumbling to his knees. Tullia reached out and received him as she would a child in want of safety. Cicero embraced her back, taking care not to hurt her delicate, petite, and suffering body. He felt her fragile rib cage in his embrace and eased his grip—this only intensified the deluge of surging emotions. Cicero, *Pater Patriae*—Father of the Country; *pater familias*—father of the family; *pater Tullia*—father of Tullia, was finally brought to his knees, weakened by love and sorrow. Love for his only daughter. Sorrow for himself and for the loss of a grandchild, the little boy that he could only dream of. He sobbed in silence, rocking gently from side to side. He wanted to speak further, but could not. His emotions would not allow it. They owned this tender moment.

Aware that all eyes were on him, feeling with him, sharing with him such a personal moment, he collected himself, brick by emotional brick. A quick sleeve wiped tears from his eyes and nose. He stood spine straight and flashed a smile to all those around. Not a dry eye revealed itself in the crowd, except for Lucius.'

"Well then . . . let us all continue on into the house, shall we?" Cicero commanded. The small gathering followed the master and his child into the domus for food and drink. Lucius and Caius followed, being the last to enter.

Unnoticed, up in a tree, near the entrance to the house, a small owl took in the emotional events down below. With her large, blinking eyes she scanned the area, rotating her head in all 135 degrees nature had allowed, evaluating her situation and looking for prey. A hint of daylight lingered in the evening sky, and so she would have been regarded a bad omen if her presence had been detected. At this time of day, the superstitious Romans considered her a funerary bird, not the symbol of wisdom and the arts; luckily, no one heard her mournful calls announcing doom for some unlucky soul. Fortunate still, the young bird did not care for this particular hunting ground—not just yet anyway—and flew to another, where she would continue her cries.

She would be back though.

———

Trophies and memorabilia looked over his shoulders as Pompey busied himself with old documents. They were from a time when he was in charge of the grain distribution for Rome. The dim flickering oil lamp on his desk challenged his reading. Words would not make themselves clear, no matter how much he squinted. He pinched the upper bridge of his nose and massaged his eyelids with small circles of thumb and forefinger; it didn't help.

If Antonius gains control of the grain in Egypt, life could get difficult in the city. This must not be allowed, he told himself.

Cornelia materialized from the darkness like a heavenly being, oil lamp in hand. She found Pompey consumed in deep thought; he didn't hear her soft feet. "Husband, you should come to bed now, let your eyes rest, as well as the rest of your senses. You look tired, and besides, you said you have a busy day tomorrow—a meeting at the Philippus Domus?"

Pompey looked to his wife. "Yes, you are right as always," he said, putting aside the documents and scooting away from the desk.

She offered a slender, delicate hand. He smiled and extended a large, manly one. Their fingers reached out and touched, and when they did, a hard rope of a long scar across the top of Pompey's right hand stole the moment.

"At least I have my hand—the other man does not," he boasted.

"Does it pain you, my husband?" Cornelia asked, rubbing the scar with her fingers.

"No, not tonight. Only when it gets cold and damp," he said. "Besides, your touch is the best medicine for my old wounds."

"Come then, let me massage all your wounds, dear husband,"

she said playfully.

"You know, I've actually been struck by javelins—twice, in the chest, and each time the gods felt compelled to protect me," Pompey commented, his trailing voice repelling off the walls as the couple paraded down the darkened hallway for the bedroom. The gilded light from the oil lamps and the man and woman's silhouettes followed.

Surrounded by comforting walls and pleasant aromas of home, the master, his freedman Tiro, and his tired guests commenced shedding layers of weariness of travel. The villa staff darted about, attending to the immediate needs of the spent travelers. The rooms grew dark and all needed oil lamps.

Cicero and his daughter clung to each other; they'd been apart far too long.

"Lucius, my dear fellow, this is my lovely daughter Tullia. Is she not a prize?" the excited and proud father asked. If Tulia had more blood circulating in her, she would have blushed a little more. Despite being wan of color, her delicate skin had a hint of natural beauty. The old man had reason to be proud of his daughter.

Tullia cast a soft and beguiling smile to Lucius. Her dark eyes captured Lucius with a stare that lingered a little longer than it normally would have—or should have. There was interest there; a forbidden interest. Lucius noticed it well but took the initiative to avert his gaze, casting it away to the floor, especially with her father standing there before him.

"It's an honor to meet you, Lady Tullia, and I wish you well," the cripple said when again he locked eyes on her.

Tullia returned his greeting with another entrancing, dimpled smile and coquettish eyes that suddenly found something to smile about; it had been a long time. She and her father moved on to greet Tiro, but not before she turned to sneak one more glance at and offer yet more feline eyes to Lucius. He returned the smile with another of his own. The dance of smiles ended when Caius came to Lucius' aid.

"So, I see you met Tullia. Pretty, isn't she? Too bad she's married to such a man as that Dolabella. He doesn't deserve such a treasure. He's a two-headed snake and both will bite if you're not careful. He'd sell his soul to the highest bidder, if he had one," Caius said, taking care that no one heard his words. "Yes, over to the 'Street of the Etruscans,' he could sell himself there, easily," he whispered.

"Sounds like you don't like him, Caius."

"We deeply respect the master, and we all know how much he loves his daughter, so it grieves us all to see, or hear, of his womanizing and other misdeeds. If Caesar were alive, you'd see Publius Cornelius Dolabella slithering over to his camp, licking Caesar's boots. He has no principles, no shame, no morals," retorted young Caius.

Caesar—there he is again, in the shadows of Lucius' brain. He could not shake an uneasy feeling whenever that man's name contaminated the air. His ghost always lingered about, uninvited.

"Something pains you. Are you ill?" a concerned Caius asked.

Lucius offered a small lie. "No, it's just my ankle again. It's beginning to hurt a little." In the next breath, Lucius' mind left the present and he could see the javelin thrust into the air, leaving his extended fingertips, the tail end wobbling as it began its flight upward into the dust-filled sky—and then the blackout. He gave his head a slight shake to clear his thoughts.

One of the house slaves converged on Lucius and Caius and offered his services. He showed them to their rooms and prepared them for the night. They went willingly, tired and in need of sleep and rest.

CHAPTER
XIX

Gaius Octavius sat impassive by a window, his blank eyes absorbed in lazy clouds parading past and his mind wandered somewhere within those meandering clouds.

His right hand toyed with the amulet around his neck. The little *bulla* was cast from silver, not of wood or cotton like the lesser families; his family could afford silver or gold. His index and middle fingers rubbed mechanically against the face on the amulet while his thumb held it in place. It was a small coin with the face of Alexander the Great on the obverse side. Grandma Julia placed it around his neck just after his birth, and there it stayed. Most childhood amulets were meant to ward off evil spirits; Grandma Julia said that this one anointed him with greatness, like Alexander himself.

Soon, he would give it up and put it away. That's when he would officially take his place among men. Some boys his age had given up their amulets nearly two years ago. Not Gaius Octavius; his mother wanted to keep him a boy a little longer.

Grandmother Julia, sister to Julius Caesar, would have pushed for his toga virilis, his transition to manhood ceremony, sooner if she had not died four years earlier. Gaius missed his grandmother. He missed her love. He spoke at her funeral, offering as fine a eulogy as any adult could possibly have uttered in eloquence and praise, causing many a tear to flow. His Uncle Julius took note. The hurt in the boy's chest resonated in his words as he spoke of his beloved grandmother and the void created with her now gone. Life changed when he and his sister, Octavia, had to move in with their mother, Atia—and stepfather Philippus.

Just an hour before, he had been re-reading one of his favorite Greek manuscripts but yielded to daydreaming and amusing ideas. The passing clouds made him think of the future—his future. The tufts of white and gray reminded him of a gigantic puzzle and he tried to imagine how all the pieces would fall in place—or be made to fit; a tight knot needing to be unraveled. And then he thought of the Gordian Knot. If necessary, he would use the Alexandrian Solution—a sword—to solve the puzzle, or undo the knot. Yes, a sword, meaning an army—Caesar's army. They would follow him if he could prove to be like his uncle. A good army, that's what he needed. Loyal soldiers like Alexander's.

"I'm young. If I start now, I could be like Alexander and take it all; but I will not die young. I've much to do before I die," he whispered to the clouds.

Something broke his musing: the sound of rushed sandals scampering about in urgency. The nomenclator's irritating voice echoed along the walls; company, a guest in the house.

Pompey, accompanied by Philippus, briskly marched in, taking command of the very air in the room. Atia trailed behind at a quick pace. Octavius knew why they were here. *Should I feign surprise?* He contemplated. *No. I will offer them nothing.*

He decided it would be best to stand and offer some display of respect; he would demand it of others someday.

"Good day to you, Gaius Octavius," Pompey said.

"And to you, Good Sir."

"Your father and I have come to discuss a matter of some great importance to you that has recently made itself known," Gnaeus Pompeius started.

Octavius looked to his stepfather and screamed in his head to all in the room: "he is not my father!" His face hid the shout behind a boyish grin.

"Your great-uncle, Gaius Julius Caesar, has left—"

"A will . . . I know." The words dropped from his mouth unhindered and unintended. He couldn't help himself. A flash of excitement blazed across his face; faster than either of the two men could catch in combined blinks.

Silence engulfed the room.

Philippus and Atia looked at each other, puzzled. Pompey cast a hard look at the boy; he would not be surprised. His intuition about this young man may be right-on. Pompey's patron, Lucius Cornelius Sulla, was intuitive about another young man many years before. That young man was a young Gaius Julius Caesar, someone to keep an eye on. And now time and events are repeating themselves. This young boy needed watching, too.

Pompey approached the boy.

Octavius did not flinch, not a muscle, and stood his ground. He would not be intimidated by this hulk of a man.

"Do you know the contents of this will?" Pompey asked of the young boy before him.

"No."—His first lie.

Pompey circled Octavius, measuring him from top to bottom. Was this a future threat and adversary, or somebody who could be controlled and managed? His immediate instinct: caution and forbearance.

"It seems, *boy*, that you have inherited some money, position, and loyalties," Pompey said. The word *boy* burned like a sting from a wasp to the neck.

"I shall not be a *boy* for much longer," Octavius replied, his face burning with contemptuous pride. The right corner of his thin, flat grin twitched uncontrollably in small ripples.

Pompey glared full force.

Atia rushed to her son's side, grasping his shoulders in a protective embrace. "Octavius, the general has come to bring news of the will and to wish you well, I'm sure," his mother said, her edginess obvious to all.

"Yes, I've come to congratulate you, Gaius—Julius—Caesar—Octavianus," Pompey proclaimed, slowly and deliberately spewing each *praenomen*, nomen, *cognomen*, and *filiation* as one might toss logs onto a funeral pyre—one by one.

Philippus stepped forward. "General, I'm sure Gaius is extremely honored that he should be mentioned in his uncle's will, but I don't think he makes anything serious of this. As you say, he's just a boy. He's much to learn. Wouldn't you agree, Octavius?"

Octavius offered his next lie—"Yes."

Man and boy remained locked in hard stares. The adolescent wolf would not cower and lie down submissively on his back with throat bared to the much older adult, alpha male.

"Yes, perhaps," the general said—for now anyway. Pompey disengaged from the stare. "I shall have the will brought forth and the details made available." With that, Pompey pivoted sharply and marched away. He stopped, turned, and addressed the other two adults. "Lucius Marcius, Atia, I wish you well and a good day to you," he said. He shot an oblique gaze to the boy, but said nothing more. Atia accompanied the general to the door, wishing him well and offering blessings on to his lovely wife Cornelia.

With Pompey gone, Atia darted back to Octavius and Philippus. "Octavius, dear, wasn't it nice of your uncle to include you in his will? Surely, you wouldn't make much more of it than the good fortune of some money and advantage to further your education," Atia said, stroking at his hair.

"There's more there than just money and advantage," Octavius said above a whisper, again staring out to his future, playing with his amulet.

"Octavius, your mother is right. I agree, there should be nothing more to make of this than what is necessary," Philippus added.

Octavius aimed glowering eyes at both adults standing before him. "It's time for the toga virilis, time for me to begin to do the things I must."

"Octavius," Atia said, her voice strung tight, "let's discuss this later, when—"

"Mother, I've made up my mind. It's time," the boy cut her short.

"Well, then," Philippus said, "you'll need a sponsor, a mentor. I would be willing, if you wish—"

"NO!" The boy shot back. "I mean . . . no thank you. I want someone well versed in the art of rhetoric, oratory, and law, someone like . . . like Consular Cicero."

Philippus' eyes and mouth went wide, then narrowed, and finally transitioned to resolved acceptance. Cicero wasn't really a bad choice. The old consular and Pompey were amicable. He certainly was not pro-Caesar. He did know the law well. And certainly, he could speak to almost any topic with sound reasoning and logic. Yes, Philippus thought, Cicero would be a good choice. He would take well to the boy, too. Cicero enjoyed the company of young men yearning to learn and hear his philosophies; anything that stroked his ego.

"An interesting choice, Gaius, but a good one," his stepfather said. "I'll arrange it immediately." Philippus regarded the boy for a moment further. "Gaius, I do wish . . . I so would like for us—"

Just as if on cue, Gaius Maecenas and Marcus Vipsanius Agrippa, Octavius' friends, cohorts, and brethren made themselves present. Octavius turned his back to his stepfather, gathered his companions and left. Out the door they disappeared, to their den, their wilderness.

CHAPTER
XX

Lucius was there to greet daylight when it unfolded across the villa. It was a perfect morning. He stood there, just outside the villa walls, allowing his senses to take in and capture all the beauty that surrounded him. He took special note of all the colors that nature had to offer at this early hour of the new day. Voices from the past—his and his mother's—whispered in his head: "Look, Lucius, do you see the trees?" she had asked.

"Yes."

"What color are the trees?"

"Green."

"Look again, son."

Like those of a falcon searching for prey, his eyes had searched the foliage. He focused hard on the trees and wondered what it was that had eluded him.

"You're looking too hard, son, relax and look at ALL the colors," she had continued to press.

The landscape before him had morphed into a whole different world, a world of perfect colors on a living canvas. He hadn't noticed the pleased smile that eased across his mother's face when the enlightenment flashed across his face.

"Yes, I see the colors now," he had exclaimed excitedly.

"Tell me, Lucius. Share with me. What do you see?" his mother asked with equal excitement.

"There are many greens! The tree is deep with dark leaves and shadows, not yet receiving the sun, very dark green, the darkest of greens. The outer leaves, in the sunlight, are bright and shiny. They're the lightest of greens, almost sparkling, like new coins. Then there are all the others in between. Hmmm . . . some of the leaves aren't even green at all. Some are brown and yellow. The colors of the branches are different, too."

Everything had changed around him after that magic moment. The little house he had lived in took on a palette-full of different browns, mixed with grays, greens, blues, and reds. In the fall, the trees would appear to be in flames, burning in luminous crimson. Others were surely made of gold. All the amazing reds, oranges, and yellows would dazzle him. He had lived in a much more complex world than he had realized. It had always been there, he just had not seen it.

Crunching footsteps broke up the musing and memories of the past. Soldier-like reflexes kicked in and muscles became tense and ready.

"Good morning, young Lucius," said the patron of the villa, Marcus Tullius Cicero. "And how are you this fine, beautiful morning?"

"Fine, Good Patron." His body relaxed and the tension melted.

The old consular closed his eyes. His chickpea-nose flared and pulled in the morning by aromas, letting them out reluctantly. "It is such a delight to do nothing but breathe, to take in nature at its best, through our senses. It's good to see a young person such as yourself greeting the new day and our goddess of dawn Aurora. Who knows what's on her agenda for us today, huh?" Cicero said. The old man's left hand grabbed his right wrist, he tucked his arms to his sides, and then buried his neck into his shoulders to stave off a quick shudder against the early morning air.

"One never really knows, I guess," Lucius answered.

Cicero surveyed the villa and countryside as if it was his first time seeing it. "So much beauty to behold, yet ignored by youth. We old people know how to appreciate it. We grow old with the days and our eyes grow older yet with the seasons. The beauty of it all escapes us. Even now, at night, when I see that great orb, the moon, looking down upon me, I see it mostly in my memory. For now it's becoming just a big, fuzzy ball of light. No longer can I see the craters and the seas as before," Cicero lamented.

"So, Caius has told me much about you on our trip to our dear villa," Cicero said.

Lucius glanced at the elderly man in a discomfited silence.

"Oh, nothing bad, young Lucius. He told me about the sea journey and how the good Fortuna snatched you from the grips of Neptune. Now that is good fortune, is it not? That will be a story to tell your grandchildren. Do you have children, Lucius?" asked Cicero.

"No, good Patron, I have no family of my own, yet."

"Ah . . . well, when you do, that will be a most memorable story to tell. That young Caius thinks highly of you, Lucius. I sense he has become quite attached to you. It's good to have loyal friends like him. Friends you can count on, in good and in not so good times. He's a good boy, rich in morals. That's what makes a good man, you know. A good man rich in morals is a happy man. A man rich with gold and wealth is not as happy or content. He may think he is, but he's not. He is always with worry. He's consumed with anxiety and concern, concern that somebody will want his riches. Thus, he has no real friends for he trusts no one. Yes, the man rich with high morals knows he is indeed the happiest of men. His morals can't be stolen from him. Of course, he could sell them, but then he becomes the unhappiest of men, knowing he sold his high ideals and principles.

"For the man who never had principles to begin with . . . well, he would suffer no consequences at all after selling himself— except for the law maybe. Even then, with enough wealth, he could buy other men willing to help the cause of unprincipled, avaricious, and dishonest men," Cicero said, his eyes fixed in thought.

"That rings true. My father would have agreed with you," Lucius said.

"There you are. Another fine and happy man," Cicero replied. "Caius told me of the stay at your home in Venusia. Your mother impressed him much. Your father is . . . is not with us, is that right?" he asked.

Lucius nodded and offered a half-smile with down-turned eyes.

"He was a soldier?" Cicero inquired.

"Yes, retired from Sulla's time."

"Ah, yes, a dangerous time. I hope we never see the likes of that again, huh?" Cicero added, as he chewed on a stalk of grass. "You were a soldier like your father?" Cicero asked.

"No, I could never be like my father. But I was a legionary, for a while anyway; for a very short while."

"And skilled with the sword, huh?" Cicero probed.

"More skilled with the javelin. My father taught me," Lucius answered, flushed with pride.

"Ah, *Pilatus*—skilled with the javelin. Well, then, we'll just have to call you . . . Lucius Pontius Pilatus . . . Lucius, skilled javelin thrower," proclaimed Cicero with a smile.

The hair at the back of Lucius' neck stiffened as if he felt a presence—a ghost. Cicero's keen senses noted the sudden change in Lucius' demeanor.

"What is it, Lucius? Did I offend you?"

"No, Sir. It's just, well . . . I can't explain it," Lucius started. "Throwing my javelin was my last memory of the battle at

Dyrrhachium . . . and knowing that's how . . . oh, it's nothing; truly, it's nothing," Lucius dismissed the subject at hand.

Cicero looked hard at Lucius. Something had disturbed the pleasant conversation, a sudden noticeable change. And then Cicero himself experienced a haunting thought: he recalled an image, an image of Caesar with a javelin impaling him at the neck, lying across Pompey's horse, like prized game on a return from a successful hunt.

Now Cicero's hair tingled at his neck.

The three stood there in silence—Lucius, Cicero, and the ghost of Caesar.

Cicero placed a hand on Lucius' shoulder. "Come, let's see if Pulvilla can find us something warm to drink. I suddenly feel chilled, even though it's pleasant out. Maybe even some nice cabbage, huh? You know, cabbage is good for you. It's medicinal." Lucius welcomed the thought of at least something warm to drink; the cabbage he wasn't too sure of. The two headed for the main domus, exchanging more small talk.

Later that afternoon—

"Here, try some of this cheese. It's excellent; especially made by some of our people here at the villa, goes well with the bread and those little olives over there next to the sliced ham. Go on— taste it taste it taste it!" Cicero commanded.

Lucius reached for and took a bite. His eyes fixed upwards, looking for the taste.

"What does it taste like?"

"Like cheese," Lucius answered.

"No no no no no—taste it again. And then follow it with a little of that wine."

The cripple took another nibble and let it set longer in his mouth, this time letting his tongue play with the morsel. He stirred in a little wine to mix with the remnants of the cheese before washing down his throat.

"Yes, now I taste it. It tastes like—countryside and sun."

"Yes! Yes! Yes! Very good! Splendid, my good fellow, splendid! We'll make you a Tusculian yet," Cicero said.

The day remained pleasant; so much so that Cicero had decided that the afternoon meal would best be enjoyed outdoors in the courtyard. Tullia and her mother, Terentia, were seated at the table as well as Felix and Pulvilla. Three house slaves hovered over the table and food to keep hungry insects away.

"Hmmm. This is good. There's a little tartness to it that . . . that tickles the tongue," Lucius said, his mouth full of the delicious cheese. He followed the cheese with a slice of ham and wedge of apple to tone down the tartness and smooth it out with a little bit of sweetness. Crusted bread soaked in rich, spice-treated olive oil followed. And then a goblet of blood-red wine washed it all down. Life was good.

A large shadow passed overhead, pleasantly chilling the air as the party savored and praised the food. Cicero looked up and made a comment that good Ceres had peeked in on them to make sure that the mortals were delighted with her fruits. Irregular-shaped clouds with gray underbellies continued to glide over the villa but dared not disturb this perfect afternoon.

A slave hurried over to the party of festive celebrants in the courtyard being entertained by the good master.

Cicero stood at the end of the table and placed a hand over his heart. "In honor of one our guests, Lucius—Pontius—Pilatus," Cicero started, "I'd like to recite a little poem I wrote as a young boy—*Pontius Glaucus*. You'll enjoy it, Lucius; it's about a young man who throws himself into the sea." At that, the contented party laughed. Lucius and Caius exchanged glances. Caius smiled and shrugged and feigned innocence.

"Excuse my intrusion, Dominus," the slave interrupted, "but there is a courier with a most urgent message."

"Well, then, we'll just have to put off our little poem for a minute or two," said Cicero, slightly disappointed in not being the center of attention again. He strolled over to where the courier waited.

"Please excuse my intrusion, Consular, but a message from Lucius Marcius Philippus," the courier announced and handed a scroll to Cicero.

Cicero took the scroll, broke the seal, and attempted to read its contents. The print was too small and the ink too light for the elderly statesman to read clearly. He could make out parts of the message, but not all of it.

"Thank you, I'll take this to my tablinum," Cicero said. With that, the messenger saluted and left the grounds.

"Tiro! Tiro!" The patron went to his reception room and called for his secretary. "Where is that man," he muttered. Tiro could not be found in the domus, so Cicero ventured back out to the courtyard. "Tiro!" Still, no response.

"Can I be of service, Patron?" asked Lucius.

Normally, Cicero would have capitulated to vanity and would have declined Lucius' offer; however, the old man had already alluded to his poor eyesight earlier and decided there would be no harm. "Why, yes, Lucius, if you wouldn't mind. I seem to be having a little trouble reading this document. Would you?" the old patron asked.

Lucius took the document and began reading, silently at first.

ANTHONY MICHAEL VILLANUEVA

"Sir, Senator Lucius Marcius Philippus and Atia respectfully request you consider sponsoring Gaius Octavius for the occasion of his togas virilis." He read a little further. "And there is mention of a will, the will of Julius Caesar, naming Octavius as heir."

"Heir? Did you say—heir?" exclaimed Cicero.

"Yes Sir, Lucius Marcius Philippus wishes to meet with you to discuss the details," Lucius said. "There is one more item, Sire . . . the good senator wishes to inform you that Gnaeus Pompeius Magnus has been appointed dictator by the Senate."

"Dictator? Heir? By the gods, what mischief is this?" Cicero asked.

The old man brought his right hand to his mouth and chin, unconsciously sliding it down to his throat—guarding it—then paced back and forth, obviously deep in thought.

"To Rome. We must go to Rome," muttered the old consular.

Hurried sandals from behind announced Tiro's arrival. "Oh Favorite Son of Apollo, I came as soon as I heard you needed my services. What biding do you have for me, Dominus?" Tiro asked, panting as if he had been racing Mercury himself.

Cicero waved Tiro off with a hand; the biding had been taken care of. "No need, Tiro," Cicero said, ignoring the panting servant.

Tiro noted the document in Lucius' hand. His rapid breathing miraculously ebbed and his subservient mask turned to one of concern. Narrow, daggered eyes scowled at Lucius.

"Tiro, make ready, we're off to the city," Cicero commanded; there was only one city—Rome.

Tiro's obedient countenance returned; the master needed his services after all.

Cicero marched off in the direction of the domus to do some quick work in his reception room. Tiro waddled after him, turning briefly to throw Lucius one last glare.

Lucius shrugged and returned to the table to enjoy the company of those still engaged in conversation, laughter, and good food. He sat back down next to Caius and helped himself to more delicious cheese and ham.

At the end of the table a smiling Tullia flashed flirtatious eyes at Lucius. She actually appeared to have more color to her than usual. Lucius noticed the fleeting smiles and returned hers with some of his own, despite having a mouthful of cheese and ham—he looked like a squirrel hording nuts. His puffed cheeks flashed red as if he'd been caught spying someone in a compromised position. What he needed was more wine to wash down the mouthful of food. The magic of the wine gave him courage to continue the flirtatious game. But when he looked over to where Tullia had been sitting, he found only an empty chair.

Ruefully, he refilled his wine goblet and settled for some sliced apple to accompany the wine and cheese, his face awash with disappointment, but still flush—this time from the wine.

"I said come on, I've something to show you, Lucius," Caius said. In the moment of the magic that Tullia had captivated Lucius' attention, he hadn't heard Caius trying to tell him something of importance.

"What? What is it, Caius?" he asked, his voice rasped in irritation.

"Come on, I said. I've something to show you."

Lucius obediently followed Caius out of the courtyard, down a corridor, and into a new part of the villa under construction that would be attached to the domus. The odor of fresh plaster and cement greeted them as they entered the room. With the aid of many oil lamps, they could see it was a large room, destined for dining and entertainment.

Caius walked up to one of the main walls, turned to Lucius, and said, "This is your wall, to do as you wish."

It took a minute to make sense of Caius' words, and then he understood. Lucius approached the wall, reached out, laid his hand on the damp surface, and swept gently from left to right, up and down.

Somewhere in this wall an idea waited, a picture, a story. The blank wall hid a secret, a secret wanting to come to the surface to reveal itself. Lucius studied the wall from top to bottom and thought of his mother. He asked her for inspiration. In his mind a thick fog thinned and then cleared, revealing the drama he etched in the dirt back at Dyrrhachium. It blazed through and then scorched the back of his mind. He stepped back measured the breadth of the mural with all-seeing eyes: the battle; men fighting; the horses; the living and the dying; and, of course, the javelin coursing through the heavens. He could see it all coming together, it was all there before him: The figures came to life and began to fight; shields clashed, blood sprayed; horses screamed and reared in fright; dirt and blood consumed everybody and everything; the air bellowed in a hideous clamor, a deafening roar; and the javelin—the javelin sped toward, toward—

"Yes," the cripple uttered, seeing what Caius could not.

Soft sandals broke the trance. Lucius and Caius turned to see who entered.

Tullia.

CHAPTER
XXI

Lucius and Caius found themselves on the road again, this time on horseback. They trailed the horse-drawn coach that carried Cicero and his secretary, Tiro. The four of them headed for Pompey's Rome residence, the Domus Rostrata. Though the trip from Tusculum to the Esquiline Hill would be not quite fifteen Roman miles, it would be a full day's ride by horseback and coach.

The sun to their backs, they descended from the rim of the old volcano crater and wound through the beautiful landscape of the Alban Hills until they reached the main road to Rome, the *Via Tuscolana*.

Caius engaged Lucius in small talk, mostly about the reconstruction of the Cicero villa after over-zealous thugs sacked it during the time the senate exiled Cicero some ten years past. All his precious statues and other valuable possessions acquired from Athens were plundered by a man named Gabinius. Those were bad times; ugly times. Caius spoke as if he were there; he just repeated what he had heard from the household staff. Another group of thugs torched the master's house in Rome, acting under the orders of another one of Cicero's nemeses at the time, Publius Clodius Pulcher, and a religious temple was built in its place. Cicero had found himself entangled in a sticky web of political intrigue and subject to a law of vengeance especially aimed at him for the prosecution of some Roman citizens who were put to death without a real trial. Leaving Rome seemed the only viable option at the time.

Lucius listened with half an ear. His brain busied itself with thoughts of Tullia. The day before returned to him, when Tullia had walked in on him and Caius as they examined the wall. Caius' voice faded away, hers drifted in . . .

"Is there something wrong with Papa's new room?" she had asked in a voice soft and pleasant to the ear.

"No, no I don't think so," Lucius had answered.

"Your father has allowed this wall to be painted by Lucius," Caius interjected.

Lucius went mute and let his eyes feast on Tullia as she stood in front of the doorway, more a dream than a silhouette: the outer layers of her hair like gold filaments floating in the air as the sunlight skimmed past and around her; the shadowed figure of her body a statuette veiled by her *stola*—her sheer, longer pleated outer garment without the *palla*; and her face painted by gilded light from the oil lamps in the room. One could not tell that she owned six years more than Lucius or Caius.

"What color are you going to paint Papa's new room?" she had asked.

Caius laughed. "No, Lady Tullia, he's going to paint pictures, people, you know, portraits and the like."

"Oh," Tullia replied, embarrassment in her voice. "I would like to see it when it's done," she said.

"Well, I'm not sure just how it's going to—"

A stern voice from outside interrupted the moment. It called for Tullia.

Tullia turned an ear to her mother's voice. "I have to go now, but I really would like to see it when you get started," Tullia had said as she glided from the room. She looked back once with that beguiling smile of hers and then disappeared like a phantom.

". . . You're not listening to me again, Lucius," Caius said, a bit perturbed.

"Sorry, just thinking of something."

"Or somebody," Caius retorted.

Lucius found himself embarrassed again.

"Tell me again, why are we going to Pompey's domus? Doesn't the master have people to handle his affairs . . . you know . . . those lictors, or that Tiro? What purpose do we serve?" Lucius asked, changing the subject.

"The master has his reasons, Lucius," Caius answered. "A wild guess? I think you remind him of his cousin of the same name—'Lucius.' He's been dead these past nine or ten years or so, maybe more. Cicero still misses him deeply. I sense it when he and his brother Quintus are together and reminisce on past times. There's always that little silence after they include their dear cousin in their conversations—like saving a place at the table."

"Hmm, another one of those bright stars in that Greek Milky Circle," Lucius whispered. "That place is getting crowded."

They continued on, spines and hips rocking and swaying with the jerky movements of the horses' hindquarters.

———

They came in from the southeast, arriving much sooner than expected. Cicero used the trip as a day of work, dictating letters to Tiro, who could keep up easily with his special shorthand technique, hampered only by the rocking and bumping of the coach on the sometimes-rough road.

"By the gods, what is that smell?" Lucius asked as they approached the Esquiline Hill. Black smoke drifted over a hill and charged at the visitors like ghosts. "Smells like pig dung and rotten meat!"

"Get used to it, Lucius," Caius said. "That's Rome you smell. Everything and anything, including the dead, got dumped here at one time or another."

How anybody could possibly be drawn to live in a city that reeks so of putrid filth was beyond Lucius.

Caius must have been hearing his thoughts. "Don't worry; it's not always this bad. It's just the winds. You'll get used to it, or this stench will just be replaced with another," Caius said with authority.

They came to a stop at the Esquiline entrance of the walled city. The master had decided it best to leave the animals and coach there and walk the remainder of the way to Pompey's residence. Tiro took care of the business of securing temporary custody of the animals until they returned: A father and son team seemed honest enough to watch the horses and possessions at a way station—especially with the promise of another sack of coins in addition to the one they received as a deposit. The coach driver stayed behind for insurance.

Cicero's small ensemble commenced their trek through the narrow streets that, for the most part, were not very straight—very contradictory for Romans who had a passion for straight lines. At one point, they came to a slight turn where the wall of a building bulged outwards, as if it were to collapse or burst at any moment.

The smells and clamors of the city were a stark contrast to those of the peaceful countryside from which they had just traveled. They navigated numerous zones of scents and sounds as they marched inward: enticing aromas of something delicious just cooked or baked; ugly, caustic fumes of something unidentified smoldering nearby; perfumed whiffs from burning incense to mask the unpleasant Esquiline Hill; pungent vapors from human wastes at nearby communal latrines and adjoining streets; and the occasional pleasant fragrances from colorful flowers suspended from windows above. The echo of an old man belittling someone who obviously had incurred his wrath could be heard resonating along the walls of a narrow alley; a small child's playful laughter from somewhere above from an unseen window emerged through and replaced the old man's bellicose cries; off-key notes from someone attempting to play an out-of-tune lyre drifted from another window; and the amorous moans of a couple reaching the zenith of their love-making finished the carnival of sounds serenading the troupe as they paraded along the streets toward the final destination.

They reached Pompey's residence and were greeted by a pleasant bouquet of honeysuckle and more burning incense. A subtle murmuring from a moderate-size crowd drifted toward Cicero and his men as they approached. The mumbling emanated from Pompey's clientela who had come to see the patron. Most immediately recognized Cicero and either acknowledged him cordially or gave him the evil eye.

Cicero's group worked their way toward the great bronze door of the house, parting the sea of clients like a small craft attempting to navigate upstream. Three, large lictors—more muscled bodyguards than civil servants—and two centurions stood guard at the door.

"Pompeius Magnus is not seeing anyone today," declared one of the lictors without any attempt whatsoever to offer any semblance of respect for a former consul of Rome who was entitled to his own lictors.

"He will see me!" Cicero avowed calmly with document in hand. "He has specifically sent for me by courier."

The lictor scowled at the former consul, looked out to the silent crowd taking this all in, awaiting the outcome, and then regarded Cicero again. "Wait here." Not—"Please wait here," or "I beg your indulgence, Sir, if you don't mind waiting for just a minute." Just—"Wait here," then disappeared behind the great bronze door.

After what appeared to be at least five minutes filled with the buzzing of flies, the soft ruffling of scrolls, and hushed whispers, the stone-faced lictor returned from behind the door and gave a slight nod toward the atrium. Cicero smiled and boldly entered the domus. Tiro, Lucius, and Caius followed the patron but the guard blocked their path. "Not you," the ogre of a man shouted.

"No, they must accompany me," Cicero exclaimed. "They are very important in the business to be conducted." Of course, that was not necessarily true, but he thought he could get away with the little lie. Cicero needed to control the situation with calm assertiveness and not anger the man.

The lictor looked over the trio and with another nod of the head let them pass. The crowd exploded as the trio entered and joined their master. The mob became animated and rowdy, complaining vehemently, and waived their petitions at the lictor. The door slammed with a resounding clang!

Once in the atrium, the nomenclator greeted the consul and his "staff."

"Greetings, Senator . . . excuse me, Consular Cicero," he said as he bowed. The man was not of the same ilk as the lictor outside controlling the crowd. "Pompey will see you shortly. Please, make yourself welcome. A chair perhaps?"

It pleased Cicero to see that Pompey had some staff with etiquette. The creatures outside were more vicious watchdogs than indispensable employees. He considered Tiro and his young Caius the acme in administrative aides; young Lucius would be groomed to be part of his special team, too.

The reverberation of heavy boots announced Pompey's arrival. "Marcus, *quid agis*—how are you? I'm glad you could make it," the large man said, greeting an old friend not seen in some time. "And Tiro, it's good to see you again, too." He did not address Lucius or Caius, but did cast a curious look in their direction. He acknowledged their presence with that awkward silence that usually precedes an awkward situation. Fortunately, the great man did not recognize Lucius as one of his former legionaries—one of his many thousands of legionaries. And no one from the small party of visitors volunteered that information.

"Oh, forgive me. This is Caius Terentius and Lucius Pontius, scribes on my staff especially chosen to learn Tiro's special short-hand technique."

A fleeting wave of shock flashed across Tiro's face. Lucius and Caius exchanged quick glances. It was a complete surprise to all three, but they knew better than to display it. Tiro offered an over-exuberant diplomatic smile to Pompey when the large man looked over to him.

"Well, indeed, perhaps your man could teach my scribes that special writing technique, huh?" Pompey said and then offered a disarming smile.

"We could discuss some sort of arrangement, I'm sure," replied Cicero, always looking for the *quid pro quo*—a favor for a favor.

"If you don't mind, I would like to speak to you in private. Of course, if you need the ingenious services of your man, Tiro, that would be acceptable," Pompey said, hesitantly. "This way to my private office." Pompey gestured the way with a wave of his hand.

The three left the tablinum and marched down the corridor. "By the way, forgive me, my congratulations to you on your appointment to . . . Dictator," Cicero offered as they disappeared from view. A more serious opinion regarding the dictatorship would have to wait for another time.

Alone in the reception area, Caius took a seat as Lucius limped about the large room, surveying the surroundings. The cripple's sandal slapped and echoed along the mosaic floor as he lotered about. All about him treasures and trophies from Pompey's triumphs and conquests made their presence known: shields, spears, and swords of different shapes and sizes from different armies; helmets with and without plumage; wooden masks and ivory carvings; and urns and vases with Hellenistic pictorials and Egyptian figures. Lucius' excited mind couldn't keep up with his wide eyes.

Then, like a creature lying in ambush, one object jumped out at him and grabbed hold. It held him captive, immobilizing him completely. Lucius eased his way forward, as if walking on fragile ice. The object beckoned him and drew him in. He recognized it immediately when he neared. It pierced his soul and held him in total disbelief.

Suspended on the wall before him glowered part of a javelin—the killing part, the tip and part of the shaft—the rest was missing, or broken off, as designed. The piercing point appeared rust-colored in places. Lucius' right hand reached out and crept upward; he couldn't have been more cautious if he were approaching a deadly asp. Terror pumped through his arteries. The thought of the javelin coming alive with a single touch crossed his mind—he withdrew, thankful that the javelin didn't turn and strike him dead.

Lucius didn't hear Caius draw near.

"What is it?"

Lucius' shoulders lurched as if being pierced in the back by an unseen javelin. The back of his neck seared in a hot flash. And his bounding heart prepared to leap from his chest.

"Jupiter, Juno, and Vulcan!" Lucius cried out in an exasperated voice. "I told you never to do that, coming up from behind me like that. Do you want to get yourself killed?"

"*Mea culpa,* mea culpa—I'm sorry," Caius said, ruefully, "but you seemed so . . . so mesmerized by that spear, like Odysseus and the Sirens."

"It's not a spear, it's a javelin," quipped Lucius, his eyes returning to the venerated object.

"Javelin, then," Caius corrected himself.

"I feel I know this relic," Lucius uttered in a whisper.

Caius studied the cripple and then brought his own gaze to the javelin. No matter how he turned his head he could not see what Lucius could see.

Voices floated into the large reception room from the corridor. Pompey, Cicero, Tiro, and Venius, Pompey's nomenclator trailed the voices. "It's settled then; you'll take that young boy and mentor him well. I can't think of any one better qualified than you. Who else could possibly instill the good ideals of the Republic in such a young person," Pompey said.

Cicero studied the floor and his feet moved him along, his mind a battlefield of thoughts and contemplation: mentoring Octavius; Pompey a dictator; Marcus Antonius still on the loose and with a large army. The weight of it all pressed hard and caused a fissure of pain at his right temple. And then flashbacks of the camp encounters with Pompey at Dyrrhachium infiltrated his mind; this dictatorship was really no surprise after all. Now the other temple ached.

Caius and Lucius clustered at the wall drew Pompey Magnus and Cicero's attention. Of all the magnificent trophies in the room, the two scribes seemed enthralled only with the javelin. Cicero took note of the relic immediately. He, too, became fixated and pulled to the object. He looked to Lucius. Their eyes met and shared a secret: a silent recognition of something cryptic and haunting.

"Do you recognize that particular trophy, Marcus?" Pompey asked. "It stopped the battle at Dyrrhachium. The end of Caesar's luck, remember? Who knows what the world would be today if that implement had missed its mark. You could be dealing with Julius Caesar, Dictator of Rome. And maybe even that Marcus Antonius as his right-hand man. And I might be the one occupying the throne of the urn. Poor Cornelia. But at least there would be my sons, Sextus and Gnaeus."

The javelin had the eyes and attention of everyone in the room. It was in command now.

CHAPTER
XXII

Forty thousand hobnailed boots shook the valley. The low, rhythmic rumble could have been a gigantic millipede winding its way through the countryside. But it wasn't; instead, it was the army of Marcus Antonius.

Sthenelus Regulius marched along in the belly of the giant millipede, nearer to the back. His numb mind had ceased to be enslaved by the hypnotic cadence of the marching boots for many miles; it now wandered out in the fields. He resembled a ghost, pale and lifeless, a ghost walking along with other ghosts. Once, for a fleeting moment, when he spied a shoot of vegetation that had miraculously survived the grinding and stomping of many tired boots, a smile crept along his subdued face, only to slide away when the legionary flanking him crushed the life from the living shoot, leaving just a green smudge on the bottom of a boot.

Behind him were auxiliary troops, speaking in their Gallic tongue. And behind them all, the baggage train and siege equipment, pulled by hundreds of mules. Sthenelus now belonged to the *3rd Gallica Legio*—ironically, a legion levied by Pompey sixteen years ago in the northern territories of Gaul. Most of the original surviving legionaries had retired, but a few were called back to duty, or just volunteered. Julius Caesar had just levied the new legion the previous year to fight Pompey. It was a mix of soldiers from other legions whittled in number by battle—Lucius' unit included—new recruits, and old vets; they were all Antonius' now.

Publius Ventidius and Marcus Aemilius Lepidus, two trustworthy generals in the service of Marcus Antonius—"Antoni" to his friends, led the army. Antoni had secretly slipped away unseen and sailed for Egypt with one under-strength legion weeks ago as part of his plan to gain control of the exported grain to Rome and to secure more wealth to pay the bonuses he promised his troops. Only the smallest contingents of legionaries were left behind in the North to man important garrisons and serve as reserves as needed.

The troops marched under an umbrella of low, gray clouds. The blanket of gray let loose some of its moisture in sheets of light showers, ideal conditions for the least amount of dust kicked up and cool temperatures for marching—the generals took it as a good omen.

Antoni's plan: move the bulk of his troops from the east and west of Northern Italy, converge at Placentia, and then pivot south to Mutina. The legionaries had marched for a good part of the day at an easy pace, packs, weapons, and helmets slung over shoulders and covered shields at their sides. Standards and eagles for each unit led the way. The animal-skin-covered *signifer* carried the standard; the aquilifer carried the eagle. The twin bulls of the *3rd Gallica* bobbed up and down along with the ever-present eagle in front of Sthenelus' unit.

The symphony of crunching rock and dirt underfoot, slapping leather, clattering metal, clopping horse hooves, and creaking wagon wheels all came to a halt with a raised hand from General Ventidius when he reached the rise of a sloping piece of ground. The general's tribunes gathered up front, awaiting orders.

The distinct outline of a walled-metropolis stretched out before them in the distance—Mutina. Spirals of black smoke rose from behind the walls; the city was alive. Orders were given, trumpets blared, and soldiers dispersed. There were trenches to dig, earthworks to build, streets to mark off, tents to erect, and a command post to assemble.

Cicero and his entourage left Pompey's home after conducting business with the newly elected dictator. Cicero agreed, of course, to mentor young Octavius, for the good of the Republic. And, of course again, no one could do it better than he.

Cutting through the throng of Pompey's clientela outside the dictator's home, the old consular and his crew found their way to the streets and headed back for the horses and coach they had left at the gate entrance. The narrow avenue had come alive and crowded since they last navigated through this part of the city. Someone else's clientela added to the congestion and chaos. The crowded populace absorbed Cicero's clan and swept them away in a river of bobbing heads and mixed shouts of *"where are you"* and *"over here."* A tangled mess of clumsy bodies with priorities seemingly more important than the cripple's, blocked and bumped Lucius unceremoniously. He stumbled and fell behind, lost at sea again, but this time in a sea of chaotic bodies. He lost sight of his comrades and patron the same way he lost sight of the ship during the storm.

His heeling ankle had been kicked and he had to swim from the middle of the rushing river of humanity to the side of the street to recover. He limped his way around a corner to an empty side street as the mob continued on its way like a herd of cattle blindly channeled to the *Forum Boarium* for slaughter.

The cripple leaned against a wall and panted wheezed breaths, the results of equal parts exertion and pain. The din of the city seemed to be sucked away and replaced with a thick, eerie stillness. He regained his senses and slowly opened his eyes. That's when he saw her.

She was old—very, very old, sitting under a makeshift canopy of an old hide. Some would have called her an old "hag." Her head sat in the middle of her shoulders, forced forward by the huge hump at her upper back. Her wild and dirty hair of white draped her ancient face that looked like aged wood. A prominent nose that was too big for her small face connected arches of dense brows. Deep crevices for wrinkles carved her almost pink skin, especially around her eyes and mouth. The rims of her droopy eyelids were nothing more than blood-red lines with very few lashes. Her bottom lip jutted beyond her upper lip and her mouth churned in circles. A large flap of skin suspended from under her chin swayed from side to side as she ruminated. Her crooked skeleton-like fingers held a small bowl with a few bronze coins resting at the bottom.

Lucius passed slowly, scrutinizing her with a hard, oblique look as a sailor might a hazardous rock at sea.

"You have had a long journey, my son," the old woman managed to emit with a tired, raspy voice. "You took one life, the gods took the other."

A web of magic had been spun and Lucius could move no further.

He fixated on her. Under her thick and bushy brows he could see her eyes: opaque pupils filled with tiny clouds. "What is it you are saying grandmother," Lucius finally uttered.

She continued to ruminate and stare past him.

Streams of sweat tricked down his face, armpits, and back.

She raised the bowl a little higher with trembling fingers. He reached in his belt, withdrew a few coins from a pouch, and placed them into the tremulous bowl.

"The one on the road invited the sword. He had bad intentions . . . evil intentions. The one the gods took, they took with the javelin. He spent all the luck they had given him. But he shall become a god in turn, and he shall have a son . . . *Divi Filius*—Son of God, and the son will turn mud and brick into marble and stone. *Pax*—peace, the son shall bring to the world with the sword and javelin and he will become the savior of Rome. And in his reign, and in his son's reign, there will be another savior—a savior of man. And he, too, will be 'Son of God,' with promises of peace, not by the sword, but by the sign of the . . . "

The seer searched her darkness, her contorted face straining for the answer. The look on her knotted face gave hint of only confusion as her opaque eyes danced under angry looking brows.

Lucius awaited the answer.

The unsettled look on her face transitioned to one of resignation.

"One of Poseidon's creatures . . . the sign of the . . . of the . . ."

"Tell me, grandmother, tell me."

"The fish," she whispered. Her truncated answer puzzled her as it did Lucius. Her pained expression suggested that there should be more to come.

"You confuse me, grandmother. What is it you are telling me?" Lucius asked.

She looked to the sky as if she saw something frightening, something terrifying.

"Beware the javelin, my son . . . beware."

"And the fish? What of the fish, grandmother?"

She spoke no more. Her face returned to her darkness.

Lucius looked about. Very few people passed by. And those who did pass ignored the cripple and the old hag sitting on the ground with the extended, twitching cup.

He had to catch up with the others before they got too far ahead. Lucius peered around the corner and could see that the street had thinned out, time to go, so he stepped out into the light human traffic. He felt compelled to take one last look at the old hag around the corner, but resisted. Go—go now, he commanded himself. He staggered as fast as his aching ankle allowed.

The cripple hobbled ahead stiffly, recognizing familiar scents and signs from earlier. He had covered twenty paces when he stumbled upon Caius marching from the opposite direction.

"Lucius! What happened to you? You disappeared!"

"I got cut off by the crowd and then kicked at my ankle. Had to stop and rest. That's all."

"Can you make it back?" Caius asked, looking down at Lucius' again-swollen ankle.

"Yeah, not a problem," Lucius said, beads of sweat above his brow and the pallor in his face begging to differ. "Come on, let's go. Can't keep the others waiting too long. Let's go, let's go, Caius. I'm fine."

The pair met the others at the gate. It hadn't been that far off from where Caius found Lucius limping on the street.

Tiro leveled a cutting glare at Lucius for making the master wait. The secretary didn't say a thing. He didn't have to. The look in his eyes, that piercing, evil look said it all. The temperature of the air surely dropped several degrees.

"Lucius, are you okay?" Cicero asked, truly concerned.

"Yes, Dominus, forgive me. I got lost in the crowd, and then my ankle . . . but I'm fine. Sorry for the delay."

"Well, we're all together and that's what counts, so let us make our way back to the villa. Shall we?" Cicero said—a command more than a question.

Cicero had a house on the lower slope of the Palatine, once burnt to the ground and rebuilt at public expense. They would not go there this day, but they would another.

The driver, having taken a good nap in the master's absence, was fresh and ready for the return trip home. The livery owners, having been paid the remainder of the fee, were happy, too. And the young scribes, having had enough of the city for one day, were on their horses, eager to go.

The journey home to Tusculum seemed longer than the trip

ANTHONY MICHAEL VILLANUEVA

to the city—it always seemed that way. Cicero asked Tiro to read back the notes he had taken during the discussion with the dictator. The old statesman listened intently with closed eyes as the coached rocked him about.

" . . . In short, Dominus, after Gaius Julius Caesar Octavianus celebrates his toga virilis, we . . . excuse me . . . you will proceed to Puteoli whereupon the mentoring of young Octavius will commence . . . ." Tiro regurgitated all the important points and plans from his notes taken in his special "shorthand," etched in his folded wax notebooks that he always kept with him. In the debriefing, the planned strategy stressed the importance of the Republic. Gaius would be guided in the right direction, the way of the constitution—nothing was more important.

Pompey did not argue the point with the poor man. He would let Cicero believe that all was well and that the Republic was healthy and alive; besides, young Gaius had not yet been infected with the philosophies of the "Caesarians." The optimates would continue to have their Republic, their properties, and their wealth protected at all costs—at least for a little while more.

<hr>

Pompey and Cicero were not the only ones who had it in their best interest to watch over young Gaius Julius Caesar Octavianus. Known to both the old consular and the general were Lucius Cornelius Balbus and his associate Oppius: Julius Caesar's men. Skilled at financing, organizing, mediating, and advising, they had been his trusted aides and advisors for many years. They were the heads of his loyal staff and knew everything. The staff made everything work when Caesar lived. Now that he was dead, they had a void to fill. They needed purpose. They needed Octavius.

CHAPTER XXIII

Lucius woke to the sound of rain, more a recital of harmonies and rhythms than just rain: a soft restlessness of tiny raindrops tapping on roof tiles above; the rhythmic bombarding of water droplets splashing into a basin outside his window in a metric beat; a lively collection of water sluicing and cascading through pipes along the wall; the harmonizing pitter-patter of the rain pelting leaves on a nearby tree; and the slow cadenced beat of dripping water leaking from the ceiling into a clay pot in an adjoining room.

Initially, the rain had awakened his senses, but the musical resonance of it all beckoned him back to sleep. Heaviness overwhelmed his eyelids, making it impossible to keep them open. Each blink grew heavier and more difficult to open. Somnus—the god of sleep—had crept into his room and used his magical stick to pour water from the river Lethe over Lucius to call back sleep again. And surely Hypnos—Somnus' Greek cousin—worked in league with him as his co-conspirator; the urge to sleep overpowered Lucius and he could not open his eyes again, no matter how much he willed them. He was drugged. That soporific drug—that soft symphonic sound of rain—had induced slumber once more, and he slipped into a dream state with ease.

In his dream, he walked down a corridor of yet another darkened alley—always the darkened alley. A few oil lamps from windows above cast the faintest color of pale wheat to the passageway. And as he walked along, he came upon someone sitting alongside one of the partially lit walls: the old hag from the day before, her trembling cup held out for more coins.

His eyes met hers, which were brilliant with light. He felt

himself being drawn into her luminescent but cloudy eyes. The clouds thinned to a mist and he broke through. After clearing the mist, he found himself yet in another alley, similar to the one he had just transited. At the end of the alley were two legionaries, one with sword in hand, and the other with a javelin. They saw him and advanced his way. Lucius backed away from the oncoming soldiers. He turned and craved to run as fast as he could, only his legs were solid stone and would not obey. As much as he willed his legs to move, they would not. The soldiers had no trouble running and would be upon him in seconds. The one with the javelin stopped, took a stance, aimed his javelin, and then let it fly with a mighty thrust. Lucius could clearly see the javelin fly, faster and faster, coming straight for him. The tip of the weapon flashed a glint of blinding light as it coursed through the air. Just as the javelin arrived, Lucius commanded himself to wake. He sprang forward with labored breaths and the javelin vaporized, inches from his chest.

The nightmare ended.

The music of the rain returned, as peaceful and innocent as before. Somebody stood at the door.

"Are you going to sleep all morning or what?" Caius asked.

"Sorry . . . I just feel really tired this morning. Hard to get up," Lucius said with a groan.

"Yeah, it's the rain. It can do that. Hate to disturb your sleep, Adonis, but we have real work to do today. Tiro is going to start instructing us in his special shorthand technique. Master Cicero was serious. We start today," Caius said with excitement in his voice.

"Finally. some real work. I was wondering when we would start doing something of substance," quipped Lucius as he labored out of bed.

"Well, at least it's something different than just copying letters over and over again. It's something new . . . like a secret language. No one can do it other than Tiro. Soon, we will be the only other two who will have this special knowledge," Caius said.

"That would make us very valuable then, wouldn't it, Caius," remarked Lucius.

"Yes . . . I guess it would."

"Good thing we're not slaves."

"What do you mean?" Caius asked.

"Oh, nothing."

"What nothing, Lucius?"

"Nothing, Caius, nothing. Leave it, okay?"

"I know what you're thinking, Lucius. Master Cicero would never do that. He cares for his people too much to do anything like that. Tiro was a slave and the master gave him his freedom and kept him on with pay. Cicero is a good patron, Lucius."

Lucius decided to let his friend have the last word. He wanted to retort with the fact that Cicero was just another man who happened to own other humans, no matter how nice he was. Some owners were good, kind, and affectionate with their slaves; others treated them with the same indifference as the livestock.

Lucius washed—more a ritualistic splashing of cold, refreshing water to his face and head than a good wash—and changed into a warmer tunic. He met Caius in a small dining area, adjacent to the outside kitchen oven. A quick meal of sliced apple, bread, and olive oil satisfied their morning hunger and prepared them to meet with Tiro in one of the comfortable big rooms in the villa.

Colorful scenes of deer and birds decorated the big room, as well as laborers working fields with sickles and rakes, harvesting and collecting wheat. A still scene of a fruit-filled basket and wine vase caught his artistic eye. The quality was too one-dimensional for Lucius' taste. He knew he could do better, he could feel it deep down within. His head turned in a slow, measuring arch as he gazed at all the frescoes adorning the room and his eyes silently critiqued the artwork of the craftsman—he wasn't willing to recognize the painter as an artist just yet.

A deliberate clearing of the throat drew Lucius back to the moment. He turned and found Tiro's beady eyes glaring at him. Lucius surrendered and offered his full attention. Caius let slip a snicker, which caught the same beady eyes full force from Tiro.

"The master . . . in his infinite wisdom . . . has asked me to instruct you on the workings of my . . . shorthand, my method of condensing many long words into short strokes, or special letters, thus being thrift in time, letters, and wax. Strings of common expressions represented in a single symbol or caricature." Tiro scrutinized Lucius and then added, "It is a form of art, converting a thought, an expression, an idea, to a meaningful symbol or group of symbols."

A hard frown on Lucius' face melted away as the concept impacted his brain. He let an understanding smile cross his face as he met Tiro's hard eyes. The secretary's expression did not change a bit.

The secretary—now teacher—continued for hours, breaking briefly only at times to take care of bodily needs. Both students absorbed the new language with eagerness and anticipation. By the end of the evening, the first of many sessions ended, as did the rain.

For a week more, the scribes increased their knowledge of the new language and quickly became proficient at "taking letters" and were equally adept at transcribing notes into complete and accurate documents, and with very few errors.

Tiro was skeptical at first about giving away his special language to Lucius and Caius, but it was what Dominus wanted. Secretly, he prayed that the two young scribes would fail miserably.

His pessimism slowly surrendered to something akin to pride—not for the scribes, but for himself in that he could actually teach the likes of these two—nothings—such technical feats. It never occurred to him that they might have the cerebral capacity to actually learn something so unique; he professed only that their success was nothing more than a reflection of his expertise and skill in teaching. He could hold his head—and thus his nose—a little higher than before.

The students reported for lessons after a day off for market day, ready to learn more. They waited. And waited.

Finally after about an hour by the water clock, Tiro appeared. "There will be no lessons today."

The students exchanged quizzical glances and awaited further information.

"There's been a change in schedule. The good master will be leaving Tusculum. He'll be traveling to his residence in Puteoli. Caius, you and I are to accompany him and assist in his work there," Tiro said, impassively.

Lucius looked to Caius and gave a shrug.

"Lucius, you are to remain here and start on the wall, the new addition to the villa. I have arranged for assistance with the coloring and painting material. They are slaves . . . workmen, with skills in painting and artwork. You, of course, are to do the main work. They will assist. You are to supervise them as to what suits you.

"I'm sure . . . you will not let us down." Lucius received the words as intended: an imperative; a command; an order; an—"or else."

The cripple sat cloaked in dejection; yet, a sense of excitement began a slow burn within. In his mind's eye, he could see his mural: the great battle he had sketched in the dirt at Dyrrhachium. It formed and came together on the wall like a great stain that morphed and revealed something wonderful, something glorious.

The good consular would be pleased. More importantly, Lucius would make his mother proud.

Back in Rome, Pompey's residence received another courier with news of a great army outside Mutina, preparing for a siege. By coincidence, Pompey had some special guests that particular morning—besides the ever-present clientela.

Lucius Cornelius Balbus met with Pompey, at the dictator's request, for some very important business discussions: the future of young Gaius Julius Caesar Octavianus. Balbus had been a good and intimate friend of Pompey Magnus as well as the private secretary for the deceased Julius Caesar. He had also been a talented negotiator with people like Cicero. Magnus considered Lucius Cornelius to be a valuable asset for the re-organization of the Republic and the needed change for the good of the people of Rome.

"It seems that Antoni's army has made its way down from the north of the Po to Mutina," Pompey stated as his eyes scanned the document handed him by the courier. He dismissed the courier with a wave of a hand as if swatting at an annoying fly.

"What took him so long?" Balbus said, not really expecting an answer.

"It is of little consequence. My troops will hold his legions where they are."

"May I ask who is in command of your legions there in Mutina?"

"Titus. Titus Labienus," Pompey answered.

"Titus? I thought—"

"Africa? Yes . . . everyone thought he had gone to Africa. Titus is in charge again."

Balbus flashed furrowed brows and a far-off stare, but said nothing.

"Labienus is a good general. I trust him. His son, Quintus, is a promising military man, too. A bit young, but he will do well, you'll see," Pompey continued.

Caesar trusted Labienus as well, Balbus thought to himself.

"I have a concern, Magnus. Antoni may outnumber you in legions."

"I have an excellent source that says Antoni is not with his troops," Pompey said. "Who knows what they might do, or to whom they will give allegiance . . . if offered the right incentive. Many of those troops were mine, once. They may want to come back if they have the opportunity."

"This is true," Balbus said. "The days of the citizen-soldier are over. The army is different. It was Caesar's personal belief that the armies would make the future rulers, not the politicians, or the people."

"He may have had a point there. Take care of your legions and they will take care of you," Pompey responded.

"And Antoni . . . you say he is not there?"

"That's correct, Cornelius. We believe he has ventured to Egypt . . . for control of the grain and access to money."

"Hmm . . . our sources concur. He slipped out of Patavium in one of his many disguises, a fisherman I believe, with a small contingent of his most trusted men," Balbus replied.

Pompey seemed surprised for a second, but only for a second; Caesar did not surround himself with stupid or incompetent men. The dead general's staff, with Lucius Cornelius Balbus at the helm, was superb. Who knows what Caesar might have accomplished with such a loyal staff, as well as a loyal army? If it wasn't for that unfortunate incident with the javelin, that moment when his luck ran out and the gods made a different choice, then he, Gaius Julius Caesar, would be dictator now—not Pompey. For now,

Pompey would do the best he could with what he had.

"Are you by chance in the services of anyone . . . currently?" Pompey asked.

"Currently—no."

"I could use someone with your talent and experience, Lucius Cornelius," Pompey said, attempting to appear more occupied with the document he had in hand, perusing for the third time.

"Well, as I currently find myself unemployed, perhaps I could be of some service then," Balbus offered.

"Good." Pompey nonchalantly walked over to his trophy wall and focused on a mounted javelin piece. "There's a matter of a young man, or soon to be young man . . . someone related to your former employer."

"Ah—young Gaius Octavius," Balbus proclaimed.

"Yes," Pompey said, eyes glued to the javelin. "Octavius."

CHAPTER
XXIV

The slave responsible for receiving visitors moved hurriedly to the loud knocking at the thick, wooden and bronze door, the door belonging to Lucius Marcius Philippus. Someone beckoned.

"I'm coming, I'm coming," he murmured to himself as his sandaled feet carried him swiftly, half-shuffling and half-running, to the summoning. "You'd think they were the gods themselves the way they bang on that door. Why don't they just knock it down and do us the favor of—"

The slave opened the door to find Consular Cicero, his aide Tiro, and the usual gaggle of followers.

Tiro stepped forward and announced: "Consular Marcus Tullius Cicero to see Senator Lucius Marcius Philippus." The secretary moved to the side to allow his master entry. The slave bowed respectfully and then flew away to announce the presence of the very important visitor, his voice echoed throughout the house.

An adolescent male walked in from an adjoining room.

"Ah, young Octavius, it is so good to see you," Cicero said as he walked up to the youth and patted him firmly on the shoulder.

The youth offered a transient, friendly, and disarming smile. "And it is good to see you, Consular."

A stagnant moment lingered between them, both just smiling. Cicero nodded his head repetitively to pass the time. The awkward moment passed when Lucius Marcius Philippus arrived, chased closely behind by Atia.

"*Ave*, Marcus Tullius. Welcome. Please, do come in. My home is yours," Philippus said with a broad smile.

"Thank you. You know, these days one needs to be careful to whom he makes such an offer. It may come to pass," Cicero jested with a wink and a broad smile.

"So true, so true. But, nonetheless, you are always a welcomed soul in this house."

"I am honored. And Atia, good day to you as well," Cicero added as he bowed.

"Thank you, Consular. It is good to see you, too. And Lady Terentia, she is well I pray?"

"Very."

The room filled with an awkward silence and clumsy smiles, except for Octavius, who offered nothing.

"Ahem—well then," began Philippus, "I believe we have some business to discuss. Let us proceed to the tablinum, shall we?" Philippus gestured the way with a slight wave of his hand, letting his guest lead. "Oh, Octavius, you need not join us just yet. We'll send for you shortly."

The group assembled in the reception-meeting room and gathered around a small table, fidgeting to find comfort. Tiro sat behind Cicero at one end, his ever-present stylus and wax tabloid at the ready. Philippus placed himself at center. And Atia stood next to him at the other end. A servant brought wine, fresh baked bread with olive oil, cut cucumbers, a small plate of olives, and, of course, good wine. They all should have been relaxed—but they were not.

"So, Marcus, have you considered the sponsoring of our young Gaius?" Atia asked.

Cicero offered a prolonged smile, letting it linger there for affect. "Yes, of course; it would be an honor," the old man said.

Atia let out an inflated sigh of relief that had been holding her erect and followed with an elated grin. "Wonderful, wonderful. It will be so good for Gaius."

Plans were discussed: the ceremony for the togas virilis would be held on Octavius' birthday, a week before the *Kalends* of Octobris. Not only would he shed the bulla and his bordered toga with the crimson stripes for the pure-white adult toga, but it was also agreed he should follow through with the ceremony for the position of pontiff as stipulated in Caesar's will.

The idea of having the ceremony in the Forum made Atia and Philippus uneasy. Concern centered on the large, anticipated crowd. Cost certainly was not the issue, but rather the exposure to the public. Normally, a family would look forward to having its clientela show in number—a sign of prestige and status. Atia, however, still harbored reservations in offering her son up to Rome, especially now as the son of Caesar. The multitudes could only be imagined. He would not only attract Philippus' clientela, but Caesar's as well—a large following for sure.

The agenda had been formulated and agreed upon: the togas virilis ceremony would start at the House of Philippus with the parting of the bulla and the striped toga of youth; a sacrifice would be made at the Field of Mars; the sacrificial offerings would be presented to the Temple of Liber on the Capitoline Hill; and a formal presentation of his "coming out" to be conducted in the Forum, followed by a ceremony inducting him into the college as one of the new pontiffs. It would be a busy day.

While Cicero conducted business in Rome, Lucius busied himself at his wall in the new addition in Tusculum.

The cripple's hands attacked the center of the wall with charcoals, laying down a basic background and etching in figures for his great battle scene. Details would be added later. Great arches and wild slashes flew across the wall and motes of black charcoal floated in the room's dank air. Now and then he would stand back and check his proportions and depth of field; it had to be perfect.

Drab stick-like figures marched on and took their positions on the wall—the beginnings of men and animals. In his mind, he could see real people in color: legionaries covered in sweat and blood and clouds of air-borne javelins in the sky. The din of battle was faint and distant, but as the mural progressed in color and depth, the sounds grew louder and clearer. In the end, he knew he would smell the battle as well as hear its roar. It had to be so. The spirits of the fallen would be there to guide him.

Through the entranceway a familiar figure appeared, her scent announcing her presence. Lucius ceased his sketching and welcomed her with a warm smile.

"Lady Tullia," he said in genuine surprise.

"*Ave*, Lucius. I hope I'm not disturbing your work."

"No, not at all. Welcome, welcome."

Tullia wandered in, her wide eyes absorbing the etchings on the wall. "Your people are all so . . . dark."

"It's just the base work. We're all just dark shadows of ourselves until light is shed upon us, then our true colors are exposed for all to see." Lucius could hear his mother's voice within his as her words left his lips.

"I didn't know you were so . . . poetic," she replied with a half-grin.

"No—no, what I mean is . . . here, let me show you." He wiped his hands clean of charcoal dust and gently grasped her hand. He pulled her close to one of the oil lanterns. "A moment ago you were no more than a silhouette with more dark umber about you. But see, next to the light, your true colors are discovered. Your eyes become much brighter, your hair like honey, your skin . . . well, I hope you know what I mean."

Tullia held fast and did not let go his hand.

Unease washed over Lucius and hot flashes began to consume him. He commanded himself to move away, back toward the wall.

Tullia followed, gliding like a phantom.

"Your father is still in Rome?" He already knew the answer.

"Yes."

"And . . . Lady Terentia?" He was running out of small talk quickly.

"Oh, she's out and about, getting ready for the trip to Puteoli with papa."

"Yes, the trip to Puteoli. I understand that's a nice place to visit . . . the hot springs and all. I'm sure you'll have a nice time there with your family," he said nervously.

"Oh, I'm not going. Not right away that is."

Captivated by her soft voice and beguiling smile, Lucius' brain locked. His mouth waited for more words to come. Transfixed like an immobile bird hypnotized by a stalking cat, he stood spellbound.

"Well then . . . your husband, Dolabella, and you—"

"Dolabella is too busy bedding Antoni's wife these days. I have no idea when he and I will do anything together," she quipped as she touched the wall where his figures lived.

Lucius remained motionless, mouth slightly agape, truly without words this time.

She turned to him. "My mother and father don't think I know, but I do. They try to shelter me and keep me as their . . . 'little girl.' I know more than they would like to think I know.

"And who do you bed, Lucius? Do you have someone in Rome? Or do you go to those disgusting places where they have those pictures and numbers on the walls? Those pictures of various . . . offerings."

He had no answer.

Lucius saw before him a different Tullia then the one he encountered upon first coming to Tusculum. Who, or what, is this person in the form of a little goddess to Cicero, he pondered. The answer rested simply in the fact that she was a product of her father's success: In all the compulsory time and all-consuming energies needed for his ascent up the political rungs and his law profession, her father could not always be there to protect her from life itself. If he could, he would have lived her life for her and made all the right decisions and shielded her from the evils of the world; but he could not. It took much time, energy, and sacrifice to become a *novus homo*—a new man, and get to where he was now and be able to ennoble his family. Success did not come without a price to pay somewhere along the line.

Tullia approached Lucius gracefully, as if floating on air, her scent leading the way. He did not offer a retreat, but stood his ground. She placed her hand on his chest as if to verify that Lucius was real, a mortal and not just some spirit or specter of her imagination. If she could not feel that pounding muscular organ in his chest on the other side of her delicate hand, then she, too, had to be nothing more than an apparition herself. Her hand glided from his chest to his flushed face. The stubble was soft. And then she wondered—were his lips as warm as his chest and face?

She had to know.

CHAPTER XXV

The day arrived.

In the early morning, as per custom, young Gaius put aside his bulla, his little amulet, with the *Lar* of the house—the house and family protective spirit—for safekeeping. It would be retrieved later.

He donned his adult toga, his togas virilis, and shed his toga of youth. The new toga was pure white and soft, made of especially fine material. Philippus and Atia could afford it. Slaves danced around Gaius Octavius as they plied the toga around him, making sure the pleats were perfect.

A large crowd gathered outside the house and followed the family to the Field of Mars where the sacrifice would be carried out and offerings made to the gods, and later to the people for feasting.

This brisk Septembris morning wore a fine coat of wispy clouds. The augers had sanctioned it an auspicious day, a good day; a flight of morning birds had declared it so. The procession of bobbing heads, clapping hands, and colorful togas snaked its way through the streets. They sang, beat small drums, and forced harsh notes from fluted instruments—more commotion than music. Some offered prayers and threw flower petals to soften the footfalls of the young man and his family.

The mass of joyous humanity finally reached its destination: the place where the sacrifice would be made and the conversion from boy to man would be official. The pageant poured from the city streets and fanned out onto the field. The festive noise settled down to a solemn hum of sober prayers. Octavius, the adolescent, proceeded to change out of his rich clothes and into something practical for the ensuing deed.

The air stilled, as did the crowd.

Gaius Octavius began a cautious but sure-footed march toward the sacrificial animal: a good-sized bull that appeared larger with each encroaching step. The adolescent—soon-to-be-man—could smell the beast before him. The animal's recently cleansed and brushed hide emitted a perfumed odor of clean straw; this, however, did not mask the scent of its raw power. The animal's conformation was as perfect as it could get: a straight spine from head to rump; a nice crest to the neck; perfect hipbones; and legs supporting its body in faultless alignment. The animal's shiny coat gave off a subtle radiance as its well-defined musculature shuddered with quick tremors under its skin.

A strong cage held a firm grip around the powerful animal's torso and its neck was yoked so it could not move freely.

A wide, white fibrous eye with its ebony center locked onto Octavius, watching the youth's every move as he approached. No fear flashed in the eye, just curiosity. It followed the young human as he intruded in the animal's safe space. The animal's nostrils flared and took in the scent of Octavius, that semi-acrid, sweaty odor of a young, nervous adolescent human. The beast stomped his right foreleg and jerked its head up and down as much as the yoke allowed, but to no avail; the youth kept coming. A powerful snort emanated from the beast and a long string of mucus reached for the floor.

Octavius, the adolescent, moved closer still, in calm, assertive steps. He would be master of the moment, not the beast. Now within arms-reach of the beautiful animal, he stopped, planted his feet, and readied himself. He postured a noble stance, head and chin up, breaths allowed in controlled, relaxed bellows, and eyes looking calm and regal—as if the world was his to command. He wanted to reach out and touch the stiff fibers of the animal's hide but disciplined his hand to stay at his side. Instead, he extended his nose and inhaled the beast's closeness.

The two stood there, beast and boy, waiting for the moment when they would become one. One of the priests slid in from behind and placed a sacred dagger into Octavius' right hand.

Time moved with the wispy clouds above, and no faster.

The beast became as calm as a bull loitering in a meadow and no longer struggled. It offered a few twitches of its ears to bat away the flies and that is all. His eyes returned forward, long-lashed eyelids blinking softly, resting at half-lid. The beast graciously awaited his predetermined fate but didn't know it.

Octavius stealthily reached over with his left hand to cloak the blade of his knife and raised the dagger to the level of the animal's neck that should be most lethal. Surprisingly for Octavius, his hands were calm and responsive to every command his brain issued.

The boy's heart galloped in place.

His lungs ceased their rhythmic breaths.

A spirit within his chest banged on the walls with clenched fists in an attempt to free itself.

The molecules in the air aligned themselves perfectly and time slowed.

Octavius' pupils dilated, his jaws clenched, his chest sucked in the animal-scented air, and then he lunged forward, thrusting the dagger into the side of the animal's neck. He used his left hand to support his right hand at the wrist and with a manly grunt, heaved with his body weight to push downward and finished the slitting of the throat.

The startled animal jumped and yawed. Its big eye flashed to Octavius with a look that displayed disbelief and betrayal. It kicked and jumped again within the confines of the cage that barely held together under the brute strength of the dying animal. A priest came to the aide of the animal and plunged a special knife into the bull's neck near the shoulders to severe the spinal cord. The beast collapsed but not before spraying Octavius with its warm blood. The cage bulged with the dead weight of the formerly beautiful animal.

The boy moved on to manhood.

The last image to fall upon the dying cells of the bull's retina was that of Octavius, the man, his face and chest sprayed in a crimson crescent. The fading image glared back with dagger in hand. The animal could no longer smell Octavius as nothing moved between its large flaring nostrils and its collapsing lungs. And the strange noises from the humans that had once roared faded as if sucked into a tunnel, ebbing to a faint drone. Octavius' image smudged to black. Warmth waned to cold. Silence took hold—dead silence—black, cold, nothingness silence.

After the sacrifice Octavius cleansed himself with water and perfumed oil. He re-donned his adult toga and marched off to the Forum to be formally presented and enrolled as a new patrician of Rome, as stipulated in his uncle's will.

Cicero gave a stirring speech referring to this "boy sent from heaven" and called upon the gods to guide Octavius in becoming an honorable and noble Roman citizen, and that he, Cicero him-self, as a friend of the family and humble servant of the Republic, would do all he could to guide and mentor the youth in the ways of a respectable "man" of Rome.

"People of Rome, I present to you—Gaius Julius Caesar Octavianus!"

The crowd erupted into an earth-shattering roar that echoed to the heavens and back. Hands were held high in praise. The sea of heads and extremities undulated like quick white-capped waves on a brisk windy day.

Somewhere within the crowd came a muted chant. It started off softly at first, barely audible in all the cheering. It grew louder with each repetition. It reached a crescendo. And then it took on a life of its own: *"Caesar!Caesar!Caesar!Caesar!Caesar!"*

Philippus and Atia were taken completely by surprise. They looked around. Their smiles slid from their faces and something akin to fear took hold as wide eyes locked onto the shouting masses. Unconsciously, they huddled together. Cicero regarded the raucous crowd with knowing-eyes and then slowly panned to Octavius. The scene caused Cicero to feel chilled.

Gaius Julius Caesar Octavianus stepped forward. His left arm appropriately covered with his new toga he raised his right hand to the air and acknowledged his new clientela.

The crowd crowed even louder.

From out in the adulating throng, near where the first murmurings of "Caesar" emanated, a small retinue made its way and emerged to greet the new patrician.

"Congratulations, Octavianus!" the leader of the small entourage managed to shout above the din of the noisy multitude.

"Caesar. You may call me . . . Caesar!" the still adolescent-voiced youth shouted back to the deeper-voiced man before him.

"Yes, well, congratulations . . . Caesar! I am Lucius Cornelius Balbus, and this is my associate Gaius Oppius!" he continued to shout, gesturing to the man next to him. "We were intimate friends and associates of your uncle Julius! You might say we handled some of his affairs! Our other friends here," pointing to three additional fellows nearby, "were also part of his loyal staff! We offer our most sincere congratulations, as well as our services, anytime, anywhere!" he shouted.

Octavius—now Octavianus—stepped down closer to the men

to be heard without shouting. "That is most kind of you. I will be away for a while . . . to Puteoli, actually, but I will return afterward. I should very much like to meet with you. You could tell me much about my uncle, and what he may have planned for me."

"As I said, we are at your service. Good day to you . . . Caesar, and may the gods have great plans for you." With that, the small following bowed slightly as if addressing royalty, pivoted, and slid back into the raucous crowd.

"Gaius! Gaius!"

Octavianus turned in the direction of the callers and called out, "Maecenas . . . Agrippa!" The three briefly embraced as young children, and then recovered quickly, cognizant of the new status of the former adolescent, now adult.

"It's time to put aside our childish ways; we're men now. But we can still enjoy ourselves, as men," the new Caesar said. Maecenas and Agrippa smiled and nodded in agreement. "I have much to do yet, the ceremony for entry into the college of pontiffs, but we'll get together later. We have a whole new future to plan."

The loud crowd started for the Temple of the Vestals. As they paraded through the streets, Gaius Octavianus—Caesar—spied what appeared to be seven giant vultures circling overhead near the temple. He turned to Maecenas, motioning with raised eyes in the direction of the birds. "You see that? The auspices are good. I know. And I'm not even a pontiff yet."

Maecenas observed the birds and whispered, "Yes. Things will get better."

At Mutina, the day had started with the rigors and duties of a Roman army preparing for a long siege. Siege equipment and towers were constructed, assembled, and moved into place, threatening the walled city. Scouting parties conducted sorties around the city looking for and taking note of potential weaknesses and points of opportunities. Other squads were busy with harvesting grain for food and foraging for livestock; a large army had to be well fed.

Sthenelus was part of a work detail cutting timber needed for the construction of some of the *ballistae*. And when not cutting wood, he cut stone for projectiles.

A loud "thwack" startled him as he chipped away at a stone that nestled between his knees, a stone he felt needed more roundness to it. The sudden noise jerked his head around. He turned in time to catch a glimpse of a medium-size stone, a 150-pounder, leaping skyward, looking like a small planet hurling away from earth in silence. The projectile continued to shrink in size as it sailed for the wall, diving for and impacting into the dirt short of its intended target with a mighty "thud." The catapulting machine danced about like a wild animal, a crazed mule. Its handlers jumped clear of the wild beast and danced in step with the wooden mule, trying to keep clear of its kick and waiting for it to settle down.

"Short!" called one of the handlers. It was just a test shot. Adjustments would have to be made in either the positioning of the machine or to the torsion springs.

Sthenelus regarded his stone for a long moment. After spending so much time and energy cutting and smoothing, was his stone to be flung at the wall only to fall to the dirt and lay lifeless with no effect? He decided not to put so much perfection into the next projectile; Instead, he chiseled his initials when nobody looked—a horrible looking S and an R.

One of the centurions approached the working party. At his sides were two massive dogs, *Molossers*—Mastiffs—giant Greek dogs, silent and well disciplined, like good Roman soldiers. The thick-boned monsters wore black faces to contrast with their very clean, light brown bodies. The dogs had sad-looking eyes about them; they were anything but sad. The canines looked up to the handler. With just a hard look of an eye and downward swatting motion of the hand they assumed a sitting position quietly at their master's feet.

"With results like that one, this is going to be a very long siege," the centurion scoffed. He issued another silent command with his hand to his guards to stay as he marched over to inspect the machine. "Hmmm, you need horse hair of better quality here. Did you get this off some old, dead mare? Reinforce it and try again. If you can't get it to work, I can find some other work for you. We need more trench work for *lavatrinas*. The flies are getting unbearable from the old ones, even for a Roman soldier." After his brief derision, the centurion commanded his guards with a wave of his baton to follow. They marched off to inspect another station.

"This is going to be a long siege," Sthenelus murmured.

CHAPTER
XXVI

The only way the evening could have been more perfect was for the gods themselves to be present for such a beautiful evening and auspicious occasion. It was the last day of the month of Septembris, the day before the Kalends of Octobris. The skies were painted with the richest colors the gods had to offer Pompey's guests. The deities were even kind enough to have those ghastly smells of the Esquiline Hill blown away from Pompey's house. Nobles, patricians, senators, aristocrats, all those of the same feather, arrived and gathered to honor the dictator on the occasion of his fifty-eighth birthday.

"Ave, good Pompeius Magnus, and salutations on a most happy and fortunate completion of these many years," toasted Gaius Cassius Longinus with a goblet of wine just handed him by one of Pompey's house servants.

All those around in turn raised goblets and toasted likewise, "*Felicem diem natalem!*"

"Thank you, good friends and guests. You honor me and my house today," Pompey replied. "Come, come, and make yourselves comfortable. Come recline and enjoy good company and good food." The gathering crowd migrated toward the back of the house to the larger *triclinium* just past the garden area; the regular dining room was too small for such a party.

Gaius Cassius Longinus, Lucius Cornelius Lentulus, Gaius Claudius Marcellus and his wife, the twenty-one year old Octavia Minor, reclined near Pompey and his lovely Cornelia. More guests arrived and vied for the best spots: reclining positions within line-of-sight of the dictator. If one could not be within earshot, one could at least be in a position to flash a smile and raise a goblet; one was not always a guest of the Dictator of Rome.

"You have a lovely home, Magnus. Well-decorated and with magnificent artwork on your walls," noted the wife of Lucius Aemilius Lepidus Paullus in a barely audible, mousy voice. Pompey and his wife both leaned forward to discover the source of the diminutive and timid voice.

It was true; the walls were painted blood-red and decorated with portraits of aristocratic couples, as well as game that one might find while hunting: deer, bear, and what appeared to be a giant cat.

Pompey ignored the diminutive-voiced wife and addressed her husband, "How is your brother Marcus these days, Paullus?"

"I can't say, Magnus. We do not exactly correspond on a regular basis." Most everyone around the tables knew that the brothers were like olive oil and water. "I'm aware that he is presently accompanying Ventidius up north, in Mutina, but I must confess that's all I know." He could not dissociate his blood ties, but he could at least let Pompey know where his loyalty rest, thus his attendance at the party.

"Ah, yes—Mutina. So much information comes from up that way, but very little of it reliable or useful. We all remember how much 'information' filtered into Rome when Julius Caesar came marching down out of Gaul; a lot of rumor and misinformation . . . all those 'thousands' of legionaries and cavalry that were marching upon Rome. I wouldn't have been surprised if that wise old fox didn't send much of it down himself. That's what I would have done," commented the dictator, once partner, once father-in-law, and then finally foe to Julius Caesar.

Pompey remembered Octavia's presence nearby. "I mean no disrespect for your great-uncle, Octavia," he said politely.

Octavia smiled warmly, nodded her head, and hopefully showed no offense taken. Those around Pompey and Octavia surely remembered that six years ago Octavia's uncle Julius tried to arrange a marriage between Pompey and her soon after the death of his wife Julia, Octavia's cousin; but to no avail—Pompey refused. His bond with Julia was solid and true, no matter that it was initially the cement of a political union. The would-be-arrangement with Octavia again would have been strictly political and a continuance of an alliance. This time, however, Pompey felt compelled to distance himself; fortunately, for Octavia, her marriage to Marcellus was safe—for the time being, anyway.

Cornelia gleamed affectionately at Octavia, their eyes meeting and smiles flashing with mutual warmth; Cornelia actually liked Octavia and wished her no ill fortune.

In the courtyard, conversations and mild chuckles rose from a respectable din to the occasional boisterous and raucous laughter from some of the guests as the evening aged and the amount of wine consumed increased. A zesty aroma of roasted lamb wafted over the crowd from meat skewered and cooked over open pits, turned and basted by chosen Greek slaves noted for their culinary skills and knowledge of herbs and spices. A thin veil of flavored smoke hovered above the guests outside and obscured the appearance of the first planets and stars that commenced taking assigned positions in the night sky. More and more stars appeared like invited guests where moments before there were none.

From one corner of the courtyard came an explosion of feminine laughter.

"Servilia, you can be so crude sometimes!" her half-sister, Porcia, said as she stifled her own laughter with the back of her hand.

"Oh, but it's so true. We women could be just as effective governing if we had to. You don't need that . . . that all-important appendage to be so wise and benevolent. They think they're all that much better for it. The good goddesses *Venus* and *Lucina* gave us something that all men yearn for, and we can get all those . . . those little appendages we want." Another burst of laughter erupted resulting in many heads turning in the boisterous women's direction. The guilty party quickly lowered their heads in an attempt to further muffle laughter and snorts, but they couldn't hide their blushes and wide grins.

"If our dear brother, Marcus Porcius, were here, I'm sure he'd really entertain us with some delicious commentaries on men and power," Porcia said to the small group.

"Good thing for Pompey he's not," Servilia quickly interjected.

"Good thing for his wine you mean," Porcia said as they ruptured into more laughter.

"I heard talk of a 'triumph' for the mighty dictator," Porcia said in a sober moment.

"No. There can be no triumph. Dyrrhachium was not a fight against a foreign army," Servilia said with some authority.

"Well, good then . . . I mean . . . the madness of it all . . . Roman against Roman . . . kin against kin, eagle against . . . eagle. What passions these men have . . . to what purpose? Slaves to their own . . . to their own self-interest . . . that's all." Tears started to well in Porcia's eyes.

"Be still and put that drink away," Servilia said tersely.

"I will not. Think of it . . . what Rome could have accomplished with both Caesar and Pompey . . . together." Porcia's slured.

"Or neither," Servilia said under her breath.

"What, dear sister?"

"Nothing, Porcia, nothing. I would keep my voice down if I were you."

"You think I care if he hears . . . me? Should I shudder if I hear his . . . boots? I think not! He may be dictator . . . 'kings of kings,' as my dear Domitius would say . . . Agamemnon himself . . . I will not fear him. Had I the chance . . . the weapon . . . the courage . . . that . . . that little appendage—"

At that, a burst of robust laughter exploded once more.

"Come, let's see how many of those little appendages we can get," Servilia said, inciting a continued round of laughter by the women.

Pompey and Cassius took note of the laughter floating in from the courtyard.

"Porcia and Servilia," Cassius said flatly.

"Hmm—poor women. To tell you the truth, I'm surprised they're here," Pompey said, taking a good gulp of wine.

"Surely, Servilia has let those twenty-nine or so years pass without malice since you had her husband, Marcus Junius, killed. And as for Julius, well, what could she say—she was his mistress, not his wife. And Porcia's husband, Domitius, well, he died an honorable death at Pharsalus."

"Cassius, I dare say that a woman may feign to forgive, but never will she forget. Never second guess that opposite gender. If we could only imbue the courage, spirit, determination, and resolve of our women into our troops, our armies would be a mighty, invincible force for anyone to deal with," Pompey said after another generous gulp of wine.

"My good General, I mean, Dictator—"

"Gnaeus."

"Well, yes—Gnaeus . . . I think that wine is starting to get to you," chided Cassius.

"No, no, it's true."

"If I may have your ear—Gnaeus, I've heard of rumblings, talk, nothing serious of course, nonetheless, I think . . . I think you should increase your bodyguards," Cassius said in a guarded whisper.

Pompey, eyes heavy with drink and a small belch rocking his head slightly, looked askance at Cassius and slurred, "More body-guards? I think not. I have no need of more bodyguards."

"It's just . . . well, some of us fear for your life. With Crassus and Caesar gone, some say the Republic is closer to being . . . the way it was, just one less . . . one less—"

"Tyrant?"

"Those are not my words, General."

"Gnaeus."

"Yes . . . Gnaeus."

"I'm not afraid of death, my good Cassius. We must all face death at some time. No, I think no more bodyguards. I would rather sustain twenty . . . no . . . twenty-three wounds . . . and one good death first . . . before more bodyguards."

"Why twenty-three, when only one would do?" Cassius asked, puzzled at the number.

"Surely, a man of my stature should have at least twenty-three—friends—don't you agree?" Pompey said and fixed his friend Cassius with a drunken eye.

———

Further south, at Puteoli—

"So you see, Octavius, our good forefathers knew how important it was to institute all those checks and balances into our constitution, for the good of the people, for the good of Rome," Cicero said as he finished his discussion.

"And for the good of the Senate," Octavius threw in.

"Well, yes, that too."

Silence entwined with ghostly vapors as the two sat in the bath of warm water fed from the natural hot springs that made Puteoli popular. Their vantage point offered a view of the bay off in the distance, but just barely; the evening seemed unusually steamy.

"Father, was my uncle really such a threat to the Republic as many have said?"

"Father?"

"Yes, I mean . . . you are *Pater Patria*—Father of Our Country, are you not?"

"Well . . . it is true I was confirmed by decree by the good people of Rome, but—"

"Well then, I should like to call you—father," Octavius insisted.

Cicero studied this young man before him. Something in this youth, albeit now a man, warranted watching. Another something brought back an old memory to the old man, an incident from many years ago. He recalled a day returning to his house in Arpinum after a long contemplating walk from the nearby river when he came across a docile-looking dog that stood in the middle of the dirt path. The dog wore an enchanting smile on its face and at the other end its tail wagged in a warm greeting. It even cocked its head in a most charming pose and flashed beguiling eyes to put Cicero at ease. Cicero, the boy, approached the dog with an offer of a kind hand. When he bent to pet the dog, the animal lunged at his arm and tore at his sleeve until it ripped off. Cicero managed to pull away with his arm intact but his ego mauled. He picked up a stick to protect himself from another attack, but the dog just smiled at him, cocked his head again, turned, and ran off.

The old man broke from his musing and stared at the youth, who also seemed to be somewhere else, his eyes fixed past the bath water.

"Do you know why they gave me that title, Octavius?"

"Huh? I'm sorry—what?"

"Pater Patria, Father of Our Country. Do you know why?"

"Ah . . . you saved the Republic from those who wished to revolt against it . . . that 'Catilina incident.' "

"Yes, Lucius Sergius Catilina, a rich man. A man rich in debt, a man rich in greed, a man rich in zest for power and wealth, a man who would employ any audacious deed to acquire anything to quench his avaricious appetite—a dangerous man."

Echoes from the past crept their way into his thoughts as he slipped back into the Senate House, moving speeches filled with passion—*How long will you abuse our patience? How long is that madness of yours still to mock us? Quousque . . . quam diu etiam . . . how long . . . how long?* Cicero sat there in the warm water, his blood boiling, not from the heat of the water, but from reliving the past on the Senate floor, condemning a man to death.

"My uncle . . . I mean, my adopted father Julius was there, wasn't he?" asked the young Caesar, bringing Cicero back to the present.

"Yes, yes he was there. He argued for the lesser course of action, banishment to some settlement, exile from Rome. I, on the other hand, called for the ultimate course—death."

The sound of dripping water permeated the steamy air as the old man sponged himself, a flat gaze staring into the past affixed to his tired face, his mind consumed with thoughts and memories again. He broke free once more from his spell and looked up at Octavius. A chill grabbed hold of his old, wrinkling body and gave him goose flesh when he looked into the boy's face. The boy had put on a warm smile and cocked his head in a friendly gesture. His eyes bore into Cicero.

—∞—

At the villa in Tusculum—

A young owl perched herself on a tree branch searching for movement. Any small, unfortunate rodent or creature she could feed her young ones would do.

Rustling and movement caught her attention and her head spun around half-circle: down below, a young woman creature moved stealthily to a thick-wooded area near the villa where a young man creature waited to greet her with open arms.

The owl corkscrewed her head awkwardly for a better view, bobbing and twisting, adjusting her night vision in the star-lit night. The two human creatures embraced passionately and then vanished into the darkness of the wooded canopy. Another distinct sound of rustling on the ground floor caught her full attention. This sound was more rewarding. The owl swooped down on silent wings and pounced on the unsuspecting mouse, holding the rodent firm in her talons. Her flat face and large eyes panned all around and her talons squeezed tight. When she felt safe, she took to the air and headed for her young ones, a ball of fur and a tail suspended under her.

The night was good.

CHAPTER XXVII

Nearly a month had passed. Gone were the hot and humid days of summer.

Lucius' battle on the wall neared completion. His army no longer consisted of dark stick figures crudely drawn on plaster but of men and horses with angry faces and substance to them. Soldiers pushed and clashed. Some lay on the ground with mortal wounds. Others were dismembered. Cavalry on horseback charged. Legionaries of one Roman army fought legionaries of another Roman army.

One figure on horseback at the far right resembled the once mighty Julius Caesar. In the air, in mid-flight, a solitary javelin coursed through the air in the direction of the general. The battle scene was wide, detailed, and busy. One could almost overlook the javelin in the heavens.

Lucius revealed his story in vivid colors, action, and horrific reality. The reflected light and shadows cast were correct and true in every aspect. His mother would be proud of his marvelous artwork: his fidelity to technique, his attention to detail, and keen sense of the artistic eye. His father would have hatched a crooked smile. Their son truly had a special gift.

Fresh brush strokes streaked across an adjacent wall just off to the side of the main mural; another project. The anatomic shape or shadow suggested a portrait. Bright highlights were in the process of being plied. The young artisan spent his days working on both projects, except for the evenings—those were reserved for other passions.

At the gates of the villa, a rider disembarked with a message— Cicero was returning, the visit at Puteoli complete. The excited household scampered about to make ready for the master. Fresh bread needed baking, the finest wine needed to be on hand, and the freshest vegetables harvested, including his favorite—cabbage.

Cicero and his fellow travelers had made their way from Puteoli to one of his favorite houses at the seaside resort of Formiae. The picturesque domus had been a favorite place to rest, relax, and conduct business. On occasion, during tenuous times, it had been a 'safe house.' From there, he made his way by sea to the port of Ostia, and then from the port to Rome, where young Octavianus joined his family.

The coaches made the final few miles to Tusculum under a blanket of puffed clouds that raced with the horses. The teams of horses pulled the coaches through hills alive with undulating waves of grass as the wind skimmed atop the sea of brown and gold. The stalks rolled along the landmass like ocean waves marching on to break upon a shore. The coaches sailed along with the waves, carrying the tired passengers closer to home, family, and friends.

The horses made the turn into the villa entrance, dragging more than pulling the coaches behind them. The passengers extended excited arms through open windows of the dusty coaches, hailing the waiting staff; home at last, and again.

Customary smiles, adulations, flowers, and cool water greeted the master as he disembarked from his spent coach. Tiro appeared his usual pious self. Caius looked reserved and quiet, mostly tired. Terentia was unsettled and tense. The rest of the traveling entourage greeted the waiting staff with smiles and hugs of their own.

"Master Cicero, you must be tired, come, rest. A bite to eat and some good wine," Felix offered as he assisted the venerated master away from the coach.

"Felix, as always, it's so good to see you. All these many miles and these last few steps have carried me home to you and Pulvilla. I can't think of any better end to such a long journey," Cicero said in a tired voice as he wrapped his arms across Felix's shoulder and let himself be led into the house with the rest of the tired voyagers.

The air turned cold and raindrops pelted everybody, encouraging them all to rush the doorway. The aroma of fresh baked bread, fragrant cheese, and crackling firewood greeted everyone upon entering the house. Clean clothing and a shawl warmed from the hearth made their way to the master, as well as a nice pair of warm slippers; every effort was made to make him comfortable after his long journey.

Tiro waddled over to the master, hands cupped together in prayer. "Is there anything I can do or get for you, Dominus; anything at all? It would be no effort, not at all."

"No, Tiro. All is well. I'm very comfortable . . . just a little tired," Cicero replied, looking more than just a little weary. Puffed pouches buoyed his blood-shot eyes and wrinkled lids heavy with fatigue tried to draw close. A battle to keep awake raged and weariness had the upper hand. "I just need to rest my eyes for a moment or two."

Felix approached the master and provided a fresh cup of wine as if offering a gift to a revered deity.

"Ah, thank you my dear Felix." He took a sip. It felt warm as it trickled down his throat and plunged into his stomach. Felix was rewarded with a warm smile as the elderly statesman let his body melt into the chair that he had fallen into.

"And Tullia? Is she not here?" inquired the tired master.

"No, Dominus. Dolabella has taken her into the city. He said he would return her later this week," Felix said with a deflecting glance. Cicero did his animated best to maintain the smile brought on by the wine offering and the affection from his beloved staff.

A graveyard silence took hold the room. A nearby brazier fed warmth to the sleepy Cicero and painted part of the room in gold while keeping at bay the darkness and cold of the rest of the room. A surprised pop from an ember in the brazier broke the silence and brought the room back to life.

Out of the dimness of one of the doorways a silhouette limped in. The figure brought in scents of fresh paint. "Ave, good Consul. Welcome back. It's good to see you home safe," Lucius said as he wiped his hands with a cloth of many colorful splotches.

"Lucius, thank you my son. It appears you have been very busy. Working into the late hours are you?"

"Just doing some touching-up."

"I would like to see your work," the old man said. He rocked forward several times and labored out of his comfortable chair. Felix scurried to his assistance.

"Sire, please, rest. You can see later. Tomorrow would be better," Lucius said, almost pleading.

"Nonsense, anything worthy is worth seeing now," insisted the old man as he ambled in the direction of the new room with the freshly painted walls. "Felix, bring an oil lamp, the brightest one you can find."

The walls of the passageway floated by in the guiding light of the outstretched lanterns as out-of-step sandals echoed within the corridor as the small entourage shuffled along. They entered the room together as a group, stopping just past the threshold. Cicero looked about, squinting, trying desperately to accommodate his poor vision, holding his lantern out in front of him.

Along the wide wall he could just make out different colors and patterns, but they made no sense to him. Lucius gathered all the oil lanterns in the room and made a large semi-circle of them on the floor before the mural.

At last, Cicero could make out the images before him. They were still fuzzy, but he could see them. He looked left, right, up, and down. And then he stepped back one pace to get a better prospective.

"Magnificent, young man—magnificent," he said in wonder. His head floated on his shoulders as he took in all the action; he missed the javelin spinning in mid-air.

They were about to move away and return to the main house when something caught the old man's eye, off to the side, a shape, a silhouette. He moved slowly over to where the figure loomed. He brought his lantern up to the wall where a goddess-like figure revealed her face to him. She stared back at him with the loveliest eyes one could ever lock unto. Her half-turned profile and mysterious leer, as she peeked over her shoulder, were heightened with a gentle, beguiling smile that begged the question: *what secret is it that she's hiding?*

Cicero recognized her: Tullia; but not Dolabella's Tullia. A child's sparkle gleamed in her eyes. There was warmth, there was happiness, there was . . . love. It was Tullia alright; but a different Tullia. She smiled not for her husband or her mother or her father. She smiled for—someone else.

He gazed at her for the longest time, and then turned to Lucius. The expression on the old man's tired face bordered on confusion. His eyes interrogated the young artist's eyes, searching, asking, seeking an explanation. Lucius' eyes fended off each inquiry with an evasive glance.

"It was to be a surprise," Lucius said.

Cicero returned his gaze back to the image. "This is truly amazing. You seem to have captured her so . . . so surprisingly well. Yes, it is a surprise, a pleasant surprise, but Lucius—"

"I hope you are not offended—I mean with me using this wall as well. I should have asked permission first," Lucius said, blushing with embarrassment. "I'm sorry."

"Are you sure you were just a soldier? I mean . . . you have a gift. A gift from the gods themselves," Cicero said—a different question than what he had on his mind.

"I like to think the gift came from my mother," the young soldier-cripple-scribe-artisan replied.

"Then, your mother must be a goddess in disguise."

"Yes, Sir. She is to me."

—

The spent travelers slept well that night; like corpses in a grave-yard. The sun had been up not more than two hours when Dolabella and his wife crashed through the doorway. Tullia tramped into the domus donning a frown and charged her way to her quarters. Pulvilla scrambled after her to see to her needs. Dolabella marched in and assumed a military stance as he munched on an apple.

"Felix! Felix! Some wine, Felix!" the young aristocrat shouted.

Tiro walked past with deliberate indifference, not even a glance.

"Where is everyone?" Dolabella demanded to know.

"Everyone is in the new addition, admiring the 'wall,'" Tiro said without losing stride and on his way to join the others.

"Wall? What wall?"

"In the new addition . . . Lucius' wall," trailed the reply from Tiro as he continued on his way to the exhibit.

"Lucius?"

Dolabella started slowly after Tiro, his curiosity getting the best of him. He stalked the secretary to the new room where a small crowd loitered, admiring the painted walls. He walked over to the large mural and examined the scene.

He was impressed.

It wasn't the quality of the artwork that awed him, but rather the battle scene itself: its horrors, the weapons, the soldiers—the killing, all of it so, so exciting.

Yes, he was very impressed.

He could envision a scene like this on one of his own walls—with him fearlessly leading the legions himself. Even the nice little touch of placing a single javelin in the air seemed proper. He would have put more in the air—many more; a black-cloud-full more.

Dolabella mauled his apple with clenched teeth as he strolled over to the adjoining wall, the smaller one. The few people nearby parted, scampering off as if they suddenly had important unfinished business to tend. He planted himself in front of the portrait.

The apple core dropped from his hand, his face turned to ashen stone, and then seconds later to a blushed red.

"Who is this . . . Lucius?" he murmured.

Soft sandals announced the presence of another critic.

"What do you think of Papa's new room?" she asked as she planted herself next to her husband.

She looked to the portrait and her jaw fell. "Is that me?" she asked no one in particular. She felt awed, flattered, embarrassed, and—frightened; but not for herself.

"It seems you know this Lucius . . . well," Dolabella said, more to the portrait than to the mortal standing next to him.

Tullia lacked for words. She dared not utter a single one, just to be safe.

Tiro waddled over to the pair and gazed upon the "goddess" on the wall, not for the first time.

"He's very good, it seems, at what he does," Tiro said.

"And just what is it . . . that he does?" Dolabella asked the wall.

"Scribe, paint . . . everything," Tiro replied; he, too, addressed the wall.

Dolabella swiveled his head to Tiro with eyes that wanted to know more.

"Everything," Tiro said again, cocking his head to the side for a different assessment of the portrait.

CHAPTER
XXVIII

"Dominus sure wanted us out of the villa in a hurry. Do you think I upset him with the mural? I thought for sure he would like the work," a dejected Lucius complained.

"I'm sure he likes the art, Lucius. It's good. Perhaps maybe too good!" Caius replied.

"What do you mean?"

"Tullia!"

"Tullia? You don't think it looks like her?"

"Lucius, the art work is good. How you see her and put her on the wall for the world to see is much different than how the rest of us see her. Who knows what Dolabella thinks?

Lucius went quiet with thoughts. Caius joined him in the quietude.

"Well, at least we don't have to walk; though I think I prefer walking over horseback. I'm not sure which is worse, the sore ankle or the sore butt."

"We'll find out by the time we get to Rome," Caius answered as he shifted about on the back of his animal, looking for comfort.

"Are these documents all that important that we need to get them to Octavius today?"

"They must be or we wouldn't be on the road right now. Master Cicero is very much concerned that that boy. . . I mean, Caesar, gets as much material as he can handle to help him on his way up that cursed cursus honorum," Caius said as he continued to shift about in his saddle.

"I have a feeling in the pit of my stomach that . . . that 'boy' will make it to the top without the master's help," Lucius said.

"He's just a boy, younger than us, Lucius. It'll take years and a lot of luck, more luck than his uncle had, that's for sure," Caius said with much confidence.

Lucius looked over to his friend with a look that wished that to be true. For now, they just needed to complete the task of delivering the documents, and then proceed to Cicero's Rome house to await further instructions as ordered.

The two riders headed for Rome huddled in their thick cloaks, hiding their heads from a cold, brisk wind that found them out on the open road. The landscape had changed: no longer green and lush as before. The evening hours changed, too: shorter, gloomier, and colder. Tree limbs resembled outstretched arms and hands with knobby, arthritic fingers reaching out to grasp any innocent victim that chanced to come along.

"Shouldn't be much longer now, Caius. I think I can see the walls up the road through the gray haze."

"I hope so. My fingers are numb and slow to move. It feels colder than usual."

"Do you remember how to get to the master's Palatine house from the Philippus house?"

"Yes."

"That's good."

"Well, at least I think I do," Caius said catching Lucius' eyes dead on.

They reached the walled city, passed through one of the main gates, and made for the domus of Lucius Marcius Philippus. The city streets were barren and cold, as if a funeral procession had just passed through. The gray frigidness added volume and echo to the horses' clopping hooves on the cobbled streets. They traveled through a maze of angled streets until they came upon a house that looked familiar to Caius.

"I think this is the place," Caius said, more certain than not.

"I hope you're right, my little friend. It isn't getting any warmer or any lighter out."

"Yes, I'm sure. This is the place. You'll see."

Caius banged on the large door and waited for a response. It did not take long for one to come. A household slave creaked the door open and showed his eyes.

"Caius Terentius with some important documents for Gaius Octavianus from Consular Cicero," the young scribe announced without missing a beat.

The doorman eyeballed the young man with a satchel at his side, filled with what appeared to be documents, scrolls of assorted densities.

"Wait here, please," said the doorman as he allowed Caius entry into the atrium. At least the doorman was kind enough to let him wait on the warmer side of the cold. Lucius was left standing out in the thick of it with the horses, all of them—horses and man—shuffling their feet on the frigid ground.

"You have something for me?" a question from one of two approaching youths.

"Documents for Gaius Octavianus," repeated Caius.

"Those are for me, then." The fairer of the two came forward and took the scrolls from the young scribe. He opened each document and briefly read the beginnings, his face displaying disinterest and boredom. "Is that it? Is there nothing more?"

Caius shook his head and looked to the pouch to see if he had missed something; there was no more.

Gaius Octavianus Caesar inhaled deeply the surrounding air and let it out nasally, a hint of a frosty mist floated toward Caius like a veiled, evil spirit. "On the Republic," Octavius said to his close companion, Maecenas, who stood next to him with documents of his own under his arm. "Tell the good consular that I offer my sincerest thanks and will put these documents to good use," the grateful youth said—the brazier could use more fuel this cold day.

Caius said nothing, offering just a nod and half a smile. The dark-haired youth accompanying Octavianus departed his friend's side, brushing against Caius as he exited through the doorway.

Lucius wondered how long he would need to keep the horses company out in the frigid cold when the door to the house opened. Maecenas exited and walked past him without as much as a nod, but he did flash a smile to the horse. Caius soon appeared, trailing Octavianus' friend.

"That's it, then?" Lucius asked.

"Notice how these cold days bring out the warmth in people?" Caius quipped. "It's as warm out here as it is in there," he said, gesturing to the doorway with a tilt of his head.

"If it's all the same to you, I'd like to head for the master's house now, if you don't mind. Perhaps it will be warmer there," Lucius said, as he thrust himself up onto his horse. The horse objected briefly with short side steps and jerky motions of its head. Caius, likewise, mounted his horse, which complained less.

Caius noted several documents strewn on the ground just as they started for Cicero's Rome house. They looked very much like the documents Octavianus' friend carried under his arm. He jerked his horse to a stop, dismounted, and retrieved the scrolls. He examined one of the discarded scrolls quickly and then cast a puzzled expression to Lucius. He rolled it back up and placed it and the other in his empty pouch.

"Something obviously troubles you."

Caius looked to his friend but offered no reply. "Let's go, Lucius, it's getting colder and darker by the minute."

Without further discussion, they headed for the master's domus.

Mutina was just as cold, if not colder—and wet.

"Hector! Ave, Hector! Are you in there? Come out and meet Achilles! Don't be afraid!" yelled Sthenelus, one of three scouts hiding behind a large boulder that broke through the ground forty yards from the city wall. The other two scouts thought the cold must have gotten to Sthen's brain to make him act so brave—or insane.

"Your mother was a sow and you don't know your father!" echoed a distant and faint reply from the topside of the wall. Laughter erupted from both sides—the wall and down below behind the boulder.

The encroaching darkness and cold air made the mud much more miserable. The muck sucked the warmth from the three scouts' legs faster than they could generate it by rubbing their arms with frozen hands.

"Who in Hades is 'Hector'?" asked a soldier shivering next to Sthenelus.

"Hector! You know—Hector and Achilles—Helen and Paris—Agamemnon and Menelaus—the siege of Troy. Don't you know this story?" Sthenelus asked in disbelief.

"Eh, yeah . . . sure I know it. I know it well," the soldier lied. Sthenelus looked with disgust knowing full well the legionary knew nothing of Hector, Achilles, or Troy.

"Maybe we can build a large horse and sneak into the city," said the third legionary.

"That would have to be a very big horse, my friend," Sthenelus said with rolling eyes and a shake of his head. The confused soldier, not knowing of Hector and the others, looked to Sthenelus and the other soldier, not knowing why they would need a horse.

"Ave, Achilles!" a shout rang out from up behind the parapet, from a silhouette in one of the crenellations, calling out to the Romans below. "Do you know of Beatus from Antium? Tell him his brother, Corvinus, says to take care. Tell him is his mother is well!"

The three scouts had gathered as much information as they were going to get about the partial breach in the wall in front of them, and besides, the mud got thicker and harder to move around in. As it was, they were now with bare feet; their boots had been sucked off and were lost in the thick sludge, leaving cold and cramping feet.

"Maybe we could just ask them to give themselves up," Sthenelus said with all seriousness, at which the three laughed after a few seconds. The laughter broke up when they heard the familiar humming of incoming arrows. It sounded like a breeze at first, a soft wind, increasing in intensity to a calamity of a swarm of bees. The three soldiers ducked behind the rock.

The arrows pelted the rock in a wild clamor, splintering and bouncing in all directions, except those that struck the mud.

"No, I don't think they plan to give themselves up to us," Sthenelus said. "I think now is a good time to head back to camp and give our report. We can't wait for it to get darker, it's too cold. If the gods permit, one of us might make it back alive."

The three made a run for it, traveling at the speed of a wounded turtle as the mud grabbed their feet; it was like running in a dream—a nightmare. They found some good hard ground and made better traction, but not before another volley of arrows found them. The gods found reason to have pity on them and spared two of the three; Sthenelus and the other believer of Troy made it back to their camp.

Lucius and Caius found the master's domus in Rome before the city and the skies turned completely black. A few daring torches had continued to flicker along some of the city streets to offer guidance, all the while cold, blustery winds whipped around and found their way through the city like long icy fingers, extinguishing the weaker ones.

They pounded on the large wooden and bronze doors until somebody answered. The slave opened the door cautiously. No one should be knocking at the door at this hour.

"It's Caius, scribe for Dominus Cicero!"

The slave recognized the voice but not the face—it was too dark. He thrust a torch in the direction of the caller's face. The dancing flames made Caius' features appear as some theater mask used in Greek plays.

"Master Cicero has sent us on a mission. We are to wait here for further instructions," Caius said with some impatience.

The slave thrust the torch in the direction of Lucius.

"He's Lucius Pontius. He also works for the master. Let us in, it's getting colder by the minute!" Caius demanded.

"The horses!" yelled the slave, as if yelling would protect him from harm. "You can't bring in the horses!"

"Well, then, would you like to take them to some stable, at this time of night, in these streets, in the dark?"

The fear in the slave's face said no. Anyone with a sober brain knew it was dangerous to be in the streets this late, unless they were in large groups, and with protection.

"We could let them stay in the courtyard until morning and then move them to some stables when it's light and safer. Wouldn't you agree?" Caius suggested. "We wouldn't want anything to happen to the master's horses—would we?"

The slave shook his head, more a shudder than a shake. The horses were valued property, more so than the slave himself.

Lucius and Caius led the horses in through the large doors, into the atrium, around the *impluvium*—the reflecting pool that collected rainwater and reflected light during the day. Horse hooves echoed throughout the atrium as they clopped upon the master's black and yellow squared mosaic floor on the way to the courtyard. The slave kept looking behind to see if any of the animals damaged the floor, or left waste to be picked up.

Two more servants arrived, one appearing to be in charge—it was the way he carried himself.

"Caius. It's good to see you again. You may not remember me; I'm Elius, nomenclator for the master here in the city."

"Yes. I remember you. I apologize for such a late calling, but the master has sent us, Lucius and me, on an urgent and important mission, and we are to wait here for further instructions. We've just come from the domus of Senator Philippus on a mission to deliver documents to Gaius Octavianus."

"I see . . . Octavianus . . . the new Caesar," Elius said with the much practiced smile that Tiro liked to use. "Well, then, come make yourself warm.

"Darius, go . . . go get some bread and honey for our guests . . . and some wine." The diminutive slave scampered away without a word, just the slapping sound of his slippers to keep him company.

"Come, I'll show you to your room."

"Sorry about the horses, but we had no choice. It got late and dark."

"Of course; the horses are important. We'll see to them in the morning." Elius led the cold and tired scribes to a room just off the courtyard. The room was small, but comfortable; more importantly, it had a brazier to keep them warm.

Darius arrived with some crusty bread, a small bowl of honey, and a clay jar of wine. He departed as quickly as he came. Elius wished the two guests a good and warm night and ventured off—but not very far.

Lucius sat near the brazier and savored the small but tasty meal. It was the best he had had all day—it was the only meal he had all day. Caius nested next to an oil lamp. From his satchel he retrieved the scrolls he had found earlier on the street and then began to examine the text again. He dipped his slice of bread into the honey and fixed his eyes on the documents, looking from one scroll to the next, and then back again.

"Is it important?" mumbled Lucius with a full mouth.

Caius ignored him and continued to examine the documents with a hard scowl on his face.

"Well?"

"They look like drafts of a . . . a will—Caesar's will."

"What do you mean?"

"Caesar's will, but with changes. Some of the wording is marked through and changed. They're drafts."

"Well, how would Octavianus, or his friend, get copies of such drafts?" asked Lucius. "Unless they're—"

Caius cocked an eye to his friend for the answer, a different answer than the one they were both thinking.

"Caius, let it go, at least until morning. I don't know about you, but I'm really tired and my head and my bones could use a little rest."

Elius inched away from the doorway where his ear had been leaning.

Caius smothered the flame of the oil lamp and invited the night and dreams into the room.

The shifting of hooves and nervous snorts from the horses covered Elius' retreat from the courtyard.

CHAPTER
XXIX

A nervous Maecenas paced about the room like a caged animal. "Are you sure they're not here?" he asked Octavius for the third time. "I had them the other evening before I left. I know I did! At least, I thought I did. They must be here!" He rummaged through Octavius' things in a near panic again for a second time.

"You must be mistaken, Maecenas," a less worried Agrippa said as he examined the contents of Maecenas's document pouch.

"When did you see them last?" Octavius asked.

"I'm sure I had them to take back with me the other night when . . . when that scribe came knocking . . .with those scrolls for you from Cicero."

"Well, there you are. They must have been with those scrolls, the ones I tossed in the brazier," a confident Octavius said. "They've been taken care of nicely, and we have nothing to worry about, Maecenas. Relax."

The nervous youth, his chest heaving, looked to Octavius, the alpha leader, for reassurance.

"Maecenas, Octavianus is right. All is taken care of. Relax," echoed Agrippa. "Have some wine. Read some of your poetry or something."

The dark-haired adolescent closed his eyes and brought his breathing and anxiety attack under control.

The waning tension in the room amplified again when the nomenclator announced a visitor, somebody to see . . . Caesar.

Lucius Cornelius Balbus marched in with sure-footed steps and a congenial smile visible within his thick dark beard.

"Greetings, Caesar." He looked to the other two youths nearby. "And to you, Maecenas, Agrippa," he said in his Iberian accent, nodding slightly to each. It unnerved Octavius' friends that Balbus would know them by name. "I hope I didn't disrupt anything important," the Iberian said. He regarded the three young men keenly as if he had caught three deer in a clearing by surprise.

"No, not at all, Octavius answered. "How may I be of service to you?"

"Oh, but it is *I* who may be of service to you," a jolly Balbus said with an all-knowing smile. "Are we alone . . . I mean . . . your stepfather, mother?" he asked as he surveyed the immediate area.

Octavius looked askance to his friends. "Except for the slaves and my good friends, yes, we're alone."

"You never know when the walls might have ears," Balbus said looking around again. Octavius walked to the hallway and checked for listening loitering souls. He found none.

Balbus paced about the room, measuring its dimensions it seemed, taking in its contents, evaluating inventory. Three fixed sets of young eyes followed him; one set confident and secure; one set beady and suspicious; and the other—on guard and ready.

"When we first met, if you recall, it was on the occasion of your togas virilis." He waited for some acknowledgement before continuing. It came in the way of a nod from Octavius. "You may also recall that I said I was part of your great-uncle's staff. With all great humility, I would say that we—his staff—were quite good at what we did. We had excellent . . . resources for knowing important matters . . . a situational awareness if you will, for all that was necessary to know. We had—'sources'—for everything and anything we needed. Most countrymen thought the gods gifted our dear Caesar with an abundance of luck. Granted, he certainly had his share, and more. But it was his sources that made things work efficiently." Balbus stopped, turned, and faced the three young men, pausing for effect.

"Some of those . . . sources are still in place. It is through one of those . . . sources that I bring some information for you. It may be nothing, really. But what is nothing to me may be very important to you. You will soon learn, if you haven't already, that information is *everything*. Sometimes more valued than gold itself."

The three remained riveted, motionless, and expressionless.

Balbus continued. "It has been brought to my attention that there has been found . . . what was it? . . . oh, yes . . . some documents that appear to be . . . drafts of a will."

Maecenas broke from the pack and paced again in tight circles. Pallor washed over his acne-plagued face. He had to sit, or fall if he didn't. Agrippa displayed neither fear nor apprehension, only a casual glance to Octavius for a sign of action, or inaction. Octavius, his face chiseled in marble, except for a minor twitch at the corner of his mouth, looked over to and zeroed in on Maecenas. And Balbus took in all three. He measured the effects of his words on the three rapidly aging youths.

"These . . . 'drafts,' you have them in your possession?" asked Octavius, his mouth and throat dry like old bread.

"No, not yet; but I can get them easily enough," Balbus answered, flashing a disarming smile.

"And . . . are you seeking an interested buyer?" Octavius came right to the point.

"By the gods, no!" he thundered in his ebullient laughter. "As I said before, I am at your service, Caesar. They are yours for the asking."

Maecenas jumped to his feet. "Perhaps, we may see them . . . to study them . . . for authenticity. They may be forgeries! Yes, we must protect our dear friend from . . . from unscrupulous people, people wishing to do harm to our dear . . . 'son of Caesar.'"

Balbus' eyes trained on Maecenas like the tip of an arrow aimed at prey, drawn taut and ready to fly. A smile grew in Balbus' broad beard and transitioned to a smirk—he had measured this one well. He turned to Octavius and said, "I will have them brought to you in short order, a gift from a friend to a friend, and as I said before, I am at your service—anytime."

"Lucius Cornelius, I mean no disrespect, but . . . why—"

"Why bring this information to you and not someone else who would know what to do with this . . . piece of wealth?" Balbus shifted his weight and assumed a relaxed stance. With pursed lips and knitted brows, he offered a mask of contemplation—the facial expressions seemed to help formulate his words. "Your uncle, your name-sake, Julius Caesar, had a special place for you in his heart. Ever since you gave that eulogy for your grandmother, he knew, the gods knew, you were to be his heir and continue his dream for Rome, the Romans, and the world. No one else could have expressed the love and devotion he had for his sister, but you did, and you did it eloquently. He knew from that day onward that you would be the one." He adjusted his stance and continued.

"We mortals think we can change the course of history with violent acts, devious mischief, or simple misdeeds—including changing legal documents and such," he said as he shot a keen glance at Maecenas. "But the gods have it all planned, you see. It is in the nature of their way. If a mighty river wants to reach the sea, it will do so by whatever means nature—and the gods—allow. It may take the natural course provided. It may take the path of least resistance and go around obstacles. Or, it may make its own path, swallowing any obstacle in its way. In any case, that river will reach the sea. What is to be—will be. The gods have already decided. We mortals are just unsuspecting implements in their true designs. For you, the gods have provided information for you to act on, or not. As I have said and truly believe, the gods have already decided."

"And what of the . . . 'source' of this information, the one who has knowledge of these documents?" Agrippa asked in almost a whisper, stepping forward to be heard. "Can he be trusted?"

"Perhaps not. But, I have other sources for that, too," Balbus said with a wilt of his head and kind smile nesting in his beard.

"The fewer people who know, the better," Agrippa said with some implied authority.

Balbus, Agrippa, and Maecenas turned awaiting eyes toward Octavius.

Octavius' eyes met Balbus' squarely. When quivering at the corner of Octavius' mouth ceased, he gave a barely perceptible nod to the Iberian.

The large bearded man acknowledged the nod, pivoted sharply and marched briskly to the door; a man on a mission.

"Lucius Cornelius," Octavius cried out.

The burly man stopped, turned, and waited for a comment, or question; neither came. Octavius couldn't bring himself to say it. Balbus, for his part, understood what was not said and just smiled, continuing on his way.

Balbus headed for the Forum to conduct further business.

Not long after leaving the door of the Philippus domus, he met with some associates occasionally used in times of need. They materialized out of nowhere, out of the very walls, falling in step behind the Iberian, a miniature army joining him on his brisk walk.

"A fine warm and sunny day to you gentlemen," Balbus said as he continued his brisk march. He did not lay eyes on them, but did acknowledge their presence with one of his smiles. The associates returned his salutation with nods and smiles of their own. "Much more pleasant than the other day, wouldn't you agree? Yes, so much warmer today," he added. He looked skywards, shielding his eyes with his hand for confirmation.

"I may have some work for you, gentlemen."

"It's always a pleasure to be in your service, good Patron. Your work—our pleasure," the leader said, the one with a scar crossing from forehead to cheek, sparing his right eye.

CHAPTER
XXX

The nomenclator had a few morsels left in his bowl when the persistent banging at the door began. The other slaves at the table froze and locked to Elius with wide eyes. He met theirs in silence and pushed from the table.

"Don't they know the master isn't here?" he grumbled in irritation to the walls. He made his way to the door, whining the entire way. "First those scribes, unannounced, now what?" Life was always so much easier when the master was away and the slaves had the domus to themselves. The emaciated-looking man with a huge shaved head, prominent cheekbones, and wild eyes opened the door just enough for his large, bug-eyes to be seen. "Yes?"

"Elius?" the man outside asked.

Elius stood rooted like an ancient tree. The man before him had the appearance of an old soldier, the scar across his face a badge of valor earned from some former battle. Or, he could also have passed for one of those gladiators that fought in makeshift arenas near the Forum.

"Are you . . . Elius?" the man repeated.

"May I ask who is seeking him?"

The stranger offered a half-smile. "I have an important message from my employer."

"And, who is . . . this employer, may I ask?"

The messenger broadened his smile and looked back over his shoulders, scanning the street. "Let's just say he is the one you approached with some rather . . . important information, some documents? I believe you are in a very good position to . . . improve your circumstances, substantially. He has been known to exchange some very heavy purses for good information . . . and highly important documents."

"Ah, yes, Lucius Cor—"

"No no no no," the messenger sang. "No names please." The man with the scar across his face shook his head, closed his eyes, and then wagged a finger, as if scolding a child.

"No, no—of course not," Elius parroted. "No names."

"He will be expecting you then . . . with the information . . . in hand? The documents?"

Color waned from Elius' face and he burst into a sweat. "I . . . I don't actually have the documents with me . . . but, I can get them, soon."

"My employer was led to believe that you had the documents in your possession," Scar-Face said. He discarded the smile and replaced it with a leer.

"I do, I do . . . indirectly. I mean . . . they are here with me . . . just not in my immediate possession . . . yet."

"Can you explain yourself?" Scar-Face asked with a tilt of his head, trying to see things a little bit more clearly.

Elius looked behind him where the answer lay. "I will get my hands on them shortly. I just need a little more time."

"Tomorrow, before the sun sets below the city."

"But—"

"Before the sun sets, Elius. You will bring the documents," Scar-Face ordered. The smile returned, accompanied with a quick wink, despite the immobile scar and brow.

The petrified slave closed the door and locked it with trembling hands. He slammed a locking bolt of metal into place, preying to keep out a monster of a situation created by his own greed and self-importance.

"All will be well, all will be well," he whispered. "It will be easy. I will simply deliver the documents and be rewarded for my efforts and still be in the good graces of Balbus," he said to his shadow, gesturing and talking with his hands all the while.

Fear gripped Elius all night long. It slept there in bed next to him, constantly breathing down his neck. When the slave's eyes closed, Fear placed a hand on his shoulder to remind him of what he needed to do—or else. The slave tossed with every passing minute of darkness and his heart pounded in his skinny chest. He got up and paced the room as Fear lay there in the bed, gawking at him with a cruel smile on his face. Elius climbed back into bed and peeked over his shoulder. Fear was still there in the dark, sleepless, relaxed, and waiting.

Elius' eyes blinked open slowly, and then exploded when he saw a sharp blade of light piercing the hallway darkness outside of his sleeping quarters. He sat bolt up and listened. The sounds of morning routines echoed down the hallway from the cooking area near the outside ovens.

He moved like a cat for Lucius and Caius' dimly lit room. He found it empty. Over on one of the cots rested Caius' satchel. Elius couldn't have been more careful if he were walking on clouds. Stealth tip-toes carried him to the satchel. Trembling hands reached for the satchel as alert ears concentrated on any sound signaling approaching footsteps or voices. He bent over in an awkward arch and peered into the pouch.

Nothing; it was empty as the room.

He let go the satchel as if it had taken a snap at him. Nausea and a searing hot flash overcame Elius and his head spun. *Those papers! I need those papers!* his mind screamed. *Footsteps! They're coming back!* Elius flew to the doorway and waited.

"Oh, there you are," he said in one of his finest performances—Tiro would be jealous. "I came to see if there was anything I could get you this early morning." The slave was quick to note that Caius had the documents in his hand. "I see you are busy working. Something for the master?"

Caius slipped the papers behind him, out of view. "No. We're fine, thank you. That's very kind of you, Elius, but we're quite fine."

"Well, if there is anything . . . anything at all, please let me be of service."

"We're good," repeated Lucius.

Elius loitered for several breaths before ebbing backwards into the morning dimness outside the door; the shadowed courtyard pulled him away until he became just a silhouette with large eyes; and then those, too, just—disappeared.

"That man is creepy, Caius," Lucius confessed. "He reminds me too much of Tiro. And two Tiros are one too many."

Lucius crawled back onto his cot, curled up with his arms hugging himself for warmth, and closed his eyes, still chilled from the night hours; Tullia was there to greet him with that smile of hers. He needed her. He wanted her. He missed her. He missed her ways; the way she would tease him, play coy, and then ravish him, leaving him dazed and spent. He imagined her body weight resting upon him, her breath and her moist damp hair across his face. It was wrong—for both of them—he knew it. It would only lead to no good. If only she were a slave, or at least of the same class as he, then things might be different and less complicated. Why did she have to belong to Dolabella? His affairs were perfectly acceptable—he belonged to the aristocracy and took advantage of his circumstances. Life was unfair.

"—And the 't's, they look suspicious, too. I'm no expert, but there seems to be a lot of an Etruscan flavor to these letters. There's something not right here, Lucius. I can feel it in my bones. Lucius? Lucius! Did you even hear anything I said?"

"What? Oh, sorry, Caius. My eyes were resting."

Caius knew very well what Lucius was doing. "Do you think I should take these to the master? He may find them—interesting," he mumbled.

"Personally, I wouldn't make anything of it, Caius. It will only invite trouble, I assure you."

"But, it may be important, Lucius."

"Think it through, Caius. If you give the papers to Cicero with your suspicions, he may feel compelled to act on them, and by the gods what a bag of maggots that will be. Leave it, Caius. The gods will know what to do. I'm sure they have already decided.

"I'm hungry. Let's go see what we can find to eat."

Caius followed his friend, but paused briefly to retrieve one of the two documents from his satchel. He wanted to scrutinize it further. In less than a minute, they were out the door.

Elius emerged from the morning shadows and watched the scribes leave. Again, he crept into the room, went straight for the pouch, and stuffed it under his arm. He dashed for the door in choppy, disjointed skips. His large rigid eyes gawked in every direction like a panicky lizard making an escape for his life.

The slave wasted no time scurrying through the streets and alleyways. He moved quickly, avoiding direct eye contact with those few he passed. His large feet moved his skinny body along the cobbled pathways with urgency. A weighted sun climbed through a haze at a slow pace and peeked upon the city. Elius felt comfort in that he had a large head start on the sun and would complete his task with time left to spare; Fear would have to find something else to do to occupy his time, Elius thought and allowed a smirk. He sprinted on, faster, breaking into a well-deserved sweat.

At an uninhabited junction, he came upon a flock of large, black ravens fighting over something that once possessed life but now existed as nothing more than a few tufts of fur and blanched bone. Three of the large birds hopped and skipped away, protesting; one larger bird stood its ground and with wild screeches and extended wings challenged Elius.

Elius hesitated a brief moment before shooing the bird away with wild caws of his own and darted around the left-over clod of fur and bone. The slave moved nimbly, casting a fleeting look now and then to his rear.

He finally reached his destination, exhausted, yet excited—he had raced possible death and won. The nondescript house on the far side of the Aventine Hill stood at a place where birds once gathered in large numbers. The street's width allowed no more than three men to walk abreast and existed in perpetual shadow; dark-green moss grew everywhere.

Elius grabbed hold of the large brass ring on the door with his spindly fingers and summoned the nomenclator. It took many poundings of the brass ring to get a response. The door creaked open. In the wedge of the open door stood a giant of a man. He had long, blond, stringy hair; gray eyes of a wolf set in a stone face; and clothes that once were forest animals.

Elius cranked his head and looked up to the monstrosity rooted before him. "By the gods . . ." he whispered.

Gray, wolf-like eyes bore in on Elius, but no words followed.

"I'm here to see Lucius Cornelius—"

"Wait," the giant commanded and shut the door.

An invisible hole sucked at the surrounding air and Elius swore he could see the walls across the way moving in on him with each breath. Beads of sweat returned to his head and burst into streams, cascading over his eyes, cheeks, and neck. The door opened again. Scar-Face's figure emerged and replaced the giant's. Elius' chin fell back to his chest to face the man with the scar.

"Elius, please, do come in."

The hesitant slave took several deep breaths and obeyed. He entered and looked around for the giant. The giant was nowhere to be seen.

"I believe you have something for us?" Scar-Face said.

"Lucius Cornelius . . . your employer . . . he is not here?"

"Other business called, but he left me with instructions . . . and a heavy purse of coins. You have the documents?"

Elius' skinny neck stretched, balancing his large head at the end and his probing eyes continued to search for the giant.

"The documents?" Scar-Face said again, the timbre in his voice not offering another option.

Elius slid his hand into his cloak as if reaching for his heart. His eyes continued their search for the giant of a man in fur.

Scar-Face pulled the document from Elius' hand before it could cool. "There seems to be only one document here. Were there not more?"

"I . . . I . . . I will have to bring the other later, at another time," the terrified Elius managed to eke out from his trembling lips.

Scar-Face flashed hard, keen eyes at the slave for a long minute. "Very well, here is your compensation, as promised."

The slave's spindly fingers snatched the bag of coins in a blur and flew in a panic, returning the way he came.

He reached the spot where he had encountered the birds feasting on their meal. It was not birds that confronted this time but two men, men that looked very much like Scar-Face; former soldiers maybe. They leaned against the walls, waiting. Waiting for something—or somebody. One of them had an old javelin that he toyed with, pricking at its tip with his fingers. The men cast oblique eyes to Elius; eyes that sent shivers down his spine and made his hands tremble even more.

He froze. Sweat flowed into his eyes but he ignored it. He would have to thread his way through the two men and there was not much space for that.

His money sack suddenly got heavier.

Elius smelled danger and pivoted sharply to take an alternate route. At the completion of his turn, he ran head-on into an enormous fur-covered animal. The slave's large eyes climbed an enormous chest of a man; it was the giant from the house. A pair of massive hands grabbed Elius and wrapped around his head and neck. The slave's scrawny long fingers clawed at the large hands in a frenzy to get free of the hold and his feet left the ground and kicked at the air. He fought for his life, a battle he feared he would not win. Next, he felt the massive, meaty hands grasp just his head and lurch it to the left. Before he could catch another breath, his head snapped to the right. A grinding crunch stunned him. Every vessel and sinew in his limbs and torso vibrated in a horrible, tingling shock wave, all up and down his body. Elius had become a bag of dead weight, a bag of skin containing useless bones, muscles, and blood. The giant's hands let the slave's awkwardly angled head, attached to a useless body, slump to the filthy ground and rest at the giant's feet.

In futile desperation Elius' mouth gasped for air. His mouth worked feverishly, like a fish out of water, but his lungs refused to draw anything in. He willed for his chest to inflate, but it would not, numbness had taken hold his arms and legs. His brain screamed, commanded, craved for air, but only a sense of fullness and confusion ensued. Elius had become a heap of rumpled clothing with eyes glassed over. With his ear planted to the ground his whole world turned on end. He scarcely registered the approach of the other two men; they were nothing more than two ghosts walking on a wall towards him. The images of the men tunneled to a blur. The hammering pulse in his ears slowed from a gallop to an anguished throb, a feeble pounding of a fist to the earth. His heart struggled to release each quavering beat and each pause between the dying beats stretched further apart. Somewhere, birds cawed. And then, like a sacrificed animal's end, the last trembling beat fell from his heart to the floor of his chest and died. Elius didn't even feel the lifting of the moneybag from his tunic.

A gathering of clientele assembled and loitered around young Caesar's front door like bees tending a hive; his inherited prestige grew rapidly.

It had been three mornings since Balbus appeared with an offer to provide some missing documents. And now he returned. A paid guard at the door recognized Balbus and escorted the important caller past the collective petitioners and into the house, which earned him disgruntled leers from those who were there before him.

"Good day to you, Caesar. I see you have quite a congregation already," Balbus said with a pleased smile.

"And good day to you, Lucius Cornelius. It's good to see you as well," Gaius Julius Caesar Octavianus replied, offering the bearded man a mutual smile. Maecenas and Agrippa followed not far behind. Balbus greeted each with a nod.

"I have something for you, as promised."

He handed the pouch over to Octavius.

Maecenas slithered next to Octavius. "Are they there? Are the documents there?" he whispered.

Octavius extracted the lone document and unfurled it.

Maecenas' eyes went wide with excitement. He grabbed the pouch from Octavius and reached inside. It was empty.

"Where is the other? There has to be another!" Maecenas said. He paced in small circles, searching and scrapping the inside of the bag, hoping by magic another would appear. All eyes fell on Balbus.

"That's all the source had on him."

"There should be more!" Maecenas almost screamed. "I'm sure there was another," he said, a little less agitated, his flushed face betraying his artificial calmness. "Perhaps we can contact the source again for . . . the other document?"

Balbus gave hard looks to the three youths starting with Octavius; to Agrippa; to Maecenas; and then back to Octavius. "That source no longer exists. I thought you understood. I thought that was your wish. This is not child's play. You have entered the realm of the real world, Octavianus. These are serious matters— business matters, dealing in currency other than gold or silver."

Octavius' cheeks blushed. He averted his angry eyes to the floor. He felt compelled to utter that universal rejoinder used by all youth whom somehow possess that supreme body of total knowledge they are inexplicitly gifted with: "I know that."

"If you find the other document, does that mean another . . . life spent?" Octavius asked Balbus, wishing he hadn't after the words left his mouth.

"That's up to you, Octavianus."

"It's Caesar."

"Caesar—would have known what to do . . . or what must be done," Balbus shot back.

Octavius' twitch returned. The corner at the right of his mouth danced as if a hook snared it and some unseen line pulled and tugged at it.

"Then do what must be done," Octavius commanded after some silent thought, the twitching ceased at his decision.

Balbus started for the door but stopped abruptly and turned to the youth-in-charge. "It gets easier each time, Caesar. After a time, you won't even think about it." The man let his hard eyes burn into Octavius before continuing on his way, his footsteps firmer and heavier than before.

Pandemonium ruled Cicero's house in Rome. The master would soon be home and no sign of Elius. A young slave boy had been temporarily answering the door; the other slaves did not want the responsibility.

An agitated Caius paced about the house. "How dare someone get in my things?" he repeated. "If I get my hands on him . . . I'll—"

"You'll what, Caius?" Lucius said, affording to be calm; he had nothing taken from him.

"It had to be that Elius!" Caius cried. "He's been gone since the disappearance of my pouch. It had to be him."

"To what purpose?"

"What else, Lucius—money!"

"Listen, Caius, I have told you to let it go, now let it go, let it be."

"The master will know what to do."

"Caius."

"Fine. Fine. As you wish."

"You don't sound very convincing, little brother."

'Little brother' caught Caius off guard and he ceased his ranting. He looked over to Lucius who appeared to be engrossed in a broken sandal and let the agitation dissipate. A smile snuck on his face.

A whirlwind of commotion greeted the master and Tiro at the door.

The servants assaulted him with cries of woes and confusion as he made his way toward the tablinum. They had not seen or heard from Elius in three days and there had been no direction in the household. Tiro led interference for the master and dispersed the slaves.

"Order! Order! Order in this house!" Tiro boomed. "There will be order in this house—now!" The fractious household settled down. "Now, then," Cicero continued, "one at a time. What is the problem here?"

"Elius has vanished and we haven't heard a word of him," began the servants.

"The grain supply wasn't delivered—"

"The wine is low—"

"We have no food for tonight—"

One by one, the servants cast complaints and grievances.

"*Fini! Fini!*" Tiro jumped in again, asserting his authority.

"Tiro, please sort this out and take care of things, will you?" commanded Cicero.

"Immediately, Dearest Son of Rome. Immediately."

Tiro herded the gathering of servants toward the cooking area of the house as one would herd hungry cats with promises of milk. They followed obediently, echoing previous complaints.

The noisy band of servants maneuvered around Lucius and Caius, completely disregarding the two and leaving them in the wake of their shuffling sandals.

"Ah, Caius, Lucius, so good to see you. What in Hades is going on within these walls of my domus?"

"It's good to see you, too, Dominus. Since the disappearance of Elius, the household has been in a state of disorder and confusion," Caius answered.

"Disappearance? Elius disappearing? Is anything missing of value from my tablinum?" Cicero asked with a worried look.

"I don't think anything of yours is missing, Sire. But—"

Lucius cleared his throat with a stifled cough and cut off Caius before he could finish his report. The Cicero's eyes moved from one scribe to the other, waiting for more information.

None came.

The Domus Rostrata on the Esquiline Hill had a visitor—Gaius Cassius Longinus.

"Gaius, my good friend, do come in. May I offer you some wine?" Pompey signaled to one his people to fetch the wine and with an outstretched hand offered a seat to his visitor.

"Thank you very much, Gnaeus. That would certainly soothe the bite of this cold and chilled morning."

"So, what brings you out on this miserable foggy morning? It surely wasn't just to see an old friend."

"Gnaeus, I heard a rumor . . ."

"Another rumor?"

"Yes. Only this time—"

"Antoni?"

"Yes. Is it true? Is he making his way back to Italy?"

"Word has it he indeed has sailed from Egypt. Making his way north through Syria. That'll work well for him as Herod is no threat to him."

"What of Egypt? The grain supply?"

"That, my friend, is as foggy as the outside cold air. We will have to wait and see. Evidently, the family feud has been temporarily settled with the youngest daughter at the throne with her brother. She's young. But I understand she is extremely intelligent and capable. If her loyalties stay strong with Rome, we should be all right."

"If not?"

"Then, I shall go to Egypt and fix it myself."

"Hmm."

"You doubt me, Gaius Longinus?"

"No, no Gnaeus. My doubt is with the Egyptians."

"Don't forget, my good friend, they are Greek really, and have more in common with us than the people they rule. Alexander himself lies with them, still ruling, even in death."

"So true, so true. So . . . what do you think his plans are?"

"Antoni? I would think he would try to get back to Mutina. The siege remains unbroken. He may want to pick up more troops along the way."

"I could offer my services, Magnus. It's only been a handful of years since I held reign in Syria. The legions there should be loyal to me. I could go and make a presence, slow him down, or at least prevent him from levying more troops."

"This is true, Gaius, you could. And we do need to stop him," Pompey said as he walked around his desk and over to his trophy wall, looking up at his most recent addition, massaging his chin, thinking, contemplating, scheming.

Gaius Longinus Cassius stood waiting, waiting for an answer.

"There is another way," Pompey said looking up at the javelin.

"You have a plan?"

"I have thoughts, Gaius—thoughts." Pompey reeled around and planted his hands on his desk. "We'll send Caesar."

"Caesar? But, he's . . . Are you suggesting young Octavianus?"

"Why not?" Pompey shrugged.

"He's just a boy."

"A boy with a name, Gaius."

Now it was Longinus' turn to scratch his chin. "Hmm, he is gaining popularity and does have quite a following, mostly his uncle's clientela and loyal veterans. It's possible."

"Julius has . . . that is . . . *had* many vets in Campania and Brundisium. They could be coaxed to come over to young Caesar. Young Caesar could be coaxed to gather his own personal army and meet Antoni, slow him down, do some damage," Pompey continued to think aloud.

"His own personal army?"

"Why not? I did it, didn't I?"

"This is true, Gnaeus, but—"

"We shall resurrect the ghost of Julius Caesar and send him to Antoni. But this time on the side of the Republic. It could work. What's the worst that could happen?"

"He could win, Gnaeus. What if he were to succeed . . . be more than victorious?"

"Like I said, he's just a boy with a name, Gaius. He has no experience."

"True; experience—none, but he has potential and plenty of future, if the gods so desire. We, on the other hand, have plenty of experience, but who knows how much future."

The two old men stood in silence, sharing the room but not their thoughts. They thought of old battles, political victories, failures, and near failures; it all went so quickly.

CHAPTER
XXXI

The cold and wet end of Decembris did not keep Cicero from doing what he loved best: he worked the Senate; he persuaded; he cajoled; he debated; he scored points; and he kept keen at mind.

"What a day, Tiro, what a day."

"One of your finest, Dominus, if I may say so."

"A good day, but I'm afraid it took quite a bit out of me. Oh, for the stamina of youth," the elderly statesman said as he slid into his chair by the brazier. "I think I surprised even myself a little by wheedling those . . . fellow senators . . . in bestowing propraetor status upon young Caesar. Pompey will owe me much for that one."

"Masterfully done, O Son of Rome, such art of persuasion; the Greeks would be put to shame, Dominus."

"And I've only begun to let them know how I feel about that renegade—Antonius. I'm awed that they would not heed my words and would insist on sending a delegation to meet with that . . . that drunkard. They will see. He will not give up his siege on Mutina."

"And putting forth the motion to change the month of Quintilis to Julius at the bequest of young Caesar was noteworthy, Dominus."

"Yes, Tiro, and a bit tricky. Pompey had in mind the very same idea. Of course, the idea to bring the calendar back in line with the seasons was mine all along. We just let them believe what they wanted."

"So true, Master. Your words are like . . . like magic itself," Tiro gushed.

"You know, Tiro, and I don't intend to boast, but it is said that Caesar—Julius that is—once said that my words conquered more for Rome than his armies ever did. It's sad that such an educated man as he would have abandoned the Republic for ideas inconsistent with our belief in a country governed by men it voluntarily elected as its leaders. There are laws. There are . . . obligations. Yes, that what's important—obligations!"

Tiro wanted to clap, but instead just stood there, hands clasped, head tilted, working up some tears to gloss over his eyes.

"Tiro."

"Yes, Dominus."

"I need to dictate a very important letter. Gather your instruments and meet me at my desk."

"Right away, Sire, right—"

"Wait," Cicero said after a thought flashed across his countenance. He put a finger to his lips. "I'll write it myself and have it delivered. Send for the boys."

"Yes, Dominus, right away."

<hr />

Another mission for the master, another trip out into the cold; Lucius and Caius no sooner returned from the Forum when they were summoned to take an important message to Pompey, the contents unknown to anyone but Cicero, the scroll secured with wax and his seal.

They walked fast, counting on the extra tunics and thick cloaks to keep warm. Caius looked over his shoulders every seven to ten paces. His face wore a mask of unease and Lucius noticed.

"What are you looking for, Caius?"

"I can't shake the feeling we're being followed, Lucius."

"Can you see who it is?"

"No. But they're there. Remember when we were on the road? Tarentum?"

Lucius' acknowledging gaze made it clear he'd rather not recall it.

Now they both sensed the men following them and decided to quicken the pace. Lucius' foot slapping started and became very annoying. Caius was too nervous to notice. The quick walk morphed into a trot and fear replaced anxiety when they finally saw the faint images of two strangers following, emerging from the grayness of the day like ghosts, matching stride for stride.

They pivoted sharply into a narrow alley. Lucius regretted the move in the first footsteps; the cobbled stones were grossly uneven and slippery from tossed waste from above. He slipped several times. Caius caught him each time and kept him on his feet. The deeper within the recess, the darker the shadows became.

"I don't like the feel of this, Lucius."

"I know, I know. I feel I've been here before."

They stopped to assess their dilemma. Puffed clouds of vapor looked like menacing, small ghouls surrounding them as they panted.

"Look for a doorway, Caius."

The scribes probed the walls when silhouettes appeared at the far entrance of the alley. Lucius expected them to separate with one of them marching toward him; somehow, he knew that's what was going to happen.

It didn't. They both started in his direction.

Caius found a locked door that would not give.

The ghostly figures continued their slow march.

Caius banged on the door and yelled for someone to open the

damned thing. "Open the door!" he screamed as he measured the advance of the two men.

The door sprang open in sudden disbelief. A dirty-faced boy in rags stood at the threshold with wide eyes and a blank stare. They all stood facing one another in silence, time measured in rapid heartbeats.

Lucius and Caius broke the spell when they forcefully invited themselves in and shoved the locking mechanism of the door in place with authority, securing it behind them.

"We need out, quickly. Which way?" Lucius asked the boy in a calm but serious manner.

The boy pointed up to a stairway that ascended and disappeared into darkness.

"Be a good boy and show us," commanded Lucius.

The pair followed the boy up several flights of stairs and landings, twisting and turning. Each successive flight ascended through assorted stenches and increasing conditions of deprivation and squalor.

They climbed the steps of brick two at a time, the small boy out in front, his skinny bare feet working madly to try and keep ahead of two adults at the rushed pace. Before they all reached the very last floor, the boy stopped and pointed in the direction of an unlit hallway. Movement in the semi-dark caught Lucius and Caius' attention and they braced themselves for the worst.

In the corner a disheveled woman with an infant at her breast sat in the semi-shadows. She showed no fear, just a blank expression on her dirty face that matched that of the boy's. The boy moved to her and took his place next to her, on the floor, knees drawn to his chest, and head resting against her other breast. The boy pointed again to the darkened hallway. Lucius and Caius exchanged glances and scurried into the darkness.

Their probing hands followed the walls until they found another set of stairs. They descended in slower footsteps until they reached the level of the insulae where windows appeared, letting in enough light to guide them the rest of the way to the bottom floor where shops occupied the most valued space. The two scribes navigated their path down the stairwell using walls as guides and when they reached bottom they found the palms of their hands thick with years of accumulated dirt, grime, and soot; unfortunately, it left a trail of their escape route.

The scribes came out from a backroom of a small shop. Rows of amphorae that reeked of *garum*—the ghastly, smelly fish sauce that the populace just couldn't live without—lined the wall. Lucius' head made contact with a suspended ornament that rang out loud like a bell when he exited the shop, startling both intruders.

Caius turned to see what it was that gave them away. A large, bronze penis with bells attached swayed to and from as the little bells clamored in protest. "At least one of us will be lucky," he snickered.

"What are you talking about?"

"The good luck charm; you've been blessed," Caius said.

"We'll see how lucky we are when we get back to the domus," Lucius chided.

They looked about but didn't see anybody matching the appearance of the two strangers that had stalked them; just other strangers passing and melting into the cold mists. It felt safe enough to go on in a slower but watchful manner.

The nervous evaders turned a corner and encountered the distinct wafting of animal scent—hides and excrement. From the partly broken mist came the bleating and mooing calls of goats and cattle.

"We must be near the cattle market. How in Hades did we come to be near the Boarian Forum?" Caius asked, more to himself than Lucius.

"You tell me."

"It's all right, follow me. Once we get to the market, I can get us back home."

"Fine, little brother, you lead the way."

They walked silent and vigilant. The stink and sounds of animals greeted them as they neared the pens. A fog developed and muffled the animal noises and painted everything gray and cold. The mist even absorbed their footsteps. It was quiet—too quiet.

Caius lurched as if someone had pushed him forward with a forceful fist to his back.

Lucius recognized the sudden, impacting thud but his brain refused to accept it.

Caius crumpled to his knees on the wet, dirty ground with shock, fear, and disbelief rippling across his face.

"Lucius . . . I can't breathe," he gasped in almost a whisper, his face turning as gray as the fog. In his back, a javelin protruded like a giant stinger that some ghostly insect had left as a calling card before fleeing back into the ghostly fog. Lucius saw that the Javelin was embedded in Caius deeply, too deep to be withdrawn without doing more harm.

"Go . . . run, Lucius . . . live," ordered Caius through wet, guttural whispers. "Liv—"

Lucius heard the unmistakable footfalls of marching boots in the thickened fog, marching straight for him. He looked to Caius who mouthed the word "go." The cripple cringed in indecision and wanted to yell at the world; instead, he gently laid his friend to the ground and hurried for the holding pens, looking back to see his friend disappear in the fog.

The shuffling of large animals broke through the mist in front of him. He jumped into one of the open pens and crawled to the far end. He sprawled out as flat as he could and covered himself with straw. He hated himself for cowering like a rodent in a bed of straw but it at least gave him time, if only a few seconds, to think. If only he had a weapon.

Anger and confusion racked his brain as he lay prone under his blanket of amber; anger for leaving Caius, confusion as to why he had to. The turmoil coalesced and disappeared when he heard boot steps nearby.

Through a triangular opening in the stalks of straw resting against his face and amid the thick and muscular hoofed legs of nervous cattle, Lucius saw two pair of human legs walk into view, just outside of the pen's wooden crossbeams. One pair stopped in front of the pen, the owner listening and searching. At his right lower leg, a crude tattoo of a snake crawled out of the man's boot. Whoever this person was, he made the animals nervous and they moved away from him.

It was then that one of the large, stirring beasts backed up and pinned Lucius' left hand with a hind hoof. Lucius pinched his face in pain and used the knuckles of his right hand to stifle a cry. When the animal let out a loud, mooing cry, Lucius allowed himself a small grunt, the grunt masked by the animal's noisy complaint. The owner of the boots with the snake crawling out left to catch up with his partner. The animal moved forward, freeing up Lucius' hand. Except for the animals, it was quiet again. Lucius crawled out and went back for his friend.

He came upon Caius' crumpled body shrouded in the fog. It had been moved. The javelin was gone and its tunics were in disarray—it had been searched. Lucius tried to arouse Caius. The cooling body only rocked with each little push, returning to its fetal position each time. The pain at Lucius' hand waned and vanished, replaced instead by an excruciating ache in his chest where his heart beat in shredded pieces.

Several shadows materialized at the other end of the mist but stopped in their footsteps. The figures made a snap turn and faded back into the grayness, not wanting to be any part of whatever had taken place. Lucius knew he had to leave, too. Despite a nearly-crushed left hand, Lucius hoisted Caius' dead weight up and onto his shoulders, securing the left arm and leg of the body with his strong arms. Together, they headed home, to Cicero's domus.

CHAPTER
XXXII

The kicking at the door would not stop. It was a persistent, annoying, and louder-by-the-second kicking. Tiro decided to take care of this nonsense himself.

"Who is creating such a rumpus this late in the evening and why doesn't somebody answer this damnable door?" he shouted.

He eased the door open and peeked from the edge.

The disfigured silhouette before Tiro resembled a monster with huge, misshapen shoulders and grotesque, multiple upper limbs. Tiro thrust a nervous lantern before the creature and found Lucius—with what appeared to be a body draped around his neck.

"By the gods—"

Lucius charged in before Tiro could say anything more and limped for Caius' room with his burden on his shoulders. Tiro chased after with the lantern, casting solemn silhouettes on the walls.

Lucius let the lifeless body of his friend fall onto the bed in one, smooth, graceful motion, covered him with a blanket to keep warm, and then stood over him, keeping guard.

"By the gods," Tiro repeated, "what is going on here?"

Lucius remained in a trance, his troubled eyes fixed on his friend.

House slaves appeared seemingly out of nowhere, colliding to a standstill when they saw Caius, glassy-eyed, lips of blue, and skin almost gray.

Cicero arrived, having been summoned by one of the other slaves.

"What is this—mischief." His last word trailed and fell from his lips, like a leaf floating to earth.

Reflected flames from lanterns danced in Lucius' glistening eyes. He turned to the Dominus and whispered, "It's Caius, he's——dead."

"But how? What happened? Are you sure?" Cicero insisted on knowing. "Maybe he's just hurt, Lucius. Tell me what's going on here."

"Javelin."

"What?"

"A javelin. He was struck with a javelin."

"What are you saying? A javelin? Are you sure? How could that be? Do you know what you speak? A javelin?" The salvo of questions came as a fusillade of javelins themselves.

"A JAVELIN! I KNOW WHAT A JAVELIN IS! It was a javelin," he said with clenched fists.

Cicero moved in measured steps to Caius and gently touched his hand. It felt cold and stiff.

"No, no, no, no. Oh, my poor boy, no . . . my poor, poor boy. What has happened to you? Why—"

"We were followed," Lucius said in almost a whisper. "Why were we followed?"

"Followed? Who followed you? Did you see who it was? A thief? Were you robbed?" Again a barrage of questions filled the air like a cloud of arrows. Lucius rode out the volley hunched and with no answers.

Cicero noted Lucius' bruised and partially bloody hand. "Oh, my boy, are you hurt? Forgive me, I didn't think to—"

"No, I'm fine."

He was not fine; he was gravely hurt. Pain swelled in his chest.

"Did they take anything?" a voice asked from behind the master, Tiro.

Both the master and Lucius turned to the secretary.

"I was just wondering . . . if he was robbed, that's all," Tiro said, shrugging.

"Of course he was robbed! He was robbed of his life!" Lucius said with the intensity of heaving his own javelin.

Tiro took a step back into the darkness and the room filled with a sad, prevailing calm. Sullen shadows of Cicero and Lucius, wavering on the walls from the flickering of the lantern flames, looked down upon the body of Caius.

"I'm sorry, my dear boy, but we need to know what became of the scroll I gave Caius. Was it lost? Stolen?" the master asked, placing a gentle hand on Lucius' shoulder.

"I don't know . . . I'm sorry, I just don't know."

Tiro crept from the shadows toward the body on the bed.

"It may still be on him—"

Lucius pounced like a caged animal and blocked his approach.

"Don't—touch him! Don't even think of it," he snarled, the icy words shooting through clenched, wet teeth. Narrow, glinting eyes met Tiro full force, reinforced with clawed hands at the cripple's sides, quavering with controlled rage. Wolves in the wild would have cowered and trembled before him.

Tiro froze. Fear prevented his feet from carrying him any further.

Cicero again patted Lucius on the shoulder. "Allow me, son, please."

Lucius moved aside and allowed the master to pass but kept his eyes trained on Tiro.

The elderly master searched Caius gently and respectfully, affectionately caressing the boy's matted hair with trembling fingers afterwards. Again he whispered, "My poor, poor boy."

Cicero found nothing. His freedman Tiro and the house slaves drew back slowly, heads bowed, silent. Lucius remained at the side of his friend, guarding "little brother."

The centurion with the special guard dogs summoned and then ordered Sthenelus Regulius to follow him to Commander Publius Ventidius' tent. There they found a handful of other legionaries waiting inside. No one said a word. They just stood their places and awaited further orders.

The tent flap was thrown back with a stiff crack as Ventidius charged in, followed by two subordinates. The legionaries snapped to attention.

"At rest," the commander ordered, and the men relaxed again. "Some of you know Tribune Popillius Laenas and Centurion Herennius."

Only a few heads nodded—Sthenelus was not one of them.

You've been selected to be part of a special unit to gather information and perform some . . . other essential duties for General Antonius. Details will be explained at the appropriate time," the commander informed the small group as he paced before them, eyeballing them, measuring them, and looking for possible flaws.

Ventidius stopped and planted himself in front of Sthenelus. "You're Regulius, are you not?" he asked.

"Yes, Sir," Sthenelus answered with a smart salute, his stare fixed straight forward.

"You did well the other evening. Good report. Can I trust you to continue to do well?"

"Yes, Sir." His eyes started to dance around as he began wondering what was to become of him.

The commander retraced his steps back to the beginning of the line.

"Tribune Laenas and Centurion Herennius will give you more information and orders in due time. You will vacate your present quarters and move to a new tent this evening. That is all for now. Laenas, they're yours now."

The tribune offered a smart salute and ordered the men out, giving instructions to gather their gear and meet at their new quarters, a tent down at the end of the row. The only thing left to do now was to hurry up and wait.

CHAPTER XXXIII

Caius lay in state in the atrium at Cicero's Rome house for six days instead of the customary seven; the cremation took place on the seventh.

On the eighth day, the master's coach made its way to Tusculum, a trip made many times before. This time, however, the riders rocked and swayed in silence. The urn sat cradled in Cicero's lap, held in place with loving arms. Lucius sat across the way, his total concentration locked on the urn. Tiro fixated on the weather outside the coach. Gone were the vibrant, breezy spring days, the happy hot summer days, and the colorful cooling days of fall. All the shades of gray and cold made it perfect for a day for mourning.

"Many thanks to the gods it's not pouring rain or our ride in the mud would be maddening," Tiro muttered.

Silence answered his observation.

"We should have a fine feast tomorrow . . . the wake and all."

Silence.

"I dare say we shall have difficulties replacing him. He was such a fine scribe."

Lucius shot a look to Tiro that was as piercing as the sharpest gladius in the whole of the Roman Republic. Dark gray, rain-swollen clouds outside the coach occupied Tiro and he didn't feel the lethal thrust of the keen gaze from the former young legionary.

The coach—turned hearse—arrived with the usual expectant crowd waiting, with Felix and Pulvilla at the front. Absent was the cheering. There was only sadness and bereavement. Tiro exited the coach first, followed by Lucius, who took the urn from the master as he stepped down. The elderly master retrieved the urn and then led the somber procession into the domus.

"Papa, Papa," cried Tullia as she rushed over to comfort her father. Lucius stood his place with a warm smile and a flushed face when he heard her voice. Tullia did not let it go unnoticed as she embraced her father, meeting Lucius' eyes with her own.

"My child, my child, my dear Tulliola. It warms my heart to see you. And your mother?"

"Here, dear husband. I am here," Terentia announced as she slipped into the room from the dark. "I pray you had a pleasant journey?"

"As pleasant as one could have with Charon ferrying us home," he managed to say with a straight face. The journey certainly had the feel of a slow crossing of the river Styx, and there was plenty of coin to pay the fare.

The retort stunned Terentia momentarily, but she recovered.

"I only meant—"

"Dear Felix, please take . . . place the urn in the atrium. Be careful with our dear lad," the master of the house said as he passed off Caius' ashes to his trusted house slave. "Now, where was I? Oh, yes, thank you for your concern, dear wife. It's good to be home. It's been a very long day, and these weary bones are crying out for a nice cup of good wine and a warm bed." He headed for his room.

Alone with Tullia and her mother, Lucius painfully excused himself and headed for his room and bed upstairs. The pounding in his chest confused his brain; he didn't know if his heart ached more for the want of Tullia, or the loss of his friend—he wanted to be with both.

He lay in his bed, thinking, reminiscing, imagining. He tossed about like a floundering ship in a storm. He peered through the darkness looking for comfort but found only misery. *Where are the good times? The fun times? Why did life have to be so painful?* He wondered.

Frustration commanded him out of bed and pulled him to the window. No moon, only more darkness. A stirring at the doorway made his muscles go taut and the thought of Caius flashed across his brain. But it couldn't be his friend. The door creaked open and a silhouette glided toward Lucius. *What ghost is this? Caius? Caesar? Who?*

He recognized the scent when the apparition closed within inches—Tullia.

They attacked each other like animals trying to take each other's souls. Mouths locked, hands grabbed, and arms caressed. In desperation, they tried to become one.

"Your parents," Lucius managed a whisper in between kisses.

"I have a servant at the doorway," she whispered back. "Better than a guard dog." She tried to guide him to his bed, but he refused to move.

"No. The leather bindings make too much noise," he gasped.

They settled for the wall and the cold floor, neither of which was a hindrance. The first time was hard, fierce, ruthless, more combat than lust—taking no prisoners; the second was tender, loving, passionate, and repentant on Lucius' part. Masks of pain and anguish were anything but; instead, they were exclamations of exploding ecstasy.

"I missed you," the spent Lucius whispered as Tullia rested her head on his chest, listening to the "flub-dubbing" inside his chest.

"And I you."

"I'm sorry for being so . . . rough. I don't know why—"

"That's okay. I'm use to—"

"Tullia, we need to talk. Your husband—"

"Sssh, not now. Not yet."

"Lady Tullia, lady Tullia, there is someone down below," a low female voice alerted the pair from the doorway. "We must go, Domina."

"I have to go. I'll see you at the morning's light," she promised as she got up and disappeared into the night, leaving only her scent and sweat on Lucius' body. He lay on the floor, neither cold nor uncomfortable, only happy again, despite the loss of his friend.

His friend.

It crossed his mind how the rage in his lusting of Tullia was most intense when Caius lingered in the periphery, just off in the outer reaches of his mind. Lucius wanted revenge, but not against Tullia. He began to feel guilty again.

The next day dawned without the ugly, cold, gray, and rain-filled clouds. The air smelled fresh and fragranced. And life resumed in Cicero's house. Lucius lay in bed and listened to the increasing bee hive of activity below, remembering the night before. The thought of his friend, the voyage across the sea, the storm, the road to Rome, the stay at Venusia, the concern for the missing scroll—

The scroll.

Where was the other Scroll? Did the mission to Pompey's domus have anything to do with the other scroll? Does the master know? Did Caius . . . .

Too many questions, too many thoughts, all of it caused his head to ache. And he had no answers, only suspicions. A new energy drew him out of bed and filled him with a yearning. He had to find answers to questions. *Who killed Caius and why?*

That tattoo—the serpent.

"I will find that serpent," he muttered—it sounded like a promise made.

The day culminated in a subdued feast for Caius before his interment within a specially constructed tomb near the domus. The new addition with the fresh paintings was the place of tempered celebration and toasting. A solemn affair with attempts at lightheartedness interjected here and there.

The master gave a little speech and remembered Caius with fondness, closing with a special note. "We may have lost a dear and treasured member of our household, and for that we are saddened. But, I have an announcement. We are going to have an addition! My dearest Tullia is with child again. And with all the proper appeasements to the gods, we will have a grandchild scampering about." To that, everyone clapped and melancholy gave way to a subdued joy.

Surprise and shock crossed Lucius' face. He looked over to Tullia. She in turn returned his gaze with the eyes of a cat flashing submission: lids softly hooded and content, her smile just perceptible, matching the one on the wall behind her. There was an aura about her that he could not see in the darkness last night.

Caius rested peacefully in his tomb and Lucius became increasingly restless. Tullia's presence only made his agitated state worse. And the unexpected arrival of Dolabella was more than he could bear.

"So, you are the great artisan responsible for the wall paintings," Tullia's husband said, confronting the young artist-scribe in the *peristyle*.

"Well, I don't know about the 'great' part," he answered, sensing something more in Dolabella's voice than a compliment.

"You seem to know my wife . . . very well."

"She was easy to paint . . . her fine features, I mean."

"Yes . . . easy." The slow, calculated response made Lucius even more ill at ease.

"The battle scene was much more of a challenge," the young artisan said, desperately trying to avoid the subject of Tullia altogether.

"Yes . . . that, too, is well done."

"Thank you."

"In fact, you've painted the mayhem as if you were there." Dolabella squinted with the façade of a warm smile. The crow's feet at his eyes feigned the illusion of bona fide interest as they fanned out. "Were you?"

"Well, actually—"

"I would assume that in order to paint a realistic scene, or such a detailed subject, one would have . . . a close and . . . intimate experience with the subject at hand. Of course, I am not an artisan and that is only an opinion on my part." The creases at his eyes unfurled slowly, dropping away, leaving only the skin not yet tanned by the sun. His eyes were less jovial now and assumed those of a commanding general focusing on some battle soon to take place.

"One can paint trees, animals, rivers, rocks . . . whether that is being intimate with leaves, branches, and fur depends on the eye of the artisan," replied Lucius, thinking of his mother and her lessons—not Dyrrhachium—or Tullia.

Dolabella's face flashed crimson. "You make a point. Perhaps you could paint for me some time."

"The paintings were more for pleasure . . . for the consular. I'm really employed to scribe for the good patron."

"I see. And what else do you do . . . for pleasure, Lucius?" Tullia's husband asked as he started a slow circle around the young scribe.

"Oh, there you are, Lucius," Cicero said as he arrived on scene. "I must talk with you. I have a . . . Lucius, Cornelius—I hope I'm not interrupting anything important—"

"No, not at all. We were just discussing . . . intimacy and art," Dolabella said, his eyes lingering on Lucius. "We can continue our . . . discussions later." He put his congenial smile back on and walked away.

Cicero and Lucius watched him leave, each with nagging questions in their heads. The elderly man broke the trance with a sigh. "Sometimes I wish . . . oh, nothing," the old man started, awash in discontent. "Where was I? Oh, yes, I have an idea. I've been thinking . . . I have a villa in Pompeii, and as Caius' family is there . . . perhaps we could take our dear lad back home. The tomb is not yet sealed and—"

"That would be great, Sir. He did want me to meet his aunt and uncle, and to see Pompeii. It would be fulfilling a wish. He would have liked that."

"Wait until you see Pompeii. You'll love it! We'll visit my relatives when we get there."

"Are we going there?"

"Of course, we must."

"If you say so."

"If I say so—of course I say so, how could we not go to Pompeii?"

The words he and his friend had on the road so many months ago played in his head. He felt fortunate in that he could still remember the sound of Caius' voice; there were others that he could not, including his father's.

"Good, very good then. We'll plan immediately," Cicero said with uplifted spirits as he left Lucius alone with his thoughts.

CHAPTER
XXXIV

It happened as he sought devoted followers and veterans once loyal to his great-uncle in Campania.

A comet.

A sign, they said, that the young Caesar's uncle had become a god and all should follow Octavianus—his rightful heir; it was only right that all the old vets should do their duty and hitch their futures to the *Divi Filius*—the son of a god. It would take weeks—if not months—but Octavianus would have his army.

Octavianus and his boyhood companions combed the countryside harvesting men. He had gone back to wearing his bulla, the one Grandmother Julia had given him, the one with the face of Alexander the Great on the obverse side, the one that promised him greatness. He rubbed it continuously, an old habit that seemed to work magic for him in the past.

"Grandmother, you said this would bring me greatness. Let it be so. They say your son is now a god. It is only right that the 'son of god' should have greatness as well. I beseech you, O Divine Grandmother. Let it be so," he prayed every morning as the sun rose and he caressed his bulla.

Maecenas, with his silky smooth tongue, rode ahead of Octavianus to lay the seeds and spread the meaning of the comet: the coming of the 'son of god.' The prophetic words were flavored with hints of favorable compensation for those who joined him. Some of the old vets were tired of trying to make a life at farming. It wasn't the digging that tired them; they carved the earth many times, digging trenches at the end of long marches. It wasn't the sometimes harsh conditions; they'd marched miles and miles in cold rain, snow, and blistering heat. They weren't starving; the land provided for them, they had livestock and bread. But *these* men couldn't live on bread alone; they needed more; they needed something to fill a void. Maecenas gave them that something, that someone: *young Caesar.*

When they first cast eyes on him, riding majestically on his horse, they were stunned. He looked so young. He was nothing more than—a boy!

"Don't let your eyes deceive you," Maecenas would warn, appearing as a pimpled-faced adolescent himself. "Look to the men who follow him! They are Julius Caesar's men—Balbus, Oppius, and the others, his most trusted men! Do you not recognize them? They will tell you. Gaius Julius Caesar Octavianus is Gaius Julius Caesar incarnate! He is the flesh and blood of the father, the god, and he is here to lead you again! He will show you the way!" Maecenas worked himself up until he appeared mad and practically foaming at the mouth.

"He's too young," someone in the crowd shouted.

"Was not Alexander young when he ruled what Rome could only dream of ruling?" spat Maecenas.

"Are we to rule the world?" another listener heckled.

Maecenas' words collided in his mouth like cattle trying to escape through a breech in a broken corral. His frenzied words spilled forth in a rushed gallop.

Octavianus commanded his horse forward with a slight kick to save the moment.

"I'm not here to rule the world. I'm here to continue my father's unfinished work, to make Rome and Italia a better Republic. If the gods intend for Rome to rule the world . . . well, let it be so, that's for them to decide. But if they do, it will be by your hands, the people, the soldiers. Let the Senate debate all the trivial issues. It will be the armies who defeat our enemies and spread our greatness. The Senate is important, but it is not they who shed their blood on this earth, thus making the ground hallowed. It is you! You will go forth and prepare the lands beyond and sow the seeds of Rome's greatness! You will create a Republic—no—an empire, an empire like no other, and history will forever remember you!"

Like pillars of stone, some stood rooted in stunned silence. Others murmured to one another that he truly was the "son of a god." And yet, others ebbed away like a receding tide and repeated the litany—"he's just a boy."

Cicero's villa in Pompeii was smaller than his others, but had charm. Olive groves and tall cypress trees surrounded the picturesque little villa. The place reminded the old man of his boyhood home in Arpinum, a hill town some three days ride south of Rome. Whenever he visited the Pompeii villa, memorable days of his youth would flash back to him: romping through orchards, vineyards, and olive groves just above the grain fields; chasing sheep, goats, and oxen across open fields; and meandering on trails that coursed along the river Liris where giant poplars and alders thrived on the riverbanks. The trees danced and swayed with gusty breezes that tossed and flipped leaves like gold coins. It reminded him of the place where his mother brought him into this world on a cold winter morning, just like this one.

Wrapped in a thick woolen cloak, Cicero sat out on the terrace of his Pompeian house against a patchwork of white and gray clouds, the dark ones scudded swiftly under the white ones. The cold winter cloudscape draped and partially hid a large volcano. You couldn't see all of it but you knew it was there, like a giant, menacing ogre, waiting. The people weren't afraid of Vesuvius; they took the giant for granted; he was as much a part of them as the air they breathed.

"Excuse me, Master Cicero," Lucius said, feeling guilty when he saw the consular reading, or at least appearing to be reading. "I'm most sorry. I'll return when you're finished."

"No, no, Lucius. It's quite all right. I wasn't really reading. It's always comforting just to have a book in one's hand. My father once told me, 'Son, a room without a book is like a body without a soul.' He was a good man, not always in good health, but always with a keen mind, and a book or manuscript in hand. Like him, I like just to have one in my hand, too."

"I have the manuscripts you wished to be copied. I pray they meet with your approval."

Cicero took the material and scanned them briefly, squinting tightly, looking for that depth of field where he could actually see the words clearly. The old man desperately tried to read the letters with his tired eyes.

Lucius looked about and scanned the surroundings. They were alone.

"In our village there was an elderly merchant who had a certain little trick when he couldn't see the letters very well. He would put the tips of his thumb and forefinger together as if inspecting a grain of sand, like this; and then he would slide the next finger, the middle finger, back ever so slightly, thus creating a little triangle, like this; then bring his little eyepiece up to his eye, like thus; and then he could read his material clearly. It worked for him anyway." Lucius' cheeks blushed after showing the master the little trick, thinking it childish.

Cicero swept his eyes around to see if anyone observed, then slowly brought his triangle of finger tips up to his right eye, closing the left one reflexively. Adjusting his fingers slightly and moving the manuscript back and forth, he marveled to see crisp letters within the small aperture he had just created as instructed.

"By the—gods." He looked upon Lucius' face with wonder. The

young scribe shied away.

"You're busy, Dominus, I'll leave you to your reading," Lucius said as he turned to leave.

"Wait! Lucius, wait. What is it that you . . . cannot do my dear boy wonder?"

The scribe met Cicero's eyes briefly and then looked askance. *I cannot be the soldier I wanted to be for my father. I cannot be your son-in-law. I cannot bring Caius back. And I cannot change the things I have done*, he silently thought to himself. "There is much I cannot do, Master. Much."

"Come, my lad, let's go get something warm to drink, eh?" the elderly statesman said as he wrapped a comforting arm around Lucius' shoulder.

They started for the warmth of the house but stopped when the dogs in the neighborhood began crying. They whimpered like pups or howled like wolves. Some ran in packs for the marina. Flocks of birds leapt for the skies and fled for the north in clouds of black.

And then the floor under Cicero and Lucius shifted under them. They both felt dizzy and off balance when the floor next decided to roll. Loose items nearby rocked gently just after a slight rattling.

"What was that?" Lucius asked.

The old man's eyes flashed, scanning the skies. He then looked over to the cloud-enshrouded mountain. "That was either our dear friend cloaked in the clouds over there," Cicero said, gesturing his head in the direction of Vesuvius, "or our other dear friend, Pompeius Magnus, stomping his boots, calling for more troops. I would have less concern for the former and more for the later. There is nothing more harmful to man than man himself, my boy, remember that."

"I've heard that the new Caesar is raising troops not far from here, in Campania," Lucius said.

"Yes, I've heard the same. Young Caesar fancies himself the son of a god, or at least that is what his followers are calling him—Divi Filius."

"What?" Lucius stopped cold.

"Divi Filius, Son of God, " the old man repeated.

A flash of an image stabbed at Lucius' mind—the old hag in the alley. What was it she said? *"He shall become a god in-turn. And he shall have a son—Divi Filius. And the son will turn mud and brick into marble and stone. Pax—peace—the son shall bring to the world, with the sword . . . and the javelin. And he will become the savior of Rome . . . ."*

She had said more, but he couldn't remember exactly what it was, something about *another*—"savior."

"What is it my boy? Something troubles you," Cicero asked with curiosity.

"Oh, it's nothing, Sir. Truly, nothing," Lucius answered, his face betraying the lie.

They walked in silence into the tablinum and found one of the house servants picking up scrolls from the floor and placing them back in the pigeonholed-racks from where they were tossed.

"Oh, Master, that was a strong one. We usually don't experience tremors like that one in the cold months, only the warmer ones."

"Is anything broken? Any of my pieces from Greece?"

"No, Sire. Everything is intact," the slave said before he scampered off.

A scroll under his desk had been overlooked. Cicero picked it up with indifference to put it away but was moved by a thought.

"Lucius," the elderly man said as he planted himself into his chair behind the desk, "There is something I've been meaning to ask." He fixated in the space before him and then to the scroll in his hand. "Caius came to me with a . . . concern. He said he found something that troubled him: some scrolls that he found after visiting young Caesar."

Lucius wanted to deny any and all knowledge of the scrolls, but couldn't. Not to this man.

"I know of the scrolls. I don't believe they were anything of importance, Sir. I told him they would only cause trouble. I told him to let them be," he ended in a tapered whisper.

"Trouble is not the word I would have used, Lucius. Peril would have been more appropriate."

Lucius' face contorted in anger. "I should have destroyed them. It would have been better if I had."

"Only the gods know that for sure, Lucius." The tired old man got to his feet and paced around the small room. "When I sent you and Caius to the domus of Pompey with a . . . a certain document, I should have known better. I was not prudent. I put you poor boys in harm's way. I hope Caius can forgive me. When the time comes and I cross the river Styx, I will get down on my hands and knees and ask—no, I will beg forgiveness from young Caius when I see him on the shore. I sent him to his death as surely as if I had thrown that javelin myself."

"That document you sent us with, was that the remaining draft we had found?" Lucius asked with glistening eyes.

"No. But it had suggested its existence," Cicero replied.

"Then the draft still exists?"

"No. That went with Caius to the afterlife. The gods have possession of it now."

Cicero and Lucius spent the following day searching for the

home of Caius' aunt and uncle and seeing the sights of Pompeii. Everybody seemed to be out enjoying the sunshine and warmth, a much different day than the one before. Even Vesuvius presented itself in its finest greens, looking majestically down on all the of the city's inhabitants.

The cerulean sea behaved itself and sparkled with flecks of bright sun. Flights of pelicans flew in perfect formation, each bird following in precision the maneuvers of the bird in front. With outstretched wings the birds glided on unseen air currents inches above the waves, they disappeared behind waves only to reappear again unscathed—what an example of discipline in this Roman world. Only people like Lucius would take note of such beauty and splendor in nature's wondrous displays.

Cicero took Lucius past a large and beautiful villa that was notable for the fine art works within its confines.

"Lucius, there is beauty your eyes would feast upon within those walls in the form of paintings and sculptures. You would be intoxicated with awe and wonder. In the impluvium itself there is a bronze statuette, a small mythical creature, a faun, I recall, dancing on the water, greeting all who enter. And on the floor of one of the rooms there is a mosaic battle scene with Alexander and Darius fighting for the world. And do you know, that mosaic existed as the greatest battle scene ever, until you painted that wondrous battle scene on my wall in Tusculum. If Saturnius were ever to see my wall, well . . . well it is best he didn't. Jealousy can evoke the cruelest of intentions and malicious acts—believe me."

Their stroll finally led them to the residence of Caius' guardians: Livilla Tercia and her husband, Terentius Nero. Livilla was the eldest sister to Caius' mother. She spoke softly, her words pleasant to the ear.

After introductions, Cicero explained the reason for the visit and offered condolences. The old consular and Lucius opted not to tell the aunt just exactly how Caius met his end, but rather what a great friend he had been to Lucius and what a valued employee he was for the elderly statesman.

"That sounds like our young Caius," Livilla remarked after Lucius related the sea journey and how his friend had saved his life. "At least now he can join his parents in the afterlife."

Cicero and Lucius were escorted into the triclinium for refreshments. On one of the walls, a crude portrait of what appeared to be Terentius and Livilla—he with scroll in hand and she with a booklet and stylus in hers—jumped out at Lucius. There couldn't possibly be any more space left in Lucius' chest for hurt. He had promised Caius that he would paint the portrait himself, and here was somebody else's rendition. His head sank to his chest and he glanced toward the painting every few seconds, thinking—no, knowing—he could have done better.

He ate in silence as Cicero and Caius' guardians talked of worldly events and the Republic. The conversation hummed on as Lucius drowned in his failures of the past year. He failed his father miserably, no matter how skilled he was at the javelin; he couldn't save Caius' life in return for his friend saving his at sea; he let Tullia into his life with no reality of happiness; and now, he couldn't keep a simple promise of painting a portrait as asked.

"Lucius, Lucius, are you all right?" The question broke through the humming. "Good Livilla asked about your mother," Cicero said, sounding concerned.

"My mother? Oh, my mother. She's fine, thank you."

"The good consular says you have inherited much talent from her—your paintings," Livilla said, referring to something said during the droning conversation.

"Yes, a gift from my mother. She taught me to see the world the way it really is, the colors, the scents, the changes, everything. And then, she taught me to express it with my hands. I wish you could see some of her works."

"Perhaps you could do something for us one day," Livilla said.

"Yes, perhaps . . . one day," he said as he turned and looked intently at the small portrait on the wall.

"And your father, what did he leave you?" Terentius asked.

"He taught me to be skilled with . . . with the javelin," Lucius replied as he stared into the past.

"Ah, Pilatus—skilled with the javelin. And you were a legionary, were you?"

"Yes, yes I was. Now I scribe for the good consular. My javelin throwing days are over. I'm doing more productive things with my hands now."

"And your mind, Lucius; don't forget your mind," Cicero added. "What's more, he has learned that magic shorthand language of Tiro's. As far as I know, there are only two people in the Republic, or in the world for that matter, that can master that secret language, Tiro and our young lad here. And, if I may say so, there is no greater artisan that I know of that can match this young man's talent."

"I'm sure our dear Caius is . . . would be very proud of you, too," Livilla said.

Everybody looked over to Lucius and beamed with pride.

An invisible weight eased from his chest and gave way to a welling of pride. Things would change. No more self-pity. His father would forgive him—it was not Lucius' fault that his ankle gave way, changing his career as a legionary. He would do his best at scribing and the art of shorthand. He would do it for Caius. He would find someone of his class to settle down with and provide grandchildren for his mother. And the affair with Tullia would end; it could never lead to anything of substance anyway. Yes, his world would change and self-pity would be the first to be tossed overboard to lighten his load. Life was too precious to waste. There was much to see, hear, taste, touch, and experience. There had to be a reason why

Poseidon or Neptune or whomever threw him back into that boat at sea; a reason he defended himself so well on the road and killed the thief trying to take his life; and a reason the javelin took Caius and not him. There were deeds yet to be done and reasons to live. The gods had his fate in their hands for a purpose. He never felt surer of anything else.

CHAPTER XXXV

Months passed, many months. But they did not pass easy.

Gaius Julius Caesar Octavianus had gathered his private army of loyal followers and now had at least two full legions.

Titus Labienus stealthily abandoned Mutina. His troops refused to battle kin and compatriots and rumblings of mutiny were too much to tolerate. The troops opened the gates to Marcus Antonius' troops—and just as well as Antoni's troops also sounded discontented. The semblance of control of Antoni's army existed only by the threat of "decimation" and bludgeoning to death every tenth member of one's unit did not sit well among the legionaries.

Pompey's cordial relationship with the Senate waned. Not only had he not taken care of Marcus Antonius as a threat, but his trusted general, Labienus, abandoned Mutina to Antoni, thus lending a greater threat for Rome to contend. The dictator persuaded young Caesar to march down to Mutina to check Antoni's change in good fortune; a veiled threat, of course, for most could anticipate what would happen when Octavianus' Julian troops would meet Antoni's Julian troops—nothing.

A fully pregnant Tullia wanted a divorce from Dolabella. The divorce lingered on Dolabella's list of things-to-do as he busied himself with canvassing and bribing—the hard work needed to be elected one of the next consuls. He actively pursued the dictator's support but Pompey proved reluctant to lend it for rumors flew that the debt-ridden candidate planned to run on a platform calling for debt cancellation.

And as for Sthenelus, he found himself in the vicinity of Rome, following orders.

Cicero and his young scribe enjoyed their stay in Pompeii but needed to return to Tusculum. They would do so, but first visit Formiae on the way, a seaside resort where Cicero maintained another villa, a cherished villa, nothing large but comfortable, peaceful, and quiet—almost. The plan was to rest at the Formiae villa for several days and then move on.

The morning started off well enough at the seaside resort, but then fell into chaos.

A flurry of activity outside Cicero's bedroom window beckoned and his instincts insisted he investigate. He stuck his head out the window to better hear the commotion brewing down below.

"Pompey is dead!" yelled a bearded old man, clothed in a tattered old tunic. He shuffled up the inclined dirt road and repeated his news with every other, gasping breath.

"What?" the consular—not trusting his hearing—yelled back from his window to the old man on the road.

"The great Pompey is dead! They murdered him!"

"Who murdered him?"

"They—the Senate!"

"What nonsense is this you speak? Why would the Senate do such a thing?"

"I only know what I've heard."

"Have you nothing more specific, man?"

A small crowd of field workers gathered around the dusty old man.

"A handful of senators led by Marcus Brutus killed him, in the Forum!"

"Brutus you say? Are you sure?"

"That is what is being said," the tired old man exclaimed as his words became as dry and brittle as parched leaves. "Brutus led the pack of wolves that killed the dictator." The old man's voice finally gave out.

"Brutus? More like Servilia I think. A revenge killing," Cicero muttered to himself. "A killing for a killing, a father for a father, a husband for a husband. It never ceases."

Tiro came running into the master's chambers. "Master! News from Rome!"

"I know, Tiro, I know."

"Can it be true?" the excited secretary cried. "The dictator?"

"Only the gods know. It could be true. We need more information—confirmation."

"Absolutely right, Master. I said the very same thing myself and have sent one of the servants down to the docks to get whatever he can from the boats coming in," Tiro said.

"Good, good," mumbled Cicero as he looked about his room, searching for something of importance, he couldn't remember what—oh, yes, his clothes.

Hours passed and there was nothing more to do except wait.

"Surely, someone must know something, anything," Cicero murmured aloud to the walls as he paced to and fro, up and down. Hours passed.

"Master! Master!" Tiro exclaimed excitedly as he scrambled into the house, waddling and flapping like a duck fresh out of water. "You'll not believe who has arrived! Sent by the very gods themselves, I'm sure! Your friend—Figulus! He comes from Rome this very day!"

"Publius Nigidius? Are you sure?" Tiro's master asked in disbelief.

"He comes this very moment, up the road, not very far at all."

Cicero ran to the window and saw a litter being carried towards the house. Somebody of importance certainly was on his or her way.

"By the gods . . ."

In no time, the litter reached the house. Cicero rushed out to greet his old friend and augur, Publius Nigidius Figulus. "Welcome, welcome, my old dear friend," the consular said. He greeted his guest with open arms and a warm embrace as Figulus stepped out of the litter.

"Marcus, my old trusted friend. You will not believe . . . the turmoil that embroils Rome."

"Is it true? Magnus is dead?"

"I dare say it is so. As dead as Caesar—Julius that is. I forecasted the event two days before the very act," boasted Figulus.

"You saw it?" Cicero asked, enthralled to hear the rest. "Do come in and tell me the details, spare nothing. Tiro, some wine for our guest. The good stuff!"

"Well, I got up very early, as I often do, to read the morning heavens. I should have paid closer attention to Mars than I had—something was just not right. Shooting stars filled the heavens, hundreds at a time, like flaming arrows during a siege. And then two days ago, as our dear Aurora brought in the new day, I witnessed the most spectacular red dawn imaginable. It seemed as if Rome itself was consumed in flames and dying. I didn't like the flights of the birds that particular morning either—they appeared panicky. The whole nature of the morning did not set well with me. Something did not set well.

"The worst had yet to come," Figulus said and then took time to sip his wine. His eyes stared out into the distance while his mind recalled the facts as he thought he remembered them. The suspense made Cicero fidgety. "I went to the pens to offer sacred cake to my chickens . . . Oh, the horror of it all." The augur stopped for more wine. "Hmmm, this is very good—"

"Go on Publius, the horror of it all," Cicero demanded.

"Yes, well, when I got to the pens, what did I find?"

Silence—his audience waited in anticipation, ready to catch the next morsel to spill from his mouth next.

"There . . . in the pen . . . were a pair of foxes . . . with my prized chickens in their mouths. One fox had eyes of fire, eyes of evil. The other fox had young, innocent looking eyes, I am sure he was the cleverer of the two. They weren't satisfied to have just one chicken each. No——they slaughtered all my chickens and left them strewn around the pen, blood everywhere. It was horrible. And after they fled, I came upon one of my prized lambs I was saving for a special sacrifice, mauled and mutilated, for no other purpose— I'm sure—other than for evil. I quickly made a sacrifice to Jupiter Optimus Maximus himself of one of my surviving animals to ward off any further evil, and upon reading the liver . . . of course I am better at reading the heavens then the *haruspices*—the reading of livers—but it was clear; the signs were ominous."

Silence followed as the storyteller drank more wine and stared in another fixed gaze.

"Speaking of the heavens, Publius, how do you read that celestial body, that comet, the one that recently appeared in the heavens?" Cicero asked.

"Ah, the comet. It is said that it is a sign that the gods have welcomed the deceased Julius Caesar to be among them, being that he comes from a family line of gods from birth. The other augurs of the college and I have debated this for days, and they are in total agreement amongst themselves that this is so. I, on the other hand, have a different opinion," the augur said.

"And that is?" Cicero asked.

"It confirms what I discovered in reading the heavens some sixteen years ago, Marcus, during the time of your consulship with Gaius Antonius Hybrida, a week before the Kalends of Octobris, upon the birth of—young Octavianus."

"Octavianus?"

"Marcus, the heavens predicted that a ruler would be born who would change our world as we know it. He would do so at a very young age and his reign would last for many years. A sign would be given just before the beginning of his sovereignty."

"Reign, sovereignty? You're talking kingship, Publius," Cicero exclaimed, being just a little rattled.

"Yes, but no. Not a king. It was all so confusing. There were suggestions of a king, but not Octavianus. A king would be born in his reign, but it would not be young Caesar . . . Oh, all so confusing. My head ached for days," Figulus concluded.

"Publius, your story is as clouded as . . . as that Greek Milky Circle," Cicero said to his friend. "What do slain chickens and the lamb have to do with Pompey's death and Octavianus?"

"Why, do you not see, Marcus? The lamb represents Magnus and the chickens are the people of Rome!" replied Figulus, feeling slightly insulted.

"And the foxes?" questioned Cicero.

"Why, Marcus Antonius for one. The other—I need more consulting with the sky, but from what I have seen in the stars and have heard in the thunder . . . it all points to . . . Octavianus."

"Octavianus? Why, he's just a boy, Publius; just a boy," retorted Cicero.

The augur turned to his friend with oblique eyes.

"Just a boy? I wonder . . . ."

CHAPTER
XXXVI

"Tiro! Tiro!"

"Yes, Dominus?"

"Pack our things. We go to Rome!"

"But, Dominus, do you think it's safe to do so?" the secretary said, drumming his fingertips together. The façade of the smile he flashed could barely hold on to his face.

"It's never safe to go to Rome, Tiro."

"So true. I'll prepare for our immediate departure, then."

The father of his country felt compelled to know more of the situation in the city. It was his duty. The Republic may be in danger and his services may be needed—at least that's what he told himself. It's time to save his country again.

The good consular, his loyal secretary, his scribe, and a handful of trusted servants gathered themselves and their belongings and headed for Rome. Tiro kept looking back at Formiae with a long face and sad eyes as it shrunk behind them.

They charged into the mountains up the Via Appia with their backs to the sea. The entourage traversed and snaked through the valleys, their eyes ever scanning the hills for threats. They ignored the large carrion-eating birds that circled overhead and that had followed most of the way. They didn't feel safe until they were out onto the open plains. Once on the plains, they headed for Fundi for a brief meal and some much needed stretching and a chance to send a message in advance to Cicero's household and family that they were on the way. The carriage headed west, leaving Fundi in their wake and their dust. They hugged the base of the mountains and slung around the last sentinel—La Casina, where the hill put the squeeze to all travelers as it met the sea at Anxur.

After rounding the hill at Anxur, the travelers again pushed on to an open sea of flat land, heading north. They kept the mountains to the right, as a ship might do plotting a course along the coast, using the mountains as points of navigation. Another sixty miles or so and they would be in Rome—the gods allowing it so.

"Forgive me for inquiring, Master, but are we venturing to Rome in response to the letters from young Caesar?" asked Tiro.

"In part, yes, Tiro. I've received letters from Balbus and Oppius as well. It appears my opinions are highly valued as of late."

"It is rightly so, as you are the 'Father of Our Country,'" Tiro beamed.

"Hmm—'Father,' yes. It seems that title so easily rolls off young Caesar's tongue. I can almost feel his webs pulling at my skin as he draws me near," Cicero whispered, just barely an audible murmur. "More importantly, Tiro, I've received word that my 'Tulliola' may be ready to give me a grandchild again, soon—that, and the want of a divorce from that husband of hers, Dolabella."

That roused Lucius' ears, but he kept silent and recalled his vows of change. Cicero looked skyward for any further sign of the vultures that had accompanied them; they were there, still following.

"I sense we will find great turmoil in Rome, Tiro. Great Turmoil."

———

Contractions increased in intensity and frequency. Memories of the last pregnancy flashed through Tullia's head like spirits. Emotions of joy and fear each took a turn assaulting her—the joy of seeing the newborn, and the fear of the impending pain.

"This time will be different. It will definitely be different," she whispered to herself as she paced the small room. "Please dear good Juno Lucina, let this time be fruitful and easy. I promise you anything, anything at all, any sacrifice," she pleaded. The idol perched upon the pedestal before her remained silent and offered only a vague smile.

The evening hours came to the house of Dolabella in the fashionable district on the Caelian Hill like visitors bringing more unwanted offerings of pain. A rider on a very tired and frothy horse arrived with word that Cicero, Tiro, and Lucius were on their way and soon would be home. Terentia informed her daughter. The news pleased her immensely and temporarily distracted her from the labor pains.

The minutes of contentment were short-lived.

One of the young Greek slave girls breezed into the room with fresh water. It startled Tullia to see that the young girl had her hair tied at the back of her head.

"Your hair, your hair! You still have your hair braided! Don't you know that all knots have to be untied? And your apron! Untie it! Good Lucina will not take it well!" Her voice boomed louder and louder as she became more agitated.

Althaia, the Greek midwife who had attended her before, came running to the room, beckoned by the commotion.

"Althaia, she's not untied her braids and knots!" Tullia screamed. "Doesn't she know?"

Althaia escorted the young slave from the room and reminded her of the Roman belief of the "knots," that any entanglement inhibited the progress of the birthing and prevented the child from coming to the "light."

"Lady Tullia, all is well. I've seen to the knots. All is well," promised Althaia in a calm and reassuring voice, her own hair combed straight and without tangles or braids, her clothes loose and not a single piece of fabric tied. "The young girl, Elpida, has just recently lost her own child and is still grieving. She forgot. She's very sorry. It won't happen again."

"Oh, Althaia, I just want things to be different this time. Better. I so badly want this child. This child will be special. I know it."

"Yes, my lady. It will be. All will be well. Here, come lie down and rest."

The hours labored on and the contractions increased in intensity and frequency; everything went as nature—and the gods— had planned. Althaia, Terentia, and the others attended to Tullia, submissive to her every demand.

Dolabella sat impassively at his desk in his tablinum, reading documents he already knew by rote. It gave him something to do. With each scream down the hallway where Tullia labored, he would simply take another gulp of his wine, and he had refilled his goblet many times thus far. The scurrying of footsteps back and forth to her room disinterested him totally and only served to distract his reading.

"Althaia! Althaia!" he called.

The Greek slave-midwife came scurrying.

"Yes, Dominus?"

"What's going on in there? Shouldn't you be done with it by now? What's taking so long?"

"Sire, Lady Tullia is having a difficult time. Same as before," the midwife replied.

"She's too old to be having children," he lashed back. "What-ever was she thinking?" *Ha! Whatever was I thinking, taking a bride six years older than me*, he thought to himself.

Terentia hurried into the room. "Althaia, we need you. I think things are about to change. Hurry!"

"Seems your daughter is not much for birthing, Terentia. Not like your sister, the good Vestal Virgin . . . excuse me . . . former virgin, Fabia—"

"Half-sister."

"Very well, then—half-sister. A good wife she was. Good enough to give me a proper son."

"But not good enough to stay married to, Publius Cornelius?"

"Dear Terentia, please . . . let's not—"

"Domina, Domina . . . the baby is coming! It's coming!" one of the house servants screamed. Dolabella's former sister-in-law—now mother-in-law—pivoted sharply like a soldier and hurried to her daughter.

Fabia had no problems giving me a son. And she was much older. Thank the gods she had enough sense to give way to her niece, Tullia, and the old man. I needed a good lawyer more than a good wife. And Cicero wasn't all that much help during the Claudian trials. Still, little was better than none. More wine followed his thoughts. The irritated young husband grunted and ran a hand through his thick, wavy, red hair, which he took much pride in. His other son had his thick, red hair as well, as did much of his family; it was their pride and legacy, that flaming red hair.

He needed to get up and refresh his senses with some cool water. But before he could stumble very far—

"Sire, Sire! You have a son!" called Althaia, as she brought the newborn before him to be placed at his feet. Gently, she lowered the bundle and unfurled the linen wrap, exposing a beautiful little boy, still covered in nature's white casing, umbilicus freshly cut and tied.

The infant complained violently about the cool air, and his

small lips curled and quivered as he cried.

Terentia marched into the room to witness the ritualistic claiming of the son by the father.

Dolabella looked down at the screaming newborn. He cocked his head to the side, but the child looked no different than before. Everyone waited for him to reach down and pick him up. To take claim. To rejoice.

But he did not.

Instead, he gave a quick snort and walked away.

"Publius Cornelius," Terentia shouted, surprising even herself. "Your child! Your son."

He sauntered back and looked at the child again.

"That . . . that thing is scrawny . . . and has—black hair. It looks nothing like me at all. It doesn't look anything like a future . . . consular to me," he said as he rocked back and forth slightly. "You know what to do with it," he said, flipping and waving his hand in the direction of the door.

Althaia's heart raced and her eyes flooded with tears. "But, Dominus," she pleaded. "What am I to do, what do I do?" she cried as she turned to Terentia for help and back to Dolabella again. She knew what she was supposed to do—the unthinkable.

"To the streets . . . to the fields . . . to the dogs, I don't care. Just do it!" He turned and marched away, searching for the last drop of wine in his goblet.

The unclaimed and innocent child was banished to the streets or nearby fields, to let nature claim.

Althaia couldn't do it.

Not this child.

This child was much too beautiful and healthy to leave for the elements. Neither the sun nor the cold nor the stray dogs would claim him. The midwife faced Terentia again, casting beseeching eyes, shaking her head, speechless, panic fast approaching.

The women stood in shock and silence for a long moment, trapped in time gelled by fear. The baby complained of the cold and broke the women from their trance. They bundled the cry-ing child and headed for Tullia's room when they were confronted by a hysterical servant, running, calling for help. Tullia needed Althaia—again!

The women ran to the room where Tullia grunted in pain and began pushing—again.

"Oh, by the gods . . ." Althaia thrust the re-wrapped bundle into Terentia's unsuspecting arms. She placed her hands on Tullia's rolling abdomen and repeated her exclamation, "Oh, by the gods . . ." Althaia placed a hand between Tullia's legs and examined the girl's bloody perineum. Tullia screamed. Again, she couldn't help but push. Althaia called for more linen. Terentia cradled and rocked her grandson as she watched in terror—and excitement.

The midwife deftly guided the second child out and repeated the warming and the cleaning as with the first child. This time the placentas appeared normal and were intact. The second child, a girl, did not complain as much as her older brother. She was as beautiful as he, if not more so. She had dark, soft hair, just like her brother.

Terentia and Althaia both knew they could not mention this second child to Dolabella. The women entered a silent and sacred bond with just an exchange of serious glances; they knew what they had to do; and they had to do it soon.

Terentia sent for a slave runner.

She knew who would save these children.

He had to.

CHAPTER
XXXVII

The first layers of night began to shroud Rome when Cicero and his fellow travelers made it to the gates. It was late. The darkness cloaking the city was more an ominous shadow than an end-of-day nightfall and an eerie calmness pervaded. The streets bore less than the usual night traffic with very few merchants moving about. Citizens hurried to and fro quietly, unease and suspicion rested in their eyes. The consular and crew merged with a few brave caravans of merchants easily enough from the Via Appia and made their way toward Cicero's domus on the Palatine.

Lucius and the others did not see the huddled cluster of two women slaves, each with tiny bundles in their arms, and two burly slave-escorts stealthily cross behind them, traveling on the Clivius Scauri, headed for the suburbs on the west side of the Tiber. The tiny cries emanating from the bundles sounded more like kittens as their muffled cries echoed off the walls at the intersection.

Darius, the new nomenclator, greeted the weary travelers with warm welcomes and water. He had replaced the missing Elius, who was never heard from again since his disappearance. There were rumors that he may have been one of the many bodies found in the Tiber, but the body was too unrecognizable to be certain.

"Master, it is so good to see you, Great Son of Aeneas." Darius emulated the ways of Tiro and Elius; he had learned well. "I will arrange for some food and wine, Dominus," he said. The slave bowed reverently and wore a perfect smile. Tiro lifted a single eyebrow and followed Darius' every move.

"Darius!" Cicero called, stopping the slave in mid-stride. "Is there any word from my wife?"

"Why, yes, Sire. Domina wishes to see young Lucius as soon as he is able, at the domus of Dolabella, on the Caelius."

"Me?" Lucius said, turning to Cicero for some clue for the summons.

"Is there not more?" the master asked.

"No, Dominus, just that Lucius should seek her out at his soonest opportunity." With no more said or asked, Darius scampered off at a quick pace, head held high, shoulders back, and spine lordly, to finish his tasks.

"Tiro."

"Yes, Master?"

"Arrange for a litter first thing in the morning," Cicero commanded as he sank into a chair. His eyes scanned the air as if reading an important document.

Cicero stopped Lucius before he reached the door. "It's neither safe nor a good time to travel in the city at this hour, Lucius. In the morning would be better."

The young man nodded and heeded his employer's words. "In the morning then, early."

The night hours lingered for eternity. Each time Lucius opened his eyes—if they ever were really closed—the darkness looked the same. No amount of tossing and turning hastened the arrival of the morning hours at all. He thought he could hear vague sounds of screaming and shouting in the night but wasn't sure—fatigue and weariness had distorted everything; sight, sound, and time.

The first changes in a pale morning sky commenced when Lucius' eyelids finally gave way to fatigue and refused to cooperate; a fretful unconsciousness ensued. The sound of his own stertorous nasal snoring startled him and he felt intoxicated from sleep deprivation.

A quick body wash with cold water stirred the senses. A change of fresh clothing and Lucius was ready for his walk to the Caelian Hill. But before he could begin his quest, an early morning visitor was at the door with a message for Lucius.

"Lucius Pontius?" a brawny messenger asked.

"Yes."

"A message from Domina Terentia," the muscular slave said and handed over a rolled parchment, sealed with red wax.

Lucius broke the seal, unfurled the parchment, and read the contents. He read it twice to make sure he did not miss anything important. "It says that I am to accompany you. Alone."

"Yes. When you're ready."

Cicero entered the atrium just when the two were leaving.

"Lucius, if you wish to wait, you can accompany me as I, myself, am going over to Dolabella's to see my daughter," Cicero said.

"There's been a change, Sir. I'm to go to a different location, per Lady Terentia's request."

"Terentia's request? Where in Hades is she sending you, and why?"

"I don't know just yet," Lucius replied.

"What is she up to?" the elderly man murmured, rubbing his chin, deep in thought. "Very well. But do be careful. I heard a lot of unusual street noises last night. This city seems a restless volcano, more so than Vesuvius itself. Oh, and Lucius, watch your back, my son," Cicero added with concerned eyes.

Lucius nodded with a sliver of a smile and then disappeared with the messenger.

The two men snaked their way through the streets, ever vigilant for anything that did not look right. Lucius' senses were especially keen as they passed along the Forum Boarium, where Caius was murdered. The scent and complaints from the cattle brought a knot to his stomach and the taste of bile to his mouth. When they reached the spot where Caius had been slain, Lucius stopped and studied the ground. An irregular, dark smear reignited a fire of emotions causing Lucius to tighten his jaw and clench his fists. The guide studied Lucius and saw the fire in his eyes, the eyes that were fixated on something on the ground. After several moments, they continued on until coming to a stone bridge, the Pons Aemilius, arching over the Tiber.

On the other side of the stone bridge the messenger-guide escorted Lucius down a long, narrow, and twisted alley, surrounded by old dwellings. It was dark and dank. Clothing and bedding hung suspended in layers like dirty streamers. After a short walk into the maze, the escort stopped, peered around for unseen, prying eyes, and then assertively pushed Lucius into a doorway, through a wall of suspended, colorful beads.

Lucius' young eyes adjusted quickly to the darkness. A backroom was aglow in yellow and gold and elongated shadows slithered across the walls. A gentle nudge from the escort encouraged Lucius to continue on toward the warmly lit backroom.

What he saw when he entered the room surprised him: two small women were responsible for the deceptively large silhouettes cast on the walls. They were as startled as he when he walked in on them. The messenger-escort followed right behind Lucius and signaled with a reassuring nod that he had nothing to fear.

Movement and a small cry from a bed of straw in the corner interrupted the awkward encounter. One of the women obediently responded to the beckoning and picked up the small bundle. It was an infant—a very small one at that. She took the infant over to a chair and cuddled the crying child, lovingly offering a breast. The other women cautiously approached Lucius. She, too, had a bundle in her arms, but this infant was quiet.

"I am Althaia, of the house of Dolabella, sent here by Domina Terentia, to protect and hide some very valuable treasures," she said softly. "She has asked that you . . . that you help us, please." Fear and hope filled her face at the same time.

"What is it that you . . . that Domina Terentia . . . would have me do?"

"We need to have the valuables moved from Rome, to somewhere safe," Althaia beseeched.

"And what valuables are you talking about?" Lucius asked suspiciously. "And why me when she could hire armed guards?"

Althaia looked deep into his eyes. She then let her gaze fall to the bundle in her arms, gently folding back the linen blanket from her charge. Lucius followed her gaze to the blanket and found a newborn infant. The baby moved her little fingers around in the air as if performing magic or casting a spell. The woman's pleading, imploring, hoping eyes met Lucius' confused eyes.

"A child?" he cried, taking a step back. "A child?" He began to pace around the small room, running his hand through his black hair and then wiping his face with the back of his hand. "A child? Hah!" he exhaled stoutly. "Is this some kind of joke, or trick?"

"No, Lucius, this not a joke, or some trick."

"And . . . and just what, or where, am I to take this child?" he asked sternly.

"Children."

Lucius flashed an incredulous, defiant stare and his head flinched.

"Children?"

Althaia looked over to the other woman, a young girl really, breastfeeding the other baby. Lucius' eyes followed.

"Two? No! No, no, no!" he exclaimed, pacing even more frantically than before. "What do you think I am?" he said as he moved about like a caged wolf. "I'm no smuggler or trader of slaves. I'm just a scribe! No! Less than that!" he shouted. "Who do you think I am anyway?"

"Their father."

"What?" His feet lurched to a stop. His knees felt weak and unsteady. He felt like an unsuspecting animal just brought down by a hunter's arrow. Any sense of reason evaporated from his brain as he stood in place, numb and void of all sensory awareness.

"These are Lady Tullia's babies . . . but they are not Dolabella's," Althaia said. "He has not only disclaimed them, but has cast them to the streets, to the elements."

"What makes you think these are my babies?" he asked cautiously after a moment of silence.

Althaia did not answer, but looked to his eyes, pleadingly.

Lucius allowed his feet to carry him over to the infant and cast eyes on the infant. The infant looked up at Lucius, blinking her little dark, sparkly eyes and smiled. A vague memory from somewhere deep in the past tried to breakthrough from Lucius' gray matter. Those eyes made him think of his sister from years long past. Something in his core said that this child shared the same substance of his being.

From the corner of the room the young girl came forward and unfurled her bundle. Another little face caught Lucius' eyes. The baby ceased his fussing and offered a smile of his own.

Lucius gingerly took the girl infant from Althaia and held her close. He sighed deeply, closed his eyes, and knew he had no choice. The logic of the heart won over the logic of the brain. He wanted to rub his nose, but his hands were full.

CHAPTER XXXVIII

Lucius had to get back to the master's house, formulate a plan, make arrangements, and think. He commanded the burly slave to stay with the women until he could return. The slave was reluctant, but relented.

The father of twins gathered himself and started for Cicero's place on the Palatine. He crossed the bridge and re-entered the city with his mother's words seeping into his head like vapors seeping in through an open window.

You better be careful, my son. I feel Rome is no different than a battleground itself.

His nervous eyes scanned every edifice, street, and alley he passed. He felt naked without a weapon.

He saw himself and Caius seated at the small table eating his mother's food and feeling safe, Caius noting the handprints on the wall.

The larger ones are mine.

And the others?

My sister's.

He remembered her sorrow at the death of the little girl.

Sandals scuttled hurriedly on cobblestone behind him. He turned to see a man and his wife scurrying past with two small children in tow. They eyed Lucius with fear. Each wore their own individual masks of dread.

Find a good woman and give me a grandchild . . . no . . . many grandchildren!

The terrified family was strung together by tight handgrips and they slithered away like a large snake.

You don't worry about me, Mater. I will take care of myself.

Lucius picked up his pace and hurried. He neared the Forum Boarium and the scent of cattle wafted through his nostrils, settling in, taunting him. His mind went busy again with thoughts and promises. A pressure inside his head intensified and seemed to push goblets of sweat—or blood—through his pores. What were once vapors seeping through the windows of his mind turned to seawater. A trickle at first, then a mad release of gushing torrents: thoughts and promises he'd made to himself of no more self-pity; an unrelenting suspicion that the gods had spared him for a deific purpose; a promise of revenge that must be kept; the knowledge that he'd been given a reason to live—at all costs. He felt like he was back at sea once more, drowning.

There had to be a plan.

And then the thought of his mother came to him yet again.

Mater! His mother! Yes, that must be part of the plan. Take the children to Venusia—to his mother!

Lucius was almost at a trot now.

———

The first one startled him, causing him to stumble to a stop; the second one was less threatening and he continued on; the third, just part of the landscape.

Bodies appeared along the streets as he neared the Palatine; in pools of blood, dark and thick. Crows called from rooftops. A few of the birds were brave enough to glide down to the corpses for a closer inspection. They hopped and marched around with

ANTHONY MICHAEL VILLANUEVA

stiff, stick-like legs and out-stretched wings making claim to their property.

Thin, fast moving scuds of smoke shot over the rooftops of the insulae and sporadically hid the sun. More screaming echoed in the near distance. It was mid-day already but the brown sky made it appear much later. Lucius finally made it to the master's domus. House servants darted about like members of a frantic fire brigade attacking an out-of-control fire. They were securing the master's important documents, placing them into leather buckets for easy transport. Some carried clothing to be packed. And others just dashed around in confusion.

Tiro issued commands for packing valued wine when Lucius walked in.

"What's going on, Tiro? Where is the master?" the tired scribe asked.

"The whole world has gone mad. Dominus has sent word to gather all his writings and make ready for transport to Formiae," the animated man said, thrusting his dancing hands into the air. "It's not safe to be in Rome anymore," he said in a panicky, breaking voice.

"And Tullia?"

"He didn't say," the freedman said as he continued to direct servants. "However, Domina Terentia has another message for you. She informed us that she has arranged for a horse and cart to be available at the Porta Latina and that you . . . you would know what to do," Tiro said with suspicious eyes and chin thrust forward. "You know, we could use that wagon for the expensive Greek art pieces and other household goods we need to transport."

Lucius ignored Tiro and flew to his room to fetch his own meager belongings. When he returned, Cicero was there giving orders, too.

"Lucius, my boy. I'm so glad to see you."

"As I am to see you, Good Sir. Lady Tullia . . . and Lady Terentia, they are safe and well?" the young man asked immediately in his next breath.

"Terentia is fine—busy, busy. I've never seen her so—busy. Odd, that she is so . . . composed with all this upheaval and madness," Cicero remarked.

"And Lady Tullia?"

Sadness washed over her father. "She is not well, Lucius. She lost the baby. She does not talk. She does not eat or drink. She just stares. She's empty. She's but an effigy sitting in bed, not really alive, just existing."

"Lost the baby?" Lucius asked with a confused look; then it dawned on him—Cicero doesn't know.

"And what's more, that . . . *Moros* . . . that personification of vileness . . . that contemptible, nefarious . . . noble . . . that . . . that . . . red-headed son-of-a-jackal was not willing to claim the child had it lived. May he and all his red-heads go to the depths of Hades and live eternally!" Cicero exclaimed as he closed his eyes and shook, his face flushed and contorted, veins in his forehead bulging. Everyone in the room stood in stunned silence, imitations of his Greek art statuettes.

"And what's more, he has gone over to Antoni! Can you believe that? Bedding his wife was not enough, no——he had to jump in bed with that . . . that . . ." It took several deep breaths to wash away the purple hue from his face. "To add madness to this world, it is said that young Caesar—oh, I was suspicious of him all along, his activities, his intent—he has gone over to Antoni as well. Can you not believe that as well?

"His age; we all put so much faith and capital in his age, his years, his name, yes—his name." Cicero paced in oval circles, finger poised upwards as if making a point to his fellow senators in the Forum. "He is certainly not without intelligence, that sly young fox —" He froze in mid-stride as if being struck by a javelin at close range. Enlightenment flashed across his face. "Nigidius, you old . . . you were so right. You truly can read the heavens." Cicero stood in quiet solitude, privately with his thoughts for a long moment, spellbound, in a trance.

He continued again as if he had just finished the last word a second ago. "Octavianus has met Antoni in the vicinity of Mutina, the legions refuse to fight, and they have formed a *Triumvirate* of sorts. Another Caesar-Pompeius-Crassus monster, only this time, Marcus Aemilius Lepidus is the third head of the monster. Julius Caesar is alive and well in the form of Roman legions—and he marches on Rome."

The elderly statesman awkwardly realized it was his loyal staff surrounding him, not the Senate. "Forgive me, we have much to do," he said as he flew to his study.

Lucius felt compelled to tell Marcus Tullius Cicero all that he knew about Terentia's plan and the babies, but decided that it could wait. First he had to get the infants to safety. He gathered what few possessions he had and headed for the door. A shout came from behind as he reached the threshold.

"And just where do you think you are going? We have work here!" Tiro said with implied authority stamped on his face.

With eyes of steel and defiance, Lucius glared at Cicero's freedman and then disappeared into the chaos of the city, leaving Tiro seething.

In the power vacuum created by the murder of Pompey, Rome had become a prize for the Triumvirate. The murderers of the dictator had fled the city with much of the Senate. And those left behind were at the mercy of nature's law—survival of the strongest, or best protected. Word was out and those who had wealth and property found their gravest suspicions confirmed: the proscriptions were back—the legions needed to be paid.

In the streets again, Lucius moved swiftly and with purpose, completely ignoring the wailing of terror, the smell of smoke, the people running past him, and the bodies. His mind was fixed— if it didn't relate to the babies, any superfluous thoughts weren't allowed. He retraced the path taken earlier with the escort as much as he could. Some stretches needed to be avoided because of fighting, blood curdling screams, and heavy smoke. Streets that earlier were empty were now filled with an army of fleeing citizens. The hours of the day evaporated quickly into minutes. Evening hours descended early, enveloping the fleeing masses in darkness and panic. The situation grew as dark as the evening.

CHAPTER
XXXIX

The cloudscape above the city reflected crimson red. The ominous red glow reminded Lucius of the morning when Julius Caesar was put to the funeral pyre; odd, that he should remember that now.

Caesar's legions under Marcus Antonius, Gaius Julius Caesar Octavianus, and Marcus Lepidus advanced on the city. Anybody with wealth feared they were on somebody's proscription list and needed to be anywhere but the city. Crazed citizens ran clutching prized possessions. They bumped, shoved, and tripped as they fled in panic. Litters that once carried somebody of importance lay strewn, crumpled, and abandoned in the cobbled and cluttered streets. Not far behind the fleeing citizens, small legions of rats scampered past, ignoring Lucius as they fled for safety, away from the spreading flames. Lucius was just an obstacle in the path of those fleeing. He felt it best to move to the side and steer clear of the maddening crowd; the only real possession he had was his life.

To add fuel to the fire, rumors were rampant that special "hit squads" operated in advance of the ensuing troops to expunge certain individuals and secure prized properties and valued assets. No one and nothing was safe.

"Citizen! Citizen! Have you seen a woman with child past this way? The woman in a *stola* of . . . of bright red and green, I think, and the child, a little girl with golden, curly hair. Please, tell me, have you seen them?" a frightened man with terror in his eyes asked as he stopped and clutched at Lucius' tunic.

"They've gone that way with the crowd," Lucius said, not knowing the truth but hoping it was so. Scores of people had run in the direction he pointed to—including the rats.

"Oh, thank you young man, thank you," the terrified man said and then fled in the direction of the pointing finger.

Up the street upon the taller buildings, helmeted silhouettes with weapons in hand appeared and loomed large on the walls. Two, three, and then more shadows, all coalescing into one hideous looking monster. It was time to go.

The cripple started at a slow trot and was thankful his healed ankle was cooperative. Shouts and screams followed not too far behind and pushed him to quicken his pace, moving him faster along. His footfalls and breathing bellowed in his ears as he hurried along.

Loud bashing and crashing followed by wild-eyed looters jumping out of windows into his path from a nearby shop startled Lucius. The looters paused briefly to regard the cripple. Challenging and crazed eyes warned him that the merchandise in their hands now belonged to them. They fled with their new treasures, disappearing into the shadows. More shouts came from the direction in which the thieves fled, accompanied by the unmistakable din of scuffling and painful screams.

Lucius knew he had to hide, and quickly. He ran into one of the freshly looted shops and climbed over toppled goods and furniture, inadvertently dropping his personal bag. He started for his bag but stopped when he heard approaching hobnailed boots. Survival instincts kicked in and he dropped flat and rolled under a partially collapsed counter. He rolled again until he was flat on his stomach. A bolt of cloth lay nearby. Stealthily, he pulled at it, unraveling the material ever so slowly onto him, stopping only when he heard the boots enter the shop. The crunching of broken shards under foot from broken pottery was deafening as the boots made their way into the ransacked and dimly lit shop.

Rivulets of sweat coursed down Lucius' face, flowing like lava, burning across his cheeks towards his dry mouth where he allowed the warm, salty streams past his parched lips. He willed his chest muscles to move in shallow, controlled, and gentle bellow-like movements; just enough to move some much needed air.

The boots paused, turned, and grated more clay pieces underfoot. More deafening than the grating was the silence that followed. Lucius squeezed his eyes shut and allowed no more breathing.

The boots started another pass—parading past the partially hidden ex-legionary. Incredibly, they crunched right past him. It was if by keeping his eyes tightly closed he had willed himself invisible. Again, the boots stopped. Lucius' eyes flashed opened and stared straight-ahead—waiting.

His heart pealed within his chest and he could feel every fistful of pulsating, red-hot blood explode from his heart chambers and surge into the rest of his body. His ears pounded. His fingertips throbbed. Sweat dripped from the tip of his nose; he so desperately wanted to rub the wetness away with his finger.

A glint of light caught his eye. Near the partially unfurled bolt of linen lay a knife with what looked to be a very sharp and curved blade. And it was within arm's reach.

Again, the boots made a grinding turn and marched back to make yet another pass in front of Lucius. This time, Lucius didn't close his eyes but fixated on the knife. Something grabbed at his mind as the boots paraded past—an image.

His whole being came alive with controlled rage. There before him was the tattoo of a snake climbing out of the boot: Caius' killer.

A sudden and loud crashing at the front of the shop caused the boots' owner to crouch and prepare for action.

A panicky squealing rat scrambled for the doorway as fast as his little feet could carry it, knocking over more pottery to the floor and leaving broken debris in its wake.

The tattooed legs wearing the boots relaxed and straightened.

During the rat's noisy exit, Lucius reached over and grabbed the knife from the floor just a foot away from the owner of the boots. The ex-legionary lurched for the boot-wearer and with one swift, sweeping motion sliced the intruder's Achilles tendon of his left leg, followed by another slicing sweep of the tendon on the right, both swipes cutting clean through the leather boots effortlessly, like cutting wheat stalk, he thought to himself.

The intruder in the boots crumpled to the debris-strewn floor like a screaming colossus falling to earth in a cloud of dust. Lucius scrambled atop of the fallen colossus, covered the man's mouth with a free hand, and plunged the cutting knife into his neck, severing his trachea with small twisting motions. Lucius could feel the cartilage crackling and hear the escape of pink-frothy air hiss and spurt from the wound, like an angry volcano. He averted his eyes to avoid the crimson spray, pulled the knife out of the spewing neck wound, and plunged it into the man's chest where the heart, if he had one, should have been. The fallen man's eyes went wide with surprise, as did Lucius'. They gazed at each other in recognition.

In front of him lay the "general" from the way station so many months ago. It was there where he had first encountered this demon. The demon was one of the four vets bringing horses through the stations. The leader wore a scar across his face, sparing the eye. It made no difference. Lucius felt no remorse, not for avenging the death of his friend.

The man on the floor stopped moving and went flaccid; the blood that spewed from his neck sputtered to a trickle; his pupils dilated wide; his eyes drifted to that faraway look; and his lower jaw rested open. Lucius scanned his surroundings like a wild animal hovering over and protecting a fresh kill from other predators. It was clear. Looking down to the face of the man who had taken the life of Caius should have made Lucius feel elated, but it did not. Absent was the sweet taste of revenge; perhaps later.

He gathered himself and his personal belongings and went back to the street. And each time he came upon stragglers, they would stare at him with terror and flee in the opposite direction; his blood-soaked tunic and knife in hand did not make for a good image.

The cripple shuffled his way along many winding streets and alleys, followed by continued haunting screams and the clamor of breaking structures. Evil spirits pursued and stalked him, he was sure of it. His own ghoulish silhouette cast evilness on adjoining walls as he passed burning shops. He cloaked himself in shadows and kept well-hidden.

He found the stone bridge at the Pons Aemilius. The water flowing under the arched stones ran black with red and orange streaks, reflections from the inferno engulfing him. He reached the entrance to the alley that hid the tenement and the waiting women, slave, and "treasures." Searing waves of heat, smoke, and the acrid stench of burning flesh assaulted him and dared him to pass. In the next few breaths, the alleyway imploded on itself, sending flaming timbers crashing to the ground and glowing cinders exploding in all directions.

Lucius flung his arm across his face to shield himself from the heat and smoke and felt the grip of sheer terror grab hold of him as he tried not to think of the unthinkable. He tried thrusting himself forward into the firestorm several times but the wall of super-heated air he so painfully tried to breathe repelled him each time. It singed his hair and burned his eyes. His heart raced, his lungs hurt, and his skin burned. He could only call out to the gods and beg for their help—or curse for their deception. He had failed his father. He had failed Caius. He couldn't fail the babies—and live.

He was about to make one last sacrificial offer of himself to Vulcan and enter Hades itself when a hand grabbed him from behind and yanked, sending him flying backwards to the ground. Lucius looked up with his burning, watery eyes to see an outline of a human-like form. Was it one of the gods? Was it a ghost? He blinked his eyes clear. The slave that had brought him here earlier to his children stood over him.

"The babies! Where are they?" Lucius screamed to be heard in the maelstrom of fire and wind around him. The slave, covering his own eyes with an arm, beckoned Lucius to follow, pointing back to the other side of the bridge.

They ran back across the stone bridge, hunched over, as hot burning debris flew over them like birds of prey. The slave grabbed Lucius by his tunic, yanked and then guided him to a building nearby that was intact and free from flame. There he found the women and babies safe, for the time being.

"Are the babies all right?" he screamed.

The women nodded.

"We need to leave this place! Cover the babies well!"

He turned to the slave and asked him his name.

"Lysandros! Lysandros of Creta," the slave yelled over the din of the firestorm.

"Well, Lysandros of Creta, do you know the way to the Porta Latina?"

The slave nodded.

"Good, we have to make our way there, now! Oh, and . . . thank you," he said; another debt owed.

Lucius, Lysandros, the two women, and the babies started for the gate where a wagon and horse would be waiting—the gods willing.

The city looked different in the chaos of the night with the fires and smoke adding distortion and confusion. The ex-legionary handed Lysandros the cutting blade that he had used earlier. It was caked in dry blood. The slave looked at the bloody blade and then to Lucius. The ex-legionary returned the look with shrugged, muscular shoulders.

"Had to use it," was all he offered.

They scampered on, occasionally stopping and hiding within recessed doorways along the way, poking their heads out, looking like little animals spying for signs of danger. Some stretches of buildings and streets were completely normal looking, except for elongated silhouettes running along tall walls, chased by other silhouettes with weapons in hand. Other stretches were ablaze and chaotic with citizens running or pushing small carts piled high with possessions, or looted goods along the narrow streets.

Lucius and his band of refugees reached a critical juncture—the intersecting crossroads at the Vicus Longus and Clivus Scauri. They needed to continue south to reach the Via Appia, but they were forced to stop. Ahead, a group of soldiers rummaged through piles of wares and scattered apparel while motionless bodies lay on the ground. There was no alternative but to turn back and find a way to circumvent the intersection and head south again. Lysandros led the way; Lucius followed the women and babies.

New fires were encountered where before there were none. Howling winds and the roar of a dying city assaulted the foursome and their bundles at every turn. Ash and soot rained down upon them. The women covered themselves and protected the babies the best they could—for a time anyway. Althaia's head covering smoldered then burst into flames. She screamed. Lucius ran to her and pulled the burning cloth from her smoking hair. She held tight to her bundle the whole time without a second thought. The rain of ash and cinders was relentless, forcing the troupe to move faster.

Running at a full trot and with Lucius up front with Lysandros, the tight cluster of fugitives blindly collided with two soldiers coming out from an alley, their shields up over their heads covering themselves from the same falling hot debris.

Lysandros was the first to react when the fog of confusion

cleared. He leaped forward onto one of the soldiers and wrestled his sword from him and then pinned him in a one-handed chokehold. The other soldier cleared his sword from its sheath and plunged it into the slave with unbelievable swiftness. The slave cried out in anger more than pain but did not release his death grip on the first soldier's throat. Lucius grabbed the nearest weapon within reach, a javelin, and thrust it into the second soldier's abdomen and upward into his liver.

In all the upheaval of the roaring fire, collapsing buildings, and raining ash, the four bodies posed motionless in time, resembling an exquisitely chiseled Greek marble sculpture, a monument to fury: the dead soldier with a hand wrapped around his neck, the dying slave with gladius in his lung, the dying second soldier with javelin in his liver, and the much alive ex-legionary, all frozen in the moment with the thundering fire, wind, and eerie reflections from light and shadow. The gods must have reveled in their masterpiece.

CHAPTER
XL

The laws of chaos and chance funneled Lucius, the women, and the babies into the direction of the Esquiline, not their intended escape route. The inferno diminished as they neared the Esquiline. There were signs that fire brigades had controlled some of the fires in this area; for once, the Esquiline smelled better than the rest of the city.

Lucius and the exhausted women stopped to rest, all deliriously tired. Sweat drenched their clothes and soot caked them in black. And all were thirsty. The surroundings looked vaguely familiar to Lucius. A gift from the gods for their valiant efforts came in the form of a broken fountain with cool, flowing water. The adults took turns quenching their ravenous thirsts, sipping water from palmed hands past their parched lips and tongues. The women used their knuckles to trickle cool liquid into the tiny mouths of the babies.

Lucius faced a minor dilemma: discard the shield and a javelin he had taken from the dead legionaries where Lysandros had given his life and take his chances with the Fates, or come up with some reasonable explanation as to why they were in his possession if he happened on another patrol. He opted to trust the Fates.

The tired refugees continued on for a short distance more along the deserted street when Lucius came upon another familiar landmark. He found himself facing the large front doors of Pompey's domus on the Esquiline. The doors were scorched but appeared intact. The unmistakable clopping of horse hooves approaching from somewhere up the street unnerved him. He gathered his little tribe of fugitives and ushered them out of the immediate area. They found refuge in the shadows again, following an adjoining wall into the abyss of a dark alley.

The horses stopped and a rider shouted commands for guards to post at the doors. More orders followed, but Lucius couldn't quite make them out. He motioned to the women to go first; they started a slow retreat deeper into the alley. Lucius followed the wall with his hand while facing the passageway entrance. He moved like a thief into the darkness, trying not to step on any feet behind him as he blindly paced backward.

The wall transitioned from brick and mortar to wooden slats after a slight depression—a door. At the same time that Lucius found the door, a legionary appeared at the entrance of the alley, facing one of the walls—he was relieving himself. This all seemed so eerily familiar to Lucius, as if he'd done this many times before. But he couldn't have, unless it was in one of his many recurring dreams.

Lucius stilled himself and became statuesque, leaning slowly rearward to become part of the door. The door creaked and he felt himself falling backward into the dark void of a room. He quickly regained his balance, but the noise drew the attention of the dark figure at the entrance of the alley and Lucius knew his situation was dire at most, alarming at the least.

He ushered in the women, closed the door, and fondled for a locking mechanism. He found it, but it was broken. Reaching out with his hands, he found what felt like a large barrel. He tilted it on end and rolled it in place to brace the door shut. With the barrel out of the way, he noted a sliver of light at the bottom of another doorway. He covered the floor in quick steps in the direction of the faint light, found the handle, opened the groaning door to allow just a stab of light in, and then listened. He thought he could hear distant voices, but wasn't sure. The first door that he had blocked was being tested from the outside. Lucius knew he had to do something. He ignored the groaning of the second door and entered a courtyard.

Billowing orange smoke towered over the courtyard walls and

black and gray ash rained down on him, again, but in lesser quantity. He signaled for the women to follow and dashed for the main structure, entering the domus proper. Within seconds he found himself in a familiar room. War trophies and finely painted frescoes decorated the walls. Despite the anemic light he could see where he was—it was the tablinum of Pompey's home. The women uncovered the babies, who up to this point had been quiet, or couldn't be heard over the chaotic events of the night, but now cried of hunger.

From the direction of the atrium, an ominous figure appeared. His boots resonated loudly. He walked and smelled like a legionary, but looked more a mercenary than one of Rome's soldiers. His face captured the light exposing a large cleaving scar across a mean eye. The eye looked hard upon Lucius, and then over to the women.

"What are you doing in the domus of Marcus Antonius?" the apparition asked.

Lucius looked around quickly. "I thought this was the domus of Pompeius Magnus."

"Not any more, thief," the mercenary declared.

"Thief?—I'm no thief," Lucius said. He followed the ghoul's fixed gaze to the bloody, burnt, and torn tunic that draped Lucius' tired body. The cripple instinctively wiped some of the drying blood off his chest. "I was attacked. I had to defend myself." It wasn't true, but he didn't really care.

The mercenary moved closer, cocked his head and focused deeper on Lucius. "Do I know you?"

"No." Which was true. The man didn't really know him, Lucius thought.

"I know faces. I've seen you before, boy," insisted the man with the scar across his right eye.

"You're mistaken."

"Just as well, I guess," the mercenary said as he reached for his sword and slid it from its sheath.

From behind Lucius another ghostly figure appeared out of the dark and into the weak light, his face just a shadow. He, too, had the silhouette of a legionary.

"Where've you been?" asked the mercenary.

"I followed someone in through the back way, through the courtyard, had the door blocked with a barrel," replied the other specter, his sword already drawn.

"Well, I found him for you," said Scar-Face with a half-smile. "And I'll take care of him for you, too."

Lucius stepped back away from both men, hemmed in by the trophy wall. The women moved to a dark corner, covered the babies, and shook with uncontrollable fear.

"Lucius? Is that you, Lucius?" the silhouette asked. The legionary stepped forward into the light. It was Sthenelus Regulius.

"Sthenelus." The name spilled from Lucius' lips.

"You know this . . . this thief?" Scar-Face asked.

Too shocked to answer at first, Sthenelus looked hard at Lucius.

"Sthenelus? Yes, it's me—Lucius," proclaimed the bloody, disheveled, and tired acquaintance.

"Well? Do you know him?" Scar-Face asked again.

"Yes," answered Sthenelus. "He was a legionary—"

"*Was*—is right. Now, he's a no body, just a common thief, taking from our good General Marcus Antonius," exclaimed Scar-Face.

"I told you, I'm not a thief!" Lucius shouted.

"Makes no difference to me, ex-legionary, your fate is sealed, here in this room," Scar-Face pronounced. He advanced toward Lucius and pointed a sword at the young man's chest.

"Wait!" Sthenelus called out. "Let them go. What harm can they do? They're not a threat to us. He's not even on the list."

Scar-Face changed direction and charged at Sthenelus. "Who put you in charge? Did you forget your place, you poor excuse for a . . . dog! I say who lives and who doesn't, list or no list. Understand?"

Sthenelus stood motionless, eyes wide, jaw tight, and handgrip on his gladius white-knuckled. Scar-Face turned on Lucius again. The former legionary backed away, back-stepping into the wall of trophies.

"This won't hurt a bit, ex-legionary. You do want to die honorably, don't you, Lucius—whatever your name is—with some . . . *dignitas*?"

Althaia and the other young girl whimpered louder. "Please don't hurt him, please. We need him," the younger of the two cried.

A strange calmness fell on and cloaked Lucius. The same calmness that took hold of him when he thought the sea was about to claim him. He had no fear. What he did have was his reputation, his honor—his dignitas. He would die honorably for his father. He would miss his mother, but he knew he would see her in the afterlife.

"I said, leave him be," commanded Sthenelus, making a move on Scar-Face.

That serene peacefulness that had cloaked Lucius disappeared on hearing Sthenelus' voice. It fell from his body like a discarded toga. A sense of resoluteness and purpose, together with an inordinate amount of courage, washed over him.

The mercenary turned on Sthenelus, thrusting his sword with a strong, experienced arm. Sthenelus repelled each attack with his own sword, the bones in his arm vibrating and his muscles aching with each deflection as sword clashed with sword. Agility and youth took on experience and strength, each man fighting with their best assets. Scar-Face surprised Sthenelus with a sweeping leg maneuver. The stunned youth faltered and stumbled to the floor. He dug in with elbows and heels and scooted on his back, retreating from the thrusting and slashing weapon that desperately tried to penetrate his body. Sthenelus blocked each thrust from the mercenary's gladius with his own but tired quickly. Another blinding kick sent Sthenelus' weapon flying through the air and it disappeared into the darkness.

The women screamed in terror and the babies wailed.

Scar-Face stood over Sthenelus. He poised his gladius high in the air, aimed and ready to strike like a bolt of lightning. "You can't defend yourself let alone that friend of yours . . . that ex-legionary . . . that Lucius—"

Time gelled as Lucius reached up from behind, grabbed the trophy javelin from the wall with both hands, pirouetted through the air, and then lunged for the mercenary with all the force that broiled within him. Every fiber of his being worked in perfect synchronicity to do what had to be done.

"It's Lucius—Pontius—Pilatus!" he spewed through clenched teeth as he spun, flew through the air, and plunged the javelin into the mercenary's throat in one single motion. The force and velocity of his leap caused both to crash to the floor. With stunned eyes, Scar-Face looked up to Lucius' face. He tried to rock himself free from under Lucius, which only made the ex-legionary push harder with the javelin.

"It's Lucius—Pontius—Pilatus," he said again in a harsh whisper that sounded like stone grinding on stone. The ex-legionary's eyes, like those of a demon summoned from Hades, bore into the mercenary's shocked, glistening eyes.

Scar-Face's rigid muscles thawed and his eyes glazed over.

Lucius could see his reflection in the vet's dilating pupils, a reflection he did not recognize, but a reflection his father just might be proud of.

Sthenelus helped his friend to his feet and offered a sword. They both looked to the dead mercenary. Lucius waved off the sword. He didn't need it. The javelin had done its job again.

"That was an honorable kill for a legionary, Lucius. Now, let's get out of here before the others come," his friend said.

Lucius gathered the terrified women with the help of Sthenelus and fled from the domus, to the courtyard, and out the door leading to the alley. Sthenelus motioned for Lucius and the women to stay put as he marched to the entrance where two other soldiers approached. Sthenelus talked to and gestured for the guards to enter the house through the main entrance. As soon as the guards ran in the given direction, Sthenelus signaled for his friend and the women to come forward.

"Go, Lucius. I don't know if I'll see you again, but I owe you," Sthenelus whispered.

"Take care, my friend. We'll meet again, I promise," Lucius said with a mutual firm and lingering wrist grip. "I promise."

Lucius called for the two women with their bundles to follow, retreating south again in the right direction. They had not yet traveled very far when they heard hobnailed boot steps running up from behind.

Fear grabbed hold and they froze, awaiting their fate.

Sthenelus appeared out of the darkness. "Wait! I couldn't let you go without protection. Let me go with you, until you're safely out of the city," he said, panting from his sprint to catch up.

"Are you sure it's safe for you to—"

"I'll take my chances, Lucius."

There was nothing more to be said. Mutual smiles of each man said it all.

"So, tell me my friend, just what am I chancing anyway? Who are these women and why are they so important?" Sthenelus asked without addressing the bundles.

"It's not so much the women, but the treasure they carry."

"Treasure?" A look of disappointment flashed across Sthen's face.

"No, it's not what you think. These bundles contain something more precious than any gold or silver. These treasures have been put in my care for safekeeping and to get out of the city, at all costs."

The boy baby cried and drew Sthenelus' attention. The legionary cast a puzzled look at Lucius.

"Sthen, these are my children. These are *my* treasures. They are my future."

Lucius' declaration left Sthenelus speechless and confused. Burnt falling timber in the dark broke the few breaths of silence that had followed.

The refugees started down the debris-strewn street with Lucius in the lead and Sthenelus taking the rear. The fires had consumed much in the way of old and easy combustible fuel, leaving only smoldering ruins in the stretch of neighborhood where earlier the small band of survivors had been pelted with hot cinders and ash. The group came upon the crumpled heap of bodies—Lysandros and the two soldiers—covered by a thick cloak of gray ash. The women turned away and hid their faces.

"Lysandros was with us until we ran into these soldiers," Lucius informed his friend.

Sthenelus reached for one of the soldiers, the one the slave had killed by choking. He removed the dead man's body protection and *gladius*. "Here, take these and put them on. You're going to be a legionary again for a while, Lucius."

The uniform fit well, as did the helmet. If felt strange to be in uniform again. His immediate thought was of his father—he would be proud.

"You look good and proper, Lucius," said his fellow legionary.

Lucius drew the gladius from the scabbard, causing the two women to eye Lucius in a different light; they cradled the babies tighter to their bosoms and stepped away from him. Lucius gave a head gesture for the group to move again. Anyone watching would have seen two legionaries escorting two women in guarded movements.

Their subdued trek connected them with the Vicus Longus. Discarded clothing and the occasional body littered the street.

"Sthenelus, what's going on?" Lucius asked after passing more bodies.

His friend briefed Lucius on what had taken place after his capture at Pharsalus, his long march up to Italian-Gaul, his march down to Mutina, and the failed siege. He relayed what he had heard about Octavian forces merging with Antonius' and that there was a new pact: Octavianus, Antonius, and Lepidus. He couldn't address the politics of it all—that was beyond him, he was just a legionary, following orders. He informed Lucius of the special squads sent in advance of the main force to secure certain properties and eliminate certain individuals who were on "proscription" lists.

" . . . And that's why I was at Pompey's domus. Marcus Antonius took the house for himself. I was given over to work with a team of mercenaries already operating in Rome—not the sort you'd catch me drinking with," Sthenelus finished. "By the way, legionary Pontius, where are you going? What are you going to do, other than take these 'treasures' out of the city?"

"I've got to get to the Porta Latina, Sthen. There's a wagon and horse waiting, or at least should be. I have no idea what I'll find there now after what I've seen and heard," a worried Lucius said.

Sthenelus promised he would escort them to the gate; he owed him that much.

Lucius, Sthen, and the two baby-carrying women continued on in a guarded march. They scanned every direction, peered in every shadow, and listened for what they could not see. The gods, in their graces, felt compelled to escort them, for there were no further threats until they neared the juncture where they would enter onto the Appian Way and turn east for the intended destination, the gate in the wall referred to as the Porta Latina.

When they reached the juncture of the Via Appia, they eased their pace and kept to the darkest of shadows until they confronted the walls that were part of the Circus Maximus. Fires highlighted the wooden structure and collected voices and screams emanated from the other side.

The escorting legionaries and the two women skirted the wooden structure as silently and discreetly as possible—but failed.

"Sta! Where do you think you're going?" said a booming voice from a uniformed figure emerging from the darkness. "Take them in through the north gate," the ghost-like figure commanded as he approached in assertive steps accentuated with authority—a centurion, his face cloaked in black.

The legionaries stood silent, the women slid in behind them.

"Where are you taking these two anyway?" the centurion asked, stepping closer to the two legionaries, revealing two slits for eyes that glared at them.

The hair at the back of Sthenelus' neck bristled when he recognized the baton-carrying centurion—it was Herennius.

The gods must have been entertaining themselves divinely this evening for Herennius did not return the recognition of Sthenelus at all. Or, perhaps, it was the caked soot and dirt on the young legionary's face that saved the moment.

"Well?" Herennius asked, again. "Where are you going with these women?"

"Nowhere, centurion. We just . . . we just wanted to taste the honey first," Sthenelus retorted with the biggest grin he could get his face to conjure up. Dimples bracketed his white teeth.

To add more folly to the maddening moment, the gods blinded Herennius to the two infants cloaked deep within the women's garments. Lucius moved not a muscle but screamed inside his head at the lunacy of it all. How long could the insanity of this moment last?

That the strangest events could take place in the most serious of moments gave proof that the gods did indeed have a sense of humor after all.

The centurion came very near allowing a twisted grin to grace his hard face, but his large square jaw fought back and remained taut. He broke the spell after several hard breaths, pivoted sharply to an about-face, and returned to the shadows. "Be quick about it—"

"Always am!" Sthenelus shouted, motioning with a fast pawing hand to Lucius to move the women quickly.

"And get them back behind the walls," the fading voice commanded from the darkness.

Sthenelus, Lucius, and the two women with babies scrambled as fast as they could down the Appian, each peering back, not knowing what to expect in the next moment, but hoping only for the best.

The night lasted longer than any the fugitives had ever experienced in their lives. The city, painted in a dull orange glow, became more distant as the foursome laid down many fast footsteps between them and the Circus Maximus—and Centurion Herennius.

Sthenelus thanked the gods for not allowing the centurion to recognize him. That their luck would be the envy of even Julius Caesar—had his not run out so early—would be something to toast to. He tried not to think of what would follow after he kept his promise to Lucius. He knew he had to go back to the city, back to his elements, back to whatever the gods had waiting for him—there had to be a severe debt owed for the more than generous gift of luck granted. Sthenelus would pray and sacrifice, give thanks, and ask for more. And he hoped Herennius would not remember him, or the women.

They moved like bandits with stolen goods, ignoring unfathomable fatigue, thirst, and hunger. Each head filled with pounding thoughts, thoughts that weighed heavy on them. Their feet were in charge for the time being and met the old road in quick paces; they allowed their brains to do other things.

Lucius thought of poor Tullia, not that he missed her amorous ways, but that she must be suffering without her babies. Or maybe, she suffered no more; in any case, poor Tullia. He wondered what his mother would say about all this. She would not ponder it for very long once she looked into the eyes of these babies—that much was sure.

The gate should be near. They would get the wagon and go on to Venusia, to his mother, to safety, and a new beginning. The women were tired, thirsty, and knew that the babies would need to feed soon, or all would be for naught.

Althaia wondered if she had a place to return to. What would happen to her now? Whose slave would she be? And what had happened to Terentia and Tullia? She prayed for the gate to be close at hand. After that, she would have to accept whatever happens. She would either be blessed, or cursed.

The younger slave thought not much at all, save taking care of the babies and wondering where she was bound for next, after the gate.

They reached the Porta Latina gate just as the new morning began to chase away the dark of night and offer promises of another day, a new day, hopefully a better day. Everyone's fate now belonged to the good Goddess Aurora.

The fatigued refugees approached the gate with caution, swords drawn and at the ready. The babies fussed—they were hungry. The younger slave had all the nourishment needed for the twins, to the point where she hurt from engorgement. That she had unfortunately lost her own infant just prior to the birth of the twins and was still lactating was again a sign of the gods working in mysterious ways.

The eastern side of everything began to glow yellow and gold, as if heated by a great oven, and elongated shadows of early morning began to recede and hide.

"Lucius, there's no wagon. No horse," Sthenelus said, stating the obvious. "Do you have the right gate?"

"Yes, I'm sure of it. The Porta Latina," he said as he scanned the area. "This is the place."

The sun continued to rise and offer warmth and gold to all—man, vegetation, and stone; but nothing more.

The infants fed one at a time with the help of Althaia. Lucius walked over to the wall where the young slave held the baby girl to her breast like only a mother could do.

"He looks really hungry."

"She," said the slave.

"Oh, sorry," he said with an embarrassed face. "You know, in all this turmoil, I've yet to know your name."

"Elpida."

"Elpida? Sounds Greek. What does it mean?" Lucius asked.

"Yes, it is Greek, and it means—'Hope.'"

"A good name, Elpida. We certainly need that, don't we?"

"Lucius, I don't know how long our rope of good luck is, but it must have an end. Where's the wagon?" Sthenelus asked again.

Lucius offered a face laced in pain. He had no answer.

With the question still fresh in the air, commotion emanated from the west side of the wall: creaking wagon wheels, clopping horse hooves, and several people with raised voices.

"We need that wagon for the master's personal goods! I told you to turn it around and return to the house. Stop this nonsense. I order you!" The familiar voice of authority belonged to Tiro.

"No! I have strict orders from Domina Terentia to bring the wagon here," yelled the driver.

"How dare you, you impudent son of a . . . ! You will pay dearly for this . . . you insolent fool!" shouted Tiro, trotting at a fast clip, trying to keep up.

Lucius, with Sthenelus in the lead, appeared from behind the wall, still in uniform and sword in hand. Tiro and the driver froze as the wagon came to an abrupt stop. The horse snorted and bobbed his head in thanks for the chance to rest. Tiro and the driver wore masks of panic as they registered the approach of two legionaries, headed straight for them.

Lucius walked up to the motionless and speechless driver.

"Are you Lady Terentia's man?"

The man could only nod.

"I believe this wagon is for me, then. I'm Lucius Pontius."

"Lucius?" Tiro was all in a twitter as he waddled in a tiff over to the young legionary, gesturing the whole time with his hands. His fingers flew and danced in the air as he tried to explain that he needed the wagon for the master's precious cargo.

"I have my own precious cargo, Tiro," Lucius said in a calm, assertive voice.

Tiro glared back with eyes that were ready to burst from his face.

"The master shall hear of this! You . . . you . . . " he stammered.

"My authority comes from a higher source, Tiro," Lucius Pontius Pilatus said calmly.

Silence and icy stares followed. Sthenelus crunched the ground under him and closed in on Tiro with a look confirming Lucius' resolve. Tiro backed off and stumbled to the ground.

"The master will . . . hear of this. You wait and see. This is not the end of this . . ." he shouted as he got to his feet and ceremoniously brushed himself off. "You will see." The secretary started back for Cicero's house, complaining with each step.

Lucius and his legionary friend loaded the wagon with the two women and the precious cargo and prepared to leave. The end of their incredible luck most likely was very near at hand, they were sure. How much more would the gods possibly allow?

"May the gods protect you and get you to your destination safely, my friend," Sthenelus offered.

"And you as well, Sthen," Lucius said. He removed his legionary body gear and tossed it to the side, save the gladius.

Lucius looked to the driver. "And you? Are you coming or staying?"

The driver shook his head emphatically. "No, no thanks."

One last smile, a flip of the reins, and the journey to Venusia was on.

CHAPTER
XLI

Much had happened in the Roman world since Lucius and his family traveled south on the Via Latina. They continued to be graced by the gods with much luck. The ex-legionary, the two women, and the babies traveled for days without incident. They finally reached Venusia in safety and received a mountain of love from his mother. Great joy and happiness overwhelmed her when she saw her son again, but what followed when she gazed upon the little innocent faces of the twins went beyond words; her world changed.

Marcus Antonius remained in Mutina. He carried on a correspondence war with the Senate, or what few senators remained in Rome. More squads operated in and around Rome, including the nearby villas, eliminating and procuring.

Antonius tolerated Octavianus, a much younger adversary and a minor nuisance, someone to manage from a distance. His troops and Octavian's refused to fight one another, all being faithful "Caesarian" troops. Didn't they know the man was dead?

Octavianus took refuge in a fortified mountain villa in a place called Arezzo with his loyal staff: Agrippa, Maecenas, and his other advisors, Lucius Cornelius Balbus and Gaius Oppius. The bulk of his legions made haste, slowly, toward Rome. At the same time, an advance "flying force" neared the outskirts of Rome to the north. His advisors had counseled the young Caesar to be patient and wait out Antonius. Antonius was self-destructive, they said, and the fates would tip the scales in Octavianus' favor. In the temporary vacuum created by Pompey's death, a delicate balance of power existed until such time that young Caesar could take advantage of the opportunities provided by the gods.

In the interim, young Caesar's sister Octavia was offered to Antonius as wife to cement a fragile treaty between Marcus Antonius and Gaius Julius Caesar Octavianus, much the same as Uncle Julius did with Gnaeus Pompeius Magnus, offering daughter Julia.

In the House of Dolabella, Tullia occupied a bed, covered with clean linen, head to toe. No one knew exactly why she died. She had no spirit to survive, nor live; her body gave up her soul so easily to that great Milky Circle of the Greeks in the heavens. Her mother mourned for the appropriate number of days for the loss of her child, but she remained resilient; she had something to live for.

On a road leading to a coastal villa in Astura, Cicero noticed towers of billowing clouds ballooning loftily to the cerulean blue skies that watched over Tusculum.

"I refuse to believe young Lucius would steal from us," a saddened Cicero lamented.

"Oh, it's so true, Good Son of Aeneas. I tried to stop him, but he pulled that sword on me and threatened to kill me, why—after all I . . . I mean . . . we did for him. That cart could have carried much more of your precious Greek art pieces that your good friend Atticus acquired for you over the years. May the gods show the likes of that thief no mercy, no, none at all," Tiro had said. Tiro wouldn't lie. He'd been Cicero's trusted aide for all these many years. He even stayed behind to watch over the villa in Tusculum and protect the property and belongings until the master could return, when the danger would be over, and his name would be cleared from the proscription list.

The villa at Tusculum was nothing more than a fiery, funeral-like pyre. In the great room, the beautiful frescoed wall was at the mercy of the uncontrolled fire. The blackened fringes of destruction crept upwards toward the great armies in battle. A menacing conflagration surrounded and then engulfed the men, the horses, and the armies as it climbed the wall; the general on horseback, resembling Caesar, was the last man consumed. The flames reached the lone javelin in mid-air but oddly enough skirted around it. The portrait of the young Tullia also vanished in the soot and flames. The searing edges had just reached her dreamy, mysteriously lidded eyes when the wall collapsed with what could have been perceived as an angry wail.

Felix and his wife stood not far from the burning structures and watched in silence and horror, clutching one another—their only wealth—as their home roared and crackled in flames. Small explosions sent sparks and embers in all directions. The walls fell inward, one by one, and what remained of the domus sailed upwards to the heavens in the form of flame, soot, and billowing black smoke—an offering to the gods.

The tribune, centurion, and young legionary who had come looking for Cicero cared less about the fires they had set, they were just following orders. They headed for the coast to catch their prey, in the direction that the ex-slave Tiro had pointed—the points of a gladius and a javelin could be extremely convincing.

The three armed agents for Marcus Antonius raced for most of the day, working their horses to the brink of exhaustion. They finally caught up to their prize.

Sthenelus followed Laenas and Herennius, snaking around trees, avoiding low limbs and branches, and came upon Cicero's slow moving horse and carriage in a small shadowed clearing. The centurion burst forward in a surging gallop, blocked the carriage's path, grabbed the reins, and stopped the complaining horse. He leaped from his horse and took control of Cicero's horse. Sthenelus and the tribune caught up and rested their horses by the tree line.

The tribune dismounted and leisurely made his way to the carriage.

Cicero closed his eyes and rested his chin on his collapsing chest. A single tear escaped one of his tired eyes and followed a pleat along his "chick-pea" nose. The rolling tear coursed along a crease formed from years and years of smiles and laughter; from years and years of dramatic expressions put forth in years and years of rhetoric and great speeches; from years and years of living, living for—what was it his father had said? Oh, yes, living for "always being the best . . . and being brave . . ." And for the Republic. The single tear completed its final journey at his lips where he tasted its sweetness, as well as its bitterness. The tear was not for fear of death, but for his beloved Republic.

Cicero broke from his moment of solitude when he heard the familiar voice of Popillius Laenas calling out to the driver.

"If you value your life, now would be a good time to leave this wagon!"

The carriage rocked as the driver leaped for the ground and fled. It was a gentle, comforting, rocking little motion, like a cradle.

Old, tired eyes fell upon Tribune Popillius as he neared, soon joined by Centurion Herennius.

"I know you. I once defended you in court . . . and won," Cicero said. His cheeks lifted again to a gentle, serene smile. He then looked over to the centurion, but did not recognize him. "I know what you've come to do. And it is not a proper thing that you do," the old statesman said with his chin up. "But do it if you must, only—do it properly."

———

Sthenelus held the reins of the three horses as the tribune and the centurion confronted Cicero at the carriage. He could not hear the conversation from the tree line, only the forest breezes that made peaceful sighs as they whispered through the branches and twirling leaves above. The gentle breezes lulled Sthenelus to daydreaming. He thought of Lucius and hoped his friend had reached safety with his treasures. He thought of his circumstances and what lay ahead for him in these chaotic days. He thought how nice it would be to just sit down on the grass, lean against a tree, and nap.

The serenity of it all shattered when out at the clearing, at the carriage, the centurion drew his sword and whacked at the elderly man's neck, taking many swipes to decapitate him. Even then, he had to use a dagger to finish the job of severing. Blood spewed everywhere and on everything, including Antonius' agents.

The horror even shocked the horses. They reared and tried to run. Sthenelus used all his might to control them but couldn't. He let go to keep from getting trampled. He and the horses had witnessed a terrible thing, an ugly thing, a thing not done properly.

Worse was to follow.

The centurion severed the old man's hands and placed them in the same sack as the head.

Back in Arezzo, next to a very comfortable and warm hearth, Lucius Cornelius Balbus and his associate, Gaius Oppius, toasted each other with fine wine and confident smiles. "Here's to us, Gaius. All seems to be working as planned."

"To you, Cornelius. Julius would be extremely proud of you. His mortal self may not be here to enjoy the fruits of his endeavors, but his immortal being must be in shear bliss. All has gone accordingly."

"To Caesar!"

"To Caesar." Balbus returned the toast, clinking goblets in a raised salute. "May he reign for countless years to come."

The wine went down smoothly.

"What's to come of Julius' will?" Gaius Oppius said after consuming his wine and refilling his goblet.

"Which one? The real one? Or, Octavius' forgery?"

"The real one."

"We'll save it for a rainy day, my friend, for a rainy day."

Both men raised goblets to the heavens once more.

"Hail, Caesar!"

EPILOGUE

Forty-nine years later—

It had been a long journey for Lucius Pontius Pilatus as he traveled to the coastal city of Caesarea in the dusty country under the Augustan umbrella of power—Judea, to visit his son Caius. At sixty-six years, and then some, traveling long distances was no easy task for Lucius. Travel by sea made him especially nervous, causing him to rub his nose almost raw; but it was worth every mile to see his son and grandchildren. This trip would be extra-special as his daughter and her children would be there, too.

Caius had accomplished much in a short lifetime. He worked his way through the *cursus honorum* and then secured an assignment to the magistrate staff of the governor of Judea in an extraordinarily short time; the gods had let fall all obstacles in his path. He was smart, energetic, and graced with much luck—an incredible amount of luck.

Caius' twin sister Junia had arrived earlier in the month with her family. She married a fine and loving husband with connections in the Imperial Palace and had children of her own. Caius and Junia had always been inseparable since birth, as were their children.

Lucius walked into the large palace and proceeded towards a majestic dining room where the family was about to dine. Beautiful tiled-scenes of ocean creatures bedecked the floor and exquisite frescos decorated the walls. Though his vision faltered with age, the old man still had an eye for art.

The finest silk curtains swayed, fluttered, and fanned everyone with refreshing cool sea breezes. And handsome servants attended to the every need of the family. In a lovely portico facing a spectacular cerulean, white-capped sea, children played and sketched pictures on parchments, giggling and telling their stories about the drawings. It was there where Lucius found his grandson, Lucius Pontius—named after the patriarch. Little Lucius was bit of a surprise, coming late in Caius' life. He was the youngest of all the brood.

Little Lucius was telling his picture story to his cousins in animated excitement, heaving an invisible object into the air. The story was of a victorious Roman battle somewhere in the Roman world. The boy gleamed with pride over his sketching: a line of stick soldiers, launching javelins in battle, a cloud of them, but with one higher and bigger than the others. Another picture story lying at his feet told of a drowning man in the sea, surrounded by large waves and a boat next to him. A giant sea god with trident in hand stood next to the drowning man. The giant looked angry. And yet another drawing lay partially covered and hidden nearby, a drawing of a large star suspended in the sky over the mountains, pointing earthward.

Little Lucius turned to catch his grandfather emerging from the glimmering sunlight as if a god had entered the house. Parchments and screams flew through the air.

"Papa . . . Papa," the boy screamed as he ran—he called his grandfather Papa. "Did you see it? Did you see it? The star! The star! Did you not see it?" the child shouted as he slammed in to the elderly man and wrapped his arms around the grandfather's legs. He grabbed his grandfather's old hand and didn't let go. The star he carried on about was the brightest star anyone had ever seen, suddenly appearing in the East. It hovered for days and appeared to touch the ground.

"Yes, little one . . . I did see it. Wasn't it bright? It lit up the whole sky."

"Papa . . . Papa, will it come back? I want to see it again."

"Perhaps, my son, perhaps. We'll just have to wait and see," said Papa Lucius.

The boy's father came trailing after the little one. It was time for everyone to sit down to eat and celebrate the arrival of the beloved father—and grandfather—and to give thanks for all that they had. The family would toast to Lucius Pontius Pilatus, who was responsible for their good fortune. And later still, they would gather and listen to stories about how grandfather was tossed into the sea during a great storm and how Poseidon threw him back into the boat. After that, there would be stories about the once great Roman Republic, and the man who tried to save it—Marcus Tullius Cicero.

But, for now, it was time to eat.

Little Pontius rushed for his drawings left strewn on the floor, but his father called him back.

"Pilate,"—they called the boy "Pilate," short for Pilatus—"it's time to eat. Come . . . come wash your hands!"

Finis

ACKNOWLEDGMENTS

My collection of history books stands shoulder to shoulder in my bookcase, proud that they were able to serve me well. Over the years, they gave me facts, names, and dates that I dutifully clung to so that I could bore my family at birthday celebrations—Cleopatra died on my wife's birthday; Caesarion (Ptolemy XV) was born to Cleopatra on my daughter's birthday; Caesar Augustus died on my birthday; on and on *Ad infinitum et Ad nausea*.

Then I got tired of the same old *Et tu Brute?* In reality, Caesar most likely called out in Greek—*Kai su*. The point is—does it really matter unless one truly gets offended by the manipulation of history for the sake of creativity and the want of a good story?

I have to thank my family for suffering me and tolerating my history lessons. They endured well.

I especially need to thank my wife, Jeanette, who stood by me as always, pushed me, and made me work hard for my words; good enough was never good enough. She was not as generous with praise that other family members felt compelled to bestow. She made me work.

I would like to thank my son-in-law, Joe Burns, for the original book cover design. Also, Lisa Ham for taking the cover to the next level.

I need to say a very special thank you to Robin Martin of Two Songbirds Press for treating my story with care and maintaining my story voice. In addition, many thanks for her work in enabling me to get this story to a reader's hands.